THE CAD AND THE CO-ED

RUGBY SERIES BOOK #3

L.H. COSWAY

PENNY REID

THE CAD AND THE CO-ED

RUGBY SERIES BOOK #3

L.H. COSWAY

PENNY REID

COPYRIGHT

This book is a work of fiction. Names, characters, places, rants, facts, contrivances, and incidents are either the product of the author's questionable imagination or are used factitiously. Any resemblance to actual persons, living or dead or undead, events, locales is entirely coincidental if not somewhat disturbing/concerning.

Copyright © 2017 by Cipher-Naught; All rights reserved.

No part of this book may be reproduced, scanned, photographed, instagrammed, tweeted, twittered, twatted, tumbled, or distributed in any printed or electronic form without explicit written permission from the author.

Made in the United States of America

ISBN: 978-1-960342-05-8

PRINT EDITION

DEDICATION

In no particular order: bird watching, femurs, and the sharing of embarrassing stories.
And to the city of Seattle, where one author dared another author to write "a secret baby book."

ONE
EILISH

@ECassChoosesPikachu: Dear losers who stole my PM card: you may take my EX but you'll never take my FREEDOM!
@SeanCassinova to @ECassChoosesPikachu: What does PM stand for? Prime Minister?
@ECassChoosesPikachu to @SeanCassinova: Pokémon of course
@SeanCassinova to @ECassChoosesPikachu: How old are you? 10?

I*'m a smart girl.*
  If you'd asked me prior to last night whether I believed in love at first sight, I would've replied with an emphatic *no*.
  Maybe even a *hell no*.
  I was not immune to the male form, or drooling over the male form, or even fantasizing about the male form. I'd had celebrity crushes over the years, posters of hot guys hanging on my wall. I may have recorded men's swimming during the Summer Olympics so I could ogle big-shouldered, thick-thighed specimens of fineness.
  But I was not and never had been a romantic sort with stars in my eyes and a happily ever after on my mind. The term *life partner* sounded like a life sentence. Perhaps it was due to my time at an all-female Catholic boarding school. My two best friends saw a cute boy and would lose their minds.
  Whereas all boys I'd met reminded me of my brothers. And my brothers were all stuffy arseholes who'd married for money and stature. For that matter, so were my brothers-in-law.
  With the exception of my one cousin who I considered more of a brother

than any of my own, I'd never met a man under sixty who I truly respected. Especially not one worthy of the giggling, swooning ridiculousness my classmates and girlfriends back at school bestowed on these creatures. I wasn't asexual. It's just that no opportunity—or drool-worthy man—had ever presented himself.

That was before last night.

Before I'd met Bryan Leech, *in person.* His poster had graced my walls since I was thirteen. Adolescent admiration for his form and skill had transformed into womanly appreciation for his . . . form and skill. It had happened sometime over the last six years. I'd been excited to meet him, because he was a brilliant rugby player and also—just being honest here—extremely hot. I hadn't thought in a million years he'd be interested in me.

But he was.

He was interested.

And his interest went straight to my head.

I'd even giggled at one point . . . *the horror!*

And then I'd danced with his thick thighs and his big shoulders under the influence of candlelight and champagne. He'd compared me to a rose and gazed at me as though I was flawless. He'd kissed me dizzy in the gardens. He'd spread my legs and worshipped me with his lips and tongue, seducing me beneath a blanket of stars. He'd taken me to his suite and made love to me.

And I'd lost my virginity.

No. I didn't lose it. I gave it to him.

But now it was the next morning, after the most wonderful, most meaningful, most amazing night of my life, and I was completely and helplessly in love.

I awoke with a start, disoriented at first, wondering if it had been a dream. But then I saw Bryan and felt a twinge of soreness between my legs. My heart slowed, then skipped, relief and wistful warmth spreading through my veins and limbs. He was still asleep, his long body curled around a pillow.

I couldn't help it. I exhaled a dreamy sigh and smiled, suppressing my desire to reach out and smooth his tousled hair. He looked so perfect bathed in the soft light of morning.

God! He was so gorgeous. It wasn't just his perfect athletic body, or the strong line of his jaw, or the mesmerizing jade green of his eyes. It was everything. He was everything.

I'd become what I'd scorned in the past. But now I got it. Oh boy, did I get it.

How he looked at me like I was the only woman in the world. How he'd asked me questions and listened—really listened—to me.

I'd tried to pretend I was sophisticated, telling him, *Don't be afraid to be rough. I'm tougher than I look.* But he saw through the act. How he touched me and watched my response with bated breath, like he couldn't get enough. How patient he'd been the night before, how skilled and tender. How he'd made my first time perfect.

How he'd kissed and held me after, told me he loved me, told me I was flawless.

How could I resist?

I was having the oddest, most fanciful notions. His soul was my missing piece. Our hearts found a home in each other. He was my other half. He was meant for me.

Clearly, one night together had sent me on a careening spiral of ridiculous romanticism. I could admit that, but I loved how alive I'd felt in his arms. Who knew a man's touch and attentions could make the world a brighter, better place?

Suddenly, I couldn't wait for him to wake up. I wanted to see myself reflected in his eyes, see a mirror of the love I could barely contain.

I rested my hand on his shoulder and smoothed it down the length of his impressive bicep. He was so strong. Touching him made me shiver, made my happy heart do a little dance.

Bryan flinched, inhaling a deep breath, then blinked his eyes open.

I grinned. "Good morning."

My smile widened at the sound of my words, this being the first time I'd greeted a lover. I sounded husky. I sounded older, more like a woman. At nineteen, I knew I'd already been a woman before the events of the prior evening. But I liked the way sex sounded in my voice.

Out of everything that happened last night, sex had been the most surprising. All of my girlfriends who'd lost their virginity said it hurt like hell the first time. But it hadn't hurt for me. It had been wonderful.

Maybe Bryan had a magic penis. And how lucky was I? Finding a bloke with an enchanted penis for my first time. Maybe he had a purse around here someplace with endless money, or a goose that shit golden eggs. I wouldn't be surprised if he did.

His handsome eyebrows did a little dance on his forehead as he struggled to lift his eyelids, finally managing to crack just one eye open and then immediately closing it. "Christ! It's bright in here. Do me a favor, love, and close the curtains. I've got a splitting headache."

I felt my smile falter, but said, "Uh, okay."

I moved to stand, but then remembered my nakedness, so I hesitated. I'd been shy, which Bryan had told me was normal. He'd made me feel so beautiful that by the end of the night I hadn't cared.

But now I was feeling self-conscious all over again.

"Hello? Are you still there?" he asked, covering his head with a pillow. "Are you closing the curtains, or what?"

"Sorry." The word slipped out automatically due to habit, even though I wasn't sorry. Not really. I just needed a minute to get my bearings. Rather than dither any longer, I decided to take the bed sheet with me and wrap it around myself.

I tugged the sheet, eliciting a short huff from Bryan, but he let it go. Disoriented and suddenly clumsy, it took me a moment to find the cord to pull the curtains closed.

"Done?"

"Um, yes." I stared at the bed, uncertain what to do.

He sounded different this morning.

Or maybe I was being silly and insecure.

Either way, I wanted to snuggle next to him—of course—but decided I needed some sign from him first.

He lifted the pillow and peeked at me. Or maybe he peeked at the room to make sure I'd closed the curtains. Either way, he seemed relieved by what he saw and removed the pillow from his face. He folded it and placed it behind his head, the definition of his muscles caught by the hazy, shadowy light filtering in beneath the curtains.

"Hello," he said, giving me a small smile, his eyes moving down my body.

"Hi." I waved and then fiddled with the sheet where I clutched it to my chest, feeling puerile but unable to pinpoint precisely why.

"You have red hair." His smile grew but his eyes narrowed.

I tucked my hair behind my ear reflexively, my heart fluttering happily because he'd said the same thing last night. He'd told me it was the color of lust and passion.

And then the happy flutters petered out, because telling me my hair was the color of lust and passion sounded really cheesy in the light of day. Really cheesy and *really* trite.

"Yes, it's the same color as lust and passion," I deadpanned, deciding that recycling his words as a joke would make us both feel better about how silly they sounded now.

He made a face, his nose wrinkling like I was strange or smelled bad. His reaction made the moment untenably awkward, heightening my insecurity tenfold. I wondered for a moment if he'd forgotten saying the words, then dismissed the thought. More likely I'd offended him by making the statement a joke.

I had the urge to apologize again.

"Anyway . . ." His stare lingered on me for a few seconds, and then he pressed the base of his palms into his eye sockets and sighed. "Bloody hell, my head is splitting."

I frowned, worried. "Are you all right? Should I call a doctor?"

He chuckled, squinting at me briefly and then replacing his palms. "Nah. I'll be right as rain soon as I have a drink, just to take the edge off. Don't worry about me."

THE CAD AND THE CO-ED

My frown deepened. I was still standing dumbly at the side of the bed, endeavoring to make sense of his words.

He doesn't mean alcohol, does he? He wasn't drunk last night.

"I can grab some water and I have a Solpadeine in my purse," I offered, taking a step toward the bathroom.

"I'll take the Solpadeine, but look for the minibar. Vodka will do the trick."

I gaped at him, unsure what to do or say, because unless he woke up in the middle of the night and drank a half bottle of liquor, there was no reason he should have been hung over this morning. He was completely sober last night. The entire time we were together he'd only had three—no, four—drinks. Four drinks over four hours was perfectly acceptable.

"Um, I don't think you should m-mix alcohol and pain m-meds."

"Who are you? My mam?" he spat, squinting at me again. "If you're bent on nagging you can leave now."

I gasped. "Bryan—"

"Quit saying my name. I know what my goddamn name is. What's your name?"

I gasped again, stumbling back a step. "W-what?"

"You heard me, or are you daft too?" he growled, pressing his palms against his forehead. "Shite that hurts."

"You d-d-don't know m-m-my n-n-n-n—" I stuttered, then clamped my mouth shut, not wanting to embarrass myself further.

What is happening? How—

I stared at him, wondering maybe if he was joking. Was this a joke? Best-case scenario this was his idea of a joke. Otherwise . . .

Otherwise it was one of two things: either Bryan Leech, professional athlete, had a brain injury that caused short-term memory loss. Or Bryan Leech had no idea who I was because he'd been drunk last night—pissed—and I'd had no idea.

He exhaled loudly, sounding frustrated. And when he spoke it sounded like he was trying to be gentle, instead the words were patronizing and dismissive. "Listen, sorry for snapping. I just . . . my head is bleedin' killing me. I'm sure you're a lovely girl, and I assume you had a good time last night?"

This can't be happening.

I covered my mouth with my hand. I wasn't going to be able to speak without either crying or stuttering, so I kept my mouth shut.

Apparently, he didn't require an answer. "It's pretty late and I want to catch a nap before heading out, so maybe just," he waved toward the bedroom door as he turned away from me, curling on his side, "go get a massage or something at the spa. You can charge it to the room. My treat."

I couldn't move.

I was rooted in place, my mind complete chaos. It was like one of those horrible movies or television shows where the woman wakes up and she's in an alternate reality.

Maybe I'd been drugged?

But no, I hadn't been drugged. I remembered each detail perfectly. Every look, every touch, every word, every wonderful moment.

My stomach pitched. An intense wave of nausea rocked through me. I was going to be sick. Running for the bathroom, I slammed the door shut behind me. I had just enough time to lift the toilet lid before emptying the contents of my stomach into the bowl.

As I flushed the toilet I heard Bryan's voice call from the other room, "Jesus fecking Christ, tell me you didn't vomit all over the floor. Just . . . just get the feck out of here, whatever your name is."

~Three Months Later~

I'm a stupid girl.

A stupid, stupid, stupid—

"Eilish? Hey, let me in. Is it time yet? What does it say?"

I covered my mouth to suffocate the errant sob, squeezing my eyes shut, and hoping when I opened them it would be three months ago, the night of Ronan and Annie's wedding. The night I'd fucked up so royally that I'd apparently acquired the superpower of changing the color of HCG strips with my pee.

WITH MY PEE!

Which meant I had a new human inside me.

Which explained all my other superpowers, like being a raging bitch all the time, and crying at nothing, and throwing up twice every day.

I'd totally fucked up, and now I was totally fucked.

"What am I going to do?" I whispered to no one, every nerve ending burning with panic.

Wait, that's not true. I wasn't alone in the bathroom. There were two of us in here. Granted, one of us was the size of a peanut—or maybe a lemon by now—and was swimming in amniotic fluid.

INSIDE MY UTERUS!

Why all my thoughts were in capital letters, I had no idea. Plus, every thought was followed by *dun, dun, DUN!*

"I don't want to rush you, darling. But you're making me nervous," my cousin Sean's voice called from the other side of the door.

Sweet Sean. Nice Sean. Wonderful Sean.

THANK GOD FOR SEAN!

. . . dun dun DUN!

A burst of hysterical laughter escaped my fingers. This wasn't happening, not to me. My friend Josey was the one who gave her heart too freely, not me. Never me.

Nadia was all business with confidence for miles, Josey was the romantic, and I was the subversive one, the smart-arse. Josey cried on our shoulders, not the other way around.

You won't cry on their shoulders because you can't tell them.

I opened my eyes. I looked at the white stick and the two pink lines staring back at me. It hadn't been a dream. This was real. And this was a complete nightmare.

"I'm p-p-p-pregnant."

He didn't say anything for a long moment, so long I wondered if he'd heard me or if I'd spoken at all.

I was just about to repeat myself when Sean said, "Open the door, my darling girl. Let me in."

So I did. I let him in. And when he came in, he gathered me in his arms and held me against his big chest. I didn't cry. My mind was blank.

We stood for a time, I had no idea how long, and then Sean said, "You're going to have to tell the father."

I stiffened. I heard the words. I knew—rationally speaking—he was right. But every fiber of my being rejected his assertion.

LIKE HELL.

. . . dun dun DUN!

Since that horrible morning, I hadn't seen or spoken to Bryan Leech, but I'd followed what he'd been doing—or rather, *who* he'd been doing. He had a new girlfriend. They'd been dating for two months. She was an actress. She had red hair.

Apparently, he had a thing for redheads.

Bryan had made no attempt to contact me—after all, he hadn't even known my name—so I decided not to care. This consisted of me emphatically *Not. Caring.* by going to concerts and clubs with my two best friends, drinking too much, and making out with strangers.

I AM THE WORST MOTHER EVER.

. . . dun dun DUN!

I couldn't think because there were too many things to think about. I sent a desperate prayer upward, begging God, striking a bargain: if this child was okay, if my drinking and partying over the last few months left this little person untouched, then I would never, ever drink alcohol ever again.

Please oh please oh please . . .

"Did you hear me, Eilish? You'll have to tell the father." Sean hugged me tighter.

I nodded distractedly. At this point I was fairly certain Bryan Leech had forgotten I existed. I knew with complete certainty he would have absolutely no interest in my child.

"Nothing has to be decided now." Sean kissed my forehead, prying the pee stick from my fingers and placing it gingerly in the sink. "Come have a cup of tea. Lucy sent over a new peppermint blend from that shop you like in New York, Tea and Sympathy."

Lucy was Sean's girlfriend and one of my favorite people in the world. She lived in New York and Sean lived in Dublin, except when he was traveling with the team. Sean and Bryan were teammates, part of the Irish National Rugby team. They weren't exactly friends, but they were friendly.

I hadn't told Sean about Bryan, partially because Sean had a mean streak. He was infamous for his nasty grudges and lack of conscience when it came to people he perceived as enemies. I didn't want Bryan to suffer.

That's a lie.

Part of me wanted to cut his enchanted dick off and burn it.

But mostly, after the last three months of thinking about that night way too much, I blamed myself.

I'd been sober. I'd wanted him to seduce me, and—drunk or not—he'd been an epic seducer. I'd had a crush on him for years. I'd been infatuated by the idea of him sweeping me off my feet. For heaven's sake, he had been my fantasy for *years*. That night I became that girl, the girl I'd always scorned and internally mocked.

He'd melted my cold, pragmatic, sarcastic heart. I may have regretted everything the morning after, but what had happened between us that night had been one hundred percent consensual.

At least, from my perspective it had been. But, apparently, Bryan had been so drunk he hadn't even remembered my name. Perhaps he hadn't been capable of giving consent. Maybe I'd taken advantage of him. Perhaps I'd been the seducer . . .

Ugh. I was so tired of this loop of self-recrimination and doubt.

Collapsing onto the couch, I rested my elbows on my knees and covered my face with my hands.

"Eilish," Sean prodded, "will you tell me who he is?"

I shook my head. I wouldn't. That morning had been terrible, so terrible, humiliating. Bryan's apathy and rejection had carved a hollow space out of my heart, leaving a wide, gaping hole. I'd been naïve, too trusting before. Too honest. Too uninhibited. Too reckless. *Too stupid.*

But I would never make that mistake again. I needed a plan and it needed to be a good one.

I was determined. No matter what it took, Bryan Leech would never find out about my new superpowers.

HE WILL NEVER FIND OUT!
. . . *dun dun DUN!*

TWO
BRYAN

@THEBryanLeech: The main problem with being sober: you can tell when people are faking their laughter. #MyJokesArentFunnyAnymore

@RonanFitz to @THEBryanLeech: Your jokes were never funny. #SorryNotSorry

~Five Years Later~

I hated parties.
    Well, maybe *hate* was too strong a word. It wasn't necessarily that I hated them, they just weren't my thing anymore. They were also inconvenient as they had all the stuff I was supposed to avoid: drink, drugs . . . women.

"You don't have to be here," William offered with his trademark quiet solemnity.

I shook my head but kept my eyes fixed on the closed doors at the end of the hall. "No. I wouldn't miss it." *Would rather be home in my slippers watching Judge Judy, sure, but duty calls.*

That was my style of party these days. Throw in a slice of Battenberg and some Werther's Originals and I could go wild on a sugar high. But no, today was William's birthday, so I was going to try and keep my grumpy old man behavior to a minimum.

Try being the operative word.
No promises.

My teammate, and the guest of honor for this particular party, tugged on the sleeve of my suit jacket and brought us to a stop. "Hey. Seriously. You're eighteen months sober."

"Has it been eighteen months already?" I stroked the stubble on my chin and cracked a grin. "Time flies when you're killing house plants."

He didn't need to tell me how long I'd been sober. I still counted the days, but not for the reasons people might think. Yes, I'd been sober a year and a half, and oddly enough, I didn't miss any of it; the late nights that turned into days, the constant hangovers, the inability to remember the events of the previous evening—that had been the true misery.

The main problem was other people, people who knew me as the fun-loving, party-hard bloke I used to be. They were uncomfortable with my sobriety, thought I'd gone "sad" and "boring." Kept asking me if I'd have a drink.

Go on, treat yourself.

One won't kill you.

Except William "The Brickhouse" Moore.

"You can leave at any time." His frown deepened.

I gathered a breath and met Will's earnest brown eyes. The bloke was entirely too earnest. "I'm fine. Don't worry, I'm not going to fuck up your birthday party."

"That's not what I'm worried about."

I placed a hand on his shoulder and slipped on my very best *you can trust me* expression. "You're not supposed to worry at all. This is your party. Let's go in and have a good time, knowing I'm on call to be your designated driver."

We both knew that was an empty offer as Will never drank, at least, not that I'd ever witnessed. Regardless, my teammate nodded with some reluctance and finally turned back to the double doors where sounds of the party carried out into the hall.

I eyed the doorway to the revelry as we approached, feeling nothing but grim determination. Nowadays my life consisted of training and clean living. Well, that and taking care of my mother, and she was enough of a handful for ten men. Needless to say, I was kept on my toes.

I opened the door for Will, happy to push him forward and into the fray ahead of me. Maybe I was using him as a shield, a decoy—just a little bit—but I felt no remorse. The man had the moral fortitude of a saint and the temperament of a puritan minister.

I ensured I wasn't around alcohol very often, but sometimes—like tonight—social obligations were expected of me. Will was from the States, and he didn't have any family in Ireland, so I'd be a shit not to show up. Plus, we were flatmates, having grown closer over the last eighteen months.

Although, judging from the look of the place, I doubted Will had much of a hand in planning the party. I'd bet my last jockstrap some WAG organized the whole thing.

"Nice party." I nudged Will a few inches forward; the crowd hadn't noticed us yet. "Did you demand the silver and gold streamers? Or was the chocolate fondue fountain one of your mandates?"

My teammate sighed, though it sounded more like a growl. "None of this is necessary."

I cracked a grin because Will hated excess. The man had lived in a spartan studio apartment on Baggot Street before we'd recently moved in together. Our place was right on the quays, but it was on the top floor so it was quiet. I liked quiet.

Before I could respond, we were spotted and I stiffened my spine, not quite ready to face the throng of well-meaning team members, their significant others, and *the others*—hangers-on, sycophants, and groupies.

A memory struck me of a party just like this one, where I'd met Jennifer, one of my many ex-girlfriends. Now there was a fake if ever I knew one. Unfortunately, Jennifer was a prime example of the fact that I was born with blinkers on. Couldn't see clearly when there was a pair of tits and an arse in my face—and too many pints of beer in my gut. Jennifer had gotten a good fifty grand out of me over the course of our "relationship," though long-con was probably a better description. The woman had been out for my money from the start, and given, like I said, I was born with bad judgment, too trusting, and was constantly drunk, I'd been easy pickings. A total mark.

"Well, good luck, mate." I stepped to the side and gave him a shove forward. He didn't even sway. The man really was built like a brick shithouse.

"Wait, where are you—?"

"Happy Birthday!" Shouts erupted from approaching partygoers, and I took that as my cue to abandon William to the crowd, glancing over my shoulder only briefly to see they'd placed a crown on his head.

Chuckling lightly, I pulled an envelope from my jacket pocket and set the gift—two concert tickets to Coldplay—on the table next to several large garish boxes. I hesitated, frowning at the small envelope next to the wrapped presents. Deciding it might get lost or overlooked in the pile of larger objects, I turned from the table and slipped the envelope back in my pocket just as I caught sight of a long, silky river of red hair.

That color was my kryptonite, always had been. The woman's back was to me, but I could make out a tall, willowy frame. The aforementioned hair was draped over one pale shoulder, showcasing a delicate, swan-like neck.

My eyes were glued to that neck, and I was struck with a sudden urge to bite it.

In a sexy way, mind.

And this was odd because I hadn't wanted to give anything or anyone a sexy bite in over a year. Not even a nibble. Then my entrancing view was ruined when Ronan Fitzpatrick stepped in front of me.

"You look rough. Been letting that loss get to you?" he asked with a commiserating expression.

"Isn't it getting to all of us?" I replied, suddenly grumpy at the reminder. A fortnight ago, the squad played a Six Nations match and we'd had our arses well and truly handed to us by the Welsh.

"You can't win them all, Leech. We brought the trophy home last year. Let's just focus on that."

I considered the irony of the statement, because Ronan was beating himself up about the loss far more than any of us. He was team captain, and even though he pretended not to, I knew he felt responsible. "Who are you trying to convince, me or yourself?"

He grimaced and downed a gulp of beer. "Yeah well, next year we'll bring it home again. Management is making a few changes. Did you hear they hired a new physio?"

"No, but I'm not surprised. Everybody hates Connors."

Our current physiotherapist had the worst personal hygiene of any man I'd ever met. Tell me who wants a bloke who hasn't washed his hands after using the john getting up close and personal with their glutes? *No one.* And don't get me started on his halitosis; I suspected it could be cleared up easily if he simply brushed his teeth.

Ronan nodded. "True."

"Bryan, you left before I could . . . uh, can you, ah, help me out with something?" William asked, joining us. He looked flustered, his cheeks red and his posture rigid.

"Of course. What do you need?"

He glanced over his shoulder, and I followed his gaze to where a group of girls stood giggling and whispering to one another as they sized him up. And when I said girls, I meant it. None of them could've been any older than seventeen, and still, their eyes were lit up with the promise of snagging a rube. Ahem, I mean, a husband.

"Christ," I swore. "Who let the baby WAGs into the building?"

"Don't you mean wannabe baby WAGs? Were they even invited?" Ronan added gruffly.

"One of them is Orla Flanagan's younger sister. The rest are her friends," William informed us, sounding stressed. "They want me to dance with them." He shook his head quickly. "I don't dance."

"Nor do you dance with children. Every single one of them is a *Daily Mail* headline just waiting to happen," I said, my crankiness rearing its ugly head.

I was five years older than William, but I felt protective of him. Probably because he was too nice for his own good. The kind of nice that could be mistaken for interest by naïve little girls. Or less than naïve little girls. They'd have themselves up the duff and walking down the aisle before he even noticed the holes in the condom. I may have made some poor choices in my time, but at least I could say I was never stupid enough to get anyone pregnant.

"I'll set them straight. Ronan. Make sure none of them try to swoop in by me while I'm laying down the law."

He chuckled and nodded while I turned and approached the gaggle of girls. I realized the error of my ways when their eyes lit up at the sight of me. Thanks to my highly documented party years, I was more well known than Will, and these girls obviously recognized me. Not that they saw anything of the real me. If they actually saw the real me, the shine would've left their eyes in a heartbeat, because the real me looked more like Walter Matthau from *Grumpy Old Men* than Zach Efron from whatever sappy movie he'd starred in lately.

"Bryan Leech!" one of them squealed, and I winced. Only dolphins should be allowed to achieve such a pitch.

"Dance with me?" another of them asked excitedly.

"No, he should dance with me," said another.

"Bryan, do you like my skirt? It's not too short, is it?"

"You signed a ball for me after Ireland played the All Blacks a few years ago, do you remember?"

I held up a hand, feeling a headache coming on, then dealt each of them a firm, fatherly glower.

"Firstly, leave William alone. He's not interested. Secondly, no, I won't dance with any of you. Don't be bloody ridiculous. I'm fairly certain I'm old enough to be your father." I pointed to one of the girls who couldn't have been older than sixteen. "Thirdly, that's not a skirt, it's a belt. And fourthly, most of my twenties are a blackout, so no, I don't remember every kid I've met."

One of them glared at me. Another's mouth fell open in shock. And the third, well, the third one looked like she was about to cry. Jesus Christ, this was why I needed to heed the advice doled out in my AA meetings and avoid females altogether. Sure, I'd probably been a little heavy-handed, but where the hell were these girls' parents?

Without another word, I turned and strode away, found the bar, and asked for an orange juice. Lifting the glass to my mouth, I scanned the room, recognizing all the usual suspects and trying to shake the residual guilt over my harshness.

But then, *boom*. I locked eyes with the redhead and a force or a weight drove the air from my lungs. This time she was facing me.

I inhaled a greedy breath, my chest inexplicably hot, and reined in even greedier impulses.

Fuck.

She was beautiful. Wide blue eyes, a rosebud mouth, long lashes, and flawless skin. She wore an understated green dress that exposed her shoulders and hugged her tits, which looked to me like the perfect handful.

I wanted her.

I had no business wanting her.

No, strike that, I wouldn't allow myself to want her.

I'd already killed five house plants, and in accordance with my AA sessions I had to ensure at least one survived for six months before I even considered starting a relationship. Therefore, I definitely shouldn't have been looking at those baby blues and getting ideas. But I was. I was getting *so* many ideas. Doggy-style, missionary, cowgirl, reverse cowgirl, sixty-nine, the squat, the spider.

Okay, so the spider's when you . . .

Wait a second. Why on earth was she looking at me like that for?

Gorgeous Red's eyes were wide, frightened almost. In fact, she looked like she'd just seen a ghost. Abruptly, she turned and disappeared into the crowd. I slammed my glass down on the bar and, moving on instinct, went after her.

It took me a while, just long enough to start questioning what the hell I was thinking—because I wasn't thinking—but I eventually found her chatting with a group in the far end of the nightclub. As soon as she spotted me, she bolted again.

What the hell?

She wound her way through people, slipping down a corridor that led to the bathrooms. I'd been in this club more times than I could count during my twenties, so I knew the layout. The corridors on either side of the bar met in the middle, so I hustled my way to the next one, my strides fast and purposeful. I smiled when I met her head-on and she stopped in her tracks, clearly startled. Her hand went to her chest in fright.

I closed the rest of the distance between us, leaving only about three feet of space. My eyes wandered, tracing her exquisite neck before meeting her eyes.

"Hello," I said.

What's the plan, Bryan?

I grinned, mostly at my lunacy, because I had no plan. This was crazy. I wasn't allowed to have plans. There could be no plan, not now, not yet, not until my AA sponsor and I agreed I was ready for plans.

Sexy plans.

Her mouth opened, then shut, then opened again. She seemed lost for words. If I hadn't been interested before, her reaction made me maddeningly curious. Was she a star-struck fan, or had she read about my past and thought I was a down-and-out scumbag, someone to avoid at all costs? I had to admit, the possibility of the latter irked me, because I wasn't that bloke anymore.

"H-hi," she replied finally, then moved to walk by me. I sidestepped into her path, bringing us closer. A waft of her perfume hit my nose, and I picked up the subtle hint of watermelon.

She straightened, steel forming in her gaze as she leveled me with a hard stare. "Would you mind letting me pass?"

"Why'd you run?"

Her eyelids fluttered, like I made her nervous. "I didn't."

"Yes, you did." I took advantage of our closeness to study her face, my attention snagging on her lips. "Tell me why."

"Honestly, sir, I have no idea what you're talking about."

Now I smirked, my attention moving back to her eyes. *So lovely.*

"Sir?"

She stared at my shirt collar. "I don't know you."

"Don't you?" Not to sound egotistical, but everyone here knew me. Sometimes for the wrong reasons.

Okay, usually for the wrong reasons.

Her eyes met mine again, and damn, something in them knocked me off guard for a second. A weird feeling of déjà vu hit me as I blurted, "Have we met before?"

Her expression gave nothing away, her face a palette of indifference, which again made me wonder if I was barking up a tree I'd already visited. Because honestly, I couldn't imagine a situation involving alcohol and me where I wouldn't have tried to bed a woman who looked like this one. Trouble was, there were huge chunks of my memory missing. Like poof, completely gone.

Thanks, Smirnoff.

"If we did meet and you don't remember, I can safely s-s-say it's not worth us talking now," she said with a haughty chuckle.

I really liked her voice. There was a queenly calm to it, even if she was visibly nervous. I decided she was right; we obviously hadn't met before. In spite of my old tendency to black out, I didn't think there was any alcohol strong enough to make me forget this beauty, and if I did, I didn't deserve to remember her.

"Fair enough," I said and tried to think of a way to prolong the encounter. Which, of course, was a bad idea, but there was something about her that made me feel this sense of urgency. This need to know her before she disappeared and I never saw her again.

I shuffled a step closer, feeling strangely compelled to do so, and caught a stronger waft of her perfume. Maybe it was the watermelon, or maybe it was just her, but for whatever reason I was struck with the need to lick and taste.

She didn't speak, but her lips formed a tight line, which made me think I was probably coming on a bit too strong. I cleared my throat and stepped back. A moment of awkwardness fell between us.

"So, you having a good time?"

Christ, I was so out of practice talking to women. She gave a little shrug, and I got the sense that she *really* didn't want to talk to me. It was weird, but it didn't deter me from keeping her there.

"Sure."

I laughed warmly. "You're hating it, then?"

At this she appeared surprised. She blinked a few times and shook her head. "I just don't go to stuff like this very often. I'm more of a homebody."

"Yeah, me too. I'd much rather be home catching up on my Netflix addiction."

She gave me a look of suspicion. "Really?"

"Yes, really. Why so skeptical?"

She shrugged lightly, looked to the side and then back to me. God, her eyes were gorgeous. "You just d-d-don't s-strike me as the t-t-type."

I noticed how she stuttered and wondered if it was a permanent thing or if I just made her anxious. She caught her bottom lip between her teeth and frowned severely, appearing frustrated.

"Once upon a time you would've been dead-on with that statement," I tilted my head, considering, "but not anymore."

She stared at me for a long time, longer than warranted, and for the life of me I couldn't tell what she was thinking. Maybe she was just an odd bird.

Eventually, she blinked as though shaking herself. She cast her gaze to the floor and gestured to the bathrooms over my shoulder. "Yes, well, if you don't mind. I need to go visit the ladies' room."

I unfolded my arms and nodded numbly as she moved by me, not giving me another look. I caught myself swaying in her direction as she passed, fighting the urge to grab her wrist.

Huh.

It wasn't that I thought I was the prize of the century or anything, but generally speaking, when I made the effort to chat up a woman, they were a lot more receptive than Red had just been.

Maybe I'm getting old, losing my touch . . .

Now there was a sobering thought.

I glared at the bathroom door and decided I wouldn't be that bloke who hovered outside of the ladies' like a nutcase. Clearly, my conversation and company were unwelcome.

With a frustrated sigh, I left the corridor and went back to the party, finding a few of the lads from the team and shooting the breeze for a bit.

Wouldn't you know, the first woman to catch my interest in years would rather hide in the loo than spend another minute in my company. Regardless, for the first time in over a year, I was actually thinking about watering my house plants.

Sometime later, after marinating in my bad luck for at least a full hour, our coach approached me. His name was also Bryan, except he spelled it "Brian." This was Ireland. The name was about as common as Pierre in France, or Mohammed in Saudi Arabia.

"Let me introduce you to our new physio intern," he said, leading me across

THE CAD AND THE CO-ED

the room. "She recently graduated from university in the States and comes highly recommended. She'll be working under Connors for the next couple of months."

"Really? I thought Connors was getting the sack."

Brian shook his head. "No, he's staying put. I know he's not exactly the most popular with you and the lads, but he's the general manager's cousin, and he knows his stuff."

"I just wish he'd use deodorant every once in a while."

Brian chuckled. "That's you and me both, son."

We approached a small group and the first person I saw was Sean Cassidy. Beside him was Lucy, his girlfriend and Ronan Fitzpatrick's younger sister. The final person my eyes landed on was again familiar, Gorgeous Red. I felt my mouth begin to curve into an unbidden smile as our eyes clashed. I quickly wiped my expression. She was stiff as Brian introduced us.

"Eilish Cassidy, I don't believe you've met our fullback yet, Bryan Leech. Bryan has some trouble with his knee from time to time, an old injury, so I'm sure you two will become well acquainted over the coming months."

What a second. Eilish *Cassidy*?

I glanced at Sean, who sure enough was eyeballing me all, *yep, she's a Cassidy, you horny fuck, so hands off.*

I cocked a brow at him. "Any relation?"

"We're cousins," a low voice responded, and I leveled my eyes on Eilish. Such a gorgeous name. Such a gorgeous lady.

"More like brother and sister," Sean put in. "We grew up together."

"Ah, I see. It's a pleasure to meet you, Eilish," I said, not taking my eyes off her for a second as I held my hand out. After a moment's hesitation, she took it and we shook. Her skin was cool and silky soft under my touch. I didn't want to let go, but she withdrew before I could keep hold of her. Coach started talking about something physio related, but I just stared at Eilish, not hearing a word of it.

I couldn't explain it, but I had to admit to myself that I was drawn to her. Not just because she was beautiful, but because she had a presence, an energy I found incredibly appealing despite the fact that she clearly considered me . . . scum? Unappealing? Beneath her notice?

Maybe a combination of all three.

Clearly, I thought sourly, *because she's a Cassidy.*

Her disdain for me now made sense. The Cassidys were, as far as Irish gentry goes, as high on the social ladder as one could get in Dublin society. Even if she didn't know of my disastrous past—which was unlikely—my blood was nowhere near blue enough. My father was a high court judge, but we weren't old money.

She shifted in place, eyes darting everywhere but never looking at me. She was uncomfortable, probably thinking back to how I'd cornered her earlier. I didn't like seeing her uncomfortable. I wanted to reassure her that she had no reason to feel that way. I understood how things were. I was a good guy. If she didn't want to talk to me or be around me, fine. That was her choice.

While the others conversed, I took a step closer to Eilish and placed my hand very softly on her elbow. Keeping my voice low, I bent to whisper in her ear, "Is that a vodka tonic? Can I get you another?"

She shook her head. "It's just tonic water, and no, thank you. I'm fine."

I studied her profile. "If I made you uncomfortable earlier, I apologize. I promise it won't happen again."

She blinked and glanced up at me, taken aback. Her hand shook as she lifted her glass to her mouth and took a sip, her attention moving to the party around us and snagging on a bloke passing by. I couldn't help but also notice because he was wearing a designer shirt and the tightest pair of skinny jeans I'd ever seen on a man.

I cocked a brow at the obvious grimace on the man's face and his restricted gait just as Eilish murmured something into her glass that sounded a lot like, "Not as uncomfortable as him, anyway."

I knew I wasn't supposed to hear it, but her comment made me smile a little. My first impression had been one of shyness, but maybe she had a sassy side.

"Perhaps he enjoys the tight fit," I suggested, dropping her elbow.

Eilish's gaze widened, darting to mine, then away. Yeah, she definitely hadn't meant for me to hear.

She swallowed another sip and threw back, "Keeps everything tidy and in place, I suppose."

I chuckled. "True, though I prefer to imagine he's a diehard environmentalist. Tight jeans mean less fabric, and less fabric means less pollution for mother earth."

"Or perhaps he's an elite luger. The pants could've been designed for aerodynamic purposes." Eilish threw back, and I barked a laugh.

She appeared surprised, like she hadn't expected me to have a sense of humor or something. Our eyes met and a moment passed between us. It felt more weighty than the situation warranted.

Being this close to her was magnetizing. I knew social norms said I should step away now, any second now, but I just couldn't seem to manage it. I felt a pull in the center of my chest.

If I wanted a woman, that usually meant she was bad news, and we definitely had a fuckload of chemistry going on.

I eyed her, how she'd schooled her expression, looking uncomfortable again, and shifted away from me subtly.

Maybe it's all on my end.

I was about to say something—anything—to try to soothe her nerves when my phone vibrated in my pocket. Pulling it out, I saw my mother's name on the screen. There were also ten missed calls displayed from earlier. *Ten.* Christ. I knew this couldn't be good. Bracing myself, I stepped away from the group and to a quiet corner, lifting the phone to my ear.

"Mam."

"Bryan, I decided to open that fancy bottle of Pinot Noir Tracy bought for me last week. Why don't you come over and we can drink it together, have a little catch up? I haven't seen you in a couple of days."

I swallowed down the hollow lump in my chest. *Good old Mam.*

"I can't right now, Mam. I'm at William's birthday party. And you know I don't drink anymore."

"You're at a party and didn't think to invite me?" She pretended she hadn't heard the last bit, just like she always did. When I'd mentioned the people who couldn't seem to get their head around the changes in my life, that I no longer drank, I'd more or less been referring to Mam.

"Lots of stuffed suits," I lied. "Not your scene."

I could almost hear her pouting. "It still would've been nice to be asked. Is there an open bar?"

I ignored her question and instead said, "The next time there's a party I'll make sure to ask. Sound good?"

She let out a huff of a breath. "Mm-hmm. So, are you coming over? I tried phoning Tracy and Marianne, but they still aren't taking my calls."

God, I really didn't need to hear about this again. She was currently on the outs with her two best friends, Tracy and Marianne, after getting drunk and telling them everything she thought was wrong with their lives, including that their husbands were lazy and their children were brats. Presently, I was the only person she had to talk to. Eventually they'd forgive her and celebrate with a night on the town, as was their pattern.

"I can't, Mam. Maybe tomorrow, yeah?"

"But I'm so lonely, Bryan. Please. You're all I have."

I let out a long, tired sigh and ran a hand through my hair. Glancing over at Eilish one last time, I saw her studying me curiously. When she realized I'd caught her looking, she quickly turned away.

I didn't want to leave, but I knew if I didn't go check in on Mam, she'd probably end up drinking herself into oblivion.

I let out a gruff breath and told her, resigned, "Go easy on the wine. I'll be there in twenty minutes."

She let out a happy little yelp. "Oh, wonderful, Bryan. I can't wait to see you. You're the best son a mother could ask for."

Yeah, yeah . . . maybe to my detriment.

THREE
EILISH

@ECassChoosesPikachu: Adult conversation with @JoseyInHeels in 5, 4, 3, 2...
@JoseyInHeels: I'll be 15mins late, sorry!
@ECassChoosesPikachu to @JoseyInHeels: That's fine. I'll order 7 donuts and name them Sleepy, Dopey, Doc, Sneezy, Grumpy, something, something.

"What did you do?"

Rubbing my forehead, I grimaced, preparing myself for Josey's reaction. "I went into the bathroom. When I came back out ten minutes later, he was gone."

Her mouth fell open and she gave me her uneven-eyes stare, where she made one eye slightly larger than the other.

"Don't give me that look."

"What look?"

"That look. The one you use instead of saying *you're a fecking eejit*."

"Oh, that look." She blinked and her eye sizes normalized. "Was I giving you that look?"

"Yes."

"Good." Lifting both of her hands between us, palms toward me, she said, "Let me . . . let me get this straight. Upon seeing Bryan Leech—rugby god, sex god, belt aficionado—not to mention the *father of your child*—"

"Shh!" I glanced over my shoulders around the café and its inhabitants. No one was paying attention. But still, in Dublin the name Bryan Leech was recognizable.

"BL seeks you out and you run into the bathroom?" Josey lowered her voice to a harsh whisper and leaned forward, her raven-black hair sweeping over her shoulders. BL was how we'd been referring to Bryan for the last four years. Other than my cousin Sean, Josey was the only one who knew Bryan was Patrick's father.

I met her dark brown eyes and nodded once. "Yes."

"Why would you do that?" A hint of pained desperation bled into her voice. "Don't you realize I've been waiting for this moment for the last four years? Don't you know I have been counting the days? This isn't how it was supposed to happen."

"Sorry to disappoint." I twisted my mouth to the side, trying to hide my smile. I decided I wouldn't tell her about what happened later, when we'd been officially introduced and shared a joke.

Better to not encourage her delusions.

"You should be. He did his part, noticing you right away, pursuing you through the party. But then you were supposed to take him to a quiet corner, confess the truth, and fall into his arms." As was her habit, she was moving her hands frantically between us, as though motioning to an invisible chart where the actions of the party were pre-destined and I'd failed to follow through. "And then Sean would be your best man, and I would wear that badass tuxedo bridesmaid dress. You know how much I love that dress."

I gave her a blank stare. "You are completely nuts."

"So?" Her fingers came to her chest. "This is news?"

"No. This is not news. But if you could be serious for just a moment, I'd appreciate it if we could talk about what happened without you referencing your delusions of grandeur."

"Fine." Josey huffed an exaggerated breath and leaned back in her chair. "Go ahead. Talk about it."

"Thank you. What I wanted to say is—"

"Don't mind me, I'll just be over here sobbing about the happily ever after that never happened."

I narrowed my eyes at her. "There is no such thing as a happily ever after."

"I know." She reached for her coffee, lifting it but not drinking. "But if anyone deserves to have their wishes and fantasies come true, it's you."

Now it was my turn to huff. "Josey, BL is not my fantasy."

"Lie. Liar. Lies. You used to have posters of him on your bedroom wall at school. You used to make me watch all those matches, know all his rugby stats. You used to—"

"Fine. Okay. He *was* my fantasy. But not anymore."

"Then who is your fantasy?" Josey sipped her coffee, her eyes taunting.

"A maid who cooks is my fantasy."

She rolled her eyes. "You sound like my mother."

"Exactly," I bit out, the word arriving sharper than I'd intended.

She stared at me, and a meaningful moment passed between us. Things had changed since our boarding school days, I'd changed. My priorities were different and my priorities had lost me friends, most notably my other best mate, Nadia.

But the dissolution of my friendship with Nadia couldn't be helped.

Josey's expression softened and she gave me a crooked smile. "Okay, sorry. What happened at the party?"

I gathered a bracing breath as I allowed myself to remember seeing him, seeing Bryan in person for the first time in five years. "I was surprised by him."

"I thought you knew he was going to be there."

"I did know, and I thought I was prepared. What I mean is, the strength of my. . . feelings, my response was surprising. My hands were shaking and my mind was a mess. Sure, I knew it was going to be difficult to see him, up close and in person, after . . . everything."

My friend gave me a sympathetic look. "You've avoided all mentions of him for years. Plus, you've been in the States."

"Exactly. It was easy to put him out of my mind when I was in Boston."

But since I'd returned, I'd encountered billboards of his startlingly handsome face, advertisements of his chiseled physique, and special features on the television about his role on the team. Over the last few weeks, images of him seemed to be everywhere, inescapable.

"You were hoping to feel indifferent?" Josey took another sip of her coffee.

"Yes."

"But you didn't?"

"No." I chuckled humorlessly, shaking my head.

"What did you feel?" she pushed, her ebony gaze probing.

I considered how best to answer.

At the party last week, I'd been hoping for detached disdain on my part, instead I was faced with prompt and uncontrollable lust. Usually I was so tired, I couldn't even muster the energy to feel pathetic about my boring sex life.

But in walked Bryan Leech and you're suddenly hornier than a rhino.

Just. Lovely.

I couldn't tell Josey about the lust, then we'd go back to Bryan being my fantasy and he most definitely *was not*.

I also couldn't tell her about our shared—but brief—moment of joking together, because the camaraderie and my *like* of him in that moment felt even more dangerous than the lust.

So I answered, "Flustered. Like I said, I was surprised. Also, worried. Anxious that he would somehow guess the truth just by looking at me. I know it's silly."

"No. It's understandable." She leaned forward again, lowering her voice.

"You've said yourself more than once, you feel guilty about not telling him the truth."

I'd come to realize over the last several years that, no matter what I did, I was going to feel guilty.

Agreed to give the baby up for adoption—felt guilty.

Changed my mind at the last minute because I couldn't go through with it—felt guilty.

Moved back to the States, tried to go things alone, worked three jobs—felt guilty.

Asked my cousin for help when I became ill and lost two of the aforementioned jobs—felt guilty.

Finished college with Sean's monetary assistance on the condition that I moved back to Ireland once I graduated and passed all my licensing requirements, and then allowed him to help me find a place, fronting me cash to get settled, and a job—felt guilty.

If guilt were an Olympic sport, I would have all the gold medals. All of them.

"But, let me remind you—again—you have no reason to feel guilty," Josey continued. "When you gave birth to Patrick, wasn't BL arrested for drunk driving that same weekend? He was a complete reprobate when you knew him."

"I never knew him," I scoffed. "We were together one night."

"And he didn't even remember your name the next day."

I knew Josey was trying to make me feel better, but the reminder of his indifference stung.

Ignoring the dull ache in my chest, I lifted my chin. "Exactly. He doesn't want a child."

Josey considered me over her coffee cup, her lips pressing into a thoughtful line. "He's changed, though. He's sober now, has been for months, I think. At least, that's what the papers are saying."

I gathered a silent breath and reached for my tea, mumbling, "Yes. Sean has mentioned something about that one or a hundred times."

My cousin, who I loved dearly but who was also prone to being meddlesome, had informed me several times over the last year that Bryan was trying to pull his life together. I was happy for Bryan, just like I would have been for any person struggling with addiction.

But news of Bryan's sobriety also meant I was conflicted. My course of action, namely keeping Patrick from his biological father, no longer seemed like a cut and dry decision.

"Will you see BL much at work?"

I nodded, suddenly finding it difficult to swallow. "Yes."

"You start tomorrow?"

"That's right. Tomorrow." *Tomorrow.* My heart seized. I thought I'd been ready to face Bryan, but after what happened at the party, I was dreading my first day."

She wagged her eyebrows. "And you'll be giving him massages."

"Josey—"

"Sexy massages."

"No." I couldn't contain my laughter. "I most certainly will not be giving him sexy massages."

"You're no fun." She pouted. "What's the point of giving up your dreams to become a physiotherapist if you can't give rugby players sexy massages?"

I lifted an eyebrow at her. "You know why I dropped out of the computational biology program."

"Yes. Because the physiotherapy major classes were more flexible and could be completed online," she said, her words dripping with disapproval.

"Are you ever going to get over this?"

"It's not fair that you had to change your major," she grumped, crossing her arms.

"You sound ridiculous." I laughed again, shaking my head at her. "It's been years, let it go."

"I can't. That program was so competitive, and you loved it. You're brilliant, one of the smartest people I know, and you'd be in the doctorate program by now if it weren't for . . ." Her gaze skipped away, her cheeks tinted pink.

I was glad she didn't finish the sentence. I'd made peace with that time in my life, how my situation had altered with the shift of my priorities. I loved her for being disappointed on my behalf, but she didn't need to be.

I'd been so angry at first, so frustrated that my life choices had been taken away from me, whereas the oblivious father continued on in his world, free of any restrictions whatsoever. But time, and especially time with Patrick, changed that. I wasn't angry anymore. I felt happy. Content.

. . . and horny.

My phone chose that moment to ring and I jumped, setting my tea down on the table. "Sorry, this might be Sean."

"He has Patrick today?"

I nodded, pulling out my cell and explaining, "Yes. Just like last week, but this time Lucy is with him. He and Patrick have been spending Sunday afternoons together so I can run errands."

"And catch up with old friends." Josey winked at me. "If it's him, tell him I say hi."

I shook my head at her—she'd always had a crush on my cousin—and glanced at my phone screen. Seeing who it was, I released an involuntary, "Ugh," and sent the call to voicemail.

"Don't tell me," her pretty mouth curved into a knowing smile, "that was Trevor, right?"

I nodded, then shook my head. "I already told him I wasn't interested in a second date."

"You shouldn't have agreed to the first date."

"I know that now."

Trevor had been my boyfriend from way, way, way back in the day. The relationship had been one of convenience. Our parents approved and so, why not? I'd gone against my better judgment and agreed to one date with him three weeks ago, just after I'd moved back to Ireland. He hadn't stopped calling me since.

"I can't believe he put a whoopee cushion on your seat. I mean, who does that?"

I laughed tiredly at the memory. Going out with Trevor had been like going out with a thirteen-year-old. He'd taken me to a food court for dinner and then to Pixar's latest release at the cinema attached to the shopping center. He'd put a whoopee cushion on my seat in the theater, laughing hysterically when I sat and the mock-fart noise erupted.

With the exception of the whoopee cushion, the night would have been fine and dandy as a fifth or sixth date, but I rarely had an opportunity to go out and do adult things, have adult conversations. I didn't need or want a fancy, expensive restaurant. But it would have been nice to do something less ordinary, like see a play or a comedian, or go on a hike and have a picnic.

I'd tried dating in the States, though it was nearly impossible with a baby, and then a toddler. In every case, I'd found men to be underwhelming. Underwhelming and emotionally exhausting. Like Trevor, men my age needed more from me than I could give. I already had one child; I had no desire to have a man-child as well.

I often wondered if my cousin was the only decent guy out there. Sean stood out like a neon sign as a man barometer, and sadly other men didn't measure up.

"Trevor is a good guy, but there's no spark between us. We're better as friends." I checked the time on my phone, then returned it to my bag, taking a big gulp of my tea. We only had another ten minutes before I needed to leave.

"You're too nice, Eilish."

"I can't believe you just called me *too nice*."

"Well, you are. You didn't used to be. You used to be a snarky bitch, but now you're too nice. And too responsible."

I exhaled another laugh. "Thank you."

"It's not a compliment."

I lifted my eyes to hers and found Josey watching me with a sad expression. "I'm glad you're here, in Ireland. But I still miss you. I miss my friend."

"You miss the snarky bitch?" I gave her a small smile.

"Yes, I do."

I stopped myself before I rolled my eyes. "People change, Josey. Especially after they have a child."

Her lovely dark eyes moved over my face, like I was a stranger or like she was seeing me for the first time after a long separation. "I thought things would be different when you moved back to Ireland."

"How so?"

"I thought we'd see each other more."

I sputtered on my disbelief. "What are you talking about? I've seen you every Sunday for the last three weeks."

"Exactly. Once a week."

"You know you're welcome over any time."

She made a face. "No, thank you. It's like you and Patrick are your own little club. You two are inseparable, and I always feel like the third wheel. You should come out with me more often."

"Josey . . ." I shook my head, finishing my tea. "What do you expect? Again, I have a child. I can't just meet up with you whenever I please."

"But you're completely different," she protested. "It's like some alien has invaded your body."

I gritted my teeth and pulled my bag to my shoulder. "Sorry, I have to get back."

"Don't be mad."

"I'm not mad," I lied, standing. "I just have to go."

She stood too, reaching for me and pulling me into a hug. "I just mean, you're so serious." She leaned away, holding my shoulders and my gaze. "You used to want to have fun, we used to go clubbing all the time. You used to *be* fun."

I shrugged, moving out of her grip. "I still have fun. It's just a different kind of fun."

"Going to the park and watching your kid play on the playground is fun?"

I turned and called over my shoulder, "Yes. It is."

"Liar," she called back.

I ignored her, weaving through the tables, because she was wrong. It was fun. Being Patrick's mam was awesome and fun. I loved being a parent. I loved the certainty it gave me, the heady sense of responsibility and purpose. Being a mother was *real* and *important.* And I loved Patrick, with my whole heart. He came first, always.

I wouldn't trade a day at the park with my kid for a lifetime of Josey's kind of fun. Not in a million years.

FOUR
BRYAN

@THEBryanLeech: There's nothing better in life than a cup of peppermint tea, a comfortable pair of PJs and a good book.
@RonanFitz to @THEBryanLeech: You got hacked by your grandad again. Just FYI.

I was going to murder my neighbors.
    I'd just gotten out of the shower, put on my pajamas and slippers, brewed a cup of tea, and settled in to read the next few chapters of *The Complete Guide to the Birdlife of Britain and Europe*, when the music started.
    No.
    Not music.
    Noise.
    The people who lived in the apartment at the end of the hall were having a party. As we've already established, I hated parties. Especially when they were interrupting the nice, calm, relaxing, quiet night I had planned.
    I tried to concentrate on reading but the reverberations of the bass and volume of the noise grew consistently louder, and I decided I'd had enough. I grunted, slammed my book down on the coffee table, and strode for the door. When I took a peek in Will's bedroom I saw he had his earphones in. He had the right idea.
    Still, I was in too much of a grump to let it lie. I needed those dipshits at the end of the hall to know that blaring music on a Sunday night—or any night—wasn't going to fly with me.
    I stomped out of the apartment and only realized I was still holding my half

finished mug of tea when I raised my hand to slam on the door. Nobody answered. It took several more bangs before someone finally opened it. A pasty white man wearing a beanie and an Abercrombie and Fitch T-shirt stood in the entryway, a stylish Asian woman with him. Over their heads I could see at least fifteen to twenty people partying inside.

"Yeah?" the man asked, his eyes moving over me in a judgmental fashion. I couldn't give two fucks what he thought. All I wanted was for them to quit interrupting my evening.

"You need to turn the music down," I said in a measured, albeit aggressive, voice.

The man scoffed. "It's only half past nine."

"I'm aware of what time it is."

"It's my girlfriend's birthday," he said, throwing his arm around the woman's shoulders. "And we're not turning the music down. Like I said, it's early. We'll turn it down later."

He made a move to close the door in my face but my arm shot out to hold it open. I took a step closer until I was glaring down at him from my admittedly impressive height. Less impressive, I was also glaring at him through my reading spectacles and still holding my tea.

"Turn it down or I'll go in there and throw your motherfucking stereo system out the window."

The woman rolled her eyes in a way I found obnoxious. "It's an iPod dock, grandad. Jeez, get with the times."

I shot her an uncompromising look. She was right about me being out of touch, but she was wrong if she thought I gave a shit. I was who I was, and I made no apologies. PJs, housecoat, fur-lined slippers, and all. It was funny to think that just a few short years ago *I'd* been the one blaring the music and giving the neighbors shit when they complained.

Perhaps this was karma.

Karma is a wanker.

"I don't care what you're playing your trashy music on. I will throw whatever the hell it is out the window and then you'll have nothing for your noise pollution. Now, can you turn it the fuck down so I can get back to the quiet night I was enjoying before you so rudely interrupted it?"

"Oh man, this is priceless," came a familiar voice, and I let out an irritable grunt. Why did I think it was a good idea to recommend Sean Cassidy move into my apartment building again? Not just that, but the same floor? He'd taken up residence two weeks ago, after the tenancy agreement ended at his old place.

I turned and found my teammate standing a few doors away and several feet down the hall, a smile on his face like he'd just won the lottery. "Eilish, hand me my phone so I can get this on camera. This is the stuff YouTube was invented for."

Wait, Eilish?

It was then that I became aware of the tall, willowy redhead standing next to him. I made eye contact with her and her lips parted in surprise as they traveled lower, taking in my appearance. For the first time in a long time, a measure of self-consciousness had me standing straighter. And, in spite of the circumstances, a swell of attraction stirred within me.

Fact: I found her incredibly alluring and beautiful.

Also fact: I wasn't allowed to have her.

Therefore, fact: it was painful to endure.

"What is that?" Sean lifted his chin toward my mug.

I glowered at my mate. "Mint tea."

Sean laughed, looking as pleased as I'd ever seen him.

Karma is a wanker and so is Sean Cassidy.

"Are you really holding a mug of mint tea and complaining to the neighbors about the noise?" Sean asked in amusement, tutting. "I thought you were thirty, not seventy-five."

"It's too loud," I said gruffly, glancing at him before my attention returned to Eilish. She no longer looked surprised. Now her lips twitched as though she was holding back a smile as amused as the one Sean was sporting.

"Is that a housecoat?" she asked, one side of her mouth tilting up.

My hand not holding the mug went to my hips as I answered curtly, "Yes."

"I didn't realize they still made those," she continued, full on smiling now. Sean chuckled.

I arched a brow, unable to stop myself as I asked quietly, "Would you like me to remove it?"

She ignored the question, her cheeks heating a little, and nodded to the door right as it slammed shut. "Looks like they aren't going to uphold your request."

I swore, then turned and started thumping again, but they didn't answer this time. I let out an irritable sigh, my shoulders slumping as I headed back to my apartment, her light, musical laugh trailing after me and causing my steps to falter.

Damn. Even her laugh is lovely.

This attraction for Eilish was . . . inconvenient. It was also a temptation I wasn't willing to test any time soon. I needed to get away from her. Unfortunately, Sean Cassidy wasn't the kind of person to let this amount of personal humiliation go without utilizing it.

"Why don't you call the building's management company and make an official complaint?" he suggested. "Show those pesky kids who they're messing with."

"Go home, Sean," I replied in a bored voice as I stepped inside my apartment. In my hurry to give the neighbors what for, I'd left the door open. Before I could slam it in Sean's face, he followed me in, Eilish heavy on his heels, though she did seem reluctant to come inside. It was expected. For whatever reason, I got the sense that she didn't like me, or was wary of me.

I hated how it only made me want to change her mind.

"Aren't you going to offer us some refreshments?" Sean inquired, still grinning like the cat that got the cream.

"No, because I never invited you in. This is a home invasion."

His eyes flashed to Eilish. "How exciting! What do you think, Eilish? Shall we strip him naked, tie him up, and steal his valuables?"

I shot Sean a contemptuous look. "And why would I need to be naked?"

Sean winked at his cousin. "For Eilish's delectation, of course. Not only is she a burglar, she's also a bit of a perv."

"Sean!" Eilish exclaimed. Her gaze came to me. "Don't listen to him. He's just being aggravating, like usual." Color flushed her cheeks, and it caught my interest. Was she embarrassed?

I took a step closer, tilting my head and studying her through my spectacles.

"Man, there's nothing to eat here," said Sean, distracting me from Eilish as he rifled through my kitchen. "Good God, man. Are those dried prunes? You really are on old codger, Leech. I bet you write in letters of complaint to the BBC about the inappropriate amount of leg shown on *Strictly Come Dancing*."

I groaned. He really wasn't going to let this lie. "Can you please quit bothering me and leave? I need to find some earplugs so I can get back to my book." And the longer Eilish remained in my apartment, the harder it was for me not to engage her. It wasn't simply that I found her beautiful. I wanted to get to know her, who she was, what made her tick. It was a new and unexpected predicament. There was just something about her that felt familiar, like I'd known her in another life.

Movement out of the corner of my eye had me turning toward her, and I saw her step up to the coffee table, her gaze scanning the title of my book. Her lips twitched again when she glanced back at me. There was something new in her expression, a warmth that hadn't been there before. Up until now, all I'd gotten was icy cold.

The warmth felt far too exhilarating for something so minuscule.

She held my gaze for a second longer, then went to pull Sean away from my cupboards. "Come on, let's quit torturing Mr. Leech and leave him to his evening."

"Oh? Did you hear that? *Mr. Leech.*" Sean's eyebrows jumped high on his forehead.

Eilish almost rolled her eyes. Almost. "Come off it, Sean."

My teammate relented, though still grinned widely, as he allowed her to lead him to the door. "I can't wait to tell the lads all about this in the morning."

I shrugged, not caring much, and sipped my mint tea. I'd partied more in the last ten years than the entire squad put together. I'd earned my newfound lifestyle of peace and quiet, so they could slag me off all they wanted. I looked to the door and met Eilish's gaze one last time before she went.

There was a quality in her lingering look I couldn't identify right away. Then it came to me: curiosity.

Something about the encounter tonight changed her mind about me.

Which made me wonder what her opinion had been before.

FIVE
EILISH

@ECassChoosesPikachu: I'm not crying, I just have onions, pepper spray, and severe acute depression in my eye.
@SeanCassinova: See you after work, I'll be the bloke holding the sign: Free Hugs

Today was Patrick's first day at primary school, and I was a wreck.

He seemed excited, not nervous at all. My boy rarely got nervous. He simply took new experiences as they came. I, on the other hand, felt like I had placed him in a wicker basket and was about to send him down the river. Yes, I was being ridiculous. No, I couldn't seem to help it.

"What's wrong, Mummy?" Patrick asked, his small hand tugging on my sleeve as he stared up at me with wide, concerned eyes. I dabbed at my tears and bent down on one knee to give him a hug.

"Nothing, baby. Nothing's wrong at all," I whispered, my voice cracking.

"Everything will be okay," said Patrick, patting my shoulder. "Don't cry. When we get home, we can play Pokémon with your cards."

I let out a watery laugh. Of course he'd be the one to comfort me. Some days I wondered if I needed him more than he needed me. The prospect of not being with him all day made my heart feel like it was breaking. I'd been spoiled over the last few months; finishing school with Sean's financial assistance meant I'd been able to spend all day, every day with Patrick.

Now it was time for reality.

Stupid reality, keeping it real all the time.

"We're a team," Patrick went on prosaically, and I grew even more emotional. It was something I always said to him. It was our motto. *The two of us against the world.*

Sean cleared his throat from somewhere behind us.

And maybe Sean.

"Yes, baby, we're a team," I sniffled and pulled back slightly. "You're the most amazing boy in the whole wide world, do you know that?"

Patrick chewed his lip. I couldn't get over how adorable he looked in his uniform: tiny white shirt, tiny blue jumper, tiny gray slacks, tiny black shoes. The sight of him made my heart melt. "Do you think I'll make friends?" he asked with just a hint of apprehension.

I laughed softly to cover my maniacal maternal instincts, which had me thinking, *They better be friendly to you, or else I'll be handing out wedgies to four-year-olds* . . . and likely being arrested for giving wedgies to four-year-olds.

I ran my fingers through his short hair. "I think you'll make more friends than you'll know what to do with."

He wriggled excitedly in place and started to grin. "I hope they like Pokémon."

"I'm sure they will. Now give Mummy one last hug. She's going to miss you like crazy."

He threw his arms around my shoulders and squeezed tight. "I'm gonna miss you, too," he whispered in my ear, like he was telling a secret.

Standing back after a hug that lasted too long, but never long enough, I finally let him walk into his classroom, but I couldn't bring myself to leave. I stood at the door, peering through the window, my heart in my throat.

Please be nice to him. He is my world. If you make him cry, I'll destroy you.

"Okay, Eilish. Time to go." Sean came up behind me, his hands gripping my shoulders and turning me away from the door.

"Just one more minute."

"No. We have to go. Do you want to be late for work on your first day?"

Sighing sadly, I let him steer me from Patrick's classroom, down the hall, out the door, and to Sean's car. Once we were buckled in, Sean had us back on the road.

"Oh, come now. Cheer up."

I sighed again. It was still sad.

"He's growing up so fast," I said mournfully.

"Yes. Pretty soon he'll be beating his Uncle Sean in an actual ruck, and not just ones we play on the game console."

I slid my eyes to the side and peered at my cousin. He was a trickster. Last night, as Lucy watched Patrick at my place, we'd gone to Sean's to *pick a little something up.*

The little something had turned out to be a big something.

"We're not keeping it."

THE CAD AND THE CO-ED

"I don't understand why this is such a big deal."

I coughed, then sputtered, then coughed again, finally managing to choke out, "How can you say that?"

My cousin shifted in the driver's seat, casting me an ill-tempered gaze. "You make it sound like I gave him a pony or a nuclear submarine. The Russians have several for sale, you know. You should be thanking me for not buying him one of those."

"No, Sean. Not a pony or a nuclear sub. Just a giant television and a brand new Wii U game system. That's it. That's all."

"So?" Sean's hands tightened on the steering wheel as he pressed on the gas, the car accelerating so suddenly I had to grasp the door handle.

"Sean."

"Eilish."

I pressed my lips together, staring out the windshield, attempting to arrange my thoughts. How could I explain to my cousin that his lavish gifts made me feel . . . they made me feel . . .

Incompetent. Like a failure. Like a parasite.

I released a silent sigh and closed my eyes, endeavoring to gather my scattered thoughts. "I appreciate everything you've done and continue to do for us. I do." I affixed my eyes unseeingly out the passenger side window. "You saved my life, more than once. But, you have to understand, I'll never be able to repay you, I'll never be able to—"

"Have I asked for repayment?" He slowed as we approached the light in front of the complex, gentling his voice. "We're family, E."

"I know," I said, but I shook my head at the word, because we both knew being family didn't always equal love and support.

But family meant something to Sean. And it meant something to me.

The rest of our relatives? Not so much.

"You simply must allow me to spoil my nephew," Sean demanded haughtily, pulling a smile from me. He liked to play the snob but I knew underneath all his bluster was a big old softie.

As an example, Sean—who had no brothers or sisters—called my son his nephew, though they were technically cousins. In return, Patrick called Sean "Monkey Sean," which was Patrick's version of Uncle Sean.

Again, I shook my head. "You mustn't buy Patrick such elaborate gifts. First of all, I have nowhere to put the television. My apartment is far too small."

"Then get a bigger place. There's a penthouse available in my building."

I wasn't going to dignify that with a response. "And second of all, it's not good for Patrick to be spending so much time playing video games."

Sean frowned. "It's not?"

"No. It's not, especially not on his own. Maybe . . . maybe you could keep the game system at your place? Then, when we come to visit, the two of you can play together."

"That's an idea." Sean nodded, his eyes brightening as he pulled into the parking garage. "It could be our special thing. I've already missed so much time with him."

Ugh. Right through the heart.

I suppressed the now familiar guilt Olympics.

We'd arrived at the sports complex, and today was my first day at my new job. Now was not the time for me to be simmering in my regrets.

"Sorry," Sean offered solemnly. "I didn't mean to imply—"

"It's fine." I waved away his apology, forcing cheerfulness into my voice. "I know you didn't mean anything by it."

"It's just that, I wish you would have let me help sooner." Sean pulled into his assigned parking spot but didn't cut the engine. "You are excessively stubborn."

I chuckled, my head falling back to the headrest, and repeated myself for perhaps the millionth time, "I did what I thought was right at the time, and I'm sorry I didn't come to you sooner. God, you have no idea how sorry I am."

I felt Sean's hand close over mine and squeeze. "Yes, well, never mind that. Nothing to do about it now. Just keep reminding yourself that your dashing cousin Sean is always right in all things, and life will miraculously become less burdensome."

I twisted my mouth to the side, lifted my eyelids—just a sliver—and peered at him. "Really? All things, eh?"

His lips twitched and I knew he was remembering the cornucopia of times over our childhood where he was most definitely not right in all things. I was just about to remind him of the time he'd fed our family dog orange sherbet, which had led the dog to leave orange puddles all over the carpet, when Sean's gaze sharpened, growing abruptly sober.

"What will you do if you see Bryan today?"

I winced, turning my face away, and endeavoring to mask my discomfort with a light laugh. "Bryan who?"

Oh yeah, real smooth, E.

I failed at life. More specifically, I failed at not ogling Bryan Leech.

I'd decided that's what I'd been doing at the party last week and then again yesterday. Even in his ridiculous housecoat, slippers, and spectacles the man was entirely too delicious.

And adorable.

Whoa. No. No, no, no. I pushed that thought away. I could not and would not think about Bryan in terms of being adorable.

Lust. Lust was safe. Any straight woman with a pulse would feel lust for Bryan Leech. I'd been *ogling* the man. Every time I forced my gaze away, it sought him out. I'd felt like an addict, devouring him with my eyes, promising myself that each glance would be the last . . .

But so it goes when one loses one's virginity to a mystical, gorgeous creature with an enchanted penis.

Sean heaved a frustrated sigh. "Eilish."

"Sean."

"Pretending you don't know to whom I'm referring is a shite strategy."

"Sean—"

"You should get to know him."

"Stop—"

"Ask him out for a drink."

"Please—"

"On second thought, don't do that. It would be exceptionally awkward. Poor bastard is a teetotaler now—can you believe, mint tea?—and he even seems to like it. Come to think on it, you don't drink much either."

"Sean, enough!" I snapped, immediately regretting my tone. I let my face fall into my hands, taking a moment to push back the rush of anxiety, and mumbling through my fingers, "Sorry. I'm sorry."

"It's okay, darling. I know you're not getting much sleep."

I smiled humorlessly, though he couldn't see it since my face was still hidden. I hadn't been getting much sleep. Patrick had been sick on and off for the last month with an upper respiratory infection. He was on the mend, but he was still sleeping with me. This meant I could count on being kicked in the stomach at least six times a night. For a four-year-old, the kid had massively long and strong legs.

"No, I'm sorry. I'm an ungrateful witch. I should have brought my broom to work."

"No. You're an exhausted single mother who is starting a new job today at the same place where the father of her child works, only he has no idea he has a child."

A flare of panic and guilt burned in my chest, making it difficult to breathe or think. But I wouldn't cry. Even as a kid I'd never been much of a crier. I hadn't cried in years. I'd tried, but I physically could not, not since giving birth to Patrick.

Besides, Sean wasn't the most unbiased person when it came to mothers keeping their son's father in the dark. His own mother had hidden the identity of his father for years.

"What would you have me do, Sean? He was drunk. He didn't know my name. He doesn't even remember me."

"Perhaps he'd have made things right by you," he offered solemnly, finally cutting the engine.

"I'm not interested in him doing *right by me*. Like I said, he was drunk, hardly capable of giving consent to father a child."

"You were both there, E. Perhaps if he'd known he was a father, he might have cleaned up his act earlier."

"You can't put that on me." I shook my head quickly, feeling my anxiety rise with each word. "Sure, maybe he would have cleaned up his act. Or perhaps he wouldn't have given a shit. Or perhaps he would have taken Patrick away from me. Or perhaps he would have—"

"All right, all right." Sean held his hands between us in surrender, then unbuckled his seatbelt. "I'm not going to argue with you about this again. As I've said, you're excessively stubborn."

I swallowed a retort on the tip of my tongue. If this had been five years ago, I would have argued. We would have sparred and enjoyed every second of it.

But I didn't do that anymore. Plus, I loved my cousin and didn't want to be ungrateful. I needed him to know how much he meant to me, how he'd made such an immense difference in my life.

I felt his eyes on my profile, felt the shift in his mood before he said, "I'm sorry. I shouldn't have brought this up, not now, not before your first day."

"I want you to know," I gathered a deep breath, and with it my courage, "I never told you this, but I've never regretted having Patrick. Never. He has made my life infinitely better. Loving him, taking care of him, has been the greatest joy of my life. Sometimes things were difficult, sometimes they were impossible, and I would wonder how I was going to make it through, whether we were going to have to live out of my car—"

"Oh, darling."

"No, listen. I need to say this and I need you to hear it."

He reached for my hand and squeezed it. I turned mine palm up and twisted our fingers together.

"This is selfish and terrible, but what got me through those times was knowing I had you. I don't know what I would have done without you as my safety net. If things fell apart, I knew you would be there."

He gave me a tender and pleased smile, which only served to ignite my guilt.

"It's not fair, how much I've asked of you."

"You're wrong, darling. Because loving you and Patrick, taking care of you and Patrick has been one of the greatest joys of *my* life. You are my family."

"But it's not fair, how you've placed your life on hold. You and Lucy—"

"Don't you worry about us, we're right on track, thanks to you. She adores Patrick, as you know, and he's been a most effective contagion."

"Contagion?"

"Yes. For baby-making fever."

I gasped, then laughed, because Sean was grinning devilishly. "You've been using Patrick this whole time?"

"Of course I have. But that doesn't negate my love for him. If anything, I love him more for changing Lucy's mind about having children. And, Eilish, I *am* sorry I keep pushing you about Bryan."

"It's fine."

"No, it's not fine. You should allow me to make it up to you."

I squinted at him because I knew where this was going. Shaking my head, I opened the passenger side door. "Don't you dare—"

"Come on, you know you miss shopping with me."

I jumped out of the car and called back at him, "I don't need anything."

"But you *want* something." He was out of the car, smiling at me with his small, knowing smile.

"Not a single thing." I shut the door and turned from him, employing quick steps. I didn't want to be late.

"Wait," he called after me, making me halt and glance over my shoulder. "You should let someone spoil you every once in a while."

"No, thank you. My days of being spoiled are long gone."

"You were never spoiled, Eilish," Sean said, a note of consternation in his tone, as though he were truly distressed by this fact.

"Well," I shrugged, pasting a bright smile on my face, "no harm then. I'll never know what I'm missing."

* * *

"You'll be fine. It'll be fine. You're a professional . . . you can do this." I nodded at the image of myself in the mirror while I spoke under my breath. Despite the pep talk, a little crack formed in my armor as a potent reminder drifted to my forebrain. *You didn't earn this. You don't deserve it. The only reason they hired you is because of Sean.*

"Crackers . . ." Sighing sadly, I closed the locker door, rubbing my chest where the spike of nervous energy flared and made it difficult to swallow.

I'd started saying *crackers* instead of *crap* when Patrick was old enough to repeat my words. Running after a two-year-old bellowing, "CRAAAAP!" at the top of his lungs had been a game-changer. So *crap* became *crackers*, and *shite* became *shells*, and *fuck* became *forks*.

This morning had been extremely difficult, dropping Patrick off at school and knowing he would be there all day. He hadn't been at a daycare all day for the last year, not since Sean had stepped in and insisted I take a loan from him so I could finish my degree.

This job was the first step toward paying my cousin back. But the irony tasted sour because Sean had been the one to arrange for the job that would pay him back.

I'll never be able to pay him back . . .

"Hey there, you must be Eilish Cassidy."

Startled, I glanced up to find a smiling woman with her hand extended. Remembering myself, I quickly accepted her handshake.

"Uh, yes. I'm Eilish."

"Name is Jenna McCarthy, I'm the nutritionist for the team. I know your cousin Sean. He got you the job, right? Lord, you sound just as posh as he does."

She gave me a quick once-over, but other than the bluntness of her words, I couldn't detect anything judgmental or sinister in her demeanor. Actually, quite the opposite.

"I . . . uh . . . that's right, he—"

"My brother was a coach, way back when Donovan was the team captain in the nineties, that's how I got my spot." She nodded once at this information, then turned and waved at me to follow, which I scrambled to do as she continued, "The club knows it's best to keep things in the family. It's a good way to keep it professional, you know? Otherwise the support staff would be full of fans and shite-all would get done." She chuckled and rolled her eyes.

I huffed a relieved laugh and my smile widened as my gaze moved over the profile of Jenna McCarthy. Several inches shorter than me, her tight, curly hair was blonde with healthy swaths of silvery gray, and laugh lines framed bright blue eyes. She'd led us out of the women's locker room and into a stairwell I didn't know existed.

"This is the best way to the belly of the beast." She gestured to the steps leading down. "You can avoid all the bigwigs and chatty clan in the office. Plus, you're the new physio, yes?"

"Yes. I'm—"

"Well then, Connors always takes the lift, so you can avoid him, too. Just make sure you hide your lunch because he's sort of infamous for thieving food around here." She chuckled again and nudged me with her elbow just before descending the stairs.

I moved quickly to follow her.

"He seems to be very knowledgeable." I'd only met the man who would be my closest coworker once during the interview process. All of his questions were on point, but it was made very clear that he wasn't my boss. The entire support staff reported up through the health and wellness coach, Brian Tierney.

"Who? Connors?" she asked over her shoulder, but didn't wait for me to respond. "I suppose he is. But he's also a grumpy bugger, which is how we lost the last two physio assistants, if you want to know the truth. Hopefully, you being Sean's girl means he'll have better manners."

I didn't volunteer that my cousin Sean had said something similar about Connors. Nor did I relate how Sean had told me in no uncertain terms that I was to come to him immediately should I have any issues with the senior physiotherapist. I'd smiled and nodded at the time, but secretly I was determined to hold my own. Sean had already done enough. I wanted to prove myself.

I *needed* to prove myself. He may have secured the job for me, but it was up to me to prove I deserved to keep it.

Jenna continued to talk while we took the stairs to the lower level. "I'll be happy to show you the lay of the land. This is the bottom floor, where the team's locker room is located as well as the base therapy rooms."

I listened attentively and smiled politely. Even though Sean had already given me a tour on the day of the interview, and I'd since memorized the schematic of the sports complex, I appreciated Jenna taking the time to show me around and give me these helpful tips.

"I imagine you'll spend most of your non-charting time here." She nudged me again with her elbow. "Hope you don't mind a few bare arses and wagging dicks."

I pressed my lips together and stared at her with wide eyes because Jenna had paired this statement with wagging eyebrows.

She then snorted and burst into laughter, smacking me on the shoulder. "Lord, your expression." Jenna shook her head, her face now red as she wiped tears of hilarity from her eyes.

Meanwhile, I stared at her while the words *bare arses and wagging dicks* hung heavy in the long hallway . . . no pun intended.

"Don't worry," she finally managed, "they're all just a bunch of little boys when it comes down to it."

"I'm not worried. And I'm undaunted by naked flesh." I tried to sound both congenial and professional, smiling just slightly, not wanting to seem uptight.

"Are you now?" Her intelligent eyes flickered over me. "Well, pretty girl like you being down here might encourage them to cover their assets more often. Come on, I'll take you to the base therapy room where you can get yourself sorted before the hoard arrives." Turning again, she waved me forward.

I followed. "I don't have the schedule yet. I emailed Connors last week but haven't heard back."

She gave me a side-eye squint and frowned for the first time since we'd met.

Quickly, I added, "I'm sure he's very busy, so it's obviously no big deal. I'm sure he'll have it for me today."

She grunted, continuing to squint at me, then said, "Well, if he doesn't have it for you by the end of today, just ask Alice in administration for a press-kit, it'll have the team's practice schedules. In fact, ask her for one regardless."

"Thanks. I will." I made a mental note to introduce myself to Alice.

Jenna's gaze swept over me again. "I don't know if Connors has mentioned it, but you might want to go through the team's injury sheets before you set to work. You should have been given a password to the charting system.

I nodded quickly, eager for every bit of information. "Thank you. I really appreciate the information."

"Moore has a shoulder injury that's been flaring up, Gallagher has been overdoing it with the free weights, Daly has been holding his lower back during practice, and Leech's knee needs special attention."

I stumbled at the name *Leech*, a familiar wave of both heat and frost traveling down my spine. Luckily, I caught myself against the wall before Jenna noticed.

Of course, I knew seeing Bryan, interacting with Bryan, *touching* Bryan was a real possibility when I accepted the position. But I would have been a fool to turn down the job. I needed the money and I needed the experience. Time with a professional team would be invaluable for my résumé.

I would be professional and, after the events of the party last week, I had every reason to believe Bryan would be as well.

Why wouldn't he be? *As far as he knows, he only just met me.*

The reminder of his antipathy, of his not remembering, stung—it always did—so I allowed the soothing numbness of ice and resolve to wrap around my heart.

Stopping just in front of a gray door with the word *Therapy* in black letters, Jenna's frown waned and became a small, soft smile as she gazed at my expression. "Don't be nervous. And don't hesitate to come to me if you have any questions. You seem like a nice girl, even if that cousin of yours eats more red meat than he should and acts like a posh arsehole most of the time."

"He really is lovely," I blurted, wanting to defend my cousin who'd saved my life.

And my son's life.

"He's a stuck-up snob, but—"

"You have to understand how we were raised. It's a defense mechanism," I rushed to explain. "He has the best heart, but he hides it because he has to. My family is very cold. Very spiteful and judgmental and . . ." I sucked in a breath, my heart twisting painfully at one particular memory where my mother had been both very cold and very spiteful. I shivered and once more rubbed my chest where it ached.

Jenna grunted again, not frowning, but not smiling either. "Well, tell him to lay off the red meat. He's not twenty-five anymore."

With that, she turned on her heel and walked back to the stairway, leaving me alone with my thoughts and the closed door to the therapy room.

I took a bracing breath, placed my hand on the lever, and opened the door. What I saw filled me first with disbelief, then dismay seasoned with despair, then determination.

More or less, the room was unchanged from the last time I'd been in it. The three massage and assessment tables were still in the same position, several large cabinets full of supplies were against the far wall, and two work stations for charting and researching were in an alcove off to one side.

The main difference was that instead of a tidy and clean therapy room, this place was a disaster.

Old food containers littered the assessment tables and both desks of the alcove. Empty—at least, I hoped they were empty—beer cans and bottles were scattered around floor. Dirty towels lay everywhere. The supply cabinets were all open and mostly empty.

What the hell?

Before I could fully react, the door behind me opened and I turned to find Mr. Connors, his arms full with paper bags of food and a six-pack of beer.

He stopped short, apparently surprised by my presence, but then recovered quickly. "What are you doing here?"

The vague smell of cumin and greasy chips drifted into the room.

I straightened my spine and held out my hand. "Mr. Connors, I'm—"

"I know who you are, Freckles. I didn't ask for your name, did I? Are you deaf? I asked what you are doing here." He brushed past me and into the therapy room, kicking the garbage out of his way as he went.

I frowned at his back. "I work here."

"Not here, you don't." He dumped the contents of his arms onto an assessment table and faced me. "You do your work in the locker room and gym. This is my space."

Gaping at his sour expression, I crossed my arms over my chest. "That is not my understanding of the situation, Mr. Connors. This is the therapy room and, based on my reading of the health and management standard operating procedure, all non-emergent therapy assessments and sessions must take place here."

His face grew an unsightly shade of reddish purple just before he bellowed, "You can take your standard operating procedures and shove them up your skinny arse!"

I flinched, my mouth falling open in disbelief. Jenna and Sean hadn't been lying when they'd called Connors grumpy. He was like a great, billowing toddler throwing a tantrum.

"This is my space, my room, and you don't have privileges."

The big man charged toward me. Automatically, I stepped back, holding my hands up between us.

Before I could manage another word, he slammed the door shut in my face, yelling from the other side, "And stay out!"

I'm not too proud to admit, I gaped at the door. I stared and gaped, not quite able to reconcile this version of Connors with the knowledgeable yet circumspect fellow I'd met during the interview.

I don't know how long I gaped—maybe a minute, maybe fifteen—but when a familiar voice asked, "Are you lost?"

I jumped.

I gasped.

I turned.

I found Bryan Leech leaning against the concrete wall, regarding me with a quizzical smile.

Let me amend that.

I found a grass-stained, sweaty, tattooed and shirtless and gorgeous Bryan Leech regarding me with a quizzical smile.

Ah . . . *forks.*

SIX
BRYAN

@THEBryanLeech: Delayed gratification is worth it in the end, right?
@SeanCassinova to @THEBryanLeech: Not if you're talking about the expired prunes in your cupboard.
@RonanFitz to @SeanCassinova and @THEBryanLeech: I hope that isn't a euphemism o.O

"Are you lost?" I asked, vaguely amused. I mean, I could be scary when the mood took me, but in general my demeanor didn't usually make women flee my presence like I was a hobo wearing a flasher's trench coat.

Unless that woman was Eilish Cassidy.

"No, not lost at all," she replied curtly and moved to step by me. She kept her eyes trained on my face.

Didn't want to tempt herself with the sight of my bare chest, eh? I liked to imagine that was the reason and not that my nakedness somehow offended her. *Not that I should be imagining anything at all,* I reminded myself. Female company was still off limits. Specifically, non-platonic female company, and there was nothing platonic about how I felt and thought about Eilish.

She was still looking at me funny.

Was I flying low or something? I glanced down just to be sure, and nothing obscene was showing. I was, however, dirty and sweaty and wearing only a pair of scrum shorts. I probably should have put a shirt on before coming in here, but I'd been running circuits out on the field when my trusty old tendinosis started giving me trouble.

This was why I'd hotfooted it over to the physio room to get Connors to have a look at my knee. Half of me had been hoping I'd bump into Eilish. Meanwhile, the other half knew better and wanted nothing to do with her. That would be the sane, logical half. I had no business even considering pursuing her, yet here I was, looking at her like a lion stalking an antelope. A very beautiful and intriguing antelope.

"Is Connors in there?" I asked, still a bit breathless after my workout.

Eilish's gaze flickered back to the therapy room as she nodded, "Yes, he's there."

There was something in her expression that made me wonder if perhaps *I* wasn't the one she wanted to flee. Connors was known to be a dick to almost everyone.

She moved to walk by me again when I spoke. "Don't take it personally."

Her brow furrowed, her gaze skittering over the tattoo on my arm before moving back to mine. "Huh?"

"Connors. He's an incurable arsehole. You could be Sacha Baron Cohen wearing a bikini and a smile and he'd still find something to criticize."

"Sacha Baron Cohen?" she lifted an eyebrow.

I tilted my head to one side and then the other, considering my next words. "Let's just say Connors is a big fan."

She let out a slow breath and sliced her teeth across her lip. She looked like she wanted to say something, but was holding back. Finally, she relented, "Are we talking Borat or Ali G?"

"Neither. He likes Brüno."

She snickered a begrudging laugh. "Wow. Disturbing as that is, it actually makes me feel better. Now whenever he's being difficult I'll just imagine him in pleather hot pants."

I shot her a grin, enchanted by her quip. "Happy to help."

She mustered a smile in return, but it was still wary. My eyes traced the shape of her mouth and the scattering of freckles across her nose and cheeks. In spite of everything, I was profoundly attracted to this woman. Perhaps I should pay a visit to the florist . . .

"He just seemed so different in the interview," said Eilish, breaking the quiet. "So much less . . ."

"Like the anti-Christ?" I provided jokingly.

"I wish that statement wasn't true," she went on, nodding and laughing absentmindedly.

I took a second to study her. She was all flawless skin and bright, vibrant red hair. She seemed young but mature, more mature than her years. If she was doing an internship, then she must've just finished college. That'd put her in her early twenties.

Man, she was way too young for me. Not that she was even an option. She

THE CAD AND THE CO-ED

wasn't. No woman was. My sobriety was a tentative thing, and any kind of change could upset the balance.

What were you thinking, penis-brain, going after her at Will's party like that? Yeah, that's right, you weren't.

The problem was, my penis often took over where my brain was either too lazy and too indifferent to care. Which was why I kept digging a hole for myself by asking, "Hey, you wouldn't happen to be feeling charitable, would you?"

She eyed me warily. "Why do you ask?"

In for a penny, in for a pound.

"I have tendinosis in my left knee, and it's seized up on me. I was just headed to get Connors to work on it, but would much prefer if you had a look instead. I'm willing to bet he's in a shitty mood, and I'd rather not be on the receiving end of it."

Her gaze trailed down to my knee, skimming over my chest, abdomen, and the tattoo on my arm in the process. A little buzz of awareness went through me. I liked it when she looked. I liked it way too much. She was chewing on her lip, clearly uneasy.

Abruptly, with a shrill denial, she blurted, "No, I'm sorry, I can't. I'm not set up properly yet."

"What's to set up? Everything you need is right through that door," I said, gesturing casually over her shoulder.

She swallowed visibly, and for a second I thought about giving her an out. But something inside me, either my dick or my heart, I swear I didn't know which, spurred me on. One or the other of them wanted Eilish's pretty little hands on me. So yeah, probably the former.

After a long hesitation, she glanced at the door and seemed to steel herself.

"Okay well, I can't promise miracles, but let's see what I can do for you."

I smiled widely, and she blinked as though caught off guard. Then she turned quickly and opened the door. *Don't follow her. Don't do it.*

I followed.

"I thought I told you to . . ." Connors's words petered off as soon as he saw me, which made me wonder if he'd been about to chew Eilish's head off for no good reason. What an arsehole. I'd keep tabs on his treatment of her, or at the very least mention it to Sean.

"Oh, Mr. Leech, I don't recall you being penciled in for an appointment today," he said, unkempt eyebrows furrowing.

"I'm not but my knee's been acting up. I thought young Eilish here could take a look at it, seeing as it's her first day."

She noticeably bristled at the word *young*, shooting me an irritated glare.

Meanwhile, Connors tossed her a disgruntled glance. "No, no, that's not necessary. I can do it."

"But—" Eilish started, and I intervened.

"I'm happy for her to see to me, Connors."

"Be that as it may, she isn't qualified," he sneered and looked at her like she was a piece of gum stuck to his shoe.

"I've been around the block enough times to be able to guide her myself," I said, irritated by his attitude. "So you can stand the fuck down."

"Don't you dare talk to me like that," he sputtered. "I'll have you reported."

"Oh yeah? Because you're a gleaming paragon of virtue. Go back to your six-pack and let Eilish do the job she's supposed to be training for."

"I need to oversee her work."

"Not this time you don't." I stared him down. He seemed to conclude that going up against me wasn't worth the trouble. Everybody knew I could be as stubborn as they came.

With a few unkind words muttered under his breath, he retreated back into his office and turned the TV on. I motioned to Eilish. "Lead the way."

I could tell she was upset, likely by Connors's disrespect, but was doing her best not to let it show. I made a mental note to have a word with Coach Brian about it, see if he could maybe give our physio a stern talking to. If he didn't, I was liable to do it myself and lose my temper in the process. Again.

Eilish stayed quiet as she gestured for me to sit on the examination chair. She bent low to have a look at my knee, and I swallowed tightly, my mind wandering to a place it had no business going. She was obviously young and inexperienced, and all this must've been a little intimidating. The last thing she needed was some old perv having dirty thoughts about her, even if she was unfairly beautiful. Too beautiful for a job like this. My single teammates were going to be throwing themselves at her before long. I clenched my fist just thinking about it.

You have no business clenching that fist of yours, my conscience finally intervened. *You promised yourself no women until you kept a plant alive for six months, and now look at you.*

Yeah well, where were you five minutes ago when I needed you to stop me from following my dick? I shot back grumpily.

"Which knee is it again? Your left?" Eilish asked softly, her cool fingers gently probing.

"Yeah, my left," I answered, uncharacteristically lost for words. I couldn't remember the last time I'd been touched by someone I actually wanted to touch me.

"How did you develop the tendinosis? Injury or overuse?"

I noticed her eyes move over the tattoo on my arm again, then she frowned as though the sight of it was confusing.

"Overuse, but I did tear the meniscus years ago. I pushed my body too hard for too long. I used to be a heavy drinker, you see. Substance abuse and training for six hours a day don't make for a healthy combination."

Her gaze came back to mine and she seemed interested in this information. "You *used to* be?"

"Yep. I'm sober almost two years. You wouldn't recognize me these days from the man I was when I drank." I gestured to my tattoo, the one she'd been looking at a minute ago. "I got this a couple weeks after I quit drinking for good. It's an ancient Mayan symbol for endurance, makes me feel stronger when I look at it. It also reminds me of how I never want to go back to where I was."

"Oh," she breathed, nodding thoughtfully. She was quiet for a moment as she very gently stretched my knee. She was being hesitant and far too careful in her movements, but it still helped to relieve the ache a little.

I continued talking, hoping it might make her more comfortable. "Yeah, take it from an old dog who's been through the ringer, you're better off steering clear of all that partying and heavy drinking business. People your age think they're invincible, free to do whatever they want, but believe me, there's always a price to be paid."

She stiffened at this, almost like I'd insulted her. "I'm nothing like most people my age."

Her statement made me curious. "No?"

"No," she answered, giving no insight into why.

"Yeah well, that's a good thing, I guess. I just turned thirty and only now am I starting to appreciate all the things I used to think were boring. You know Will? Will Moore, the American, built like a brick wall?"

She nodded.

"I don't know if you saw yesterday when you stopped by, but he and I live together now. And keep this between you and me, but most of the time we'd both prefer to stay in and play Scrabble than go out clubbing with the rest of the squad," I said and winked.

Then I tried not to grimace because I'd just winked at her.

Why the hell am I winking?

She gave a light chuckle, "Yeah, I think I guessed that from the episode outside your neighbor's apartment."

I didn't let her comment faze me, instead I plastered on a carefree smile. "I'll have you know women all over the country would be queuing up to catch a glimpse of me in my PJs. You should count yourself lucky."

"Oh really?" she challenged. "Who are these women? The same ones who go to Daniel O'Donnell concerts and play bingo on a Friday night?"

I glared at her playfully. "Yeah, yeah, laugh it up. I don't know why any man would sleep naked when they could be wearing a pair of flannel jimjams."

She gave me a funny look, blurting, "You're sort of unexpected, do you know that?"

I shrugged and flashed her a toothy grin. "I like what I like."

She returned her attention to stretching my leg. When she relieved a particularly sore spot, I let out a pleasurable groan. She looked up at me and our gazes locked. For a moment she appeared transfixed as her hands continued to work their magic. I knew she had more in her though, so I encouraged huskily, "Don't be afraid to be rough. I'm tougher than I look."

Something in my tone made her freeze, her hands withdrawing into her lap. A moment of quiet passed before I asked, "Eilish, are you okay?"

"Yes, I just . . . I forgot myself for a moment," she said very quietly as she shook her head.

I frowned. "You what?"

"I'm sorry, I mean, I forgot to leave off some forms at HR. I need to go."

"Right now?" I asked quizzically.

She nodded very fervently. "Yes, right now. Put an ice pack on your knee and keep off it for at least thirty minutes." And with that she hurried from the room.

. . . *Ooooookay.*

I replayed our conversation in my mind, trying to figure out if I'd inadvertently offended her. Sure, she'd gotten a little huffy when I'd stereotyped her age group, but something told me that wasn't it.

Two years ago, I wouldn't have given a flying feck if a beautiful woman got huffy with me. They'd mostly still be up for a quick shag anyway. Yeah, I wasn't that impressed with the man I was. But, I wasn't him anymore. And Eilish wasn't just a beautiful woman.

No, there was something up with Eilish Cassidy, and I'd be damned if I wasn't determined to find out what.

* * *

"What's the story with your cousin?"

"Pardon?"

"Eilish. I bumped into her earlier over in physio. She doesn't seem to like me much." I claimed the spot next to Sean on the grass and stretched.

He gave me the side-eye. "What did you say to her?"

"Oh, of course you think it's something I said. I was a perfect gentleman, but you'd swear I was Charles bloody Manson, judging by how she couldn't get away fast enough."

"She's shy," said Sean, not meeting my gaze.

Shy? Ehhhhh no.

The way his jaw stiffened told me he wasn't telling me the whole truth. My brain worked overtime, wondering if maybe some dickhead had treated her poorly and now she hated men. Or maybe she just found me "unsavory" because I had a reputation and she was a Cassidy. The family were notorious snobs.

"Well, she'll have to get over that pretty fast if she's going to work with the team. No room for shyness when you're feeling up muscled rugger buggers for a living."

"She's a trainee physiotherapist, Leech, not a goddamn happy-endings masseuse," he said.

I smiled wide, taking satisfaction in riling him. "Is there a difference?"

At this he reached over and gave me a slap on the head. "Yes, there's a difference, fuckface, and you know it. I swear if you so much as make one wrong turn with her, I'll end you." He paused, his voice lowering when he continued, "She's been through a lot."

I put my hands in the air. "Relax, I'm joking. I'll behave around her, I promise."

He made a low sound in the back of his throat and returned to stretching. I couldn't stop wondering about what he meant when he said she'd been through a lot. It was out of the ordinary for me to be this curious about a virtual stranger.

Then again, I was still figuring out what my ordinary was. Maybe I'd always been a busybody, just too shitfaced all the time to indulge the impulse.

This thought made me grin.

Later that day, when I was driving home from training, my phone lit up with a call from one of my closest friends. Sarah Kinsella was my AA sponsor. Someone who, over time, I'd become close with. She was different to the usual sort of people I met, and it was nice to have someone in my life who had nothing to do with rugby. She was one of the coolest, most honest women I'd ever known and had survived a much rougher life than mine: abusive father, heroin addict mother, foster homes, more abuse.

People like Sarah had a reason to turn to alcohol, and the fact that she was so in control of herself now made her someone I really looked up to.

"Hey Sarah, how's it going?" I answered on hands-free.

"Bryan, hey! I'm good. Just thought I'd give you a quick call and see how you're getting on."

"I'm good, could be better. Mam's been pulling her usual stunts."

"Oh no, I'm sorry to hear that," she said, leaving it open for me to talk if I wanted. It was one of the things I liked most about her. If you wanted to talk she let you, but if you didn't she never pushed. Today, surprisingly, I found that I actually *did* want to talk.

"Yeah, I was at my mate Will's birthday when she called asking me to come over. I tried to say no, but you know how she is. She's my weak spot. Sometimes it feels like I'm all she has and I can't abandon her. Her refusal to accept that I'm sober now is making it difficult to do right by her."

"Mm-hmm. That happens a lot. Usually it's the friends you used to drink with that can't accept your new lifestyle, but with you it's your mother. You were basically her drinking buddy since you were a teenager, Bryan. Plus, you not drinking anymore shines a light on the fact that she still is. Addicts don't want to see what they are, because denial is easier than trying to change."

"I just wish I could make her understand that I'm not judging her. If she wants to drink, that's her choice. I'm not going to force sobriety down her throat."

"It's hard for her. She's been in this lifestyle for a lot longer than you were. All you can do is be there for her and help her if she asks for it. If she wants to change, it has to be her choice."

"Yeah, you're right," I sighed. "Sorry for being such a depressing bastard all the time. I feel like all I ever do is vent my problems to you."

"Hey, that's what I'm here for. Besides, you let me talk to you about my failing love life. So we're both getting something out of it," she replied, a smile in her voice.

"Speaking of, any news on that front?" Sarah was a lesbian living in a small city, and I often sympathized with her given how tiny the dating pool could be.

"Not really. If you think your life's depressing, you should swap with me for a while. Even Tinder's given up and started showing profiles of people I previously swiped left. It's like it's subversively trying to tell me I should consider lowering my standards."

I chuckled at this. "Such a judgy bitch, that Tinder."

"Tell me about it. But what about you? I take it the orchid I bought you for Christmas has wilted and died since you haven't mentioned it in a while."

"Yep. Buried it in the back garden next to my dead budgie and childhood cat."

"Liar. You don't have a garden in that fancy-pants penthouse apartment. It's all sterile countertops and tiled floors."

"Well, if I had one I'd have buried it. I don't know what it is, but I think I was born with the opposite of a green thumb."

"Death thumb?"

"Yeah, that's what I've got. Thumb of death."

She laughed. "So I guess you won't be moving on to the next stage anytime soon?"

"Nope." An unbidden image of Eilish Cassidy flashed before my eyes. The back of my neck prickled, which it did these days whenever I wasn't being completely honest, causing me to exhale a frustrated breath.

"Nope? Are you sure?"

"Well, kind of. There's this girl . . . this woman who's caught my eye, but I'm pretty sure she finds me about as appealing as a fungal infection."

She let out a scoff. "Sure."

"Hey! I'm being serious."

"You didn't pull the old Bryan Leech 'Come on Stronger than Hulk Hogan on Steroids' trademark, did you? Because that only works with rugby groupies and the intoxicated. Any sane woman would run a mile."

"First of all, Hulk Hogan has probably been on steroids since the eighties, so you need a new comparison. Second of all, what makes you think I come on too strong?"

"Remember when I first became your sponsor and you fell off the wagon? I had to come drag your arse out of some hellhole pub, and since you didn't know I was gay back then you came on to me. It was sort of hilarious. You had all these lines—"

"Okay, no need to regale me." I frowned. "I'm almost home, and I need to go pick up some groceries."

She chuckled some more. "Fine, fine. I want to know more about this lady you're into, and we should probably talk a little about you taking the next step and starting up a relationship, but all in all I think you're ready."

I chewed on my lip, her words hitting a chord. She thought I was ready. *Was I ready?*

"Yeah, you're right, we should . . . talk," I said and hung up just as I pulled into the shopping center close to my apartment.

I parked my car and started heading inside when I caught sight of the florist. Plants were displayed in the window and I walked toward the display before I even realized what I was doing.

"Well, since I'm already here . . ."

A bell rang when I stepped inside the shop and the overpowering perfume of nature hit me immediately. A middle-aged blonde woman stood by the counter, offering me a friendly smile as I looked around.

"Can I help you with anything?"

I scratched my head, no idea what I wanted to buy. Plus, the place was tiny and there were shelves and flowers everywhere. I felt all big and cumbersome in the small space, like if I wasn't careful I'd end up knocking something over. "Uh, yeah," I said and gestured to the collection of plants by the window. "Which of those is easiest to keep alive?"

She obviously thought my question was odd, but she didn't comment on it. "Well, the spider plants. You see the ones with the long floppy leaves, they tend to be fairly low maintenance."

"Great, okay, I'll take one of those."

I couldn't explain it, but I suddenly felt self-conscious, like this florist woman somehow knew I was a lowlife recovering alcoholic who could barely even keep a plant alive. It was part of my recovery. I needed to learn to look after other things than just myself. So far, I had failed. But now, for some inexplicable reason, I was more determined to succeed than ever. An image of blue eyes and red hair flashed in my mind.

Yeah, I knew the reason, all right.

The florist walked over to the window and picked up one of the spider thingies, then made quick work of wrapping it and ringing up the purchase. I thanked her and walked out of the shop with a renewed sense of determination.

This plant was going to survive if it was the last thing I did.

SEVEN
EILISH

@ECassChoosesPikachu: @TheContainerStore is having a sale!!! I'm having difficulty *containing* my excitement… get it? #SeeWhatIDidThere?

Disorder was my kryptonite.
    After Patrick was born, keeping my place clean and tidy felt like the only thing over which I had any control. I couldn't control when (or if) I slept, but I could control whether or not my sock drawer was organized by sock length, thickness, then color.

"I'll just tidy up a bit," I whispered to myself, proceeding with extreme caution. I knew Connors was gone for the rest of the afternoon, I'd overheard Alice in the office say he'd taken time off.

Alice, the lead admin on the top floor, had allowed me to use one of the shared office spaces so I could do my charting for the past week. She'd shown it to me during my first day; it was a welcome and quiet alternative to Connors's dodgy physio room. As well, according to Connors, I still didn't have privileges. I wasn't going to make a fuss over it; if motherhood had taught me one thing, it was to pick my battles. If there's a workaround that's almost as good, do that.

So I'd been using the gym and locker room, no big deal.

But maybe if I straightened the place out, ordered and restocked the supplies, and demonstrated that I could be an asset, he would relax a little and stop freaking out every time I neared the physio room.

Or maybe he's got an unknown object stuck so far up his arse, he's just going to be a fecking wanker for all eternity.

. . . shame on me.

"That was unkind, Eilish," I muttered, stepping into the therapy room and flicking on the light. As soon as the space was illuminated, I took a step back. The sight before me was—as it had been the week prior—daunting. And disgusting.

Plus, I thought I spotted what looked like Jenna McCarthy's lunch container, open and empty on his charting area.

He stole her lunch!

"That forking freak," I said before I could catch myself. I scrunched my face and shook my head. "Stop it. If you can't say anything nice, don't say anything at all."

Fine. I'll just think it. He's a fecking freak and a fecking slob.

"Best not to think about it," I told myself, pushing those thoughts—and the usually dormant portion of my personality—to the back of my mind. "Just clean it, organize it, and take inventory."

The sound of footsteps from behind had me leaning out of the doorway and peering into the hall. I spotted William Moore coming my way. I'd learned over the last seven days that the tall American flanker was basically the nicest, most polite person on the face of the earth.

His eyebrows lifted high on his forehead and he slowed as he approached. "Hi, Eilish. How are you?"

"I'm well. And you?"

"Good, good. And your son? Patrick is his name, right?"

"That's right." I smiled quizzically at the big guy. "How'd you know that?"

"Sean was telling us about how he'd bought him a tuxedo."

A trickle of fear between my shoulder blades had me standing taller. "Who? Who was he telling?"

"Just me and Ronan."

At that I relaxed and smiled my relief. Ronan was the team captain and—as an aside—also happened to be the spitting image of Colin Farrell. "Yes. He likes to buy Patrick suits and matching pocket squares. I'm running out of closet space."

Patrick's existence wasn't a secret, but I thought it prudent to leave pictures of him at home.

William's attention skipped to the room behind me and then back to my face. "Are you finally allowed inside?"

I gathered a breath and debated how best to respond.

I must've taken too long because he said, "You should let us speak to Coach Brian about this, about Connors and how he—"

"No. Don't do that. I'll take care of Connors, I will. I'll get him to see reason. I've only been here for one week, I need more time."

William made a face, and I thought for a moment he was going to argue, but then he took a step back, nodding. "Fine. Well, the guys are just down the hall and Ronan's with them if you change your mind."

"Thanks, William."

"See you later." He nodded politely.

"See you." I gave him a little wave as he left, his footsteps retreating down the long hall.

Turning my attention back to the disaster area known as the therapy room, I made a quick survey of what needed to be done and in what order.

Trash first. Then supplies.

Stepping forward, I kicked a pile of takeout containers to one side, wanting to clear a path to the cabinets so I could look for latex gloves. But then I stopped, stiffening, an odd scratching sound coming from the pile I'd just nudged with my foot.

Turning back to it, I crouched on the ground and lifted a greasy paper at the top of the mess. And that's when I saw it.

A cockroach.

In Ireland.

A giant behemoth of a bug, the likes I'd only ever seen on nature programs about prehistoric insects.

Okay, perhaps I was over exaggerating its size. Perhaps not. Honestly, I didn't get a chance to dwell on the matter, because the roach-shaped locust of Satan hopped onto my hand.

I screamed.

Obviously.

Jumping back and swatting at my hand, I screamed again. But evil incarnate had somehow crawled up and into the sleeve of my shirt. The sensation of its tiny, hairy legs skittering along my arm had me screaming a third time and I whipped off my shirt, tossing it to the other side of the room as though it was on fire.

"What the hell is going on?"

I spun toward the door, finding Ronan Fitzpatrick and Bryan Leech hovering at the entrance, their eyes darting around the room as though they were searching for a perpetrator. Meanwhile, I was frantically brushing my hands over my arms and torso. I felt the echo of that spawn of the devil's touch all over my body.

"Cockroach!" I screeched. "Do you see it? Is it still on me?" I twisted back and forth, searching.

Bryan and Ronan were joined in the doorway by more team members, but I barely saw them in my panic.

God, I could still feel it.

I. Could. Still. Feel. It.

Now I knew what those hapless women felt like in horror movies when they realized the serial killer was still inside the house.

"Oh! I see it!" Bryan darted forward, grabbing me by the arms and turning me to one side.

And then he smacked me right on the arse. And then he grabbed my arse, squeezing.

I squeaked, too shocked to do anything but stare at Bryan. He met my startled gaze, apparently also too shocked to do anything but stare at me.

Then he lifted his hand, covered in roach guts, looking equal parts proud and bracing. "I got it."

"Disgusting." This came from Malloy, loitering by the entrance as though he didn't dare venture into the physio room lest more dragon-sized roaches be ambling about.

"I've never seen a roach that big before." Daly, one of the other team members, sounded positively scarred.

Realizing I was out of breath—and wearing no top but my bra—I yanked my gaze from Bryan's and glanced around the room, the burning heat of embarrassment crawling up my cheeks.

Crawling . . .

I shivered. Poor word choice.

My shirt had landed on a computer monitor at one of the workstations. I hurried to retrieve it.

"All right, all right. Nothing to see here. Crisis averted." I listened as Bryan lifted his voice. Glancing at him, I saw he had his hands up, like a moving barricade, and was walking everyone out of the room.

"Keep that hand away from me," someone said.

Followed by another of the lads chiming in, "Yeah, we know where it's been."

"Very funny. You're all a bunch of crack-ups."

Once everyone was out, Bryan shut the door. There was a short pause before he asked, "Can I turn around?"

I swallowed, my limbs feeling loose and wobbly—likely the aftereffects of the adrenaline—and nodded. "Sure. Yeah. I'm—I've got my shirt on now."

Bryan peeked over his shoulder, then gave me a sympathetic smile. "Are you okay?"

"Yes. I'm just sorry." I huffed, crossing my arms over my chest and resisting the urge to scratch my arms raw. "I'll be even better as soon as I get a hot shower."

His eyes flared and he flinched, just slightly, before averting his gaze to the floor and clearing his throat. "Uh, speaking of which. I guess I better wash this hand."

"Oh, yeah. There's soap by the sink. Miraculously."

The side of his mouth hitched ruefully and he nodded once, moving to the built-in sink along one wall, next to the supply cabinets.

I waited for him to wash his hands before I moved to the door, opening it and strolling out to the hall. I couldn't stand another second in that room. Given the fact that I had the remnants of a dead cockroach on my arse, all my plans to clean the physio space fled.

A few paces down the corridor, Bryan reached out and gripped my elbow, staying me. "Are you really okay? The way you screamed, it sounded like someone was murdering you."

Renewed heat flooded my cheeks and I released a self-deprecating laugh. "Did you see the size of that thing? It was larger than most dogs."

Bryan chuckled, his lovely eyes twinkling down at me, but he didn't release my elbow. "Yes. I know. I had a pint of roach innards smeared all over my hand."

"Well at least it's not on your arse." Now I was laughing in earnest and so was he.

I leaned against the wall, feeling like I needed the support for some inexplicable reason. I felt spent. Yes, I was tired. I was always tired. But I shouldn't have been this level of exhausted.

"Hey. Let's sit for a minute." He tugged on my arm, pulling me down next to him as he sat on the floor, and then relinquished his hold.

"Oh God, this is so embarrassing," I mumbled, pressing my hands to my cheeks and staring straight ahead.

"No, no. This is nothing." Bryan nudged my shoulder with his. "You don't know the meaning of embarrassing if you think this is bad."

I peered at him, a doubting frown on my features. "Oh really? Screaming like a lunatic and ripping off my shirt in front of half the team wasn't embarrassing enough for your standards?"

"Don't forget when I smacked you on the arse," he teased.

"How could I forget?" A slightly hysterical chuckle burst from my mouth. I felt like crying with the sheer frustration of it all.

Why did he have to witness me mid-cockroach breakdance?

And why did he have to be so nice about it?

And why was he sitting so close now?

And are those gold flecks in his green eyes?

I forced myself to swallow and look away. "You have to admit, my display of cockroach-induced insanity is pretty high up there on the embarrassment scale."

"Nope. Not even close."

Unable to help myself, I peeked at him. A new grin stole over his lips, also stealing my breath.

Thankfully, he didn't expect me to speak. "One time, at a victory party—of course I was shitfaced—I spilled my beer all over the general manager's son."

I felt my eyes widen. "Ah. That's bad."

"Even worse, his son was only six weeks old."

"Oh no!" I covered my mouth. "You spilled your beer on an infant?"

"Yes. And not a little spill either. The whole beer, a double pint. It was a complete accident, but I felt like such an arsehole."

"That's terrible." I was cringing but also fighting uncomfortable laughter.

"Yes. It was." He nodded, his eyes growing hazy, the smile slowly disintegrating off his face. The dissolving smile left a ghost, a pale shadow hovering behind his eyes, like the memory haunted him. Like his past behavior haunted him.

My heart chose that moment to twist in my chest, a sudden ache on his behalf. Bryan looked entirely remorseful. Witnessing his sadness made me oppressively sad. The oppressive sadness spurred me to act.

"One time, in my research methods class," I blurted and then paused, waiting until his eyes focused on mine before continuing, "our professor asked us to arrange our data sets by key demographics. So I raised my hand, and he called on me. In front of the entire class, I meant to ask him something like, *You will want to see a categorization of subjects by gender, won't you?* But instead—unthinkingly—what I actually said was, *You'll want to have sex, won't you?*"

Bryan choked on a startled laugh, his mouth falling open, then tilted his head back and laughed again, this time with gusto. The sound was intoxicating, a deep, rich, uninhibited rumble. My worry for him eased as I indulged myself in a rare moment of watching Bryan unabashedly. He looked happy, and his happiness in that moment made my heart swell.

Stupid heart. Stop swelling. Swelling is bad for you. Stay small and protected.

But I couldn't help it. His earlier guilt had struck a chord with me. My eyes trailed over the curve of his lips, the line of his jaw, his neck.

Forks, he was handsome when he was happy. *So* handsome. Magnetic. And when he laughed, he was devastating—free and open and alive—he made me feel alive in a way I hadn't experienced since . . . since . . .

That night.

I wasn't laughing and I wasn't smiling, because my heart—the one that had been twisting then swelling just seconds ago—was now lodged in my throat.

Bryan's laughter tapered, and he wiped a tear of hilarity from the corner of his eye, glancing at me. When his gaze met mine, he did a slight double-take, blinking, his eyebrows inching upward with what looked like surprise.

"Eilish?"

Any minute now, he was going to stand up. Any minute now, he was going to say goodbye. Any minute now, I was going to watch him leave.

Do something!

But what could I do? Tell him I was infatuated with him? Because that's all this was. Infatuation. Wishing. Dreaming.

I thought I was past this.

"Hey?" His eyes moved between mine, then dropped to my lips. He licked his and whispered, "Are you okay?"

I nodded, also whispering, "Yes."

He leaned forward, just a hair's breadth, his attention still zeroed in on my mouth. "What are you thinking about?"

I didn't answer with words. Instead, I tilted my chin, closed my eyes, and I kissed him.

His lips were warm and soft and essential. He smelled like I remembered, like I'd dreamed about. I would have moaned with how good he felt, except he wasn't responding.

That's right ladies and gentlemen. I kissed Bryan Leech, and he stiffened as though afflicted with lip paralysis.

It took me a foggy four seconds before I realized this as fact, but when the news finally made it to my brain, I immediately pulled away. "Oh my God. I'm so sorry." I covered my mouth with my hand, my heart beating a million miles a minute.

What were you thinking? What the hell is wrong with you?

Peripherally, I saw he'd lifted his hand and it hovered in the air as though to —cup my cheek? Push me away? Who knows? I stood and backed away from him.

He also stood, reaching out and taking a step forward. "No, no, no. I'm sorry."

I moved to the side and out of his reach, putting as much room as I could between us in the corridor, thankful that we were still alone.

"No. I'm sorry. I'm just, not thinking clearly. I'm tired. And stressed."

"It's okay."

"No." I gritted my teeth and forced myself to look at him. "It's not okay. I shouldn't have done that. It was completely inappropriate and unprofessional, and that's not who I am."

Bryan appeared to be endeavoring to assemble a reassuring smile, but his eyes were stormy and conflicted. "You're a really nice girl, Eilish."

Ugh.

A brush-off. I stiffened, wincing.

"But the thing is, I'm no good to anyone. I'm . . ." he stopped, clearly struggling, then said on a rush, "I'm too old for you. I'm all used up. You," he hesitated again, then said, "you deserve someone far better than me."

I closed my eyes, willing my pulse to slow, willing the burning in my chest to quell. This was the worst. Everything before this moment was not the worst, because this was the worst.

The. Worst.

Get out of here. Leave. Now.

Taking a deep breath meant to push back the renewed tide of mortification, I opened my eyes and lifted them to his, but didn't really allow myself to see him. "It was just temporary stress-induced absurdity. Like I said, I'm sorry. It won't happen again."

Thankfully, my phone buzzed just as I finished speaking and I whipped it out of my back pocket, not even really looking at the screen.

Bryan took another step forward and I was thankful for the distraction of my phone. "Eilish—"

"I have to go." Not giving him a chance to finish, I pasted a tight smile on my mouth as I bolted past, speed walking down the hall, through the stairway door, climbing the stairs two at a time.

At least now you know, a voice whispered between my ears, *now you know. Even sober, he doesn't want you.*

EIGHT
EILISH

@JoseyInHeels: Where are you @ECassChoosesPikachu? I need your opinion about these shoes!
@ECassChoosesPikachu to @JoseyInHeels: I've been color coding my calendar.
@JoseyInHeels to @ECassChoosesPikachu: Put the highlighter down…

Avoidance was the best policy. In all things. Take now for instance.
My mobile was ringing, and I was ignoring it. The resulting guilt made my nose itch. I ignored that, too.

"You're not going to get that?" Alice asked from the doorway, lifting her eyebrows and indicating with her forehead toward the phone on the desk. "Your phone? Are you sure you don't want to pick it up?"

I shook my head. "No. It's not important."

This statement also made me feel guilty. I was a walking, talking bag of guilt these days. Since kissing Bryan three weeks ago, I'd been avoiding him like the plague and passing him over to Connors for therapy. Miraculously, I didn't feel guilty about passing him off because refusing to touch him was simple self-preservation.

But getting back to the wet blanket of guilt. There wasn't much I could do about the guilt, so I embraced it. Guilt was my constant companion, my home girl.

Finally, the phone stopped vibrating and Alice's questioning frown moved back to me.

"It's fine." I waved away her concern. "What is it you needed?"

She made a face, her eyes narrowing. "Your phone has been buzzing on and off for the last half hour, I can hear it from my desk. Are you sure you don't need to get that?"

"I'm so sorry. Has it been disturbing you? It's my mother." *And Josey.*

Both my mother and Josey had been calling me non-stop, and I'd been sending them to voicemail all day. I'd had to cancel coffee with Josey last week, and she hadn't been happy about it.

"Oh." Alice stepped further into the office I was using. "Is your mother okay?"

"She's fine. She just wants me to attend a party and I already told her I couldn't. She's been calling me non-stop to insist I reconsider." I gathered the charts I'd scattered on the desk. "Is it the office? Do I need to leave? Do you need the space?"

"Oh, no." She claimed the other desk chair and gave me a bright smile. "I just wanted to check in on you, see how you're settling in."

"Thank you." My smile grew and gratefulness blossomed in my chest. "That is so kind of you. Thank you. I feel like things are going well."

Her eyes flickered over the charts on the desk. "My, my. Do you color-code everything?"

"I'm afraid so. I'm addicted to organization." This was an understatement. These days, the fastest way to get me hot was to take me to The Container Store and hand me a gift card. I loved storage, organization, highlighters, and colored folders.

I. Loved. Them. I always had. Even more so now.

"That's grand. I know a lot of the boys have been complimentary, happy to have you on board. And Coach Brian says you're a breath of fresh air, how organized you are."

"That's great to hear." A surge of happiness warmed my heart. I hadn't realized how much the praise meant to me until she'd said it. "I've been researching alternative therapy approaches for several of the players, Daly in particular." I turned and grabbed his color-coded chart. "He presents with non-specific pain in the longissimus thoracis and iliocostalis lumborum regions, and I was thinking that a focus on lumbo-pelvic core stabilization might provide help. A paper was just recently published in *The Lancet* on the effectiveness of alternating methodologies."

"Oh. Well, that's nice. But there's just one thing," she said, holding up her index finger, her smile dropping.

"What is it? What's wrong?" I braced, staring at her, the earlier relief—which felt like wind in my sails—now dying a quick and painful death. "Whatever it is, I'm sure I can fix it." I reached for Alice, grasping her arm, fear crawling up the back of my throat. "I'll do better. I promise. Whatever—"

"Calm down, dear. I just need you to sign the new employee handbook. You

THE CAD AND THE CO-ED

returned all the pages except the signature page." Alice shook her head quickly, patting my hand.

I released the tension holding me hostage and huffed a light laugh. "Oh. Okay, yes. I can do that. Sorry."

"No need to be sorry. I'm sorry if I worried you. I've been out of sorts today, someone stole my lunch."

"Oh no!" I gave her a sympathetic frown. "They took it from your desk?"

"No. From the staff fridge on this level." Alice scowled. It was an impressive scowl. She almost looked menacing. "Once I find out who did it, they'll be sorry."

I bit my bottom lip. I had a fairly good hunch that the culprit was Connors. I debated whether or not to tattle on my unfriendly co-worker, but before I could speak, a voice interrupted, "There you are."

Sean stood in the doorway, dressed in one of his traveling suits; the sight made me grin.

"Here I am," I responded simply, appreciating the cut of the suit. It was gorgeous.

Always dressed to the nines when he traveled, Sean was the king of metrosexuals and loved to shop more than most women. Plus, his taste was impeccable.

"Alice, give us a moment." He strolled into the office, twitching his chin toward her chair. "I have business to discuss with the lady."

"Uh, sure." Alice appeared briefly flustered, then stood from the chair and sidestepped around my giant cousin. She gave me a kind smile as she reached the door. "Don't forget about the signature page. And, please, let me know if you need anything. Anything at all, okay?"

Renewed gratitude chased away the earlier nerves. "Absolutely. And thank you so much, Alice."

Her warm eyes held mine for a moment, then drifted to Sean. Alice's demeanor cooled, and her lips pinched as she lifted a disapproving eyebrow. Then she turned and left.

"Hag," Sean said, fiddling with his cufflink.

"She is not a hag, Sean. She is lovely and kind."

He gave me a grumpy frown. "She's a hag to me. Still hasn't forgiven me for that nonsense with Fitzpatrick. Holds a grudge like a cat."

"Cats hold grudges?"

"Yes. So do ravens. I can't abide either. Dogs are far superior."

I ignored this statement because I was busy and had less than fifteen minutes to finish up before my next appointment. "What nonsense with Fitzpatrick can't she forgive you for?"

"When I had it off with his unsavory fiancée."

"Brona O'Shea? That was years ago."

69

"I know. Plus I did him a favor, didn't I? Now he's married to the delectable Annie. Ronan should be sending me flowers on their anniversary."

I ignored this statement as well because I knew Sean would be happy to talk *at length* about how he'd saved Ronan Fitzpatrick from the evil Brona O'Shea by sleeping with her. Never mind the fact that Sean only did it to make Ronan lose his temper. And never mind the fact that Sean then tried something similar with Ronan's sister, Lucy. Except it backfired, because he fell in love with Lucy, and was still smitten five years later.

"That Alice is like an elephant with her memory. A dowdy elephant in need of a makeover. Horizontal stripes should be outlawed."

"I think she looks wonderful. Leave Alice alone," I grunted, frowning at my cousin's snobbery. "Now, what did you need?"

His eyes narrowed, bouncing from my face to his cufflinks, then to some imaginary piece of lint on his pants. "So . . ."

"So?"

"Here we are," he said with a plaintive sigh.

"So, here we are."

Sean bit the inside of his lip, his eyes probing. "And how are things?"

"Very well, thank you." I turned my attention back to my notes because I knew where this conversation was heading.

Bryan.

He always wanted to talk about Bryan and how steady he'd become. *He's so stable, so sturdy. He's such a durable chap,* Sean would say, as though Bryan were a table.

I felt my cousin's eyes on my profile. Not wishing to rehash the same conversation, I kept my gaze studiously forward.

"Eilish."

"Sean."

Now he grunted. Then he stood, crossed to the door, and shut it. Sean rounded on me, crossing his arms over his chest.

"It's been weeks. You've been here for *weeks*."

"And?"

"And what do you think?"

"I think things are going well."

"Not about the bloody job. What do you think about Bryan?"

I twisted my lips to the side, hoping I was able to mask the sharp pang of some unknown emotion—regret? Sorrow? Embarrassment? Longing? More guilt?

What do I think about Bryan?

I didn't know what to think about Bryan. Before I'd messed everything up by kissing him, we'd shared a few friendly moments. Over the last few weeks, while avoiding him, I'd watched him interact with his teammates; his care for them was clear and he was well liked, respected. I also felt like I knew him better now—much better— than I had five years ago when we slept together.

Mint tea, spectacles, and housecoats. I smirked at the memory of his grumpiness last month, how adorable he'd been as he complained about his neighbors.

I like him.

Yes. I liked him. And I was beyond besotted with his body.

And that tattoo . . .

Giving myself a quick shake, I reminded myself that I shouldn't be thinking about Bryan's sexy tattoo. Ever.

My voice was forced firmness as I said, "Sean, I don't have time for this. It's Friday, and I have several more appointments this afternoon. Please let me work."

"Fine," he huffed, his hands falling to his thighs with a petulant *smack.* "I'll let you work. But you should know that people are starting to notice."

A jolt of trepidation had me lifting my eyes to my cousin. "What do you mean? Who has noticed what?"

"Bryan, for one. He has noticed that he is the only one you pawn off to Connors."

"Has he said anything?"

"He doesn't have to. The other lads have brought it up a few times. Gavin asked me if Bryan had made a pass at you, if that's why you won't help him."

Guilt—always guilt—flared in my throat, making my lungs prickle, and I swallowed against the thick band of remorse.

Bryan hadn't made a pass at me. *I'd made a pass at him.*

"Shells," I sighed, dropping my pen to the desk and holding my forehead in my fingers. "I didn't mean to exclude him."

"Then what did you mean by refusing to treat his injuries?" Sean demanded with a flair for the dramatic.

I slid my eyes to my cousin, glowering at him. "That's not what I'm doing. I've never refused him. It's just . . . really difficult."

"What's difficult?" Sean asked gently.

"Honestly? Touching him is difficult. So is talking to him, or being around him, or seeing him." I re-buried my face in my hands and shook my head.

I hadn't anticipated how strongly I'd be drawn to him. Clearly, I'd been naïve. I thought I could ignore him, or get used to him at least, but that wasn't happening. Instead, he'd become an ever-growing source of longing, frustration, and—yes—guilt. Sooner or later I was going to burst with it.

When Sean spoke next, he was very close and placed a comforting hand on my shoulder. "Perhaps if you told him the truth, things would be easier for you."

A wary laugh tumbled from my lips. "I can't. I can't tell him."

Just the thought made me want to buy two one-way tickets back to America.

"Why not? He's very stable."

"I'm not worried about his stability, Sean."

"Then what are you afraid of?"

What am I afraid of?

Patrick was my life. Despite how he came to be, his sweet smile, his silly sense of humor, the way he looked at me with adoration and love . . . it's what I lived for. He was what I lived for. The mere thought of losing that daily dose of amazing terrified me. *He's my world.*

"Eilish?"

"I'm afraid he'll t-t-take Patrick away f-f-from me," I blurted, my voice cracking on the last word, my damn stutter returning in full force. I told myself to be quiet, but some force compelled me to continue. "I have n-n-nothing, nothing b-b-but this job which means I'm b-b-barely making ends meet. I could never afford a custody b-b-battle. He would win, he would take Patrick and there's n-n-nothing—"

"Shhh." Sean gathered me into his arms, pressing my head against his shoulder. "It's okay. I'm sorry. I didn't mean to push you."

I forced myself to take several deep, calming breaths, pushing the crush of anxiety away, back, and down, where my worst fears lived and simmered in the back of my mind.

"Are you going to cry?"

I shook my head tightly. "I n-n-never cry. You know that."

Sean gave me one final squeeze, then gripped my arms, holding me slightly away so I was forced to meet his gaze.

"You have me," he said, his eyes as earnest as I'd ever seen them. "And I will always help you. When you tell Bryan, because you must tell him, if he goes off the deep end—which I don't think he will, but if he does—I will help you. You have to know that."

I frowned sadly. "I could never ask you to do that."

"There will be no asking, and I will not take no for an answer." He gave me a small shake to emphasize his words, his forehead wrinkling with frustration. "But, Eilish, you need to put aside your fears and think of your son. Bryan has changed. He's not the degenerate carouser he once was. I wouldn't be bringing this up so much if I thought there was a chance Bryan would try to take Patrick, or if I thought Bryan might relapse and be a bad influence. The man has changed. Truly."

My face crumpled as I nodded and tucked my chin to my chest. "I believe you."

"Good." Sean gathered a large breath, then pulled me back into his embrace, adding, "Because Patrick deserves to know his father, and Bryan deserves to know his son."

THE CAD AND THE CO-ED

* * *

Step one, find Bryan Leech.

Step two, give Bryan Leech a massage.

Step three, improve Bryan Leech's range of motion and performance outcomes. Simple, right?

Then why was I still staring in the mirror, giving myself a pep talk?

"You can do this. It won't be at all weird, so what if you kissed him and he brushed you off? You can be normal. You'll just walk over to him and say, 'Bryan, I understand your knee continues to give you concern. If you'd like me to do so, I'll be happy to administer a deep-tissue massage and stone therapy.' And then he'll say . . . he'll say . . ."

. . . crackers.

"It doesn't matter what he says," I assured myself, lifting my chin. "Don't be so ridiculous. You're a professional. *Act* like it." Slamming the locker door, I turned on my heel and marched out of the women's locker room to the stairs. I was flying on a cloud of determination.

I would touch Bryan Leech and remain unaffected. I would help him and I would keep my hormones under control.

I would.

I will.

I hadn't decided what to do about Patrick yet, but excluding Bryan from treatment was completely out of the question. I was disappointed with myself, with my selfishness. I had a job to do and he didn't deserve to be punished for my unrequited feelings.

That stopped now.

Jogging down the stairs and out the door leading to the player's hallway, I rehearsed what I would say.

I would say, *Hello, Bryan. I have a bit of time before the end of the day. Perhaps I could take a look at your knee.*

Or, I might say, *Bryan, let's have a look at your knee. I hear it's still giving you trouble.*

Or maybe, *Bryan, I understand you're having a bit of trouble with your knee. If you have time before the end of the day—*

"Eilish."

I stopped short, almost colliding with William Moore. Automatically, his beefy hands reached to steady me.

"William. Sorry. Sorry about that." I backed up a step and out of his grip, counting three other players behind him, and swallowed with some difficulty when I realized Bryan was one of them.

"You okay?" William asked, dipping his chin to catch my eye.

I nodded, looking beyond him, and pointed at Bryan. "You."

Bryan stiffened, his eyes widening. "Me?"

"Yes. You. Meniscus tear. Follow me," I said, turned away from him, and promptly grimaced.

Real smooth, E.

Real professional.

Great job.

That wasn't weird at all.

NINE
EILISH

@ECassChoosesPikachu: On the agenda for tonight: a cold shower.
@SeanCassinova to @ECassChoosesPikachu: You really should get your pipes looked at. I know a sturdy plumber if you're interested…

Leading the way to the training room, I didn't wait to see if he'd followed. I was too busy berating myself for speaking like Tarzan.

So much for rehearsing.

But Bryan did follow. I heard his footsteps echo mine, and it sent a shiver of anticipation racing down my spine, a shiver I promptly repressed.

Yes. I would soon be touching him. But I couldn't think of Bryan as *my* Bryan, the object of my nighttime fantasies, the owner of the enchanted penis, and definitely someone I actually liked.

No.

That would never do.

Instead, I had to think of him as Bryan Leech, fullback, thirty, meniscus tear complicated by tendinosis, no scope, neutral gait.

Once inside the training room, I navigated to the space I'd been using for most of my therapy sessions and motioned to the table, taking a deep breath before instructing with forced calm, "Please lie down, face up."

I sensed Bryan hesitate so I glanced at him, finding him watching me with a peculiar kind of intensity. "Can we talk for a minute?"

"Uh, yes. Sure." I nodded, then quickly added, "Would you like to tell me about the original injury?"

"No. It's not that." Bryan's gaze narrowed on me. He was frowning, but it was a thoughtful frown rather than an upset frown. "I think we should clear the air. I know you've been avoiding me."

"Oh." I swallowed with effort, wringing my hands. He'd caught me off guard. I wasn't prepared to talk about this. "About that—"

"I'd like to apologize for—"

"Like I said," I waved his apology away, "it wasn't your fault. I was confused, I was mixed up, tired."

"But, that's just it. You weren't confused." His gaze softened as it moved over me.

An untenable stabbing pierced my heart because the softness looked like pity, or at least that's what it looked like to me.

"Eilish, you must know you're very beautiful—"

"You remind me of my son's father," I blurted, talking over him, not wanting to hear his assurances about how beautiful I was and that one day I would find someone special. God, I couldn't stand it if he said that. I couldn't deal with another rejection from Bryan Leech.

His eyes widened and he reared back, just a little. "Your son's father?"

"That's right." I fought to suppress a wave of panic. *What are you doing? What have you done?*

"I didn't know you had a son." His gaze grew more circumspect, as though he was looking at me with new eyes.

"I do. He's four. Almost five." I wet my lips, my mind a riot. Some of the players—like Will and Ronan—knew about Patrick. Some didn't. Clearly, Bryan hadn't known until just now.

Careful, Eilish. Be very careful.

He nodded, his gaze again sweeping over me, as though this information explained something critical and now I made more sense to him. I tried to appear composed while he did this, but some irrational part of me both hoped and worried this news would trigger his memory. That, miraculously, he'd remember what happened between us five years ago.

I was so weird. And a coward. *You're a weird coward.*

"You must've been very young," he murmured, like he thought and said the words at the same time.

"I was. You see," I had to clear my throat because my voice had grown squeaky and tight, "what happened weeks ago was about me being tired and confused. So, I'd appreciate it if we could move past it. Maybe we could start over?"

He was still frowning, like my words were a puzzle, but in the end he nodded slowly and said, "Yeah. Sure. Sounds good."

"Good." My knees were shaking, so I leaned against the supply counter. "Please lie down, face up."

His eyes, still cloudy with thought, moved between me and the table. "You're not using the therapy room?"

"No." I shook my head, giving him my back as I retrieved the special blend of jojoba with eucalyptus and peppermint essential oils. "I find this space better suited for my purposes."

The table creaked under his weight and I turned to find him settling on his back. "You know, I'm sure Coach Brian would be very interested that Connors is giving you grief."

Dismissing his statement with a noncommittal head shake, I crossed to the sink, ran a towel under the water, then popped it in the microwave. "I've read your chart. You tore the meniscus seven years ago, right?" I kept my tone professional and light, but felt immensely relieved that he'd let the subject of my son go without further questions.

"That's right." Bryan folded his hands behind his head, and I sensed his eyes move over me.

I drew even with his knee. "Why did you decide against the scope?"

"Doc said it healed, more or less. But it tightens up from time to time."

He grunted as I probed him laterally. His quadriceps flexed, the muscle in sharp relief.

"I'm going to guide you through complete range of motion. Just relax." I picked up his leg, sliding my hand to the back of his thigh.

Bryan mumbled something that sounded like, "Easier said than done."

I ignored it, and him, trying to convince myself that his leg was just any leg. In fact, I imagined it was separate from his body. *A mannequin leg . . .*

This helped.

The microwave beeped, and I placed the limb back on the table, retrieving and then shaking out the towel of excess heat. "Have you considered acupuncture?"

Again, Bryan hesitated before speaking. "I'm not *opposed* to it."

He sounded like he was making a face so I glanced at him. Bryan was indeed making a face—his nose was wrinkled, his mouth turned down, his eyes scrunched with suspicion—and the expression was so much like my son's *I don't want to do that* face that I fumbled the towel and nearly dropped it.

"Forks," I murmured under my breath, steadying myself against a surge of discombobulating emotion. I could do nothing about the heat claiming my neck and cheeks, or the galloping of my heart, because when I looked at Bryan in that moment, I saw Patrick.

Actually, looking at Bryan now, I allowed myself to admit that it wasn't just his expression. Patrick and Bryan looked like father and son: same hair color, eye color, bone structure, skin tone. Where I was pasty white with pale blue eyes, Bryan and Patrick were naturally bronze with jade-green eyes. They even had the same mouth.

And it was disconcerting.

My heartstrings played a morose tune of longing and regret, but I disregarded the song. Gritting my teeth, I wrapped the towel around Bryan's knee.

"Let's leave that there," I said distractedly, needing a moment of physical distance. Turning, I grabbed the jojoba oil and placed a generous amount in a ramekin, heating it in the microwave for just five seconds. But it was enough. Five seconds was enough to quash the feelings cinching my throat.

"I'll start with the other knee," I said offhandedly, keeping my eyes downcast as I approached his side and tried my best to ignore how decidedly luscious his legs were.

For the record, all rugby players have remarkable legs. They're cut, defined, corded with muscle. But Bryan's were perfection. His pronation was neutral, his femurs were long, and the definition of his quads was decidedly luscious.

A memory—just a flash, a feeling—of him moving against me, the fine hairs of his legs just the right amount of rough along the smooth bare skin of my thighs, made me shiver. The silence that followed felt thick and unyielding, though the feeling was likely all one-sided.

I was the only one who remembered.

I was the only one who still revisited the memory.

I was the only one who woke in the middle of the night from dreams of being touched by his hands, his mouth, his—

Determined, I repressed the recollections—I repressed it all—instead, counting the strokes as I dug my fingers into his calf.

He sucked in a sharp breath.

"Sorry. Too hard?" I gentled my touch.

"No. No, it feels good. I like it hard."

I nodded, my eyes on my hands and not his leg. *Anterior. One, two, three, four . . . Lateral. One, two, three, four . . . Medial. One, two, three, four . . .*

"God, that feels good." Bryan moaned, covering his face with his forearms.

I gritted my teeth, hating myself when his sounds made something twist low in my belly. *You are a terrible person, Eilish Cassidy. A terrible, terrible person.*

He moaned again. My nipples hardened.

FORKS!

"You have magical hands," he groaned.

Ignoring the raspy, roughened quality of his voice, I used my weight to increase the pressure. He'd used that very same tone during our one night together. In fact, he might have said those very same words.

"Don't stop."

I clenched my jaw, because he had said, *Don't stop* five years ago, and he'd said it exactly like he'd just said it now. Except five years ago, I'd been massaging a very different part of his body.

"So," I cleared my throat, unable to tolerate his moans of pleasure and praise any longer, "uh, what are your plans for the weekend?"

"The weekend?" He sounded a bit dazed.

"Yes. This weekend. What do you have planned? Planning on busting up any parties?" I asked lightly, not wanting him to know that I was unaccountably breathless. I moved to his other knee and discarded the towel.

"Ha. No. Not unless those wankers down the hall give me a reason to." Removing his arms from his face, Bryan's voice was thick, gravelly as he responded, "I, uh, have some furniture to assemble."

"Really?" Surprised, I stilled and stared at the line of his jaw. The creases around his mouth—when he held perfectly still—made him look mature and distinguished. Actually, they made him even more classically handsome, if that was even possible.

"Yes. Really. Two IKEA bookshelves."

I slid my hands lower, behind his ankle, waiting for him to continue. When he didn't, I prompted, "That's it?"

"No." He sighed, hesitated, then added, "I need to stop by the hardware store. The tap in my bathroom is leaking and one of the drawer handles in the kitchen is missing a screw. I just repainted the guest room, so I have to take the excess paint cans to the chemical disposal place; it's only open on Saturdays before noon. And then I promised my mam I'd take her to dinner."

My mouth parted slightly because the oddest thing happened as he rattled off his list of chores.

It turned me on.

Even more so than running my palms over his luscious legs.

That's right. His list of adult tasks made my heart flutter.

I rolled my lips between my teeth, not wanting to blurt that I also needed to go to the hardware store over the weekend. As a treat to myself, I was planning to organize Patrick's closet and wanted to install shelves above the clothes rack. Truly, Sean's penchant for buying my son designer suits and ties was completely out of hand. Without some reorganization, I would run out of space.

That's right. Organizing closets was something I loved to do. I couldn't get enough of those home and garden shows, especially *Tiny Houses*, because I adored clever uses for small spaces. I was just freaky enough to admit my passion for storage and organization.

But back to Bryan and his moans of pleasure, adult chores, and luscious legs.

I would not think about Bryan Leech adulting. I would not think about him walking into the hardware store in his sensible shoes and plain gray T-shirt— that would of course pull tightly over his impressive pectoral muscles—and then peruse the aisles for . . . a screw.

I. Would. Not.

Ignoring the spark of kinship, I set to work on his knee, again counting to distract myself. It worked until he volunteered, "I'd like to install some shelves in my closet, but that'll have to wait until next weekend. Honestly, I've been putting it off. I'd do just about anything to get someone to help me organize my closet." He chuckled.

I'd like to organize your closet.

I fought a groan, biting my lip as I removed my hands, turned from his body, and rinsed them under the faucet.

"We're, uh, finished for today. Ice your knee when you get home and use the elliptical instead of running. The less impact the better."

He was quiet for a moment, but I was painfully aware of his movements. In my mind's eye, I saw him sit up, stand, and straighten; his large form intoxicatingly imposing, coiled power behind an achingly handsome face.

"Thanks," he said haltingly, as though he wanted to say something more or he didn't quite know what to say.

I made a show of looking at my watch, turning from the sink and wiping my hands. "Not a problem. I'll check back with you on Wednesday."

Sending Bryan a quick, flat smile, I rushed past him.

I rushed out of the training room, down the hall, and up the stairs.

I ran to the women's locker room and into a bathroom stall, locking the door behind me with shaking fingers as the wave of emotions finally caught up to me.

I sat on the closed toilet lid, my elbows on my knees, my face in my hands.

But I didn't cry.

So many feelings—a potent mixture of self-loathing, desire, regret, sorrow, and shame. I wanted to cry. I tried. But I didn't. No tears would come.

I was a mess. I never used to be, but I was now. And I didn't know how to untangle myself.

I wasn't certain I could.

* * *

"Eilish, this is your mother."

Unable to help my grimace, I shook my head tiredly as Patrick and I walked into the hardware store. I shouldn't have answered the phone. Obviously, I knew it was her, and yet she insisted on announcing herself every single time. I didn't think my mother would ever get used to mobile phones.

"Hello, mother. We're—"

"I can't chat long, I have a nail appointment and lunch with Keira at the club. But it's important that you know I've informed the Donovans you'll be attending their tea on the seventh. This means you'll have to make arrangements for that child."

My smile and heart fell and my blood began to boil. I glanced at Patrick, at his innocent, happy-go-lucky expression, and embraced the resultant fierce wave of protectiveness. How my mother referred to my son as *that child* had always incensed me. It was why I hardly ever answered her calls or attended the family brunches on Sundays. It was why I avoided her and my siblings.

I was the youngest of five children and officially the black sheep. I'd always been outspoken, but now I was a fallen woman. I was a college dropout. I was whispered about. I was a scandal.

My mother hated scandals. They were terribly inconvenient.

Never mind the fact that I did eventually finish college and, unlike the rest of my brothers and sisters, paid my own way (mostly). Never mind the fact that my mother had cut me out of her life—both financially and personally—when I refused to give Patrick up for adoption.

Never mind that.

"Mother—"

"Trevor will be there. Keira said he asked if you'd be attending."

I rolled my eyes. "Please let that go. I am not interested in Trevor."

"Oh? Really?"

"Yes. Really."

"And next week, what? Will you be back together again?"

"No, Mother. We dated over the summers when we were teenagers, when we were kids."

She sighed. "Honestly, Eilish, I don't understand you. Trevor Donovan comes from a respectable family and *is* respectable. After what you've done, you should be thankful he considers you at all."

I exhaled silently and reminded myself there was no changing my mother. Best-case scenario, she saw me as damaged goods. Worst case, she saw me as one of those whores down by the docks in *Les Misérables,* just with better teeth.

Taking my silence in stride, she chirped, "I'll send the car for you at one."

"That won't be necessary. As I told you in my message, I won't be going."

She huffed. Loudly. Directly into the receiver. "Eilish. Don't be petulant."

"I have to go." I squeezed Patrick's hand and gave him a small smile, which he returned before his eyes moved over the long rows of tools and machinery.

The hardware store was his favorite place. For Christmas last year, I bought him a kid-sized apron and tool belt to match the store's employees. He'd been so excited, one might have thought I'd bought him a life-sized Batmobile, and he refused to take them off at bedtime for over a week.

"Is this because of *that* child? Do you need a sitter? Because I'm sure Circe will lend you her nanny and—"

"I have to go. Goodbye, Mother." I ended the call, my temper rising as it always did when my mother spoke of people as though they could be lent and borrowed.

Tucking the phone away, I widened my smile at my son's expression. "We need wood cut for the shelves. Do you want to do that first or do you want to look at the lawn mowers?"

Patrick pointed a beaming grin at me and nodded. "Can we ride one?"

"No. But the man said last time that you can sit on it and pretend."

"Okay." He nodded enthusiastically and tugged me toward the ride-on lawn mowers; he had the layout of the store memorized.

I followed where he led, glancing with particular interest down the aisle that held closet-storage solutions. I tried not to think about Bryan's closet. I tried, but I couldn't stop myself. He likely had a large one, maybe even a walk-in. *With lots of space for shoe organizers and scarf hangers.*

Fantasizing about his fictional sock drawer, I was unceremoniously yanked out of the daydream by the very real sound of Bryan Leech's voice.

"I brought one from a different drawer so I could find a match. I think it's three quarters." Bryan's words carried to me as a shock of adrenaline brought me to a standstill. My grip on Patrick's hand tightened and I pulled him close, picking him up.

"Mummy, what's wrong?"

"*Shhh.*" I pressed his head into my neck, fear and instinct dictating I hide his face. "Don't move; don't make a sound."

In my bones I knew if Bryan saw Patrick, he would know. He would know instantly that Patrick was his.

I had to get out of there.

I had to leave before Bryan discovered me. Discovered us.

My throat suddenly dry, I turned my head in every direction, trying to find him.

Then he spoke again, closer this time. "That's it. That's the screw I'm looking for. Might as well pick up a few extra."

I darted in the opposite direction, which thankfully happened to be toward the exit, and ran as fast as I was able out of the building. Patrick's little hands gripping handfuls of my cardigan brought me back to myself. He was still and silent. Once I rounded the corner, I leaned away to inspect his face and found his eyes wide and frightened.

My heart clenched, twisting painfully at the sight.

"Are we safe, Mummy?" he whispered.

I nodded, releasing a shaky breath before drawing him close and hugging him tightly. "We're safe."

For now . . .

I held my breath, willing my racing pulse to slow, even as the sound of it filled my ears. But my cousin's words from the day before came to me, a chant matching the cadence of my heart. *Patrick deserves to know his father, and Bryan deserves to know his son.*

What was I going to do? Hide Patrick from everyone? Never bring any pictures to work? Make up excuses about why I never brought him around? Pretend he didn't exist?

It was already too late for that. Some of the lads on the team already knew. Bryan knew. Soon everyone would know.

I'd lived the last five years in a constant state of anxiety and fear: first, fear of having a baby, then fear of failure, and now fear of having my child taken away.

Always fear. Always guilt.

Sean was right. I knew he was right. Separate from my own messy feelings, from my worries and longings, was my little boy. And my boy deserves to know his father. *And Bryan deserves to know his son.*

I winced and then nodded, because it was true. The Bryan I knew now would be an excellent father. I couldn't keep making excuses.

Even if the thought of telling Bryan—of admitting the truth—made my blood run cold with dread, I had to do it. I couldn't hide Patrick. He deserved better than a mother ruled by fear.

Bryan hadn't remembered me. He didn't remember our night together. He didn't remember making Patrick. He hadn't even remembered my name. I had been nothing to him. And maybe he would hate me for keeping Patrick from him. But it wasn't about me.

It was about Patrick.

I needed to tell Bryan the truth.

For Patrick.

TEN
BRYAN

@THEBryanLeech: Sometimes life punches you right in the face. And sometimes you end up liking it.
@WillthebrickhouseMoore to @THEBryanLeech: So that's what you're into. Interesting.

"I got a new plant, and it's been alive for a month."

"Oh really? What kind?" Sarah asked. She sounded interested.

"A spider plant. The lady at the florist said it was the easiest to keep alive," I told my sponsor as I finished toweling dry my hair—over the phone, of course. She might not be interested in seeing a bunch of men walk around in the nip, but a woman hanging out in the team's locker rooms wouldn't go unnoticed.

She chuckled at this. "I think that might be cheating, but okay."

"Hey, it's better than nothing," I defended.

"So, why the change of heart?"

"What do you mean?"

"I thought you were done with the whole *luurve* side of life."

"I am . . . sort of."

"Then why have you taken a new plant under your wing?"

"I like the challenge."

"Mm-hmm. I think you might be making unintentional plans in that head of yours. What was her name again? Eilish?"

"I'm not making any unintentional plans about . . ." I trailed off, glancing around the room just in case Sean was somewhere listening. "*Her.*"

"I think you are. I think you want to open doors for her, buy her flowers, take her out for romantic candlelit dinners, and prove that you can be responsible with a person by being responsible with a green leafy friend," she teased, a smile in her voice.

I grunted, but didn't deny her accusation because I did want to take Eilish out. I'd been preparing to do just that when she told me she had a son. But in the end, I didn't ask her. It wasn't the fact that she had a son that concerned me, not at all. In fact, my imagination rather ran away with plans after she'd said it, liking the idea of a two-for-one deal.

Maybe he likes rugby.
Of course he likes rugby.
I should get him a jersey.

But then the other part of her statement sunk in: *You remind me of my son's father.*

Jesus Christ. How was I supposed to get out of that box?

"I've always hated dating," I said instead. "In fact, if I could bypass all that *might I bestow upon you a kiss* business, I would. Why can't we all just skip to the comfortable part of relationships? Go straight to the bit where you can walk around in your undies, let farts go and blame them on the dog, and leave the door open when you're taking a piss?"

"First of all, there is no part of a relationship that should involve that last bit, and second of all, dating is the *best* part. All those butterflies and excitement, the sexual tension. Wanting to skip to the comfortable bit is laziness. It means you don't have to put in any effort to woo someone. Also, if memory serves, you've never had a relationship that lasted more than six months."

"Thanks for the reminder, oh Sarah of Ye Old Wet Blanket," I groused, but she was right. I hadn't dated anyone for longer than six months; and even then it hadn't really been a relationship with any meaningful or lasting impact.

"*Ye Old Wet Blanket* was my grandmother's name, I'll have you know."

I cracked a smile but couldn't suppress my sigh of frustration. "It's not that I'm lazy, it's just that it doesn't hold any appeal. And anyway, I'm too old for all that. Dating's a young man's game."

Dating was a young man's game, and yet I'd been prepared to ask Eilish out until her confession last week. I hadn't been able to stop thinking about her, regretting what I'd said after our kiss. But she'd avoided me for weeks, which was understandable given how I'd responded.

Or not responded.

I just couldn't believe it was happening—that we were kissing—and then it was over. Even though everything I'd said about not being good enough for her was true, the compulsion to ask her out, spend time with her, was overwhelming.

Sarah let out a sound that was half laughter, half frustration. "You *are* a young man, Bryan."

"Then why does the idea of getting to know someone feel like a chore?" *A chore when it's anyone but the one woman you can't have.*

"You're thirty years old, practically a baby. You've just burned yourself out. You need to find the excitement in life again, the thrill to be had from simple things."

"I do get a thrill from simple things," I countered. "Didn't I mention I fixed my tap this weekend? And I had Earl Grey tea with breakfast."

"Oh. Stop. Too much excitement. I can't handle it." She said this deadpan, adding, "I'm talking about finding something you enjoy doing on the regular. You know, a hobby, you nutter."

"I have hobbies. I've taken up bird watching."

"Okay, go ahead, take the piss."

"I'm not joking. I've been driving up to the mountains on my days off, when I'm not fixing up the apartment. Best few hours of the week."

"Oh . . . you're serious," said Sarah, taken aback.

"Course I am. I've taken up golf, too. Well, I like going to the driving range from time to time at least."

A sigh from her. "I take it back. You are an old man."

"Glad you're finally seeing things clearly."

"You do realize the problem with all these new activities you're filling your life with, right?"

"There's no problem. I'm quite content with my life now."

"They're all solitary. Before you know it, you'll be a cranky old hermit, shouting at kids to get off your lawn and complaining about how the postman is always late."

"Come on, you're getting a little ahead of yourself now—"

"I'm not. There's a gaping woman-shaped hole in your life and you're filling it with mundane pursuits. Soon enough you're going to realize what I already know."

"And what's that then?" I asked, getting a little irritated now.

"That you've been sober for two years and you're ready for a relationship. You're not the same bloke you were at twenty-five. You're one of the most reliable people I know, and you're too much of a good-looking son of a gun to be single. Some woman needs to be getting the benefit of that body of yours."

"Why, Sarah, if I'd only known you've been harboring this crush," I teased, my irritability fading.

"Oh please, just because I'm gay doesn't mean I can't recognize an attractive man when I see one. Anyway, I've got to get ready for my shift at work, but think about what I said, okay? You deserve someone, Bryan, you really do."

Deserve someone. Up until now, I hadn't considered I deserved someone. My mam was a prime example of someone alone, someone who had pushed nearly everyone else out of her life, except me. But was I alone? Did I feel alone? After my horrible behavior for years, I hadn't felt I'd deserved anything otherwise. *But now?*

I needed some time to think about all this.

"Okay, call me tomorrow."

"Will do. Bye."

After I hung up, I finished dressing and packing my things, mulling over her words.

Maybe Sarah had a point. Recently, I'd started having wet dreams, and that shit hadn't happened since I was fourteen. It was downright embarrassing. I swear it'd only take a light breeze to make me come these days.

I was lost in thought when I stepped out of the locker rooms and collided with a body. "Oh shit, sorry," I said right before her scent hit me.

Eilish.

"No, it's my fault," she said as she righted herself. "I wasn't looking where I was going."

"That makes two of us." I gave her a soft smile, ignoring the pull I always felt when she was nearby. There was no use.

I knew I wasn't her favorite person, but at least now I knew why.

You remind me of my son's father. . . What kind of eejit would let her go? I wanted to find the wanker and beat the shite out of him.

I moved to step by her, gritting my teeth at the unfairness of it all. Why did she have to be so beautiful? So . . . funny and clever, intriguing? Why, in spite of all the stuff I'd just said to Sarah about not wanting to go through the rigmarole of getting to know someone, did I still *really* want to get to know her? She was an anomaly and it made her dislike of me that much more of a blow.

But then she blurted, "Let's go out for a drink," and I paused mid-stride.

I turned just my head to look at her, certain I'd misheard. "Pardon?"

She chewed on her lip. "Sorry. I meant that to be a question. Do you . . . do you want to go somewhere and have a drink with me?" Her eyes were on my chin, and she spoke slowly and carefully, as though forcing herself to say the words.

I glanced around to look for cameras, because this had to be a joke. No *hello.* No *how are you*? Just straight to asking me out for a drink.

But just in case this was for real, and this intriguing woman actually *was* asking me out, I kept my tone soft as I gently reminded, "I don't drink, Eilish. I'm two years sober."

"Forks!" she exclaimed, squeezing her eyes shut. "Right, yeah. Sorry, I forgot. Well, I didn't forget I'm just—Sorry."

"You don't need to be sorry. No harm, no foul." I took a step toward her, just barely restraining the urge to place a comforting hand on her shoulder, or grab her hand, or give myself a high-five.

Whoa, don't get ahead of yourself.

She looked extremely nervous, so I dismissed the idea of a self-congratulatory high-five. Though I could have done so if I'd been quiet, she couldn't see me because her eyes were still shut.

"We could go for coffee?" she suggested, finally meeting my eyes, and there was something about the intensity in hers, almost like she was pleading with me not to make it a big deal, that had me nodding automatically, albeit warily.

"Eh, sure, coffee sounds good." *What the hell is going on?*

"Right, great. Is now okay?"

Now?

"Now?"

She nodded fervently. "Yes, now."

"Well, I'm done for the day so I guess . . . yeah. We can take my car." I was responding on autopilot because my brain was too preoccupied trying to figure out what was happening.

"All right. Lead the way." She motioned me forward with her hand and, casting her one more bewildered glance, I led the way.

Nothing about this makes sense. Unless . . .

"Hey, Eilish?"

She glanced up at me as we walked. "Yes?"

"Is everything okay? Connors hasn't been acting up again, has he?"

She shook her head. "No, no, nothing like that."

"You need a kidney, or something?"

She sputtered a surprised laugh. "Of course not."

"Blood transfusion? I'm type A negative if you were wondering."

"Bryan, I don't need an organ transplant or a blood transfusion. I don't even want you to pay for the coffee. I just need to talk to you someplace not here."

"Well, I'm definitely paying for the coffee, but what do you want to talk about?"

She glanced from side to side, like there were listening ears all about. "I'll tell you when we get to the coffee shop. Just, can we go somewhere at least a few miles away? It's a subject of a sensitive nature."

"Sure." I was even more confused now. What on earth could she possibly have to say to me that was *of a sensitive nature*?

And, so, was this a date?

Or no . . . ?

In a baffled daze, we made it to the garage and I opened her door. She slipped in, and wordlessly I pulled out of the sports complex. The car drive was silent, my mind awash with curiosity. It was also awash with plans, ways I could turn this impromptu coffee date into a real date.

I glanced at her and allowed my eyes to move over her form. Even buzzing with nervous energy, being close to her felt . . . nice.

I could do this. I could make the moves on her, show her I was nothing like her son's father. I might be rusty, but I still knew a thing or two.

Or three things. But not more than three.

I knew I should've turned the radio on when my stomach made a loud grumble. I glanced at Eilish and saw the side of her mouth had curved just slightly.

"You ever notice how your gut always waits for absolute silence to do that?" I asked lightly. "It's like it wants to achieve optimum embarrassment."

She nodded and shot me a smile. "Yeah. It used to always happen to me in school during tests." She paused, looking me over. "You haven't eaten since lunch, have you?"

"Nah, but don't worry about it. I'll eat when I get home."

She considered me a moment. "We can get something now, if you want. I don't mind."

My mouth shaped into a grin at this opening. "Is this a sneaky ploy to lure me into a dinner date? Because if it is, I'm in."

"No! It's not, I swear. This is definitely not a date. I just know how important it is for you guys to eat at regular intervals. Don't tell him I told you this, but Sean sometimes carries cooked chicken breasts around with him in sealed food bags in case he gets peckish."

I chuckled to cover my frustration at her insisting this wasn't a date. "Really? Next time I see him I'll have to ask if he'd like to share his breasts with the rest of the team."

Eilish's cheeks reddened. "Please don't."

"But it's not fair, keeping those succulent bosoms all to himself," I went on, hoping my flirting attempt wasn't unwelcomed.

"Bryan," she pleaded, and there was something about my name on her lips that woke my dick up.

Go back to sleep, eager. Nothing to see here.

"I'm joking, I'm joking. I won't out his secret to the boys. You have my word."

At this, she smiled tightly and turned to look out the window. A few minutes passed as I quietly drove. Eilish reached up to fiddle with her hair. It was in a neat bun, but she pulled out the elastic and let it fall over her shoulders. Man, that hair. I bet it felt like silk. My fingers itched to find out.

I pulled to a stop outside one of my favorite steakhouses and parked. Eilish didn't speak as I led her inside. But when I asked for a table for two, she put in, "Please, a booth at the back if you have one," anxiety radiating off her in waves.

I was still at a loss to explain what was going on with her, but I tried my best to put her at ease even though her nervousness was rubbing off on me a little.

"They do amazing chicken wings here. Louisiana hot sauce. You should try them," I said as we slid into the booth.

"Oh yeah, I might," she replied absently and took the menu from the waiter before studiously reading through the options. The tension grew thick between us, and I was at a loss as to how to break the silence. She asked me here to discuss a sensitive issue. The only person we had in common was Sean, so maybe something was going on with him. Maybe he was ill. I hoped to God that he wasn't.

"Can I take your orders?" the waiter asked when he returned. I gestured for Eilish to go first.

"I'll have the chicken wings and the sweet potato fries, please. Oh, and a Coke." Her voice was a little shaky and I felt this overwhelming urge to touch her, help her calm down in some way.

"And I'll have the sirloin. Medium rare. Still water to drink. Thanks."

The waiter took our menus and the silence returned. I couldn't take much more of it, but I knew if I pushed to know what she wanted to talk about I'd only scare her off.

"So, how was your day?" I asked. "Good, bad, average?"

"It was okay."

"My knee's been feeling great since your massage."

She shifted in place, not meeting my gaze. "That's good."

"How are you liking working with the team so far?"

"I like it."

"*Eilish.*"

Her bright eyes flicked up to meet mine. "Yes?"

In a bold move, I reached across the table and squeezed her hand. "Talk to me. Whatever you have to say, I promise you won't find any judgment here."

She let out a long, shaky breath. "Can I, um, ask you a few questions first?"

I let go of her hand and sat back. "Of course. Fire away."

"Sooo . . . eh, what do you think about kids?"

"Kids?"

She nodded fervently and leaned forward to rest her elbows on the table. "Yeah, kids."

Where was she going with this? I mean, I knew she had a son, but why ask me about kids?

Her gaze seared into mine, like my answer was a matter of life and death.

I cleared my throat, wanting to be honest but also give the right answer. "I don't really think about them much, if I'm honest, but I like them. Some of the blokes on the team are dads, and I have great craic playing around with their little ones on family days."

Eilish absorbed my answer with a serious expression. "What about the non-fun side? Could you ever see yourself caring for a child when he's . . . I mean, when they're sick? What about when they throw a tantrum and need to be disciplined?"

I raised an eyebrow. This was an odd conversation, but I went with it, curious to see what her end game was. "Again, never really thought about it, but I guess it could be rewarding to raise a little boy or girl. I've always been a very protective sort, and I think if I had a child, or the person I was with had a child, I'd pretty much do everything I could to keep them happy and safe."

I gave myself a mental high-five for that one. If this was her way of interviewing me before agreeing to go out with me, I could more than respect that. She was a mother, of course she'd want the guy she was dating to treat her son well.

Well look at you, Bryan Leech, getting one right for a change.

Feeling pretty good about my chances, I gave her an easy smile.

The waiter approached and placed our drinks down in front of us. Eilish grabbed her Coke, sucking a long gulp through the straw while a thoughtful expression crossed over her features.

After quenching her thirst, she spoke again. "So, let's imagine a scenario where you are a dad. What sort of parent do you think you'd be? Strict? Laid-back? Somewhere between the two?"

A dad? Really? I didn't say it, but I thought maybe she was getting ahead of herself.

"There must be a need for both, right? Too much of either would probably mess a kid's head up, so I'd say somewhere between the two."

"How about slapping a child when they've misbehaved? Do you think it's necessary?"

"I guess . . . no? I mean, I was slapped growing up and it never stopped me from misbehaving. I think a good talking to, or a discussion, would have worked better."

She nodded, her eyes brightening. "And you're Catholic, right? Do you think you'd raise your kids in the church?"

"I guess I would, but what—?"

"And what about phones and computers? Where do you stand on children having access to the Internet?"

"Well, obviously I think they need to be supervised up to a certain age but . . ."

"Like how old?"

I scratched at my stubble. "Fourteen?"

"You think a fourteen-year-old should have unfettered access to the Internet? Really?" she questioned, not seeming to like that answer.

"Okay, maybe sixteen then, but I don't think you can shelter them forever, either. At some stage you need to let them make sense of the world on their own."

"Huh."

A moment of silence ensued as she thought something over.

"Eilish, am I being interviewed for a nanny position or something? Because

I have to say, I've never quite had the pleasure of being asked out to dinner by a beautiful woman only to be peppered with questions about parenting." I studied her closely, noticing her blush at my calling her beautiful. She was though, and she had to at least be a small bit aware of it.

"I know," she answered quietly, her eyes a little sad. "And I'm sorry for all the questions, but there's a point to all this, I promise. I just have one more question."

I shot her an empathetic look and spoke softly, because she seemed to be hurting in some way. "Okay, one more won't kill me."

She cleared her throat. "You mentioned you struggled with an alcohol problem in the past and that you're sober now. I was just wondering what age you'd allow your child to start drinking?"

Quick as a flash my mood changed. Her question hit a sore spot. Growing up, Mam let me drink early. *Too* early. I definitely could've benefited from stricter rules.

"I don't think any child should be allowed alcohol. In fact, if I had my way we'd have similar laws to those in the U.S. that restrict alcohol consumption until the age of twenty-one."

She tilted her head, her expression curious. "That seems a little extreme."

"Yeah well, I don't think we should ever underestimate the damage drinking can do. Our mid-to-late teens are some of the most tumultuous years in a person's life. Every little thing that goes wrong seems like the end of the world, and having access to alcohol at that age can be extremely dangerous. My mam started offering me wine at the dinner table when I was eight. I know that's normal in a lot of European countries, but well, my mother's been struggling with an alcohol addiction her whole life. Before I knew it, I was mimicking her behavior, and she was too lost to care. I'd go as far as to say she was comforted by the fact that I drank with her. I essentially made her feel better about her own behavior by partaking in it."

When I paused to look at Eilish, she seemed horrified. "I'm sorry. That must've been rough."

I shrugged. "It was, but I never realized until I got older and saw how drink was ruining my life. It was stealing my health, preventing me from maintaining long-term relationships of any kind. It even stole my memories. Most things in life you can get back, but time isn't one of them, and my biggest regret is the years I lost when I could've been doing something productive with my life."

I stopped speaking, because Eilish was staring at me so intensely it almost took the wind out of me. She was truly emoting to my loss and it was completely unexpected coming from a woman I thought hated my guts.

Our gazes were still locked when she blurted, "I have a son."

I nodded once. "Yes. I know." This was old news.

"His name's Patrick."

"My middle name's Patrick," I told her with a warm smile.

She nodded, gulping in air. "I know."

Now I studied her quizzically. "You do?"

"I do." She pressed her lips together, her jaw ticked, her eyes now drilling into mine. And then she said, "Patrick is yours, Bryan."

I'd just lifted my glass to take a drink and almost spat water out all over the table. Instead, it went down the wrong pipe and I choked.

She winced.

"*He's what*?" I half-sputtered, half-laughed. She was having me on, right?

"He's your son. We have a child," she stated, clasping her hands together tightly, her tone firm. "It's the reason I've been . . . acting like a lunatic."

What the hell?

My brain simply couldn't compute what she was saying, because what she was saying was completely fucking crazy. But of course you can't say to someone, *You're completely fucking crazy.*

So instead, I decided playing things off with humor was the best approach. "I'm sorry, Eilish, but I think you're mistaken. We only just met a few weeks ago. Although I might've boasted I could get women pregnant with just a look as a younger man, it wasn't actually true, and definitely not retroactively. Certain body parts have to be in play for that to happen."

Her posture drew ramrod straight, her lips forming a tight line.

"This isn't a joke, Bryan. You spoke of your memory loss just now. Well, we've met before, you just don't . . . you don't remember me. It was five years ago, at Ronan and Annie's wedding. We slept together once, and a few weeks later, I discovered I was pregnant."

My smile faded quickly as her words sank in.

Memory loss.

Slept together.

Pregnant.

The sound of my heart filled my ears, and my vision went hazy at the edges.

Several moments passed. They could've lasted seconds or whole minutes, I couldn't tell. My brain was too busy trying to untangle the information I'd just been handed. Each piece made too much sense for me to deny. That sense of déjà vu that struck me when I'd first met her, the feeling that I'd known her in another life. The unexplainable familiarity. The pull to get to know her.

She was telling the truth.

I had a son.

I. Had. A. Son.

ELEVEN
BRYAN

@THEBryanLeech: When you realize you're actually really truly an arsehole.
@SeanCassinova to @THEBryanLeech: Aw, poor baby. Want a cuddle?
@THEBryanLeech to @SeanCassinova: Nah. Last time you got a stiffy. It was embarrassing for both of us.

"Now, folks, I believe the steak was for the gentleman and the chicken wings for the lady," the waiter said when he arrived with our food.

I gaped at Eilish as the waiter set the dishes down in front of us. Not surprisingly, my appetite had vanished. My gaze went from the earnest honesty of her bright blue eyes, to the nervous set of her mouth, to the tension that radiated off every inch of her body.

God, she really was telling the truth.

This was crazy.

I had no idea what to feel or how to deal with the bomb she just dropped.

I had a son, a son who was almost five years old, and who I'd never even met.

His name is Patrick . . .

"Bryan, say something, please," she whispered once the waiter left us alone.

I opened my mouth, but no words felt right. "I . . . I'm sorry, I need to use the john."

I stood abruptly from the table, almost knocking over my glass, and staggered toward the back of the restaurant. Eilish didn't breathe a word or try to follow me, and when I shut myself away in a cubicle, I sat down on the closed toilet seat and dropped my face into my hands.

I was dreaming.

I had to be dreaming.

For the first time in a long time, I felt like drinking. It'd take the edge off if nothing else. My brain reminded me that whenever I felt like this, the best thing to do was call Sarah, have her talk me down, so I pulled my phone out and dialed her number.

"Two calls in one day. Lots of women would be jealous," she said as she picked up. I was relieved she hadn't started her shift yet, because she always put her phone on silent when she was working.

"I want a drink," I bit out, my voice gruff.

Her tone changed from joking to serious in a heartbeat. "Fuck. Okay. Why?"

I let out a joyless laugh. "My entire life has just been flipped on its head, and I don't know what to do."

I heard her breathe deeply. "Tell me everything."

"I've just been told I have a kid, a son I never knew about," I blurted.

"What!" she practically screeched, and somehow her reaction made me feel better. I definitely wasn't overreacting here. This was *huge*.

I quickly rehashed everything that had just gone down with Eilish. When I finished speaking, Sarah was quiet on the other end. Finally, she spoke.

"Okay, Bryan, don't freak out at me for saying this, because I know you really like this girl, but you have to consider the possibility that she might be lying."

I sputtered, incredulous. "Why would she lie about something so serious?"

"Because you're wealthy and famous and it sounds like she has a bit of a crush on you, and having a child with a man like you would basically mean she's set for life. Please don't tell me you've forgotten about Jennifer, not to mention Kylie. Those two must've extorted at least fifty thousand each before you finally kicked them to the curb."

I didn't appreciate her bringing up my past, the women who'd taken advantage of my addiction in order to feed their own. Drunks and addicts attract drunks and addicts. And now I was neither.

"Eilish isn't like that."

"You hardly know her."

"That doesn't matter. She's not a liar, and besides, she comes from a very wealthy background. She doesn't need the money. Her cousin practically treats her like a princess."

A small sigh came from her end. "You still need to be wary. Even if you believe the kid's yours, you'll need to get a DNA test to confirm it. You can't just run into a situation like this headfirst without thinking things through."

I frowned. "What makes you think I'd do that?"

"Because you don't sound upset. You sound sort of happy, excited even. I know you well enough by now to be able to differentiate between the two."

"I'm not happy," I protested. *Was I happy?* How could I be happy about something this mental? And why would I feel like having a drink if I was happy about it? Then again, back when I was an addict I turned to alcohol for every occasion. Just got good news? Have a drink to celebrate. Just got bad news? Have a drink to commiserate.

"It's a natural reflex to want to drink when you get a shock or feel out of control, and you've just had a massive one. It still doesn't mean you don't like what's happening. You've been fixated on this girl, and now all of a sudden she tells you you're her kid's dad. You're excited about the possibilities of where this could lead, but I'm telling you to keep your wits about you, Bryan. Trust me. This could end badly if you don't."

I rubbed my mouth, searching through the mess in my head to try and figure out what I was feeling. My pulse was beating fast. My palms were sweaty. There was a knot in my stomach similar to how I felt right before I played an important rugby match. This was basically the Six Nations Championship level of exhilaration.

Damn, Sarah was right. I *was* happy. I was more than happy. I was over-fucking-joyed. Seriously, what the hell was wrong with me that I was overjoyed about being a father to a child I'd never met? If I ever had any doubts that I was screwed up, here was the evidence.

"You're right. I will. I'll be smart," I told her finally. "I need to go back out and talk to Eilish now. I'll call you later and let you know how things go."

"Yes, call me. And good luck," she replied.

After we hung up, I emerged from the cubicle and went to splash some water over my face to compose myself. I knew if I went out there with a big psycho grin on my face I was only going to freak Eilish out. I needed to chill, act as normal as possible.

But what was normal in this kind of situation? *Hell if I knew.*

When I walked back out into the restaurant, she was still sitting at the table. She hadn't touched her food and there were dozens of tiny pieces of tissue paper on the table from a napkin she'd torn to shreds. She was obviously anxious as hell, and I felt bad for just leaving her there. I slid into the booth and she glanced up, looking relieved to see me, yet still cautious.

"You came back," she breathed, eyes flickering over me in concern.

I ran my hand through my hair. "Yeah I, uh, just needed a minute to get my head around everything."

Eilish nodded shakily. "Understandable."

A silence fell and I struggled with what to say first. The waiter, clearly having noticed we hadn't touched our food, chose that moment to make an appearance.

"Is everything okay? Can I get you anything else?"

"We're fine, thank you," I told him, and he quietly retreated.

"Listen I—"

"It's okay if—"

We both spoke at once, cutting each other off.

"Sorry. You go first," she offered. "And I totally get it if you hate me right now."

I frowned at her. "Of course I don't hate you. Why would I?"

"B-b-b . . ." She closed her eyes, breathed in and out, then started again, slower this time. "Because I've kept this a secret from you for so long. I was young and frightened, and I had this idea of you as this wild, uncontrollable party animal. That's not an excuse. It's just, I didn't think you'd want anything to do with me or the baby. It may sound ludicrous, but I didn't want to bother you."

"Eilish, I *was* a wild, uncontrollable party animal, and I'm not saying it was the right thing to do, but I understand why you didn't tell me. Fucking hell, I don't even remember our night together." I paused for a moment, the lovely reality of *that* fact sinking in.

My eyes moved over this woman in front of me, this gorgeous, intelligent woman. I'd had her. I'd had her and I didn't even remember. This new knowledge was a special kind of hell.

Her eyes lowered and pink stained her cheeks. She looked uncomfortable. Actually, she looked mortified.

"Eilish . . ." I started clumsily, but what the fuck was I going to say? How do you apologize for sleeping with someone and not remembering?

Sorry, darling. I'm sure you were great, but I was too shitfaced for it to make an impression.

Christ. I was an arsehole.

Then again, I did have flashes, strange moments of déjà vu. She'd seemed so familiar, small memories of red hair and pale skin. Perhaps I wasn't such a forgetful dick after all.

She waved me away, a brittle smile claiming her features and a flash of unmistakable pain dulling her eyes. "It's not important." She cleared her throat, setting her teeth. When she returned her eyes to mine they were cooler, withdrawn, disinterested in a way that looked like self-preservation, and I felt the difference like a blow to the stomach. It was a look I recognized. Only now I understood why she used it on me.

"Patrick is important. We should focus on him." Her tone was firm and dispassionate.

"Yes. Of course. But I'm just saying, the way I acted is hardly a glowing recommendation for fatherhood." I sought to soften her. "If anything, it's my own fault I've missed out on all these years with . . . with Patrick. The person I was back then didn't deserve a kid."

"I should've told you." She shook her head, the line of her jaw stubborn.

"You're telling me now."

Her brow furrowed. "Why are you being so . . . so reasonable about all this?"

I smiled. "Because I'm a fairly reasonable bloke."

"But you're making me feel worse. The least you could do is shout at me, call me a few names. I deserve it." Her face crumpled as though she might cry, but then I watched as steel and resolve forced back the tide of emotion. Holy shit, behind all the nervousness this girl was strong.

I respected that strength and was drawn to it in a way I didn't entirely understand.

Acting on instinct, I reached across the table and took both of her hands in mine. She was still working on obliterating her napkin into tiny pieces, but they fell away. She sucked in a breath at the contact. Holding her soft, delicate hands in mine felt right. It felt so fucking right.

"I don't blame you, Eilish, so stop beating yourself up. This was a rough situation for anyone to be in, let alone a teenager. And it was my fault for going after you in the first place. You were way too young, but I was obviously too shitfaced to realize or care."

She shook her head now. "It's not like you forced yourself on me. I . . ." she paused, the blush deepening over her cheeks, "I wanted it."

Something in my chest unfurled. My voice was low when I spoke. "Really?"

She only nodded in response, not meeting my gaze. I squeezed her hands to let her know she didn't need to be embarrassed.

"We have a lot to talk about, you and me," I told her softly.

She squeezed her eyes shut, her head shaking in a small, quick movement.

I rubbed my thumbs over the insides of her wrists, a sense of rightness and necessity stirring my blood.

Christ, I needed to stop touching her, because if I thought she was beautiful before, the fact that this woman was the mother of my child gave her a fucking halo. I swear, she glowed. She was radiant. As magnetic as before, but also something more.

I let her hands go, because otherwise I was going to pull her across the table and devour her.

Clearing my throat, I forced my eyes to my food. "First though, we'd better eat before the waiter drives himself into a state wondering if there's something wrong with our dinners."

This solicited a small, breathy chuckle from her, and it felt good to make her laugh. We each took a few bites and a thoughtful silence fell over us, redirecting my thoughts away from *her* and back to the situation.

I still wasn't quite sure why I felt so good about all this. If anyone else had come to me with the same revelation, I'd probably have told them to pull the other one. But there was just something about Eilish, something about her earnest, open personality that made me believe her.

I wanted to do right by her.

And having a child wasn't a bad thing. It was a great thing. A gift. I was old and wise enough to see that now. If she'd come to me all those years ago, when I was still drinking and out of control, I shudder to think of how I might've reacted.

So maybe her keeping everything a secret for so long was a blessing. Maybe this was how it was always supposed to be.

I glanced at her as she nibbled on a chicken wing. Her long, thick lashes shadowed her cheeks, casting her pretty features in a devastatingly beautiful light. Just looking at her sucked all the air from my lungs.

Yeah, maybe there was a tiny, minuscule part of me that liked the idea of having a child specifically with Eilish. It meant I got to spend more time around her. Ever since I laid eyes on her at Will's party I'd been captivated, almost like my subconscious sensed our connection. And it killed me that we'd met before, spent an entire night together, and I couldn't remember a single second of it. I'd had my greedy, ungrateful hands on her—been *inside* her—but I was too wrapped up in myself at the time to appreciate how lucky I was. *Her look of hurt.* Had I hurt her? Physically? Or . . . oh shite. What would it feel like to be on the receiving end of being forgotten?

She didn't deserve to be forgotten.

She deserved to be treasured.

And I was going to do everything in my power to make up for what I'd done. But really, as delighted as I was to have this connection to Eilish, I was also incredibly eager to know everything about her son. *Our* son.

"Do you have a picture of him?" I asked, unable to hold back my curiosity.

She nodded and dabbed her lips before going to dig through her handbag. "Of course. Yes. Sorry."

She pulled out her phone and navigated to her photos. Her hand shook as she passed it to me across the table. I took it with barely concealed fascination. The picture showed Eilish with a little boy on her lap. He had light brown hair, bright green eyes, and a dimple in either cheek. That wasn't what held me captive though. It was like looking at a time capsule of myself. My heart pounded as several emotions overtook me. I hadn't been kidding that I enjoyed playing with some of the lads's kids, but this . . .

Was it possible to love him already when we hadn't even met?

I couldn't take my eyes off the photo and had to inhale a few deep breaths just to keep from embarrassing myself in front of the entire restaurant. Nobody expected a six-foot-four behemoth of a rugby player to start welling up in public.

Eilish must've noticed the shine in my eyes because she asked gently, "Bryan, are you all right?"

"Yeah," I sniffed. "It's just . . ."

"The resemblance?" she guessed. "It's uncanny, isn't it?"

I nodded and swiped my thumb over her screen, then glanced up. My voice was scratchy when I spoke. "Can you send this to my phone?"

"Yes. Of course."

"Thank you."

I held her gaze for a moment, unspoken feelings passing between us.

Fear.

Uncertainty.

Anticipation.

Excitement.

I knew that for me the latter two outweighed the former. I just hoped it was the same for Eilish. My eyes traced the elegant slant of her nose, the curve of her rosebud mouth. She was so bloody gorgeous. This was going to be very fucking complicated, that was for sure.

"Did you name him after me?" I asked.

"Yes, I did."

"Why?" I prodded gently.

"I'm not sure why I did it. Maybe it was my guilt? Or maybe I felt like he should at least have some part of you."

I chuckled softly. "Have you seen him? He's got all of me. If I didn't know better, I'd say someone cloned my younger self."

A small smile graced her lips. "Yeah, it's pretty hard to deny he's yours."

Suddenly, Sarah's words came hurtling back, urging me to take things slow, be clever, get a DNA test. I didn't want to do any of those things, because there was something about this that felt pure. I didn't want to dirty it up. Eilish must've read my thoughts because she started digging in her bag again, pulling out a small white box.

She cleared her throat. "Obviously, I understand you'll need definitive proof, considering the circumstances." She paused and pushed the box across the table. "I brought a small lock of Patrick's hair, if you'd like to have a DNA test done. Or, if you prefer, we can arrange to have a blood sample taken with you present, so you can witness the whole thing."

I wasn't sure how to feel about the fact that she'd brought it along even before I asked. Maybe she thought I'd be suspicious, but I wasn't. Not one bit. I still didn't entirely understand it myself.

Without speaking, I opened the box and glanced inside, where a small lock of hair sat on a piece of cotton wool. My chest clenched and I shut the box. I didn't know what to say, didn't really want to discuss it, so I simply dropped it inside my coat pocket and returned my attention to her.

"When can I meet him?"

She started fiddling with her torn napkin pieces again. I felt like shoving them all aside so she had no choice but to focus on me.

"When would you like to?"

"We don't have any training this weekend," I suggested. "I could meet up with you both somewhere you feel comfortable. You can even bring Sean along."

"Oh, yes, that's a good idea. Um, may I have your phone number please? I'll talk to Sean and touch base with you regarding the details."

Suddenly, the atmosphere changed, grew more formal, like she'd thrown a wall up. I didn't like it. I also didn't like the fact that my teammate had obviously known I had a kid all this time and never told me. It was different with Eilish. She didn't know me. But Sean knew I was a changed man—reliable, responsible, trustworthy—and *he'd* still kept it secret. One look at the boy and he would've known he was mine.

Yep, Sean Cassidy and I were going to have some serious words when the time came.

After we exchanged phone numbers, the waiter arrived with the bill. We both reached for it, her hands closing over mine.

"Please," she wiggled her fingers, trying to pull the check away from me, "please let me pay for dinner."

I wanted to say *NO FUCKING WAY!*

Instead, I said, "That's not necessary."

Her grip tightened, and something rigid entered her tone. "I insist."

I huffed a laugh and shook my head. "It's no big deal."

"It is a big deal." Her voice was like granite, her eyes stony and serious. "It's a big deal to me. Patrick is your son, and my hopes are for the two of you. But I . . . I don't want anything from you, Bryan."

I flinched, frowning at her, again feeling like I'd just been punched in the stomach. This last statement clearly referred to more than just dinner.

She didn't want *anything* from me.

The sudden sinking sensation in my chest caught me unawares, pushed me off balance, and she took advantage of my stunned surprise. Eilish tugged the check from my grip, slipped cash into the sleeve, and held it out to the waiter as he passed.

"Keep the change." She gave him a tight smile, then moved her gaze back to mine, but she might as well have been gazing at me from behind an impenetrable fortress. Her walls were up, and they were very, very high.

I reached for her. "Eilish—"

"I can find my own way home," she said firmly, adding as she stood from the booth, "I honestly can't thank you enough for being so gracious and civil. The secret was weighing on me. I just want what's best for Patrick. I appreciate how sensible and rational you've been, and I hope all our future interactions will continue in this vein."

Giving me another small smile that felt excessively businesslike, she turned and quickly picked her way through the tables, disappearing through the front door, leaving me staring after her.

Civil?

Sensible?

Rational?

The fuck?

I breathed out the gust of air she'd knocked from my lungs, discontent warring with a dawning sense of determination.

She didn't want anything from me?

Well, that was just too damn bad.

She was the mother of my child, for Christ's sake.

I sucked in another breath, reality having both a sobering and intoxicating effect.

I had a son.

Amazing.

Incredible.

TWELVE
EILISH

@ECassChoosesPikachu to @JoseyInHeels: Lunch? Today? Please? #Emergency

"Shite."

"I know."

"I can't believe you told him."

"I know."

Josey stared at me from across the café table, her features ripe with astonishment. I'd called her that morning, the day after my dinner with Bryan, and told her the news. I'd confessed the truth about Patrick over chicken wings and Coke.

She insisted on meeting for lunch, so here we were. Meeting. For lunch.

Except neither of us were eating our tacos. I'd just related the entire story of my dinner with Bryan, and she was clearly too agitated to eat.

"And he wasn't upset?" she asked for the third time, her face scrunching.

"No. Like I said, it was so bizarre. He wasn't at all upset."

Her face scrunched further, wrinkling her nose and the space between her eyebrows. "He wants to be a father?"

"Yes." I laughed the word, still in shock. "Or, at least he doesn't seem to be opposed to it."

Her features smoothed and she gathered a deep breath, her eyes moving over the table. "He's what? Thirty-five? He's probably ready to have kids."

"No, Josey. He's thirty."

"Really? I thought he was older."

"Nope. He's six years older than us."

"Huh." She blinked, her eyes losing focus. "This is completely mad."

"Tell me about it."

We sat in silence for a stretch, both staring into space, lost to our own thoughts.

Abruptly, she broke the silence. "This is so great."

"I know," I said, because it was great. At least, I hoped it would be great, for Patrick's sake.

"And you don't believe in happily ever afters." Josey's face split with a grin.

"What?"

My friend clapped her hands together. "You and Bryan, sitting in a tree, K-I-S-S-I-N-G—except first comes baby in your case. Then love. Then marriage. Or maybe marriage, then love. Who cares, just as long as there's lots of H-O-T S-E-X."

"No!" I rejected much too loudly, holding my hands up. My outburst earned me a few sidelong glances, which I ignored. "No, no, no. This isn't about me. Nothing is going to happen between Bryan and me."

"What? Why not?"

"Because it's not." *Because I kissed him, and he rejected me. I made a fool of myself. Again. He doesn't want me.*

She studied me, appearing disgruntled. Then, apropos of nothing, said, "Is this because of your father?"

I stiffened, my gaze lowering to the table between us. I needed to clear my throat before I could respond; when I did, my voice was much too tight. "No. Of course not."

"Yes, it is."

"It's not." I glanced at her, finding she'd narrowed her eyes.

"It is. You've always had daddy issues—and mommy issues, not that I blame you—but, Eilish, you are not your mother. For one thing, you're a lot hotter."

The laugh that escaped my lips was slightly hysterical. I suppressed it by rolling my lips between my teeth. "I know I am not my mother."

"Do you?"

I met Josey's piercing stare straight on. "Yes. I do."

"Good. Because she is unkind, controlling, and frosty as that snowman, except she's got the corn-cob pipe stuffed up her arse. And we've already established that you're too nice."

"You mean personality-less."

"No. Too nice." She waved away my interpretation of her words from our conversation weeks ago. "Being a parent didn't change your mother, didn't make her nice. She used you and your brothers and sisters, and your hot cousin for that matter. Your dad left your mother because she's a spiteful witch and he was tired of being controlled."

"Yes. He did. And he didn't love any of us enough to stay, or—I don't know—call on our birthdays." These words arrived much more bitterly than I'd anticipated. To my surprise, I had to blink away sudden moisture stinging my eyes.

Josey's face softened, and she reached across the table to hold my hand. "Listen to me, sexy lady. You are not your mother. Bryan is not your father."

"I know Bryan is not my father," I whispered, gritting my teeth. "My father didn't forget my mother after sleeping with her once."

"Oh, honey." Josey's tone was laden with sympathy, and I pulled my hand away. "He was drunk."

"Exactly."

She sighed, it sounded frustrated. "Give him a chance."

"He doesn't want a chance." I sniffed, shaking my head. "He doesn't want me, he wants to know his son. This isn't about me, it's about Patrick."

A small part of me—a very small part—had held out hope that Bryan would remember our night together once I told him. If not the full details, then at least some small glimmer of recollection. In my heart of hearts, I'd hoped that I'd made *some* impression.

Silly, right?

Pathetic, right?

Crazy and stupid and selfish, right?

He hadn't.

He hadn't remembered me at all. I was . . . completely and utterly forgettable.

But this isn't about you, loony bird. This is about Patrick.

"This is what I mean, Eilish." She motioned to me, looking and sounding exasperated. "This is what I'm talking about."

"What?"

"You're *too* nice, *too* responsible." She leaned forward, a hint of mischievousness entering her voice, and whispered, "Don't tell me you don't have the hots for this guy. He's Bryan-fucking-Leech. He's the total package. He's always been charming and sexy as hell, but now he's a reformed bad boy, and you're the mother of his child."

"So what?"

"So what?" Her eyes widened as they darted between mine. "So, get laid and report back. Seduce the man. If you don't leverage the fuck out of this, then you're dead to me."

I choked on nothing, staring at my friend, trying to figure out if she was serious. I couldn't tell.

"You're nuts."

Josey leaned back, shaking her head at me. "*Too* nice."

"You're like one of those devils sitting on my shoulder, trying to get me to do bad things."

"I am. I am exactly like that." She nodded, grinning. "Go do bad things to him, do very wicked things. Enjoy yourself for once. Use him like he used you."

I leaned my elbows on the table and let my head fall into my hands. "He didn't use me."

"He did. He used you, and he doesn't even remember doing it. This time, make him remember. Make him sorry he ever forgot."

* * *

During the rest of the week, avoiding alone time with Bryan became a bit of a game. I called the game, *Keeping My Shit Together At Work*. I even cancelled our Wednesday appointment. Every time I saw him I was overwhelmed by the urge to cry. And this time I feared I really would cry.

In the end, I didn't cry. Instead, I used the time avoiding Bryan to give myself pep talks. Every time I encountered a mirror, I mentally spoke to myself.

This isn't about you.

You don't want anything from him.

Patrick is what's important.

So what, you like him? So what, you're forgettable? So. What? I'm sure he's forgotten hundreds of girls.

Not surprisingly, this last mini pep talk didn't make me feel better. In fact, it sent me face first into a pile of night cheese and canned sardines. As an aside, I learned a valuable lesson that night: keeping chocolate in the kitchen—for emergencies—was both wise and good.

Since I was the world champion at avoiding Bryan Leech, we'd been forced to work out the details via text.

> **BRYAN**
> I tried to catch you but Alice said you already left. When can we discuss this weekend?

> **EILISH**
> This Saturday, 11. Stephen's Green Park. We'll be at the playground.

> **BRYAN**
> Do you want to talk about the details beforehand?

> **EILISH**
> I'll introduce you as a family friend. After you take some time to think things through, we can discuss next steps.

> **BRYAN**
> What does that mean?

THE CAD AND THE CO-ED

> EILISH
> Once you decide what you want your level of involvement to be, we can talk about what to tell Patrick.

> BRYAN
> I don't need time. I'm all in.

I didn't respond because I didn't know how he defined *all in*.

Worst-case scenario, *all in* meant Bryan wanted full custody and I would have to prepare for a custody battle.

Best-case scenario, *all in* meant Bryan wanted to spend as much time as possible with Patrick and be a supportive, positive figure in our son's life as a parent. *Patrick would have a dad who loved him.*

I guess time will tell . . .

Even though I'd prepared Patrick—telling him that Thursday evening we were going to meet someone new over the weekend—Saturday afternoon arrived much, much, *much* sooner than I'd anticipated.

My reasoning for not telling Patrick who we were going to meet was simply: I still didn't know Bryan very well.

What if he flaked out? What if he changed his mind and decided he didn't want to know his son? What if he convinced himself I was lying?

I couldn't bear the thought of telling my son he was going to meet his father and then Bryan not showing. If that happened, it would break Patrick's heart.

And then I'd be forced to torture and murder Bryan Leech.

So I was vague about who we were meeting.

"You should sit down." Sean's voice was softer than usual, laced with concern and something else I couldn't place.

I shook my head, my eyes on Patrick as he climbed up a ladder leading to a long, metal slide. He waved at me when he reached the top, a big grin on his face.

"I can't sit. I'm too nervous."

"That's perfectly understandable, darling."

My heart twisted. In truth, it hurt. It felt bruised and tender. I could barely breathe.

"He's here," Sean said.

I turned my head and spotted Bryan immediately, a jolt of anticipation and fear and resolve shooting down my spine, making my fingertips tingle. His eyes were on me and he looked . . .

"He looks excited," Sean remarked, his voice betraying a hint of confusion. I sensed my big cousin stand, moving the short distance to hover behind me, offering silent support. I was so thankful Sean had come. I couldn't fathom doing this alone.

"He does look excited. Excited is good, right?" I couldn't stop the worry from bleeding into my tone.

"Yes," Sean confirmed. "Excited is the best possible emotion for him to be feeling at present."

Bryan's gaze flickered over my form, then ensnared mine, but I barely noticed. I couldn't think. I was out of breath by the time he reached us, panic driving the air from my lungs.

"Eilish." His eyes moved between mine searchingly, then he surprised me by closing the distance between us and wrapping me in a tight hug.

At first, I reacted as best I could given the situation. I stood like a terrified statue and stared forward with wide, panicked eyes.

"Bryan," I squeaked as he held on, the warmth and strength of him melting my fears and succeeding where all my attempts to calm myself over the last week had failed.

He affected me.

His arms around my body, the feel of his sturdy—yes, sturdy like a table—form poked a hole in some wall I'd been hiding behind. After a moment, I returned his embrace. I held on to him. I grabbed fistfuls of his shirt and pressed my face against his chest. I leaned against him. I gave him my weight, the burden of my worries.

Just for a moment.

I breathed him in and he smelled . . . fantastic. Familiar. He smelled like my dreams. And he felt too good to be true.

He is too good to be true.

And you're forgettable.

Just like that, the moment ended, reality a cruel and painful but truthful reminder. I needed to keep my distance. I needed to be cautious and careful. Josey's loony suggestions that I leverage Patrick to seduce Bryan were just that, loony. I would never use my son that way. Not ever. My mother used us against my father, and I knew what that felt like.

As much as I hoped Bryan's definition of *all in* was my best-case scenario, there existed a very real possibility that he defined it quite differently.

"Thank you for coming," I said, pushing him away and taking a step back.

Bryan didn't quite release me, his hands still lingering on my upper arms as he shuffled a step forward, following me.

"Thank you for . . ." He didn't finish, his bright green eyes moving over my face in a way that felt like too much.

Stiffening and straightening to my full height, I lifted my chin. "Let me go get Patrick. He's right over there."

Bryan turned, his gaze sweeping over the playground, and I watched his profile. I knew the exact moment his eyes found Patrick. Bryan's expression became one of wonder.

And in that moment, I believed in love at first sight, because I'd just witnessed it.

I'd just witnessed a man fall head over heels in love with his own son.

"C-come on, I'll introduce you," I said after a prolonged moment of quiet, my voice shaky. This was just too surreal.

I led the way to where Patrick was again climbing the ladder to go down the slide.

"Mummy, look at me," he said as he crested the top, then sailed down with a delighted *wheeee*. We came to this park often, and I'd already taught him the safe way to use the slide countless times. Still, Bryan looked a little concerned that he was using it without supervision, and there was a part of me that approved of his worry.

"He's been on this slide before. It's safe," I told him quietly, and he turned to look at me. He didn't say anything, only nodded, then brought his rapt attention back to Patrick. He looked fascinated.

Patrick stared up at him, not a shy bone in his body. I guessed he got that from his father.

"Who are you?"

Bryan went down on one knee and gave him the widest, brightest, most loving smile I'd ever seen. It sort of held every part of me hostage for a moment, and I started having all these . . . feelings.

No. NO. NOOOO!

FEELINGS ARE NOT ALLOWED.

I clenched my teeth, willing the untidy feelings away. Now was not the time for messy feelings. The middle of the night was the time, when night cheese and sardines and newly purchased chocolate bars were close at hand. Not. Now.

"I'm Bryan. I'm . . ." he hesitated, seemingly swallowing with some difficulty before finishing, "I'm a friend of your mummy."

My attention wandered between the two of them, the similarity in their looks even more pronounced when they were side by side. More emotions. More teeth clenching. At this rate, I was in danger of breaking my jaw.

Patrick absentmindedly tugged on his hair as he surveyed the man before him. My heart beat fast, and I realized that, oddly enough, I wanted my son to like him. I wanted him to accept Bryan, for his sake as well as Bryan's. Although the big, hulking rugby player was doing a good job of acting calm, I could tell how much he desperately wanted the same thing.

I grew up with a father in name only, and I didn't want that for my son.

"My name's Patrick. I'm almost five. Mummy told me you were coming," Patrick answered casually, shrugging, and Bryan shot me a little grin.

"Oh yeah, what did she say about me?"

"That you're her friend, and Monkey Sean's, too."

Bryan mouthed a questioning *monkey?* at me.

I laughed softly, some of the tension leaving my shoulders. "It's how he says uncle, or uncie, I guess. I keep trying to teach him the right way but he's dead set on monkey. Drives Sean up the wall."

Bryan smiled. "I bet it does."

"Well, secretly he loves it," I rolled my eyes, "but he just won't admit it."

"Monkey Sean bought me a dickie bow," said Patrick, and Bryan turned back to him.

"Somehow I'm not surprised." Bryan chuckled, clearly enchanted.

"And a suit. All men need a suit," Patrick went on, parroting Sean's words. I laughed some more and it sounded a tad hysterical to my ears, but it also felt good. My cousin was determined to make a mini-Sean out of my son.

"Do you know how to play football?"

"I do." Patrick's eyes brightened.

"Want to play with me? Come on. Over here."

Patrick was already off the slide, grabbing his ball, and making his way over to the grassy area before Bryan had the chance to respond. I laughed at Bryan's dumbfounded expression and gestured for him to follow. Once he was gone, I stood there, watching as they kicked the ball to one another.

The scene looked so . . . right. Meant to be. I bit my top lip to keep my chin from wobbling and I released a sigh—half relief, half worry—and went back to join Sean over on the bench. I wanted to give them time without me hovering, time to know each other, build the foundation of their future relationship.

It was the right thing to do.

But walking back to Sean and trusting Bryan with my son was also the most difficult thing I'd ever done.

* * *

"Are you coming down with something?"

I pulled my attention away from where Bryan and Patrick were still playing football and glanced at my cousin. "No. I don't think so. Why?"

Sean flashed a mischievous smile, then quickly suppressed it. "It's just that your eyes are watery and you keep clearing your throat."

I huffed a laugh, sniffling, blinking away new tears. "I don't know what's wrong with me."

"Don't you?" he asked softly.

"I haven't cried in years. But this last week, since telling Bryan the truth, I've been . . ." I shook my head, turning my gaze back to father and son.

Bryan had just picked Patrick up and swung him around. They were both laughing.

I clenched my teeth against emotion clawing at my throat and choked out, "I guess I feel guilty."

"No. I don't think that's it."

"I do. I mean, I kept them apart for so long." Shaking my head, I felt the full weight of my terrible decisions. Part of me recalled Bryan's affirmation that he wouldn't have been worthy of fatherhood a few years ago, and that he understood why I didn't tell him, *but still*. "I just hope he can forgive me."

Sean was quiet a moment then gently prodded, "Who? Patrick or Bryan?"

"Patrick, of course."

"You don't care about Bryan's forgiveness?" My cousin didn't sound judgmental; he sounded curious.

I shrugged. "I guess it would make things easier if he didn't abhor me."

Now Sean released a scoffing laugh. "Bryan Leech may feel many things about you, but I guarantee none of them are anywhere close to abhorrence. Quite the opposite."

I breathed out and with the exhale I felt a little—a very little—of my worries depart. Sean wouldn't lie to me. He wouldn't soften a blow for the sake of my feelings. I trusted him more than anyone I knew, and if he said Bryan harbored no ill will toward me, then I believed him.

"That's a relief."

"Is it?" Sean nudged me with his shoulder.

I nodded, giving my cousin the side-eye. "It is. Raising a child is difficult enough without the parents constantly being at each other's throats."

"Ah, yes. A reality which both you and I have a veritable cornucopia of expertise." He inhaled through his nose, his large chest expanding with the breath. "But, that's not what I meant."

"Then what did you mean?" I was distracted, because at that very moment, Patrick play-tackled Bryan and the big man fell to the ground in a dramatic display. This of course sent Patrick into a fit of giggles.

"What if Bryan wishes for more than co-parenting?"

I turned my head sharply to look at my cousin, the simmering fear rearing its ugly head and twisting my heart. "You mean, what if he wants full custody?" I couldn't keep the shrieking quality out of my voice.

"Calm down." Sean held his hands up. "Calm down, that's not what I meant either. What if Bryan wishes to make the three of you into a family? What if his intentions toward you are of the matrimonial variety?"

My heart twisted again, in a different way but no less uncomfortable. I had to swallow before I could respond. "No."

"No?"

"No. He doesn't want that."

Sean was quiet for a beat, then pushed, "Don't be so sure."

I snorted, scoffed, then shook my head. "Come on, Sean. Don't you think you're getting ahead of yourself? He just found out on Monday that he has a son. He's just meeting him today."

"Yes, but I warned you, Bryan is sturdy."

"Like a table. You won't let me forget."

"That's right. Like a table. Or an exceptionally well-crafted chair. The point is, he *wants* to be sturdy. For someone."

"Let him be sturdy for Patrick, then."

"Being there for Patrick means being there for you. Clearly, he longs for it, for responsibility."

I shook my head before my cousin finished speaking. "I'm not his responsibility."

"He may see things differently."

"He can see them any way he likes, but that doesn't make it so. Patrick is his. He and Patrick—you were right—they deserve to know each other. But I'm not going to be with someone simply because he's the father of my child. Patrick shouldn't be a pawn. I'm not a participation ribbon he gets for having a son." I swallowed a sudden thickness and crossed my arms. "I deserve better than that."

"So you do," Sean quickly agreed, putting his arm around my shoulders and squeezing. "You deserve a prince."

I didn't reply, pretending to be too absorbed in the sight of Bryan and Patrick to respond. But what I didn't say, what I couldn't give a voice to, what caught in my throat, too heavy with emotion to be spoken out loud, was that I didn't need a prince.

I'd happily settle for someone who wouldn't forget me.

THIRTEEN
BRYAN

@THEBryanLeech: If I'd invented jet skis I would've called them boatercycles #justsayin

@SeanCassinova to THEBryanLeech: Glad to see you're spending your free time productively.

My kid was amazing.

Okay, so I wasn't sure if it was my own vanity or what, but this surely had to be the best four-year-old in the whole entire world. No other kid could compare. Not ever. I was bloody smitten and it had only been an hour.

I could've kicked a ball around with him all day.

I took my phone out for a second to check the time, and his eyes lit up. "Pokémon!" he declared and tried to swipe the phone from me. I held it out of his reach, chuckling.

"Hey now, little thief. Poke-what?"

"Do you have Pokémon? On your phone? Mummy has it but she only lets me play for twenty minutes."

Finally, I got what he was on about. Even I wasn't oblivious enough not to have heard of the craze. "No, I don't have it, but I could get it for you," I offered, already swiping to the app store to do a search.

"Yes! Get it! I want to find Bulbasaur," Patrick enthused.

"Oh, no you don't," came a sweet yet strict voice. Eilish. I'd been hyper-aware of her watchful eyes, wishing she wouldn't keep such a distance. As much as I loved spending time with Patrick, it would have been nice for her to be with us, too. Our family.

Yep. That's right. I was in this thing, balls to walls. This was my family.

"Is he trying to sweet-talk you into letting him play Pokémon on your phone?" she inquired.

I glanced at Patrick. He was shaking his head fervently behind Eilish's back. Oh man, this kid was hilarious. And a sneak. I couldn't help laughing. "He *might* be."

Patrick scrunched up his face and threw his hands in the air like I was the worst accomplice in the world. I laughed some more. I loved how much personality he had. I didn't think kids really had much about them until they were at least ten, but I could have whole conversations with Patrick and not get bored. He was like a little person. Well, technically he *was* a little person, but you know what I mean.

"As soon as he spots a smartphone he pounces," said Eilish. "He got so addicted to the game I had to start rationing his play time, otherwise he'd happily spend the entire day running around looking for creatures."

"I've found all the ones on our street," said Patrick proudly. "James from next door has only found three."

I glanced at Eilish. "I honestly don't mind him using my phone . . ."

She shook her head. "We have to be getting home soon anyway. It's almost dinner time."

"Can Bryan come for dinner?" Patrick asked enthusiastically.

My eyes shot to Eilish, and it was clear Patrick's request had taken her by surprise. Her eyebrows moved on her forehead as though trying to find equilibrium, and her mouth opened and closed. Even struggling for words this woman was gorgeous.

A tightness, an unexpected vise, constricted my chest, the suddenness of it made it difficult for me to speak, and an awkward silence fell between us.

Clearing my throat, I finally managed, "That's okay, buddy. Maybe next time."

"Well, if he doesn't have other plans," Eilish said at the same time, surprising me. I was certain she'd been about to come up with an excuse.

"I don't," I said, my tone a little too eager. I just didn't want this day to end. It was bizarre, because my life seemed set in stone only a week ago, but now everything was changing. And I didn't technically dislike the change.

"Oh. In that case, you're welcome to join us," she went on, her voice pitched high and breathy, clearly nervous. "Sean will be coming, too. His Lucy is away in New York, so he usually eats with us."

"Did you make sure to slaughter a cow this morning?" I joked.

"She slaughtered two, actually," came Sean's voice as he joined us. "And you're one to talk. I saw you put away three burritos after training last week, and you still had room for dessert."

I grinned at Eilish. "I hope you have a fully stocked fridge."

"I made pasta bake." She lifted an eyebrow at me, the side of her lips tugging to one side. "It's got four different cheeses, both sausage *and* chicken, and about a trillion calories per serving, so if you're both still hungry at the end, I'll eat my hat."

Sean smiled widely, as did I. "Challenge accepted."

* * *

Eilish lived in a small apartment just outside the city. It was in a two-story Victorian that had been split into two separate units. Eilish's place took up the bottom floor. Though it wasn't big, it was a sought-after location, so I wondered if her family was footing part of the bill. If they weren't contributing monetarily, then they'd most certainly pulled some strings to get her the place.

Not that I was judging her. In fact, I wished *I'd* been footing the bill all these years instead of her hoity-toity parents. It made me feel pretty worthless, if I was honest, and I was already making mental plans to pay her back for all the years of child support I'd missed. I could afford it, and more.

In fact, if I had my way I'd give her every last penny in my bank account by way of penance. Because that is what I owed her. She had been raising Patrick on her own. And studied. And now worked full time. *There wasn't any way I could pay her back. She had sacrificed more than money. She'd sacrificed herself.*

If I wasn't careful, Eilish Cassidy would be elevated to sainthood level in my mind. I decided I should debauch her before this happened.

Having followed her and Sean in my Land Rover, I scoped out the neighborhood and begrudgingly accepted that it was a nice place to bring up a kid. I almost wished she'd been living in a crap hole. That way I could swoop in and save the day. But no, it seemed Eilish was doing okay for herself without me.

The reality of her circumstances gave me the sense of being dispensable, and I didn't like it. A weird itching in my chest flared, one that had been present since she'd left me in the restaurant a week ago, this need for her to *need* me. I may have been entertaining fantasies for the last seven days where I was her knight in shining armor, but clearly she wasn't a damsel in distress. She'd survived a teen pregnancy and the scandal that went along with it. She'd even managed to bring up this fantastic little boy all on her own.

And where was I?

This thought made breathing difficult, but I owned it. I owned the discomfort. I deserved it for every shitty, selfish decision I'd made.

And after I wallowed for a minute, I left my car and the sense of unworthiness behind me. Patrick was my son. Eilish was his mother. I hadn't deserved them five years ago, but damn if I wasn't going to do everything in my power to deserve their trust now.

They were already inside when I made my way down the hall to her door, where Sean was waiting for me in the hallway. I paused and eyed him.

"You did very well today," he said, arms folded across his chest as he surveyed me.

"Happy to hear you approve," I deadpanned and made to move by him. He got in my way.

"I hope you'll continue this good behavior," he went on, and if I wasn't mistaken, I thought he might be enjoying this. "I wouldn't want to have to escort you off the premises."

I shot him a wry look. "Like you could."

"I'm bigger than you."

I scoffed. "By about an inch."

"Inches matter," he shrugged, "or so I've been told."

Ignoring this statement, I crossed my arms over my chest. "Look, I've no intention of doing anything to upset Eilish or Patrick. I know I'm a lucky bugger to even be in this situation, so believe me when I say I'll be on my best behavior."

Now his lips twitched, like he was trying to hold in a smile. "See that you do."

Finally, he let me pass. As soon as I entered the room I was struck by how cozy it was. It smelled like Eilish, like watermelon, like summer, like *home*.

God, I really needed to get a handle on this obsession I had with her. Maybe she was interested in me solely as the father of her son, nothing else. Nothing romantic.

Then again, maybe not.

She'd been the one to kiss me last month, hadn't she? That was something.

But I couldn't be freaking her out, not when my desire to know and be around Patrick had grown so quickly into a physical need.

Much like it was to be close to Eilish.

Speaking of, I'd been torturing myself for days trying to remember our night together, but all I got were brief flashes, nothing concrete. I rewound to Ronan and Annie's wedding, but remembered hardly anything. I could barely even remember arriving at the ceremony. It was so fucked up.

Correction: I'd been so fucked up.

But I wasn't anymore.

Still, I caught phantom images of red hair and pale, silky skin in my mind, but I couldn't tell if they were real memories or just my brain showing me what I wanted to see. I was dying to ask her. Maybe if she could recount how we met it would help me remember. It felt important that I did, but there was no way to broach the subject, not with things so tentative between us, and definitely not with Sean hanging around to supervise.

THE CAD AND THE CO-ED

Eilish was puttering about in the kitchen when I turned back to Sean. "By the way, we need to talk."

"Yes, we will. Later." He lifted his chin, then nodded soberly, understanding in his eyes.

I nodded back and then went into the living room to join Patrick. Sean went into the kitchen and I could hear both he and Eilish conducting a hushed conversation. I wondered what they were discussing. Me, most likely. Patrick seemed completely unaware of the tension, and I happily let myself fall into his obliviousness for a while.

About twenty minutes later, there was a knock on the door. I discreetly leaned forward to peek out the window and saw a youngish guy standing outside the door. He was average height with light blond hair that was attempting a man bun. I say "attempting" because it wasn't yet long enough to be tied up, and so formed a sort of nub at the top of his head. It also looked as though he was cultivating a beard, but his facial hair was too light to achieve the full effect.

Now who the hell was this nob-jockey?

Eilish's light footsteps sounded down the hall. I strained my ears to listen when she answered the door.

"Trevor. What are you doing here?" she breathed.

"Eilish, hey. You look great. I just wanted to drop by and grab that copy of *Iron Man* I loaned you."

There was a short moment of silence and Eilish lowered her voice. "Right, yes, I'll just go get it for you. Wait here."

"Can I come in?"

"No. I mean, now's not a good time," she replied, her voice strained.

Man, this wasn't her boyfriend, was it? My protective instincts kicked in, or was it my possessive instincts? She didn't sound too happy that he'd come by. Before I could think things through, I was up and stepping into the small entryway, closing the door to the living room firmly behind me.

"Eilish, is everything all right?" I asked, furrowing my brow at Man-Bun. He straightened when he saw me and gave me a quick sweep up and down, his mouth forming a tight line of displeasure.

"Yes, everything is fine. Trevor just stopped by to collect a film I borrowed from him."

I shot Trevor a hard look. "Is that right?"

He was practically scowling at me now. "Yeah, I'm her boyfrie—"

"Ex-boyfriend," Eilish cut in.

Well, there it was, my worst fears confirmed. Eilish was a million times too good for this loser. I mean, how did he even manage to score her? The bloke looked like he could fall into a barrel of tit and come out sucking his thumb. Did she have low self-esteem?

Okay, so maybe I was judging him prematurely. After all, I didn't know him. But come on, all evidence pointed to nob-jockey man-child territory.

"And who are you?" Trevor asked, all petulant. He looked like he was preparing to get comfortable, like he was going to stand in Eilish's doorway until she finally gave up and invited him in.

"Patrick's father," I shot back pointedly and heard a tiny squeak of a gasp from Eilish.

"Oh," said Trevor, the steam going out of his engine altogether.

I wondered why Sean hadn't come out yet. If I knew anything about my teammate, it was that he'd rather Eilish date John Mayer than this piece of work. I'd say he was jumping for joy when Eilish dumped him. I mean, come on. It had to have been her who did the dumping.

A moment of silence elapsed and I relished every second of it, unable to help the smug smile claiming my mouth.

"I'll just . . . uh . . . go grab that movie real quick," she said haltingly, as though she didn't want to leave me alone with her ex, but she didn't have another choice.

I wasn't going anywhere.

Avoiding my eyes as she passed, I waited until she was gone before turning my full attention to Trevor. Taking a few steps closer, I marched him backward and out of the doorway. "What's your game?"

"Excuse me?"

"Why are you here?" I asked, enunciating my words like he was slow. He didn't like that. I could tell by how the vein in his forehead popped.

"I came to get my movie back."

"Bullshit. What do you want with Eilish?"

"Hey! Our relationship is none of your business."

I cocked my head. "You don't have a relationship. You broke up, so quit finding convenient reasons to stop by. How many times has it been this week, huh? Three? Four?"

He clenched his jaw, his nostrils flaring. "Like I said, it's none of your bus—"

"Of course it's my business. We have a child together."

"She never mentioned you before."

"She didn't need to. I'm standing right in front of you now. And I'm telling you to sling your hook. Whatever went on between you, which I'm sure wasn't much, is over. I'm here now."

"You can't just—"

I stepped even closer, breathing down on him. "Trevor, do yourself and favor and leave. Eilish dumped you. Move on."

Something about the way I said it must've hit a nerve because his lip began to quiver. Without another word, he turned and stomped away.

I watched him go and . . . now I felt bad.

Well, kind of.

I shut the door and let out a heavy sigh. I didn't need him coming around bothering Eilish, especially not with Patrick in the mix. The idea of her dating, of strange men being around my kid, made me want to break something. It was a foreign sensation, and some might argue I had no right being territorial given I'd only just come into their lives, but I couldn't help it. I had a deep and uncontrollable need to protect them, particularly from unworthy arseholes like Trevor.

Needing a glass of water, I made my way down to the kitchen and found Sean sitting by the counter, a beer in his hand and a smirk on his face.

"I must say, that was quite the performance."

I grit my teeth. "You were listening."

"Of course I was. Wouldn't want to miss you putting Trevor Donovan in his place. Never liked the fellow myself." He handed me a bottle of water, and I popped it open.

"He looks like a fucking twat, Sean. What was Eilish thinking?"

"She was thinking it's none of your business," came another voice, and I winced. Eilish stood in the doorway, her expression hard. "What happened to Trevor?"

"He left," I answered simply and knocked back a gulp of water.

"What did you say to him?"

I shrugged. "A few home truths."

"You had absolutely no right," Eilish said. Her tone was calm but her entire body radiated tension.

I took a step toward her and moved to place a hand on her shoulder; she flinched out of my grip, her eyes shooting daggers.

Was it wrong I found her irresistibly sexy when she was angry?

But I didn't want her to be angry, not with me. In order to see my way safely out of this mess, I was going to have to channel old-school Bryan Leech, the charming bugger who could talk his way out of a military quarantine, not the crusty old bastard I was now.

The main problem was, I didn't know if any part of the old me was left.

FOURTEEN
BRYAN

@THEBryanLeech: Why does Dracula have no friends? Because he's a real pain in the neck. LOL.
@RonanFitz to @THEBryanLeech: I thought it was because he's always hogging the batroom :-D
@WillthebrickhouseMoore to @THEBryanLeech @RonanFitz: I worry for you both…I really do.

Careful to keep my voice conversational, I gave Eilish a smile that I hoped was equal parts charming and apologetic. "You obviously didn't want him coming around. I thought I was doing you a favor, but I overstepped the line. My mistake. I apologize, it won't happen again."

At this I heard a snort from behind. Sean. Clearly, he didn't believe me. Or my smoothing-skills were now terrible. Probably a bit of both.

"Yes, well, apology accepted," Eilish said, stiff as she took another step backward. I got the sense she didn't like or appreciate my closeness. "But I would like it if you—both of you," her eyes flickered to Sean and then back to me, "respected my boundaries. My personal life is mine."

"Right." I drank some more water while she turned to open the oven, disliking everything about this conversation. Sean appeared to be thoroughly enjoying the scene, and I didn't get it. I'd expected him to warn me away from Eilish, but he seemed almost encouraging of me being here. It didn't make sense.

I was quiet as she dished up the food, and a few minutes later, we were all sitting down to eat. I focused my attention on Patrick, amazed by how much pasta sauce he could get on his face in a matter of seconds. Every once in a while, my gazed flicked to Eilish, but she studiously avoided looking at me, instead choosing to talk to Sean about how Lucy was doing in New York, and how the long distance was affecting them.

"What do you think about Trevor?" I asked Patrick quietly while Eilish was distracted chatting to Sean.

Patrick scrunched up his brow. "Who's that?"

"A friend of your mummy's. He's got hair like this," I said and swept a few locks back to imitate a man bun.

"I don't know anybody who looks like that," said Patrick, all matter of fact, and then a second later his attention was back on his food.

Interesting.

Eilish had never introduced Trevor to Patrick. That must mean things weren't that serious between them. The idea made my chest swell with caveman satisfaction. A memory of the massage she gave me earlier in the week popped into my head, like it had been for days now. Her touch was seared into me, the way she worked my muscles over with her delicate hands. I knew I was a bastard to be turned on by it, but I was, and there'd been something in her eyes that made me suspect she was, too.

I needed her to touch me again.

She must've sensed my thoughts because her eyes flicked up suddenly and her cheeks heated when she saw how I was looking at her.

"May I be excused?" Patrick stood suddenly, grabbing his plate, his eyes darting to the small clock on the kitchen wall.

Eilish gave our son an indulgent smile. "Yes. Fine. But only one show, okay? And then it's story time."

He nodded quickly, clearing his plate and dashing out of the kitchen.

"He likes TV, huh?" I remarked as soon as Patrick had left the room.

Eilish opened her mouth to respond but Sean answered for her, "It's because she rations it. He's only allowed to watch half an hour a day."

"It's for me, too," she sought to clarify, her eyebrows drawing low in consternation. "It would be so easy for me to let him watch hours of TV in the evenings and weekends, so I can get a break. But I don't want that for him. I don't want that for us."

"When do you get a break?" I asked, trying to keep my voice casual even as guilt gnawed at my insides.

Her eyes dropped to her plate. She reached for her water and took a sip.

"Here and there." Her posture turned self-conscious.

I inched closer, trying not to show how much that answer bothered me. "That can't be very good for you," I said softly, my voice full of concern.

"I do fine," Eilish shrugged like it was no big deal, and a tension-filled silence elapsed.

"Poor old Trevor," said Sean humorously, changing the subject. "However will he spend his evening now that he hasn't got his *Iron Man* DVD to watch?"

My lips twitched in a small smile. Cassidy could be a wind-up merchant when the mood took him, but since Trevor was his target I was happy to play along. For the first time today I was glad of his presence. He quelled the tension between Eilish and I, if nothing else.

"Maybe he'll settle for *Thor* instead. Hey. I just realized who he bases his look on."

Sean snickered derisively. "Nobody would cast Trevor Donovan as Thor while I'm standing in the room."

"Please stop," Eilish scolded, pointing her fork at her cousin, though I could see she wanted to smile. "What did Trevor ever do to you, huh?"

"At Aunt Cara's, he once subjected me to a twenty-minute discussion about Xbox versus PlayStation. That's quite enough to gain my ire, dearest," Sean replied.

"He works for the games department at Google. It's his specialty."

"Taking down two-hundred-pound men with pure brawn is my specialty, that doesn't mean I go around tackling people to the ground whenever I feel like it."

"Not unless they ask nicely," I put in.

"Well, that goes without saying." Sean smiled in agreement.

I caught Eilish's gaze and her blush deepened. Was she thinking about *me* tackling *her*? Because that sounded really, really nice as long as it was on a bed and we were both naked. Sign me up.

Yeah, I was hot for her. Holding back wasn't an option anymore.

"He's a good guy," she protested weakly.

"If he's so nice, why did you break things off?" Sean questioned. I had to say, I was enjoying how he directed the conversation, even if I wasn't quite sure what he was up to.

Eilish worried her lip and stared down at her food, muttering, "We just didn't have a spark."

"Ah yes, the spark, the chemistry, the *folie à deux*," Sean crooned. "What a pity."

Eilish shook her head in exasperation. "*Folie à deux* means shared psychosis, Sean."

"And what is love but two people going temporarily insane with need for one another?"

"It's not the same thing," Eilish said.

"Is it not? What do you think, Bryan?"

I shrugged. "I wouldn't know. Never been in love."

"You haven't?" He feigned horror. "Well, that's a travesty. Isn't it a travesty, Eilish?"

"Quite," she replied absentmindedly, studying me now. She seemed surprised to hear I'd never been in love, but it was true. I hadn't been lucid for much of my adult life, and certainly not enough to fall in love with someone. Not properly.

"Have you ever been in love, cousin?" Sean continued, a shine of mischief in his eyes.

"You already know the answer to that question, *cousin,*" Eilish bit back. He was obviously getting to her now.

"I, of course, had never known true love until I met Lucy. But my, when she came into my life it was like being swept up into the heart of a tornado. Everything changed," he finished, scooping up the last of his pasta urbanely. I never knew it was possible to eat urbanely until I'd shared a meal with Sean Cassidy.

"Well, aren't you one of the lucky ones," said Eilish with a bit of sass and rose from the table. "If everybody's finished eating I'm going to start on the dishes."

Immediately, I stood, too, taking the plates from her. "Let me help."

"No, that's quite all right. You're our guest."

"And this guest is helping clean up," I replied, standing firm. When I glanced at Sean, he was swiping his thumb over his chin and smiling happily, his gaze going back and forth between the two of us.

"I insist," Eilish bit out, tugging the dishes back from me.

"So do I."

"Oh, let him help. Doing the dishes is a very admirable quality in a gentleman," said Sean, thoroughly amused.

"Fine. I'll wash. You dry," Eilish relented.

"And I'll take Patrick upstairs to change into his pajamas," said Sean, sweeping out of the room. A whoosh of air fled my lungs, emotion biting at me. I wished I could get him ready for bed, do all the mundane things I'd missed out on for years.

All that would come in time, I was sure.

But first, I needed to talk to Eilish.

I followed her into the kitchen and we worked silently for a few moments. She didn't look at me, instead keeping her eyes on the dishes. I enjoyed this, washing dishes in her small kitchen. I was big and she was tall. We filled the space, but it meant we had to be close. It felt just right.

"I really am sorry about Trevor," I said softly as I used a dish towel to dry the plates.

"It's fine. I know you were only trying to help . . . in your own way," she replied, using the back of her hand to swipe some hair out of her face. It fell forward again and she let out a huff of annoyance.

"Here, let me," I offered, setting the dish towel aside. Her hands were in the suds and she froze when I gently pulled the tie from her hair, gathered its silky masses in my hands, and tied it in a neat ponytail. It was even softer than I imagined, and so thick. I allowed my knuckles to brush against the back of her neck and thought I saw her shiver in response.

"Eilish," I whispered.

She turned her head a little to glance up at me. "Yes?"

I cleared my throat, unable to hold back what I wanted to say. "You have beautiful hair."

She stiffened, her blue eyes going wide as saucers. I ran my knuckles over the back of her neck again, and again she shivered. "And the softest skin I've ever—"

"Eilish! Where are Patrick's cowboy pajamas? He's insisting on wearing them," came Sean's voice from beyond the small space, breaking the moment.

She jumped away from me, turning her face to call to her cousin, "They're in the wash. He'll have to wear a different pair."

Her voice was strained. Had she felt that moment we just shared as much as I had? The need to touch her pulled me forward, pumped thick in my veins.

"Eilish—"

"Please be careful with that dish." Her tone was unsteady, her attention firmly set on the sink. "It's the only casserole I have and I use it every week."

Studying her profile, I noticed her cheeks were flushed. If she'd felt it, she clearly didn't wish to discuss it. Frustration built in my chest, the desire to feel her skin beneath my fingertips became an ache. I'd thought about her skin since laying eyes on her all those weeks ago at William's party.

And yet . . . maybe this wasn't the time or the place. I was only starting to get to know Patrick. Everything was still so new.

So I moved back. Knowing I'd overstepped unspoken boundaries, but unable to muster regret. Quietly, I finished drying the dishes.

Sean re-entered the kitchen a few minutes later, giving me a silent nod as if to say, *we can go have our talk now.*

"Patrick is ready for his story. Bryan and I better be off," he said, bending to place a kiss atop Eilish's head. "I'll see you tomorrow."

"Yes, tomorrow," she replied, giving her cousin a small smile before her gaze fell on me. "I, uh, suppose I'll see you Monday, then. I can do some more work on your knee if you'd like."

There was self-consciousness in her voice, and I knew it had taken courage to make the offer. I jumped on it immediately. "Yes, I'd love that. That'd be great."

"Good. Well, bye, Bryan." She nodded, apparently having difficulty meeting my gaze.

I didn't want to, but I said, "Goodbye, Eilish," and allowed Sean to lead me out of her apartment. I couldn't fight the sense that I was forgetting something, leaving something critical behind.

Once we were out of the building Sean asked, "So, your place or mine?"

"Does it matter? We live in the same building."

"Right. I keep forgetting. Then I remember you in your grandad PJs and it all comes rolling back. You'll have to tell me where you acquire such fine bedwear, by the way."

I shot him a funny look. Sometimes with Sean you couldn't tell if he was serious or taking the piss.

Twenty minutes later, we were sitting in my kitchen, two untouched bottles of water in front of us. Will was in his room, reading some puritanical tale of history most likely.

"So, Bryan, you wanted to talk," Sean began, arching a brow and clasping his hands together.

I rested my palms on the armchair. I was pissed with him, but at the same time I wasn't. I couldn't explain it. Perhaps my happiness at having met Patrick was overriding my anger at having his existence kept from me.

"Did you know I was Patrick's father all along?" I asked.

Sean casually lifted a shoulder. "Not at first, no."

My jaw firmed at hearing this. "When then?"

"About two years ago, the likeness became more evident, but I put it down to coincidence. After all, my twenty-five-year-old teammate wouldn't *dream* of taking advantage of my innocent nineteen-year-old cousin, now would he?" There was a bite behind his words, even though they were spoken calmly, and a rush of guilt and shame flooded back. I had no right to be angry at him. I'd been a piece of shit. I deserved not to know.

I hung my head, running a hand down my face. "I was a different person then."

"Yes, I'm aware of that."

"I'd never hurt her now, or Patrick."

"That, too, I'm aware of."

"Then why didn't you tell me sooner? I've been sober for almost two years."

"Two very tentative years." He gave me an arch glance. "Believe it or not, I do actually like you, Bryan. I knew laying your son on you while you were still recovering was a bad idea. That and it wasn't my place to tell you. It was hers."

Well, he had me there.

"And my duty to Eilish far outweighs my duty to you. If she wanted to keep Patrick from you forever, I would have accepted her wishes. I might not have liked them, but I'd have accepted them nonetheless."

I blew out a breath. "Right."

"So, are we good?"

I hesitated a moment. "Yes . . . well, no. I mean, we're good, of course we are, but I still want to know how it all came about—"

"Isn't that self-explanatory?" Sean interrupted with a quizzical brow.

"Not that, fuckwit. I want to know how things have been for her. How your family reacted when they found out."

"They didn't react well at all. Eilish was in college when she discovered she was pregnant. Panicking, she came home to tell my aunt, naïvely thinking she might be inclined to help. She was not. Aunt Cara wanted Eilish to terminate the pregnancy. When Eilish refused, Cara arranged for an adoption. When Eilish couldn't go through with it, her mother threw her out of the house."

Something primitive within me inwardly raged at this news. I had to force calm into my voice as I asked, "Where did she go?"

"She went to the States, nine months pregnant. She wasn't supposed to fly, but she was too bloody stubborn to take my help. So she used her savings to cover the first six months, then worked three jobs afterward to pay for school and childcare."

I glared at him. "You let her work three jobs?"

"Eilish doesn't allow people to *let* her do anything. But, no. I was unaware that she was working for quite some time. I'd been sending her money. She wouldn't spend it, never cashed the checks. In the end, I had to accept her wishes, but I found ways around it. Buying her gifts in the form of food and clothing, things for the baby helped."

"When did she come back to Ireland?"

"A few months ago. Last year, in her last semester before graduation, she became very ill and lost two of her positions. Left with no other options, she reached out to me and finally asked for help. Truly, she had pneumonia and was basically on death's door." Sean ground his teeth as though the memory still plagued him. "I told her I would only help if she stopped working, allowed me to cover her expenses until she finished school and for the next twelve months, and moved back to Ireland once she graduated. She had no choice but to accept my terms."

"I'm going to repay you every penny," I cut in, but Sean swiped a hand through the air.

"Not necessary. Be there for them now, that's all I ask."

"Sean, I'm paying you back," I grunted.

"Well, I won't accept."

"You will."

"I will not."

"God, you're obstinate."

"And you need to get off your cross. The situation is what it is and you need to set aside your guilt. Though she might be loath to admit it, Eilish is lonely. Her life revolves around that little boy, and although that is a very admirable quality in a mother, it's no way to live a life. I think you can help her start living again." A pause as he eyed me. "Perhaps you can help each other."

I knew he was referring to my newfound "boring" lifestyle. The thing was, it wasn't boring to me. I loved the predictability of it. I'd lived with the opposite for so long, and it was a welcome change. I had to admit though, his support surprised me.

I stared at him curiously. "Are you saying you approve of me, Cassidy?"

He huffed a breath, his expression deadly serious. "I'm saying I recognize the look in your eye when you're around Eilish. It's how I'd like to think I look at Lucy, full of adoration and awe. As long as you keep looking at her that way, we won't have a problem. And, to be quite blunt, you could use some happiness. You've become as palatable as those prunes in your fridge in recent months and I don't think it's the lack of alcohol prematurely turning you into a joyless old codger. So yes, I approve of it wholeheartedly. In fact, seduce her again."

I coughed, choking on nothing, and sputtered, "What? What did you say?"

"I said seduce her. And do it soon. She has more unresolved feelings for you than Perrie Edwards has for Zayn Malik."

I stared at him for several seconds, dumbfounded. "Who?"

He threw his hands up in the air. "See. This is half the problem. I should've used Jen and Brad as an example instead. You're completely out of touch, Bryan. Can you even remember how to seduce a woman?"

"Of course I can remember."

One eyebrow rose slowly.

"I'm more than capable," I insisted.

The eyebrow rose even higher.

"Hey!"

"I'm only trying to help. Maybe look up some moves or watch some videos, do whatever it takes to make sure you're not rusty and she enjoys herself."

Now I was offended. "Seriously, fuck you, Sean. Of course she'll enjoy herself. She'll like it so much she'll beg me for—"

"Hey." My teammate narrowed his eyes, cutting his hand through the air. "I don't need or want to know the specifics. I'm just saying, take good care of her. She gives and gives and gives. It's time she received, Leech. I want her to receive and be cared for. And don't be selfish."

"I won't be." I shook my head with the denial, staring at Sean.

Staring at him because . . .

Did he just tell me to seduce his cousin?

No. He'd just ordered me to do it. And then he'd ordered me to make sure she got off.

Well, hell.

I couldn't believe what had just happened.

Wonders really do never cease.

FIFTEEN
EILISH

@ECassChoosesPikachu: When you want something but you know you can't have it because it'll give you heart disease. And maybe cancer.
@SeanCassinova to @ECassChoosesPikachu: Terribly melodramatic, aren't we?
@ECassChoosesPikachu to @SeanCassinova: I meant figurative cancer, of my soul.
@SeanCassinova to @ECassChoosesPikachu: I stand by my previous tweet.

Maybe it was the full moon. Maybe someone had put chatty potion in the water cooler. Or maybe it was the fact that the first game of the preseason was quickly approaching. Whatever the reason, everyone had been much more talkative than usual.

Jogging down the stairs, I glanced at my watch and groaned. It was well past seven p.m. and I was now running horribly late for my last appointment of the day. Sean had left at five to pick up Patrick from school, thank goodness. But I felt terrible about my tardiness since my last appointment was with William Moore, who was still the nicest, most polite person on the face of the earth.

Out of breath, I burst through the locker room door, scanning the mostly empty space for the hulking flanker. My hand came to my forehead and I wiped perspiration away.

"Who're you looking for, love?"

I glanced to the side, finding Ronan Fitzpatrick pulling a bag onto his shoulder.

"Uh, William. Have you seen him?"

He shook his head and his brown eyes seemed to sparkle with some mischief. "Not recently. But he was looking for you earlier."

I groaned again. "I'm so late. We were supposed to meet at five thirty, but Daly—"

"That Daly's a talker, hopefully he kept his conversation polite." Ronan lifted his eyebrows questioningly.

Since Ronan's sister, Lucy, and Sean had become an item, I'd grown to know Ronan and his wife, Annie, fairly well. He'd put in a good word for me when I applied for my position. We weren't friends, per se, but I felt I knew him. At least, I knew him better than the other lads on the team.

"It's not really Daly's fault I'm late. I've been running late all day," I said mournfully. "Damn it. I really wanted to check on William's hamstring. He's been doing so well."

"Don't beat yourself up, just have him paged."

I studied the stocky captain, my hands on my hips, my mouth twisted to the side. "Do you think he's still around?"

"Like I said," a slow, meaningful grin spread over Ronan's mouth, making him look like he knew a secret, "Will has been waiting for you."

With one more pointed look, which I could not interpret, Ronan walked toward the door, saying as he passed, "Stay right here, I'll have him paged for you."

"Thank you." I turned to watch him go, giving him a grateful smile.

"Not a problem, kiddo." He winked at me in a way that felt remarkably brotherly, then disappeared out the door, leaving me in the empty locker room.

Shaking out my limbs, then rubbing my stiff neck, I eyed the benches. Quickly crossing to the nearest one, I sat with a sigh and continued kneading the space between my shoulder blades. My feet hurt. I'd been standing—or jogging—all day and had been fantasizing about my tiny bathtub since lunch.

Granted, my tiny bathtub wasn't really tiny. It was just tiny to me, since I was Amazonian by most standards.

"Eilish."

I stiffened, whipping my head over my shoulder at the sound of my name, my mouth going completely dry.

Bryan.

I could have said, *Hi, Bryan.*

I could have.

I could also have given him a smile of greeting, or maybe even a little wave. Both would have been acceptable.

But, no.

No.

No.

Instead, I stared at him, freshly showered, still wet hair, a white towel hanging low around his hips, baring his luscious thighs. The towel was entirely too small. It might as well have been a postage stamp.

And that tattoo . . .

This wasn't the first time I'd seen him since Saturday. Today was Tuesday, and I'd given him two massages in the gym, safely surrounded by all his teammates and coaches. We hadn't spoken much, only about his knee and how he was feeling.

But he'd texted me earlier in the day about getting together again.

BRYAN

When can I see you and Patrick?

EILISH

I'll get back to you with a time for this weekend.

BRYAN

How about after work one day this week?

I hadn't responded, mostly because I hadn't had a free moment to think all day. Skipping lunch, I'd been rushing from one appointment to the next. Therefore, all thoughts of Bryan had taken a back seat to work.

But now he was in front of me and I was a little afraid I'd just drooled on myself. This time it wasn't just his body or the memory of our night together that turned my insides to mush. It was that I knew him now, he wore a housecoat and drank mint tea and had to wear reading glasses. He'd saved me from a cockroach and shared one of his most embarrassing stories in order to make me feel better.

And it was the memory of how kind and understanding he'd been when I told him he had a son. And how he already loved Patrick. And how he'd helped with the dishes and touched my neck and called me beautiful.

No.

He didn't call you beautiful.

He called your hair beautiful.

He'd called me beautiful before, but that was because Bryan had always had a thing for redheads.

I shook myself—quite literally—and forced my eyes to his face, feeling a rush of heat flood my neck and cheeks.

"Hi," I said on an exhale, ripping my gaze away and turning my back on him, because, A) I was tremendously embarrassed by my unprofessionalism—i.e. blatant ogling, B) the reminder of Bryan's penchant for redheads had me remembering the morning and months *after* our one night together, and C) when I'd glanced at his face he was smirking.

And it was a knowing smirk, like he *knew* how the sight of him affected me.

He'd said nothing as I'd ogled him, nothing at all. Just stood there silently, almost as though his postage-stamp towel had been planned for my benefit. I covered my face with my hands, pressing my cold fingers to my cheeks.

"Sorry," I said to the room, shaking my head as I stood from the bench. "I didn't know anyone was in here. I was, uh, just waiting for William."

"Don't apologize."

I jumped and turned as he spoke because his voice was surprisingly close. Sure enough, Bryan was standing just three feet away, his massive arms crossed over his impressive chest.

Massive, impressive, enchanted.

Resisting the urge to hold my hands out between us—to warn him off—I clenched them into fists at my sides. Plus, he was still smirking. His full mouth curved to one side, his eyes hooded, one eyebrow slightly higher than the other.

"I had fun on Saturday," he said, his voice low as his eyes skimmed over my face, dipped to my neck, then rested on my lips. "When can I see you again?"

"Uh." *Crackers.* "Sure. Yes. Of course. I know Patrick would enjoy it. Let me ask Sean when he's free this week."

Bryan's eyes cut to mine, narrowed slightly. "Why do you need to ask Sean?"

"So we can . . ." My mind went blank, and I tried to swallow. I'd like to think it was because of the way his jade-green stare was focused on mine, like a probing, unrelenting drill of suspicion.

But, no.

It wasn't his eyes.

It was his proximity. And the fact that I could smell his soap. And the sexy tribal tattoo covering his arm and shoulder. And his straining towel, holding on to his hips for dear life, a single gust of wind would be enough to blow it away and leave him completely naked.

WHY OH WHY IS HIS TOWEL SO SMALL?

Oh no, my thoughts were in capital letters.

THIS IS VERY BAD!

"We don't need Sean there." His voice dropped to a whisper as he shuffled a step closer.

"I'd-I'd like Sean to be there."

"Why?"

"I don't want to confuse Patrick."

"Confuse him how?" Bryan cocked his head to the side, taking another step closer and forcing me to retreat until my back connected with a locker.

"You're the first man I've introduced him to."

Bryan stood a little straighter, and his eyes warmed at this news, his mouth once again curving with a smile.

"Have you taken the DNA test yet?" I crossed my arms, lifting my chin.

"No. I think I know my own mirror image when I see him." Bryan huffed an amused laugh, but didn't advance any closer.

"You should take the DNA test, then we'll talk about setting up a schedule."

His frown returned. "A schedule?"

"Yes. For you and Patrick." I faltered, finding the words difficult to say. "Once you take the test, we can have the solicitors work out the details."

Bryan stiffened, and scowled, rocking backward on his heels. "Solicitors? Why would we use solicitors?"

His defensive posturing actually made me feel more at ease. "It's for your benefit, Bryan. To make sure your rights are protected. I know you-you've missed out on the first years of Patrick's life, and that's my fault. You should talk to a lawyer and discuss your options."

God, that was painful to say.

But it was also the right thing to do.

Bryan's eyes flickered over me, assessing, deliberating. Abruptly, he said, "What do you want?"

I answered without hesitation. "I want what's best for Patrick."

A small smile hovered over his lips and behind his eyes. "I do, too," he said softly, taking another half step toward me. "But that's not what I meant. What do *you* want?"

My eyelashes fluttered of their own accord, betraying my confusion. "What do you mean?"

"What's best for you, Eilish?" he whispered, his gaze blazing a trail from my forehead to my chin, again coming to rest on my lips. "Who's taking care of you?"

"I am." Again, I responded without hesitation, a tremor of unease running down my spine.

"Really?" he drawled, biting his bottom lip and drawing it between his teeth in a distracting movement. "You can't take care of all your needs."

"Yes, I can." The tremor became something else—steel and resolve—and whatever sexy, voodoo spell Bryan had been so expertly weaving with his tiny towel and chiseled abdominal muscles and handsome face and love for my son quickly vanished.

Bryan's smirk returned, and quite abruptly I no longer felt flustered by his proximity. Standing up for myself while putting my foot down was an art I'd mastered over the course of my childhood.

With his eyes on my lips, he placed a hand on the locker behind my head, caging me in on one side. "I'd like to help."

"I don't need your help," I said flatly, drawing a wider grin from his gorgeous mouth.

"Let me rephrase that. I'd *love* to help." His gaze drifted back to mine and held, his meaning clear as he whispered, "I'm *desperate* to help."

Really?

REALLY?

My cheeks were red again, but this time for an entirely different reason.

"What are you proposing?" I ground out, irritated with the small part of myself that wasn't angry, the small part that was wondering if I could install a stripper pole in my bedroom before the weekend. It was also excited and completely on board with the idea of Bryan lending *desperate help.*

But mostly I was angry. Even worse, I'd skipped lunch, so I was both hungry and angry. Or *hangry.* Because, really? We had a child together—a child he didn't remember making—and now he . . . what? Wanted to hook up?

What. The. Hell?

"I could help you relax." He trailed a finger down the side of my throat to my collarbone, sending traitorous goose pimples racing over my skin, and he leaned closer, his big frame making me feel petite. "I could make you feel good . . ." He bent his head, brushing his cheek against mine. "So good."

I swallowed stiffly as he placed a scorching kiss on my neck. Actually, it wasn't scorching. It was butterfly light, but it burned like a brand.

Bryan lifted his head and our eyes tangled. His were dark with desire and the moment gave me an intense feeling of déjà vu. I could taste his minty breath, the warmth radiating from his bare skin. My heart betrayed me, racing like a lunatic. My hormones also betrayed me, heat and heaviness pooling and twisting low in my belly.

But my brain didn't betray me.

It knew better.

It remembered being forgotten.

"No, thank you," I said, slowly and carefully through gritted teeth.

Bryan's eyes twinkled as they moved between mine. "No, thank you?"

"Thanks for the offer, Bryan. But I assure you, if I required assistance in that department, you would be *the last* person I'd ask."

"Oh really?" He looked amused, delighted, gazing down at me with a big, cheeky grin and a devilish glint.

"Yes."

"And why is that?" He sounded like he was trying not to laugh.

I scowled at him, knowing I needed to make a choice. Should I make something up? Bluster my way through this? Or should I be honest? Allow myself to be vulnerable to this man who'd rejected me?

Except, I didn't want anything from him. Not really. Other than for him to be a good father to our son and to be fair in his dealings with me.

Being an adult, I decided to go with honesty.

But, being a petty adult, I decided to go with brutal honesty.

"Because I'm not so sure you'd remember me the next morning."

Bryan flinched, the amusement falling from his face as his eyes moved between mine searchingly. "Eilish," he breathed, a frown of concentration wrinkling his forehead. "I'm not that person anymore."

"No. You're not," I conceded softly. "But you didn't want anything to do with me until you found out Patrick is your son. So you'll have to excuse me if this," I waved to the tiny towel and the rest of his torso, "this act falls on deaf ears and indifferent hormones."

As I spoke, his eyebrows jumped in surprise. "Is that what you think? That I only want you because of Patrick?"

"Yes. Of course, Bryan. I kissed you and you told me that you weren't interested."

"That's not what I said. Of course I was interested! I'd have to be a bloody eejit not to be. I said I wasn't any good for you, that you were a nice girl and—"

"*Saying I'm a nice girl* is the same thing as giving me the brush-off," I scoffed.

"You are a nice girl," the side of his mouth hitched, his eyes infinitely cherishing. "You are the nicest girl. And the cleverest girl. And the most beautiful. And the strongest. And—"

"Stop. Please stop." I shook my head, closing my eyes against his handsome attack and repeated what I knew to be true. "I'm forgettable to you."

"Oh, Eilish." He sounded tortured. "I was drunk. I was an arsehole. I'd say it was the worst mistake of my life, but it gave us Patrick."

"Why can't you just let this be?" I pleaded. "Why are you doing this to me?"

"Because you are not forgettable." His voice deepened and sounded gruff with frustration. "I can't have you believing that. I haven't been able to stop thinking about you since Will's birthday party, and trust me, I've tried. I have a spider plant at home that is very much alive as proof."

"Spider plant? What are you talking about?"

"You're all I think about," Bryan threaded his fingers into my hair, tugging me forward with a subtle movement, "And I know you think about me."

I couldn't deal with this, with him and his. . . words. My heart was on a rollercoaster, bouncing between hope and levelheadedness.

"I don't trust you," I admitted, opening my eyes but unable to lift them past his neck.

He hesitated, then said, "What is it going to take for you to give me a chance?"

"It's too late."

"Why? Why is it too late?"

I shook my head once, about to cave in, about to say, *I don't know,* when William Moore opened the locker room door.

Bryan straightened immediately. It took William a moment to spot us, but by the time he did, Bryan had separated us by three steps and had crossed his arms over his chest.

I took a deep breath and attempted to find my wits, stumbling over my words. "William, I'm so sorry. I was running late and—"

"Don't worry about it." The big American smiled at me, which I understood was a rare occurrence, and stepped completely into the room. "Are you sure you still have time?"

Again, William Moore was just the nicest guy ever.

The. Nicest.

"I do." I faced him and nodded. "Sean picked up my son, so I have until eight."

I felt Bryan's gaze move between us, but I ignored it. I ignored him and his . . . offer. If I dwelled on our conversation with him so close—and wearing so little—I would become weak again. I might even give in to him, and I couldn't do that. I needed to stall, I needed time to think. Thinking clearly in his presence was impossible, and I was upset with myself for still wanting him.

Yes. I still wanted him. My hands were shaking and I vibrated with how badly I wanted him. But our first time would be our only time because I would *never* make that mistake *ever* again.

"Oh." William nodded, looking thoughtful as he stuffed his hands into his pockets. "You should go home; we can reschedule for another time."

I tried to focus on William's words but I was too distracted by my torrent of emotions. I wasn't stupid, not anymore. I knew what I'd felt for him all those years ago hadn't been love. It hadn't even been infatuation.

It had been lust.

Just lust.

Lusty lusting mclusterston lust. And that's it.

Lust was empty, and it left you cold, forgotten. It could also leave you with superpowers in your uterus.

And that's all you're feeling now. So, lesson learned, moving on.

"Wait a minute," Bryan cut in, drawing William's attention to him. "Wait a minute, are you two . . .?"

It took William longer to catch on than me, and in those precious seconds I made a decision. Was it a good decision?

Hard to say.

Actually, no.

It was a bad decision.

But I made it nevertheless.

"Yes. We are." I nodded fervently, glancing to sweet William and begging him with my eyes to play along. "We're dating. William and I are dating."

Oh my God oh my God oh my God! WHAT ARE YOU DOING?

. . . dun dun DUN!

William's large eyes moved from me to Bryan and then back again, his mouth opening, then closing. A small sound escaped his throat and I winced, crossing to him with quick steps and taking his arm.

To his credit, William didn't move away and he didn't contradict. But he did stare down at me sharply.

"We are a couple," I squeaked, then cleared my throat. "We'd like to keep it quiet if you don't mind, as it's all very new." Despite my preventative throat clearing, my voice was still strained and cracked.

"It's really new," William said flatly, glaring at me. Something in my eyes must've won him over because the big guy sucked in a large breath, wrapped his arm around my shoulders and faced Bryan, saying, "And we'd like to keep it between the two of us."

Something passed behind Bryan's eyes, some emotion I couldn't quite read as he stared unflinchingly at his teammate. Bryan's glower was menacing and the air began to press heavy, thick with unsaid words.

William stared back. The tense moment caused a twisting achiness in my chest and a spike of nervous sensation to alight along my skin.

Eventually, Bryan glanced away. His lips twisted in what looked like a bitter smile. "Well, that's nice," he said, making the words sound like an insult. "You two have plans for tonight?"

"No," I answered for both of us, guilt—always guilt, for the lie, for pulling William into my drama, for just everything—carving out a hollow space in my chest. "Not tonight."

But I need time to think! Away from Bryan and his tiny towel of doom.
Dun dun DUN!

Unexpectedly, William volunteered, "Friday. I'm taking her out Friday."

I nodded unnecessarily.

But before I could say anything, William added, "And, you know, lunch tomorrow."

I glanced at the big guy, startled, certain both question and confusion were etched on my forehead.

William turned a wry smile on me. "And maybe Thursday, too," he shrugged, his smile warming, "if I'm lucky."

* * *

"I am so sorry," I blurted, sliding into the seat across from William.

He lifted his brown eyes to me, wide with surprise, presumably at my sudden appearance, and then finished taking the sip or gulp of his drink.

It was lunch on Wednesday. William had left a message for me to meet him at a pub across the street from the complex. I had no chance to apologize the night before, since roping him in to playing my pretend boyfriend.

After making my false announcement, I'd left. I'd gone home and tucked

Patrick into bed. And then I'd lain awake half the night fretting, growing angrier at Bryan, because *how dare he!*

And yet, every time I closed my eyes I saw him in his housecoat, clutching his mint tea. Or I saw him with his head thrown back, laughing at my embarrassing story. Or I saw him in the park, when he'd first set eyes on Patrick.

Or I felt his hot breath falling over my shoulder, the slide of his finger on my throat, the aching brand of his lips against my skin.

Crackers.

Presently, swallowing his gulp of water, William gave me a small—very small—smile, and asked, "Why are you sorry?"

I stared at him, shaking my head, not knowing where to begin and finally settled on, "For this. For lying. For forcing you into going out with me for lunch."

"You didn't force me. Lunch was my idea."

I shook my head, pushing the menu to the side and folding my hands on the tabletop. "William, I am so sorry. I'm—I don't even know where to start. I'm just so sorry. I'm a hot mess and I dragged you into my messiness, and Bryan—"

"Bryan is your son's father." William placed his hand over mine.

I closed my eyes, letting my chin drop to my chest and gave him a half-hearted nod. "How did you know?"

"He told me."

My head shot up. "He what?"

William nodded. "We're roommates."

"He told you?"

"Yeah. This morning on the way in. We ride together sometimes."

I exhaled a disbelieving breath, my eyes moving unseeingly to a spot over William's shoulder. "I can't believe he told you."

The big man cleared his throat, bringing my attention back to him. His expression was patient and kind as he said in his quiet way, "I was going to ask you out."

"You-you what?"

"I was planning to ask you out," he said simply, honestly, openly, a rumbly straightforward confession. "I don't want you to think this," he motioned between the two of us, "is a hardship for me. You're lovely. And genuine and kind. I like you. A lot."

. . . dun dun DUN!

I gaped at him, unable to do anything else. I was not prepared for this.

I was prepared for his irritation. I was prepared to apologize profusely. But I was *not* prepared for this.

WHY MUST THESE MEN CATCH ME SO UNPREPARED???

His eyes darted to my lips, and his curved to one side, just subtly. "You're more than lovely. You're beautiful. But you already know that."

"William, I . . ." I shook my head. *What is going on?*

"I wanted to tell you. You have no reason to apologize," he finished gently, his brown eyes now striking me as remarkably soulful.

So I stared at William Moore. I really, *really* looked at him.

He was good and honorable, hardworking and ethical. I knew this to be true. The guys on the team respected and admired him, as did the administrative and coaching staff. And clearly he was brave, fluent in emotional maturity.

William would make a great father, the thought popped into my head before I knew I was thinking it—unbidden, honest—followed immediately by another thought, equally unbidden. *But William is not who you want.*

I gave him a warm smile that I hoped reached my eyes, flipping my hand over and twisting our fingers together. "You are a remarkable person, William Moore."

"So are you, Eilish Cassidy." He didn't smile this time as his soulful gaze moved over my face. William watched me for a moment longer and gathered a deep breath, releasing my fingers. "I don't lie. I'm not a liar."

I nodded, understanding, knowing it was for the best. I didn't want him to lie. Heck, I was already regretting the lie, mostly.

Bryan's enchanted body parts. That's why you lied. When threatened with enchanted orgasms by a cad, the best thing to do is lie.

"So we go out on Friday."

Laughing lightly, I retrieved the menu and glanced over the sandwiches. "You're funny, William."

"I'm not joking."

This had me lifting my eyes to the man nicknamed *the Brickhouse* and raising an eyebrow in question. "Don't you think it would be best for me to be completely honest? Rather than prolonging the charade?"

He shrugged. "I'll let you decide. But so long as we go out, we're not lying."

"William . . ." I didn't know what to say, so I stalled, searching the tabletop, menu, and restaurant walls for help.

What is wrong with you, E? William Moore is asking you out. You like this guy. A lot. He's kind and good, not to mention stunningly handsome.

As a matter of fact, his oblique muscles made me want to cry. Yet I felt nothing for William beyond friendship and professional courtesy. No longing. No pull. Agreeing to go out with him felt like lying, and I didn't want to do that. I hated that I'd lied to Bryan in the first place. I wasn't going to compound the lie by leading William on.

He must've recognized my inability to articulate my thoughts because he said, "Look. I know you're hung up on Bryan—"

"I'm not hung up on Bryan."

Am I?

"Let me ask you this, then. When is the last time you went out? Not even on a date. When is the last time you went out with friends—dinner, movie, dancing, a show?"

Leaning back in my chair, I crossed my arms. "Seven months ago."

"Go on."

Not allowing myself to think too much about what I was about to admit, I confessed, "I had a rare night off and my best friend's mother offered to babysit. A group of us girls went dancing and I indulged in one too many alcoholic beverages."

"Nothing wrong with that." He shrugged. "You're a mother, not a saint."

Giving him my hard stare, I continued, "I made out with a stranger on the dance floor."

A faint, approving smile tugged at one corner of his mouth. "Good. Were you hung over the next morning?"

"No. I didn't have too much to drink, just enough to lower my inhibitions for a while. I made it home by one and woke up the next morning feeling fantastic."

"See, you—"

"And promptly came down with pneumonia the next week."

He winced. Like most of his facial expressions, it was understated. "That sucks."

"It did. No one else was sick, so I must've caught it from the stranger."

William chuckled softly, like he couldn't help himself. "Geeze."

"Yeah. I took it as a sign."

"What kind of sign?"

"The universe doesn't want me to have adult fun beyond organizing closets."

"Maybe it's time to give the universe another chance."

I shook my head, glancing over his shoulder. "I like you, William. But I have so much going on right now, so many changes, so much chaos. I don't think I'm ready to engage in any adult activities beyond organizing closets."

"Fine. Then let's do that. You get dressed up, I'll take you out to dinner, and then you'll organize my closet. It'll drive Bryan crazy." He shrugged again, his face impassive as he reached for and took a sip of water.

"Why do you want to drive Bryan crazy?"

"Because he's not himself. He's not happy. He's not unhappy, but he's not happy either. He's my friend, and I want him to be happy."

"And taking me out to dinner will make him happy?"

"No. It'll drive him crazy, which should hopefully push him into doing something reckless."

"You can't want Bryan to be reckless." I squinted at him in confusion. Why on earth would William want his friend to be reckless?

"I do," he said simply.

"But he's worked so hard to be sober, to be less reckless."

"But he's not *less reckless*. He's not reckless, period. He's a boring sonofabitch and needs a wakeup call."

I huffed a disbelieving laugh. "Everyone thinks you're a saint."

"I'm no saint," he said plainly, his American accent more pronounced.

"Well then, everyone thinks you're honorable."

"That's more accurate."

I grinned. "You're an honorable non-saint?"

"More or less." Though his voice was its usual low, unaffected tenor, I detected just a hint of something new as he said, "Even thieves have honor."

SIXTEEN
EILISH

@ECassChoosesPikachu: Patrick's new favorite joke: What do you call an alligator in a vest? An "investigator" HA!
@JoseyInHeels to @ECassChoosesPikachu: The kid needs better jokes
@SeanCassinova to @ECassChoosesPikachu: MY NEPHEW IS BRILLIANT!

"Tell me again how this happened?"

My eyes flickered to my cousin's, then back to my image in the mirror. I leaned forward to apply my mascara.

"As I've told you, William said he'd been wanting to ask me out for a while. We went to lunch on Wednesday and, once you agreed to babysit, I told him I could go out tonight."

"Moore . . ." Sean said, as though to confirm. Again. "The American?"

"Yes."

"Not, say, Daly or Malloy?"

I glared at Sean. "No."

"Hrumph."

I switched to the other eye. "We're just friends."

"I don't understand how this happened," he said mostly to himself. "Moore is a saint."

My mouth curved into a smirk before I could stop it, thinking back to William's denial of sainthood status.

After lunch, when we'd returned to work, I'd called Sean and asked if he could watch Patrick Friday night. He readily agreed. I also asked Sean if he would be available during the day Saturday so Bryan could spend time with Patrick.

I'd planned to use the time on Saturday to run some errands, catch up on bills and such while the boys spent time together out and about. Patrick needed time with Bryan, they needed to form a foundation for their relationship, but that didn't mean I needed to be present. In fact, I thought it might be better if I wasn't around when Bryan and Patrick visited. That way Patrick wouldn't get used to the three of us being together.

Bryan had been cordial all week. Polite. Solicitous. And he hadn't brought up our locker room encounter. I didn't know if I was grateful or disappointed.

Presently, in my bathroom, Sean motioned to me accusingly with an outstretched hand, then twisted his cufflinks in an anxious gesture. "You look amazing." Even when he babysat the man wore cufflinks.

Glancing down at myself, I quickly inspected the jade green dress I hadn't worn in six years. "Thank you?"

"That's not the kind of dress a woman wears to go out with a friend."

"Yes, it is," I said on a sigh, closing and dropping the mascara in my makeup bag.

"It's not. It's the kind of dress a woman wears when she wants to be noticed."

"Or maybe it's the kind of dress a woman wears when she hasn't gone out to a proper dinner in years and she wants to feel pretty and special instead of like a mother. You know, covered in Popsicle goo and four-year-old boy germs."

"Fine. Or that," he conceded quietly, tilting his head to the side in a considering manner. "Have you really not gone out to dinner in years?"

Deciding that dinner with Trevor at the mall didn't count, I smiled warmly at Sean's reflection. "Yes. But, honestly, I haven't minded. I know how lucky I am to have Patrick, and I wouldn't trade my daily Popsicle goo and little-boy germs for fancy dinners in a million years."

"I know, E. I just—" Sean was interrupted by my cell ringing on the countertop. He made a face at it, then at me, and continued, "I know you wouldn't trade Patrick for fancy dinners. But have you considered maybe you could have both?"

I picked up my cell, not looking at the screen, and frowned at my cousin. "Exactly. Which is why I'm going out tonight, with my *friend*."

"Don't you want something different? Something better?"

"No. I don't. I don't need *better*, Sean. I have a great job, I have you, and I have Patrick. I don't need anyone else."

"Yes. I know. You don't need anyone. You've only said those words three point four million times. Is that what you want for Patrick, hmm? To go through life alone? I'm not saying you *need* someone to be happy, I'm merely suggesting you consider the possibility that—"

"Hello?" I answered my phone, giving Sean a look that I hope communicated my desire to never have this discussion ever again.

"Eilish, it's your mother."

I grimaced, leaning my hip against the bathroom counter. "Hello, Mother."

As soon as the words were out of my mouth, Sean also grimaced. We swapped a commiserating glance.

"I've been trying to reach you."

"Yes. I've been busy."

"This is important. A rumor has reached me, and I don't know what to think." I heard something rattle in the background, like she'd just dropped a glass onto a hard surface.

"Uh, I don't—"

"Is Bryan Leech that child's father?"

I stiffened, blinking rapidly as dread and apprehension and confusion filled my chest and made responding in a timely fashion impossible. I glanced at Sean for help, and he frowned at my expression, pulling the phone from my ear and placing the call on speaker.

". . . still there? Hello? Eilish?" came her shrill voice.

"Yes. Yes, I'm still here."

"Well? Is Bryan Leech the father?"

"I don't—I mean, where did you—?"

"That's unimportant. Don't you see? This changes everything."

"How does this change everything?" I asked, hoping to stall, needing a moment to think.

Sean made a face of stunned confusion and shook his head. I could see he was truly perplexed.

"He is a man of means, Eilish. And do you realize who Bryan's father is? He needs to take responsibility for that child. And you. He needs to take care of you."

Her words of crazy finally provided something I could respond to with clear thought. "Mother, he is under no obligation to take care of me nor would I ever ask him to. And, honestly, this is none of your business."

"It is my business. Do you know how embarrassing this has been for me? Do you know how hard this has been on your family? If he marries you—no, *when*—when he marries you, it will change everything."

Sean made a face, which I was certain I mirrored, something along the lines of, *Can you believe this bitch?*

"Mother, I have to go. Let me repeat, this is none of your business. Leave it alone."

"Wait. Wait. Don't hang up. Listen, I—uh—I need you to come to brunch on Sunday."

Both Sean and I narrowed our eyes in unison. "I don't think I can make it."

"It's very important that you come. I have papers for you to sign, regarding your trust."

I almost snorted. Almost.

"Mother, if I'm not mistaken, you disowned me four years ago and changed your will."

"I might have been hasty," she said, which was the closest thing to an apology I would likely ever receive. "I've already met with the solicitors and it's done. I just need you to come by on Sunday to sign the papers."

"Mother . . ." I closed my eyes, rubbing my temples.

"I know that cousin of yours watches the child on Sunday afternoons, so I know you have the time. Please, come to brunch. Stay ten minutes to sign the papers, then you can leave."

For cripes' sake, the woman couldn't even say Sean's name, and he was her nephew!

"I don't think—"

"And I have grandmother's ring for you, the emerald, from Egypt."

I paused, holding my breath. Sean and I traded stunned stares. He quickly muted the line and loud-whispered, "Grandmother Lillian's ring? You have to go. Go get that ring. Go."

I'd never met Lillian Cassidy, as my father's grandmother had passed before I was born, but my father used to show me the ring and tell me it was to be mine. This was before he abandoned our family years ago. He always said I reminded him of his Grandmother Lily.

After he left—and it was clear he wouldn't be returning—I never thought about it, though I'd seen my mother wear it on occasion.

"Are you there?"

Sean unmuted the phone, wiggling it, and mouthed, "Go to the brunch."

"Fine," I said through gritted teeth. "Fine. I'll go. I'll see you Sunday." I made a mental note to call Josey and cancel or postpone our weekly coffee plans.

"Wonderful. See you then. Don't be late. Ta." And with that, she hung up.

I released a tired breath as Sean set my cell on the counter.

"That woman." My cousin placed his hands on his hips. "She is a harbinger of ulcers and alcoholism."

I huffed a sad laugh and shook my head just as a knock sounded on the front door. Sean turned his head toward the sound.

"Can you get that for me? I'm sorry, I still need to finish here."

"Not a problem, darling. Take your time." Giving me one more sympathetic look, he turned and left the bathroom.

I hunted for my lipstick, trying not to think too much about the call. I didn't want to get my hopes up about the ring, and *how did she find out about Bryan?*

As I applied color to my lips, I listened to the faint sounds of Sean opening the door and greeting William. Their low, rumbly voices carried to me. I quickly dusted setting powder over my makeup and gave my wrists a spritz of perfume.

Pushing away thoughts of my mother, I didn't take a second to study my reflection. Instead, I hurried to Patrick's room and gave my son a tight hug and a kiss.

"Will you be all right with Monkey Sean?"

He nodded, twisting his arms around my neck. "We're going to eat steak and then he's going to show me how to make a full wizard knot."

"A full wizard?"

"Yes. With my necktie."

A full wizard . . . A full Windsor.

My cousin was ridiculous and I loved him so very, very much.

"Ah. Okay. Be good."

I left Patrick coloring in his room and darted to the living room, but then I stopped short.

Because William and Sean weren't alone.

"Bryan," I said on a gasp, drawing three sets of eyes to me. "What are you doing here?"

He didn't answer right away. His eyes were wide and surprised as he took in my appearance, trailing over my high heels, bare legs, and form-fitting silk dress. Self-consciously, I glanced at myself again, tugging on the hem.

Bryan's voice was distracted; as though he were talking to himself, he began, "Holy sh—"

"You look great." William stepped in front of his teammate and gave me a warm, if sedate, smile.

I frowned at William, then at Bryan—or what I could see of him behind William—then at Sean, who was inspecting my ceiling.

My frown deepened. "What's going on?"

"Oh," Sean chirped, imbuing his tone with forced lightness, "I just thought since you were going out, Patrick, Bryan, and I could have a men's night in. You know, go through the latest Dolce & Gabbana catalogue, play a friendly game of Mario Kart, teach Patrick how to hook in a scrum. The usual."

Glaring at my cousin and his fake expression of innocence, I released a pained sigh. "Sean, you should have discussed this with me first."

"Ah, I thought he had." Bryan sidestepped William, sounding apologetic. "I'm sorry, I can go."

Swallowing the sudden lump in my throat, I steadied myself, because his voice sent prickles racing over my skin.

His words from earlier in the week assaulted me.

I can't stop thinking about you . . .

When I felt prepared, I turned my attention to Bryan. His expression was truly repentant and concerned.

The sight of him, dressed so casually in jeans and a plain white T-shirt, his hair tousled like he hadn't yet brushed it, his jaw shaded with two days' stubble, shouldn't have made my chest tight and achy. But it did. He did.

My heart melted and I sighed again, waving away his offer. "No. It's . . . it's fine."

Bryan stepped completely around William and crossed to me, ducking his head as he caught my eyes and giving me a small, earnest smile. My insides twisted and rearranged themselves into chaotic knots.

"Hey. It's no problem," he said soothingly. "I thought Sean had cleared it with you, but no big deal. I can go. I'll be seeing you tomorrow, in any case. I can wait."

"No. Don't do that. You should stay and visit with Patrick." I gave Bryan a quick, tight smile, and walked around him, moving sightlessly to the door and saying to Sean, "I already said goodnight to Patrick. I'll . . . see you later."

I felt the weight and warmth of a big hand on my back as William leaned in and whispered, "You really do look great."

I smiled up at him. "Thanks."

"Have fun," my cousin said, shoving my jacket at me, his features unrepentant as I glared at him from the corner of my eye. To William, he added, "But not too much fun."

* * *

We did have fun.

Instead of organizing his closet, we went to dinner, and then to a nearby club for a few drinks—we both had tonic water, no gin.

William didn't talk much, but he did ask a lot of questions. However, when I asked him about himself, he wasn't especially vociferous with his answers.

"Where are you from in the States?"

"Oklahoma."

"Oh. I've never been to Oklahoma. Do you miss it?"

"Sometimes," he hedged. "Where did you go to school?"

"Uh, Boston. I love Boston."

"Tell me."

So I did.

And that pretty much summed up our night.

He wasn't a talker, but he was a great listener. He was still asking questions even as he walked me to my door.

"What was Sean like growing up?" he asked, opening the door to my building and placing his hand on the small of my back.

"Oh, ha ha." I shook my head, my grin automatic. "Basically the same as he is now."

"Really?"

"Yes. When he was eight, all he wanted for Christmas was an Italian suit."

William chuckled, insomuch as William chuckled, and blinked once slowly. "I believe it."

"Actually," I corrected, "he was also obsessed with the SkyMall catalogue. He loves gadgets, which is great for me because I always know what to get him. The odder the gadget, the more he'll love it."

"Like what?"

"Um, let's see. Like a waffle maker that also warms your maple syrup."

"That's not that odd. That's awesome."

"Okay, then how about a serenity cat pod?" I withdrew my keys and faced the door to my apartment, half-hoping, half-despairing that Bryan was already gone.

"A what?"

"A pod with mood lighting that makes purring sounds and vibrates. It's like a little bed, but more modern, for your cat."

"He doesn't have a cat."

"Doesn't matter. He would've loved it."

I pushed open the door, my eyes still on William and his smile. It was the largest grin he'd given me all night and it lit up his whole face, made his rigid angles soften.

"You didn't get it?" he asked, lingering in the hall.

"No, sadly. It cost a thousand euros."

"A thousand euros?" William echoed, disbelief dripping from the words.

"What cost a thousand euros?"

I glanced over my shoulder and stiffened, backing up a step on instinct.

Bryan was still there. And he was yawning, like he'd been asleep, pulling his hand through his messy hair.

"A cat pod," William answered easily, shaking his head. "Sean wants a cat pod for Christmas."

"Why?" Bryan's voice was roughened with sleep, and his eyes bounced between us. "I thought he liked dogs?"

William stroked his chin thoughtfully. "I think we should get it for him."

"I agree." Bryan strolled forward, a smirk tugging his full mouth to one side. His eyes slid to me and they heated. "Hey."

"Hi," I said, taking another automatic step away from him, my back connecting with the wall just inside my apartment.

Bryan continued to advance until he stood next to me, his gaze moving over my body unabashedly, but saying nothing.

A long, awkward moment stretched, where we all swapped increasingly uncomfortable stares but nothing was said. Or maybe just my stare was uncomfortable. Heat crawled up my cheeks and my heart beat menacingly between my ears. I couldn't think of what to say as one tortuous minute became two.

Finally, *finally* William reached for my hand, drawing my attention to him. "Thanks for tonight." He tugged me forward and placed a chaste kiss on my cheek, saying, "You're good people, Eilish."

"Thank you, William." I smiled softly as he released my hand. He stepped back into the hall.

"I'll see you Monday," William said, his warm brown eyes still on mine.

But before I could respond, Bryan said, "Yep. She'll see you Monday." And shut the door.

My mouth fell open and I stared at Bryan—shocked, horrified by his rudeness—when I heard a low rumbly laugh, a full belly laugh, from beyond the door and William calling, "Let him have it, Eilish."

Bryan grinned down at me, his green eyes dancing with amusement.

"Are you going to let me have it?" he teased, and made the question sound unequivocally scandalous.

I gathered a deep breath for patience, my attention moving to the ceiling as I quietly appealed to a higher power, and marched past him into the living room. "No. And you can leave now."

"I'm sorry." Bryan shadowed me. I felt his presence close at my back. "Us lads on the team, we're always giving each other shite."

Ignoring his shoddy excuse and his apology, I turned to the kitchen and grabbed a glass, turning on the tap. "Is Sean here?"

"No. He left an hour ago," Bryan whispered.

I nodded tightly, realizing all at once it was very dark. And, besides a sleeping Patrick on the other side of the apartment, we were alone.

In the dark.

My heart did a flip.

I gulped my water too fast. It dribbled down my chin and onto my dress.

"Oh, hey." Bryan stepped into my space as I moved the glass away; he wiped gently at my chin with his thumb, his fingers curling around my neck. "Will didn't get you soused, did he?"

I shook my head, my eyes flickering to his, then away. I couldn't hold his gaze. And he was too close. And touching me.

In the dark.

How did I get here?

Again, the moment stretched. Rather than uncomfortable, it felt . . . ripe with anticipation. I couldn't think, and I blamed the weight of his eyes on me, the heat from his hand on my neck, warming my blood. I could barely breathe.

How did I get here?

I'd been so careful.

So careful.

"I'm sorry," he whispered, still touching me, shifting his weight from one foot to the other.

"What for?" The question was out before I could catch it.

"For so many things. For not asking you out at Will's party months ago, because I wanted to. For not kissing you back, because I *really* wanted to. But mostly," he paused for a moment, his thumb sweeping along my jaw. "Mostly for ever making you think you are anything other than magnificent and unforgettable."

Oh.

Well, then.

"I'm not dating William." I blurted and closed my eyes, attempted to distance myself as the raucous chaos of my mind echoed in the beating of my heart.

"You're not?" He sounded surprised.

"No. I'm not."

What am I doing? WHAT AM I DOING?

"But you two just—"

"As friends." I swallowed the last word, balling my hands into fists.

He said nothing, but something shifted. His breathing maybe?

I opened my eyes to find he'd moved closer. Our chests brushed. My breath hitched. I lifted my gaze and he ensnared it. It was dark, but this close I could see him. I watched as some internal conflict raged within him, his glare darting over my face.

And then suddenly he wrapped an arm around my waist, crushed my body to his, and growled, "Fuck it," just as his mouth claimed mine.

SEVENTEEN
BRYAN

@THEBryanLeech to @WillthebrickhouseMoore: You up?
@WillthebrickhouseMoore to @THEBryanLeech: New phone who dis?
@THEBryanLeech to @WillthebrickhouseMoore: Ha ha. I forgot my keys. Let me in.
@WillthebrickhouseMoore to @THEBryanLeech: What's the magic word?

My houseplant was still alive. Safe at home. Watered just this afternoon. I could let myself have this, have her. I could . . .

God.

Why did she have to feel so good? I'd been born with an addictive personality, so when a woman felt as amazing as Eilish, I was pretty much screwed—and no woman had ever felt like Eilish. Touching her was a losing battle, and I surrendered willingly.

She let out a shaky sigh when I moved my mouth from hers to the hollow of her neck, sucking and licking at the tender spot, trying to consume every inch of her. I felt frantic, like time was running out and I might not ever get this chance again.

I wanted more of her sighs. Louder. I wanted her to say my name, for it to be the only name she uttered.

I slid my arms around her waist again, pulled her body flush to mine, and pressed my mouth to hers, this time deeper, opening her. She melted for me, just like I'd fantasized. The fabric of her dress was so fucking thin that I could feel her nipples brushing hard against my chest. It drove me wild.

"Bryan," she murmured, my name a breathy sigh on her lips.

Say it again.

She was letting me kiss her. Not only that, she was *responding*. She wanted this. Wanted me.

I wasn't going to push. I was going to take things slow, even though I could have us both naked in a matter of seconds. I needed to behave, and yet, my hands traveled down, down, down until they reached her thighs. Without thinking I lifted her, and her legs went around my waist.

Not once breaking our kiss, I carried her out of the kitchen to the living room, lowering her to the couch, and settled between her open legs. I was hard as a rock. Her breath hitched and she went quiet for a second, just . . . feeling me. A soft, desperate moan escaped her. I clenched my jaw and gently rocked my hips; my cock nestled right at the center of her warmth. I was desperate, but not just because I'd been celibate for so long.

I was desperate for *her*.

My hands shook.

I broke away long enough to breathe, "I want you," and then I was on her again.

"I want you, too," she whispered on an exhale. I felt twenty feet tall, invincible.

We kissed for ages. Her dress had bunched over her hips but otherwise we remained fully clothed. Bizarrely, it was enough. I could've kissed her for hours.

I cupped her face in my hands as I devoured her, trying not to think about her long, bare legs wrapped over mine. I didn't touch her there. I couldn't. Not if I wanted to maintain my control. Tilting her neck, I bit and soothed her soft skin, drunk on the feel and taste of her. I opened my eyes and her cheeks were flushed, her neck exposed, her eyes still closed. She was completely lost to this, to us. So was I.

I rocked against her body again and my balls tightened. I could come at any second. I'd hardly even touched her and I was going to blow my fucking load in my pants. Judging by the noises she was making, Eilish was just as turned on as I was.

"Please," she mewled as I bent to her neck once more and moved downward, planting kisses over her cleavage, dying at the sight of her tight little nipples straining against her dress and begging for my mouth. I looked up. Her red hair was spread around her head like a wild halo. She was beautiful. Fierce. Glorious.

I couldn't help it. I bit down hard on her nipple through her dress and she let out a startled moan. I smiled and sucked the silky fabric into my mouth as she writhed beneath me. Her eyes were open wide now, gazing at me with lust and want. Her chest rose and fell fast, her skin pebbled with goose pimples. I moved my hips again, thrusting my erection against her, and she shook abruptly.

"Bryan!" My name left her lips on a sharp breath.

Fuuuuck.

Eilish's entire body trembled as I gazed up at her darkly. I bit down on her nipple again. She sighed and I recognized the look of pleasurable contentment on her face.

She'd come.

I made her come without even taking her clothes off. *Jesus.* She was all docile and compliant when I took her mouth in another kiss, thrusting against her, drawing out her orgasm. I liked her like this—open, needful, soft.

How the hell had I forgotten her? Forgotten this?

I took her into my arms, sitting back on the couch, and she came willingly, curling up in my lap like a satisfied kitten. I couldn't stop kissing her, my own need to come suddenly less urgent. In that moment, I was too obsessed with her. Usually, she was closed off, locked up tight, but now she was giving me something rare: vulnerability. *Trust.*

Our kiss was deep at first, but then slowly tapered off into little pecks and nips. Her lips were red and bruised. Her hands trailed over the corded muscles in my neck, down my shoulders and back. Her tender touch was loving, cherishing, gentle.

When was the last time I'd been touched like this?
Had I ever been touched like this?

Christ, I sounded like a teenage girl.

I wanted her.

Her touches made a new fire in my veins, building to a frenzy, and soon I could barely breathe with how badly I wanted her. Although I would have loved nothing more than to carry Eilish upstairs to her room and make love to her for the rest of the night, I couldn't.

Not yet.

She would feel overwhelmed in the morning. Regretful, even. The idea of her regretting anything that happened between us from here on out terrified me. I wanted this to work, and for that to happen I needed to take it slow. And not just for her. For me, too. A relationship—a *sober* relationship—was uncharted territory for me. I'd pushed her in the locker room, sent her running away. I wouldn't make the same mistake tonight. I didn't want to test her boundaries before I knew for certain what was going on with us.

I needed to leave.

And if I didn't do it now, I wouldn't.

"I should go," I told her between kisses. Her eyes were closed again. I loved how lost she was in me.

"Hmm?"

"It's late, love. I should go home," I said again, my voice tight, my words at odds with my actions because I didn't stop kissing her. My hands squeezed her hips.

"Go?" she murmured and finally opened those beautiful eyes. She tilted her head, confused.

"Yes. Go," I repeated between clenched teeth.

Eilish seemed to remember herself because she flinched, breaking away and tugging on her skirt. "No, you're right, it's late."

I watched her with a sinking sense of frustration as her beautiful flush of contentment and pleasure became one of embarrassment.

"Hey," I whispered, cupping her cheek. "I'm not going to push you into doing something you'll regret in the morning."

Her eyes flickered back and forth between mine.

Say you want me to stay.
Say you wouldn't regret it.
Say you never could.

She didn't. She only nodded and answered in a trembling voice, "Uh-huh. Okay. Sure."

I paused, just a second, a luxurious moment of hesitation during which I indulged myself in the feel of her under my fingertips—her warmth, her smell. Maybe I would stay. Maybe I'd hike up her skirt and touch her, pull down her underwear and taste her.

Jesus fucking Christ.

My lungs ached when I stood, my every pore repelled by the idea of leaving her now when she was so ready for me. But I had to. I wasn't the same man I was when we first met. I was an adult now. I was a parent for Christ's sake. And I was going to show some restraint . . . *even if it fucking killed me.*

She trailed after me, and when we reached her front door, I opened it and turned back to look at her. Her hair was wild, her lips pink and raw, and her dress all twisted and wrinkled, though she'd tried to smooth it.

She was perfect.

Just . . . perfect.

Why did I have to be so bloody mature these days?

But I knew why.

I knew building something lasting with Eilish was only going to happen if I wasn't greedy. Didn't push. Let her dictate the pace. Our eyes locked for who knew how long, as though searching for answers neither one of us was ready to give.

"I'll see you tomorrow." I nodded once, making a promise.

She dropped her eyes to the floor. "Sure, sounds good."

"Hey," I said and reached out to touch her cheek one last time. "Are we okay, Eilish?"

Those intense eyes looked deep into me, cut me right to the core. I'd never get over them, not in a million years. I wasn't sure how to read her, but I hoped to God she wouldn't back down from her want. *She wants me.*

I won't mess this up. I *can't* mess this up.

"Yes, we're okay, Bryan. You're right. You need to go."

Relief. Sweet, sweet relief. I hadn't messed things up.

I leaned down, pressed a swift parting kiss to her lips, and then I left. Begrudgingly. Every part of me wanted to stay and do naughty things to my nice girl.

* * *

"I brought dinner," I called out with a smile as I let myself into Mam's house, a bag of Indian takeaway under my arm.

There was movement from the living room and my mother shuffled out to meet me, effectively throwing a bucket of cold water over my already dodgy mood.

"Bryan. That smells delicious. Come in, come in," she croaked, gesturing down the hall to the kitchen.

After my sweet encounter with Eilish last night, I'd been feeling pretty good about life in general. As I went to sleep, I replayed every moment, remembering her moans, how she felt, how she responded to my touch. *Kissing her was divine. Tasting her would have been even better.*

But then, when I'd arrived at her apartment today to visit with Patrick, she'd been nowhere in sight. Sean greeted me at the door, but said nothing about Eilish's whereabouts. She hadn't returned by the time I left.

And now this.

I followed my mother, taking in her appearance. Her hair looked like it hadn't seen a brush in days, and she wore a housecoat over what I was sure was a nightie. She also reeked of booze. Stale booze. It seeped from her pores.

Most of the time she was a functioning drinker, but every once in a while she had periods like this where she barely left the house. My chest bloody *ached* for her, because I'd been there. She'd taught me how, after all. The only difference was I'd had the strength to change. She didn't.

I hated when she got like this, but at the same time there was a flicker of anger in me. Some days I just wished she'd get her shit together and be a grown-up. Act right. Let me focus on myself for a while instead of constantly worrying about how she was doing.

I'd come to tell her about Patrick, now I wasn't sure. I'd planned to discuss it with Eilish, but couldn't as she'd made herself scarce. My mother didn't look ready to hear I had a kid, that she had a grandchild.

"You unpack the food while I grab some plates." She turned to search in the cupboard. I knew just by looking at the place that all the dishes were dirty. The sink was piled high.

Mam blew out an irritable breath when she discovered this fact, turning and casting me a sheepish look. "I-uh-I've been under the weather," she lied. "Maybe we could just eat out of the containers?"

I stared at her. Stared and stared. She was a mess. I knew this. I couldn't change her, I knew that, too. But damn if I didn't want to shake some sense into her, yell at her, threaten her until she agreed to change.

Instead, I clenched my jaw. "Go take a shower and I'll do the dishes, then we'll eat."

"Pffft," she huffed, waving me away. "I'll shower later. Let's eat now."

She made a grab for the bag. I tugged it away. "We're not eating until you've washed and put on some fresh clothes. Actual clothes, Mam, not pajamas."

Her lip quivered and I instantly felt a twinge of guilt. Since going sober, sometimes I was too hard with people. But being too soft, too easygoing, was what got us here in the first place. Maybe if I hadn't coddled her all these years she wouldn't be so comfortable living like this.

Her expression hardened and she folded her arms over her chest. "If you came here just to boss me around you can leave. I've had a rough week and I don't need this right now."

"How?"

Her brow crinkled. "How what?"

I leaned both hands on the counter. "How have you had a rough week?"

She glanced away, her lip quivering slightly. "Your father got engaged."

My eyes widened. "He did?"

She nodded, her throat bobbing as she swallowed. "To some little twenty-five-year-old hussy."

I sighed and then dropped onto a stool. This wasn't the first time my dad had remarried. In fact, if I was counting correctly, this would be his fourth wife. Mam was his first, but he left when I was a toddler. I didn't understand it at the time, but I knew he wasn't necessarily a bad guy. He just didn't like his women any older than thirty. Not exactly a praiseworthy quality.

But thanks to his career as a high court judge, we always had money when I was a kid. It would've been better to have had a male presence in my life, someone to show me that throwing parties every night of the week wasn't the norm. *Someone who gave a shit.*

I gave my mother a serious look. "And in a few years' time he'll probably replace her with a younger model, too. There's no point upsetting yourself over it."

She sniffled. "Yes, I know." A pause as she gestured to herself. "I wasn't always like this."

Her statement surprised me, and I felt my eyebrows jump. Normally, this subject was off limits. It was ignored, brushed under the rug.

I knew a little of how her drinking started, but not all the gory details. His first mistress, who was ten years younger than Mam, got pregnant. Dad promptly left Mam to go raise the baby, only it turned out there was no baby.

The woman had made the whole thing up to get what she wanted—and she did. Dad married her, then of course, divorced her several years later. Anyhow, the abandonment and subsequent divorce was what kick-started my mother's alcoholism. When she got really, *really* plastered she sometimes liked to talk about the saga of the fake pregnancy. That's the only reason I knew of it.

And yes, the irony wasn't lost on me. My dad left one toddler he barely saw to go raise another baby. Maybe he deserved to be conned. Arse.

"No?" I prompted, my heart beating faster with hope. If I could get her to talk more, admit she had a problem, then maybe . . .

"When your dad left me I felt—" She sunk into a chair, her elbows hitting the kitchen table so hard I winced. "I wasn't enough for him, Bryan. I wasn't good enough."

"Mam—"

"But I didn't feel sorry for myself. No. I didn't. I was angry." She sniffed, wiping at her nose even as she adjusted her back, making it straight and stiff. "I decided I'd teach him. I'd show him he was wrong. I was so much more than he could handle. I hate parties; did I ever tell you that? Your father, he loved them. He loved it when I drank, said it made me fun. Made me seem younger, carefree."

I bit my lip to keep from interrupting as the words tumbled from her lips.

"I saw him last week . . . at a *party*." She huffed a bitter laugh, her eyes misting with tears. "And do you know what he said to me? Said he left me all those years ago because I was a drunk. Called me an embarrassment, a waste of a woman."

I gritted my teeth against the swift slice of pain in my stomach, because I remembered this agony. I remembered the day I hit bottom, when Coach Brian found me face down on the bathroom floor before a game. It was the last straw in a long string of bad behavior. He gave me the ultimatum I needed: get sober or get kicked off the squad.

Though I wanted to protect my mother, I also knew—if she was ever going to change—she needed to come face to face with her worst moment. She needed someone to give her the tough love Coach Brian gave me.

"Mam—"

"You don't have to lie to me, Bryan. I know what I am."

"Fine." I stood, holding my hands out from my sides. "And I used to be the same. I used to be a waste, but I changed. So can you."

She shook her head. "It's too late for me. I can barely go two hours sober before I start itching for a drink. You're so much stronger than I am. You always were."

I reached out to touch her shoulder. "That's not true. You're stronger than you know."

She let out a breath. "Yes, well, maybe I just don't want it enough."

My chest ached hearing the despair in her voice. "Mam, let me help you—"

"Listen, maybe I will go take that shower," she said, cutting me off as she stood and turned from me.

I frowned, watching her back as she left the room. She always did that. Put an end to things as soon as the conversation got too real. She could talk about the mundane until the cows came home, but never the things that actually mattered. *Her. She matters.*

A minute later, I heard the water turn on upstairs so I made a start on cleaning up the kitchen. I'd done this before, too many times to count.

How many more times would I do it?

When she returned, her wet hair was parted in the middle and neatly combed. She'd also dressed in a clean top and a pair of lounge pants.

"Hungry?" I asked.

"Starving."

I dished out the food and we ate in silence for a few minutes. Seeing her condition when I arrived, I'd known telling her about Patrick would have been a disaster. After all, Eilish had been right to wait to tell me until I had my act together.

But thinking on it now, maybe it would be good to tell her. Maybe the idea of having a grandchild would give her a little push to take better care of herself. Give her a goal to work toward, the same way not getting fired had been my goal.

I cleared my throat. "I, um, actually have some news."

She glanced up from her food. "Oh?"

"I'm not quite sure how to tell you this, but I had a bit of a shock recently."

Mam tensed, her features showing concern. "You're not sick, are you?"

"No, no, nothing like that. I just, well . . ." I hesitated, then decided the best thing was to just drop the bomb and deal with the aftermath as it came. "I have a son."

Her fork fell to her plate with a clatter as she gaped at me. "A son?"

I smiled, thinking of the crazy little boy that I was still getting to know. "Yes, he's almost five."

"But-but-but how?"

"His mother, Eilish, was very young and scared at the time, and I was, well, I think we both know I was in no fit state to become a father, so she kept the pregnancy a secret. Recently, our paths crossed again. I think the whole thing had been weighing on her conscience. Seeing I'd changed, was no longer . . ." I couldn't finish the sentence with *was no longer an arsehole drunk*, so instead I said, "I'd cleaned up my act, so she decided to reveal the truth."

"Oh my goodness, Bryan. That's just crazy." She gazed at me with wide eyes, her mouth parted with the shock of it. "How do you feel about it? I mean, how do you feel about him?"

"Do you know what the mad thing is? I feel great. He's the spitting image of me, and I loved him as soon as I clapped eyes on him. It just feels right that this happened now, you know?"

Mam leveled me with a skeptical frown, as though weighing her words. I had a feeling she wanted to voice her doubts, the same as Sarah had, so I pulled out my phone. Flicking through my pictures, I stopped on a selfie I'd taken with Patrick the other day and shoved it across the table to her.

"This is him. His name's Patrick."

Mam picked up the phone, her eyes going wide. There was no mistaking the resemblance, and in a flash I saw her doubts obliterated. Her hand went to her mouth, and her eyes shone.

"He's gorgeous, Bryan," she whispered. "And he looks just like you."

I smiled fondly. "I know."

She stared at the picture for a long moment, then handed the phone back to me. "When can I meet him?"

I studied her, saw the self-consciousness in her face, the uncertainty. She didn't think I was going to let her meet Patrick. And the truth was, I wasn't, not in her current condition anyway.

"You have to get healthy first," I told her in a gentle but firm voice.

Her lips twisted into a bitter smirk. "So you're going to use my grandchild against me? You're going to hold him over my head until I do what you want?"

I resisted rolling my eyes and instead set my jaw. *Tough love, Bryan. You need to give her some tough love.* "Quit feeling sorry for yourself."

"You're just like your father," she spat, lifting her chin proudly. "Thinking you can control me into doing what you want."

I lost my temper at that, growling in response. "You know this is what's best for you. If you won't quit drinking for you or for me, then do it for your grandson." I slammed my palm on the table, making her flinch and lower her gaze. "You want to live long enough to see him graduate college, don't you?"

A tear rolled down her cheek and her lip quivered. "Yes."

"Then let me help you." I softened my voice, rubbing my hand over my face. "I've got the advantage of having gone through it all myself. I know what's ahead of you, and I know how to help you succeed, but you have to want it."

"I'm old." She shook her head. "It's not going to be the same for me as it was for you."

I reached out across the table and took both of her hands in mine. They felt tiny, frail. "You're not old, Mam. You're barely fifty-five. Fifty is the new thirty."

She cracked a half-hearted smile at this, saying nothing.

I squeezed her hands. "We'll deal with any hurdles as they come."

She met my eyes, not speaking for a moment, then finally nodded. It was a hesitant nod, one that lacked confidence. I needed to build her up somehow, show her that change was possible. That she could do anything she set her mind to.

And if Patrick was the reason to start cleaning up her act, then so be it.

* * *

When I arrived home that night, Sarah was sitting on the wall outside my apartment building. I'd just pulled my keys out when I spotted her. Dressed in khaki pants and a brown jacket, she almost blended into the scenery. I let out a breath that was half guilty, half irritated and made my way toward her.

I felt guilty because ever since I told her about Patrick, I'd been avoiding her calls. And I felt irritable because I knew without question the boy was mine and her hounding me to get a paternity test was a hassle I didn't need.

"Well, at least you don't look like you've been drinking," she said as she pushed up off the wall, eyeing me up and down.

"Quit looking at me like I'm short. Of course I haven't been drinking."

"You've been unreachable. Forgive me if I assumed the worst."

I dragged a hand down my face, feeling tired. After dealing with Mam, I really didn't need this. "Yeah, sorry about that. I've just been busy."

She cocked an eyebrow. "Busy playing daddy to a kid that might not even be yours?"

I folded my arms and met her gaze. "And if I have?"

She blew out a breath. "Bryan, I told you not to rush into this. I told you to get a paternity test. Take your time. Believe me, it might seem unnecessary but it's one little thing that could save you a lot of heartache down the line."

"Sarah—"

"No, don't give me platitudes. I know you better than you think. I'm your friend and I care about you. That means I'm gonna push you to do what's right for both you and the kid, even if you've got your head stuck so far up your own arse you can't see it."

I saw the steel in her eyes and knew she wasn't going to let this go, not tonight anyway. It was one of the reasons she made such a great sponsor. She wasn't afraid to tell me how it was and she never gave up. They were admirable qualities, just not when they were being directed at me personally.

"Fine," I relented. "I'll get the test."

"You said that before."

"I'll get it, Sarah," I told her, jaw tight. "I'll get it."

She narrowed her gaze, trying to figure out if I was fobbing her off. I was, sort of, but I was hoping my acting skills worked this once.

"Okay, I believe you," she said finally, then gave me a small smile. "Let me know if you need someone there to hold your hand."

"Piss off."

She grinned. "Hey, I know what big babies you rugby boys can be."

"Yeah, yeah. I'll call you tomorrow," I said and made my way to the lobby entrance.

"You better," she called after me.

As soon as I got inside my phone started ringing. I pulled it out quickly, hoping it might be Eilish. I hadn't called her, though I'd wanted to. She'd been the one to disappear this afternoon, and calling seemed like pushing. I wanted her to come to me, as it needed to be what she wanted.

Anxiously glancing at the screen, I saw a number I didn't recognize. This aggravating day really didn't want to end. That certainly seemed to be the case when I answered and was met with a haughty female voice.

"Hello?"

"Bryan, this is Cara Cassidy."

. . . Cara Cassidy?

Wasn't that Eilish's mother?

Oh, jeez. Having been friends with Sean for years, I'd heard many stories about what a ballbuster this woman could be.

"Cara," I said, putting on my most charming voice. "What can I do for you?"

"I'd like to invite you for brunch at my house tomorrow morning, eleven sharp. I apologize for calling so late, but I had a time locating your number."

"Yeah, I'm unlisted." I smiled a little at this woman's tenacity. Still, I wondered about the invite. "I might not be able to make it tomorrow. I already have—"

"Whatever plans you have I'm sure you can cancel them. After all, you're a father now, Bryan. It's time you stepped up to your responsibilities."

Did she really just say that? Clearly, news had traveled fast, but I couldn't think of who might've told her. It didn't seem likely that Eilish would, and I knew for a fact that Sean would rather cut off his thumbs than give his aunt information like this.

"I'm perfectly aware of that and I am taking responsibility," I replied.

"Then I'll see you at eleven," Cara finished, leaving me no option to refuse without coming across as a major arsehole.

I gritted my teeth.

If I knew anything about Cara Cassidy and her ilk, I knew that this was no innocent invitation. She had an agenda. People like her, like my father, always did. It was a good thing I was well used to dealing with her type and was immune to high society manipulations.

I was just about to refuse—and in doing so, take full ownership of my arsehole nature—when a thought occurred to me.

"Will Eilish be there?" I asked.

"Of course," Cara rushed to confirm. "Eilish has assured me she'll be in attendance, leaving your son with my nephew for the morning."

"Fine." I nodded once even though she couldn't see me. "I'll see you tomorrow."

I'd rather accede another defeat to the Welsh than go to brunch at this woman's house.

But I would go.

To see Eilish, to spend time with Eilish, my stubborn, sweet-as-hell Eilish, I'd do just about anything.

EIGHTEEN
EILISH

@ECassChoosesPikachu: If you don't hear from me in an hour, a blue blood has poisoned my tea with narcissism or strangled me with grandmother's pearls.
@LucyFitz to @ECassChoosesPikachu: Your cousin says "She better put a ring on it." Any idea what he's talking about...?

Ten Minutes.
　　I was only going to stay for ten minutes.
And don't forget, everything you say and do is wrong.
　　I reminded myself of this simple fact as I crossed the street and climbed the stairs leading to the old Georgian mansion. I'd texted Josey earlier and pushed back our Sunday coffee. The café was nearby, so as long as I left my mother's house in under half an hour, I would still make it on time.
No matter what, you are wrong. Go ahead and claim the sky is brown and the sun is purple. Just like old times.
　　Gathering a deep breath, I held it within my lungs as I stared at the huge double doors. They were imposing; at least I'd always thought so.
　　Ringing the bell, I waited, glancing up and down the road. Nothing had changed, not really. Margaret Donovan's roses were still that same color of bright pink that my mother despised and Mr. Grady's topiaries were still shaped to look like harps.
　　"Miss Eilish."
　　I turned at the sound of my name, finding Jameson, my mother's butler.
　　That's right, my mother had a butler. And he took the role seriously. Good

on him, I say. Superb butlers, according to my brother Charles, were hard to come by.

"Jameson, I hope you're well."

"Tolerably," he responded, taking my coat. "Your guest has arrived and is with Mrs. Cassidy in the blue room."

"My guest?" I frowned at the older man, making no attempt to hide my confusion.

Jameson, I suspected, disapproved of outward displays of emotion, especially confusion. Something about my face made his eyes narrow slightly.

"Indeed, Miss Eilish," was all he said, turning and taking my coat with him.

I watched him go until he disappeared, and then I turned toward the hallway off the foyer. The blue room was extremely pretty, the furniture and paintings impeccably maintained. Several of the pieces dated back to the fifteenth and sixteenth centuries and were museum worthy.

I'd rarely been allowed in the blue room.

Low voices met my ears as I approached, yet I was fairly certain the higher of the two belonged to my mother. Without knocking, I opened the door. Scanning the ornate parlor, I sucked in a sharp breath as my eyes locked with Bryan's. His were twinkling as they moved over me, and I couldn't tell if he looked amused or angry.

Or perhaps a mixture of both?

"Eilish," he stood, smoothing his hand down his tie and dress shirt as he did so, "there you are."

I gaped at him, but I did not overlook the relief in his voice or the strained lines around his mouth. And that's when my attention moved to the only other person in the room.

"Mother," I said, my tone forced lightness. "Where is everyone else?"

She smiled, but it looked more like an aggressive baring of teeth. "You never said how . . . colorful Mr. Leech was."

Colorful was my mother's code word for indecent or coarse. It's what she'd always called my friend Josey. My mother had tolerated Josey only because her father was one of the first Internet millionaires.

As my brother Charles—the banker—liked to say, "New money is still money."

Ignoring her reference to Bryan's colorfulness, I returned my attention to Bryan, wanting to apologize to him. I was certain the time he'd just spent trapped in this room couldn't have been pleasant.

"It's good to see you," I said instead of apologizing, walking into the forbidden blue room and coming to stand at his side. An odd desire to protect him from this place and the people who dwelled here gripped me.

The tense lines around his mouth relaxed as I approached, and he bent forward, placing an unexpected and gently lingering kiss on my cheek.

"I can't tell you how happy I am that you're finally here," he said flatly, his words communicating so much more than their surface meaning.

I tried to impart sympathy with my eyes while also endeavoring to make sense of his presence. I didn't want to ask, *Why are you here?* because that would give my mother the upper hand. Better that she think I knew all along that he was coming.

Right on cue, my mother asked, "Oh, did you know he would be here?" She sounded both shrewd and mildly disappointed, which was how she usually sounded.

"Eilish and I speak frequently." Bryan slipped his arm around my waist, pulling me to him.

I glanced at him, impressed by his double-talk skills and his misleading non-answer. But then I reminded myself that his father was one of my mother's type; he'd likely learned to navigate polite society and their impolite maneuverings.

My mother issued Bryan an unfriendly smile and stood from her chair, glancing vaguely at her watch. "I must check on brunch, and Circe's found a new breeder, she'll want to tell me the details."

"Wait, mother." I stepped out of Bryan's hold. "Did you have those documents? For me to sign?"

"Oh." She frowned distractedly. "They're not ready yet."

I blinked at her. Once. Slowly. And hard. "I suppose the ring is . . .?"

"At the jewelers. Being resized for you." Now she looked harassed. "Really, Eilish. I have to go."

"Go ahead," Bryan said, giving her an unfriendly smile of his own. "We'll just wait here until the food is ready."

She looked like she was going to protest. Surprisingly, she didn't. Instead, her gaze slid to mine momentarily and then she turned, leaving the room without another word. Her footsteps echoed in the marble hallway. As the sound of them tapered, I released a heavy exhale.

My mother was up to something and I knew it wasn't good, because she was never up to something good.

Bryan squeezed my waist, glancing at me from the corner of his eye.

"What are you doing here?" I whispered.

"I was invited, so I came," he said easily, then grimaced. "Worst mistake of my life."

I chuckled, facing him. "Was it very bad? With my mother?"

"Yes." His answer was immediate and full of humor. "Her talents are wasted on blue bloods, she should be interrogating terror suspects."

I laughed again, shaking my head. "I'm so sorry."

"Don't be. I get to see you, don't I?"

His words startled me, as did the smoothness and warmth with which he'd said them. I cleared my throat, glancing away, searching the blue room and its priceless antiques for something to say.

Eventually, he bent to my ear and whispered, "How did you manage to grow up here without breaking anything? This place is like a china shop on steroids."

"I didn't grow up in this house," I answered, feeling oddly breathless.

"You didn't?" He looked surprised, interested.

"No, not really. I grew up in boarding schools."

His gaze flickered over me, his eyebrows drawing together. "Boarding schools?"

"Yes." He was very close, so I took a step back and away, turning to the antique French couch and took a seat. "I had a room here, for the summers. But this is may be the tenth time I've ever been in this room."

"Huh." Bryan nodded thoughtfully, his eyes still moving over me. "What was that like? Growing up in a boarding school?"

I shrugged, cradling one hand in the other on my lap. "Fine, I guess. I imagine it was like most schools, some people were nice, others were not."

"Except, with most schools you go home at the end of the day. Not so with a boarding school."

"We were all in the same boat, so it wasn't too bad."

"What boat is that?"

"You know."

"How would I know?" He claimed the seat next to mine, sitting too close. Our thighs touched from hip to knee, but I couldn't move. I was already pressed against the end of the sofa.

"Your father is a high court judge, right? I imagine he had expectations for you."

Bryan chuckled, placed his arm on the back of the couch behind me and leaned forward, crowding me. "No. He didn't have expectations of me." His attention moved to my hair, and he tucked a loose strand behind my ear. "Once he divorced my mam, I hardly saw him. I didn't hear from him for ten years, though he always sent us plenty of cash, but I guess he had to."

"Why did he have to?"

"Court-ordered child and spousal support from their divorce settlement."

"Oh," was all I could say, because this topic felt like a minefield.

Neither of us spoke for a long moment as we studied each other.

What was he thinking? I couldn't tell. We hadn't talked about money, not in so many words, but I got the sense he wanted to contribute. I didn't really know how to feel about that. Logically, I knew it made sense. Patrick was his son. Of course he wanted to contribute to raising him.

But illogically, I cringed at the thought. Bryan had been drunk that night. He'd blacked out. I'd been sober. He shouldn't have to pay for a mistake he made while too intoxicated to remember.

Was he hoping I would bring up child support? Was he waiting for me to do it?

If so, he was going to wait a very long time. Probably forever. I'd rather take money from Sean than Bryan. How twisted was that?

Bryan's gaze drifted to my lips and I stiffened, a seductive heat whispering over my skin.

Or is he thinking about what happened between us Friday night?

"Eilish—"

"Bryan—"

We both stopped, laughing a little and swapping amused smiles.

"Go ahead," he said, his hand falling from the back of the couch to my shoulder, sliding along my collarbone to my neck. "You go first."

I swallowed and nodded. "I'm actually glad you're here."

"Really?" He sounded pleased.

"I mean, I'm not glad either of us are *here,* but I'm glad to see you. I want to thank you for your clear head on Friday."

He'd been sweeping his thumb lightly along the edge of my jaw but stopped at my words, his eyes narrowing infinitesimally.

I kept my voice even and reasonable, dropping my eyes to my lap, wanting to spell things out rationally and openly. "I think you were right to put a stop to things. Obviously, we are attracted to each other, on some level."

"*Some* level?"

I ignored the teasing edge to his voice and continued. "I've come to the conclusion that nothing can happen between us. Patrick comes first, and complicating things by indulging said attraction would be a terrible mistake. We must—"

His hand tightened on my shoulder. "No."

"What?" I lifted my gaze, surprised.

"I disagree."

"You disagree?"

"Yes," he said curtly, then leaned forward and placed a light kiss on my neck, whispering in my ear. "Nothing about you will ever be a mistake."

I shivered as his hot breath spilled over the sensitive skin, tilting my head reflexively. "Bryan, you must see that we can't—"

"No." He tongued my ear, making me shiver again, my body tense, my thighs clenching. "You're wrong. I'm attracted to you on *every* level. I want you, Eilish. I want you with every breath I take."

"Wanting isn't enough. Attraction isn't enough. We have to be adults about this." I moaned, likely negating the sensibleness of my words.

"Then let's be adults." Somehow, he made being adults sound positively wicked.

"You know what I mean." I reached for him blindly, my eyelashes fluttering as I grabbed fistfuls of his dress shirt. His hand slid up my thigh, under my skirt, his touch light and demanding at the same time.

I was going to push him away.

I was.

I was.

I was.

. . . any minute now.

"Come out with me on a proper date. I'll be good." He dipped his head again, suckling my neck, his fingers beneath my skirt, digging into my backside as though he wanted to guide me to his lap, wanted me to straddle him. I flattened my palms against his chest, preparing to push him away, but Bryan leaned back before I could.

He held my face between both of his hands, ensnaring my gaze. "Give me a chance, Eilish. Please. We don't have to say anything to Patrick. Giving me a chance changes nothing, I'm still his father, and you're still his mother. What are you so afraid of?"

I opened my mouth to respond, but the words caught.

I'm afraid you only want me because of Patrick.

I'm afraid you'll grow tired of me and of our son.

I'm afraid you'll walk away, leaving us both.

I'm afraid of what it says about me—that I'm willing to settle for your scraps of attention, that I'm my mother—if I give you a chance.

I couldn't tell him my fears because they revealed too much, so I let the words burn in the back of my throat.

"One date. That's all I'm asking. One. Date." Bryan pressed an urgent kiss to my lips, then touched his forehead to mine. "Don't make me beg. I will, and it won't be pretty. I'm loud when I beg. I'll sing. And I'm a crap singer. Your mother's dogs might like it, though."

Despite everything, that made me laugh and I covered his hands with mine.

"One date," he repeated, kissing me again.

"One date," I said before I could catch myself, the words more a wish than an agreement.

His grin was immediate, positively beaming. "Great. Grand. Fuck, this is great."

Giving me no chance to correct myself, Bryan stood, pulling me from the couch and enveloping my hand in his.

"W-Where are we going?" I asked. He pulled me from the room, down the hall, and to the foyer.

"We're leaving," he said, as though leaving my mother's house was the only option and his response the most obvious thing in the world.

* * *

THE CAD AND THE CO-ED

"Are you sure you don't mind?"

"Not at all." Bryan glanced around the café, his eyes bright and his mouth curved in an infectious grin. He'd been grinning since I'd inadvertently agreed to the date.

I'd explained to him on the way that I'd already made plans with a friend for the afternoon, but he was more than welcome to come. He'd readily agreed.

"That's our spot, and we can pull up a third chair." I pointed to the table where I usually sat with Josey. She hadn't arrived yet.

"Got it." He nodded and led me over by the hand. I tried not to dwell on the fact that he hadn't let my hand go since we left my mother's house. I also tried not to dwell on the looks we were getting from everyone in the café.

Keeping our fingers entwined, he easily picked up a wrought iron chair and added it to the small table, asking, "What's good here? I'm starving."

"Are you sure you don't want to go back and have brunch at Cassidy house?" I sent him a teasing grin as I sat in the chair he offered, feeling the loss of his palm against mine as he took his own seat.

"I'd rather eat glass than share a table with your mother."

I barked a shocked laugh, my amusement increasing when I saw the serious set to his jaw. "I know she can be unpleasant, but it couldn't have been that bad. What did she say to you?"

He exhaled loudly and shook his head. "Nothing I want to repeat." He must've seen the curiosity written on my face, because he relented. "She said that she'd spoken to my father about my behavior. She called me a drunk. She questioned whether I was good enough to be *aligned* with the Cassidys."

"Ugh." I clutched my stomach, which had abruptly soured, then reached for his hand again. "I'm so sorry. She can be really wicked. Believe me, I've been on the receiving end more than once."

We traded a commiserating gaze. "No. I'm sorry."

"What? Why?"

"I can't imagine what you went through with that woman, when you told her you were pregnant. I'm sorry you had to do that alone." Bryan reached forward, dusting my hair away from my temple and cradled my jaw. "I'm sorry I made it impossible for you to tell me the truth. But I want to be here for you now."

"Just be there for Patrick," I said, covering his hand with mine.

His grin returned and he opened his mouth to respond, but he was interrupted.

"Oh my God."

I straightened and turned at the sound of Josey's voice, finding my friend gaping at us with plain shock.

"Ah, Josey." I stood and embraced her, then turned to introduce Bryan. "This is Bryan, I hope you don't mind if he joins us for—"

"Are you kidding?" She giggled, the sound somewhat crazed, and made her flirty eyes at him. "Of course I know who you are. Everyone knows who you are."

Bryan's smile wavered, looking momentarily blindsided by her exuberance, and I tried to hide my grimace.

Recovering swiftly, he extended his hand. "It's nice to meet you."

"You, too." Her eyes grew impossibly wide, and she shuffled closer to him, maybe a little *too* close. "I can't believe I'm actually shaking your hand. I'm such a big fan. You smell so good. You're completely brilliant, and I can't believe how tall you are. I mean, you're so tall. So very, very tall." She continued bobbing their hands up and down, holding on to his far too long and clearly making him uncomfortable.

I debated whether or how to intercede, mostly just wanting to crawl under the table.

Finally freeing himself, Bryan took a step away from her and tucked his hands in his back pockets, sending me a quizzical look. "Can I get you ladies anything? Coffee?"

"Coffee would be great." I gave him what I hoped was an apologetic smile.

"Are you really going to get our order? That's amazing," she enthused. "I've never been served by a professional athlete before."

Behind her, I let my forehead fall into my hand, shaking my head, making a mental note to apologize to Bryan profusely.

"Two coffees then?" he asked lightly, being more than gracious by ignoring her loony behavior.

"Yes. Two coffees. Thank you," I answered for both of us. He nodded once tightly, bolting for the line at the counter. I didn't blame him for wanting to run—first my mother, now my friend.

Waiting until he was out of earshot, I tugged Josey on her arm and quietly demanded, "What is wrong with you?"

"What is wrong with *me*?" she asked, her rushed whisper echoing mine. "That's Bryan Leech! You didn't tell me he was coming. You didn't give me time to prepare. I'm . . . overwhelmed by how sexy he is. And it's everything; he's just so everything. He's like a vagina magnet. I mean, my vagina felt magnetized. He's so tall."

"Yes. I know. You commented on his height like three times."

"Oh no, that was weird, right? I should apologize."

"No. Don't apologize, that will only make it worse. Just act normal. He's just a man."

"Just a man?" she repeated, as though I'd called him *just an amoeba*, offending her. "That, my friend, is not *just a man*. That is an orgasm guarantee. Every. Single. Time. Probably three or four times a day. I bet he doesn't even have to go down on you first. He just looks at you and, BAM."

"Oh my God, please stop talking." My eyes flickered to where Bryan was standing—thank the Lord—now ordering, his back was to us. "You need to get control of yourself. You are a grown woman, please act like it."

"I don't know if I can." She shook her head, her eyes wide with worry. "I've never met anyone like that, let alone been with someone like that. You know how horny I am. I've always been this way. It's why I stopped waxing."

"What? What are you talking about?"

"Waxing just makes it worse, it makes me lustier."

Despite the situation, I laughed. "You are so crazy."

"I have to leave," she said resolutely. "I can't handle that level of perfection."

"He's not perfect, Josey. Stop focusing on what he looks like."

"I'm sorry, I can't. You don't understand. You've always had this confidence in yourself, and you should. You're so beautiful and tall and graceful. And smart. But you don't know what it's like for us mortals." She backed up, shaking her head. "Next time warn me, okay? So I can take a Xanax? I've got to go."

I tried to catch her arm, but she was quick, weaving through the tables lightning fast. I blinked at her back, too stunned at first to move, and then she was gone.

NINETEEN
BRYAN

@THEBryanLeech: Ever notice how pineapples are made of neither pine nor apples? #mindboggled
@ECassChoosesPikachu to @THEBryanLeech: So I come check out your feed and this is what I find. Riveting stuff.
@THEBryanLeech to @ECassChoosesPikachu: I'm riveting enough in other areas, love. xxx

I was covered in sweat after an early morning training session. The boys were bantering as we headed inside to shower, and I grinned at their antics. Put a bunch of grown men together and no matter their ages or maturity, the topic will inevitably fall to the lowest common denominator.

"Under boob wins over side boob. Hands down," said Doyle.

"No way, side boob is so much better." This was Fitzpatrick. Course it was. I could tell by the smirk on his face he was disagreeing purely to rile Doyle. The man took his under boob way too seriously.

"What about good old fashioned top boob?" I put in. "Ya can't beat a bit of classic cleavage."

"Nope. Under boob is still the best," Doyle stood firm. "It's got the most heft."

Will's face at Doyle's use of the word "heft" to describe the female anatomy was comical. He looked like he was thinking about it way too hard.

"You're the under boob of society, Doyle. Of course you're going to favor it," Cassidy interjected, taking some fancy lip balm out of his pocket and applying it to his lips. I never really paid much attention to my appearance, not like Sean. That guy had one locker for his uniform and one for his abundance of lotions.

But I decided tonight would be different. I wanted to look good for our date. More than that, I wanted Eilish to feel like I was good enough for her. I wanted her to feel proud to stand beside me when we went out.

Sean continued, "I myself have always harbored a fondness for large conservative matron boobs. Give me Pam Ferris in a low-cut blouse and I'll be a very happy man."

Fitzpatrick chuckled. "I thought Doyle had issues, but you take the cake. Does my sister know about this secret fantasy?"

Cassidy smiled with teeth. "Why, of course she does. Your sister is well aware of all my sexual appetites, *explicitly* aware."

That wiped the grin right off Ronan's face as he shot Cassidy a disgruntled scowl.

"Hey, you dug your own hole with that one," I said, casting him a look that said *what did you expect?*

We were inside now, heading toward the showers when I caught sight of Eilish. She was just finishing what appeared to be a heated conversation with Connors, and my protective instincts kicked in. Cassidy noticed the same thing, but as soon as he saw the look on my face and my determined stride, he stepped back and let me handle it.

"Everything okay here?" I asked.

Eilish jumped a little at the sound of my voice. Connors cast me an irritable side glance. When I made eye contact with Eilish, I instantly saw how stressed she was. It might not have been evident to the average person, but it was to me. I could see it in the tight line of her mouth and the crease in her brow. I didn't want her stressed, not when we were supposed to be going on our first proper date today. I could murder Connors for whatever he'd done to upset her.

"This is a matter for the physio department. None of your concern," Connors said with a dismissive wave of his hand. Had he seriously not learned by now I didn't take that kind of shit from him?

"If it involves Eilish, it involves me. Now what's going on?"

Eilish cast me a pleading expression. "It's fine. I'm fine. Go shower. I'll see you in a little bit."

I studied her a moment, then turned my attention back to Connors. "Whatever this is, give it up. We both know she's done nothing wrong, and you're just being a cantankerous arsewipe."

Connors's face turned red with anger. "She was in my space, meddling with my things. She had no right."

"I was *attempting* to clean the place up a little," said Eilish, her tone decidedly calm. I was proud that she wasn't showing Connors any weakness, even if it was clear to me she was upset.

Our backgrounds weren't as dissimilar as I'd originally thought. Her family was old money, but my father's position as a high court judge gave me some perspective on her upbringing. Both our fathers had left when we were young, leaving us to the devices of our mothers.

Still, even looking at her now, I didn't feel like I deserved her. I felt unworthy somehow, stained. She just seemed so wholesome, too noble for the likes of me. Maybe that's why I wanted her so badly. The devil always looks for virtue to corrupt.

Except, that friend of hers . . .

"There's absolutely no need to talk to me in such an unprofessional manner," Eilish lifted her chin, peering down her nose at Connors, her tone high and mighty.

"I'll speak to you any way I like. And you're one to talk about unprofessionalism. You only got this job through nepotism and spreading your legs for the players," Connors bit out, eyeing me pointedly.

Oh, hell no.

I stepped in front of Eilish and got in his face. "The fuck did you just say?"

At the same time I could hear Eilish sing-song, "Sacha Baron Cohen in pleather hot pants" under her breath.

I almost laughed at her reference, but I was still supremely pissed, especially when Connors spat back a cutting, "The truth."

"You know, one day you're going to steal the wrong lunch." I put a hand on his shoulder, ready to do something unwise, when familiar hands pulled me back.

"He's not worth it," Eilish urged. "Like you said, he's just a bully. That's all he'll ever be."

But he called my girl a whore and should be destroyed!

No one should get away with such vile speech, especially not pointed at Eilish. She was ridiculously intelligent, dedicated, and bloody good at her job.

"Bryan, *please.*"

It was her voice that centered me, her touch that brought me back to my senses. Roughing Connors up wasn't going to achieve anything. More than that, I was still proving myself to Eilish and violence would only undo all my hard work. It would show I was unpredictable, a livewire, when the person I wanted to portray was a steady hand.

But it sure would feel good.

I inhaled a deep breath and dropped my arm.

"That could be considered assault, you know," Connors sniffed.

"If you think that's assault then you need to get a fucking reality check," I shot back.

"Okay." Eilish threaded her arm through mine and pulled me away, holding me to her side. "Mr. Connors, I understand you do not wish to have me go through your things, but that wasn't what I was doing. I was simply tidying up *my* workspace, as I have every right to do. It's in the best interests of both the players and us that we treat them in a sanitary environment, so I'll be reporting the conditions of the physio rooms to HR first thing on Monday morning."

He narrowed his gaze. "You wouldn't dare."

Eilish stared at him dead on. "Oh, but I would."

With that we walked away, and I glanced down at her proudly. There was a steely reserve in the way she held herself, and I had a feeling, quite surprisingly, that Connors had met his unlikely match in Eilish Cassidy.

"That was kinda sexy," I bent to murmur in her ear. Her skin pebbled where my breath touched. "Seeing you put Connors in his place like that."

She turned to face me, a smile at the edge of her lips. "It wasn't about putting him in his place. I'm thinking only of the team's well-being."

"The team, eh?" I held the door for her.

"That's right." She nodded as we passed into the hall, turning her back against the wall to face me as the door swung shut.

We were alone, our voices echoing in the lonely corridor. That potency that always seemed to linger when it was just the two of us materialized again. Eilish's gaze traveled down my body. Her pupils dilated and her breathing deepened. My cock stirred. Of course it did.

Oddly, I thought back on the brief encounter in the café with her friend. Something about it had bothered me more than it should. Josey had looked at me with stars in her eyes and an invitation lingering behind a flirty smile. It had made me uncomfortable, and not just because she was Eilish's friend, although that was definitely a big part of it.

I knew Josey didn't see me, not truly. Best-case scenario, she saw a guy who worked hard on his body. Worst-case scenario, she saw money. I used to eat up that kind of attention. Not only that, I used to take advantage of it.

I blinked out of my thoughts and returned my attention to Eilish. She was still looking at me like she wanted to do naughty things with me. Huh. Maybe looking good for her didn't require a shower, a shave, and a sharp suit. Maybe she liked me just as well in a dirty rugby shirt, scrum shorts, muddy boots, and a layer of sweat. The way she swayed toward me seemed to confirm it.

"How's Patrick been?" I asked throatily. Maybe discussing our son would help me behave, because I was two seconds away from pushing her up against the wall.

She swallowed, her voice equally rough. "He's good. He keeps asking about you."

My heart gave one hard thump and my lungs filled with air, glancing at the wall over her shoulder.

I was constantly eager to know how he was doing, and the fact that he'd asked after me personally got my thoughts all twisted up. It was like there was a string tied around my heart and I had this need to know he was happy and safe at all times. The scary thing was, now that I knew he existed I felt like it was always going to be this way, whether he was four or forty.

"Yeah?" I asked, bringing my attention back to Eilish.

"Yeah. He thinks you're hilarious. He keeps talking about how you did this trick with your thumb to make it look like you'd cut it off."

I smiled fondly. "Most kids find that scary. But for some reason our boy thinks it's the funniest thing ever."

Something flickered in her eyes when I said "our boy"—something warm—and suddenly, I wanted to fuck her.

What was I thinking? I always wanted to fuck her. But now, right now, an urgent pounding at the base of my skull made it hard to think.

"He's something else." She chuckled, forcing my thoughts back to the conversation. "Nothing fazes him," she continued. "I left him alone in Sean's bedroom once and came back twenty minutes later to find he'd been climbing to the top of the wardrobe and dive-bombing onto the bed."

I laughed loudly. "Are you serious?"

She nodded. "Yes, I swear to God, I almost had a heart attack. He wasn't allowed sweets for two weeks after that."

"Maybe we've got ourselves a little stuntman in the making, huh?"

Eilish shuddered. "Don't say that. I'm not sure my heart could handle it."

I reached out and touched her shoulder. "Nah, he's just a little crazy, I guess. Gets it from me. I was a hell-raiser when I was a kid."

Her gaze wandered over me, her voice quieter now. "I bet you were."

I stared at her, stared until something passed between us, something heavy and needful. I cleared my throat and stepped away.

"I better go shower. Want to meet me out front in half an hour?"

"Sure. I have to go freshen up and call the babysitter to check in on Patrick," she said and then paused, biting her lip. "By the way, do you want to tell me where we're going? I have no idea what to wear."

"Something comfortable. Nothing fancy."

"You do realize that makes me more nervous than if you'd told me to dress fancy, right? I don't know how to be outdoorsy. At. All. Just giving you fair warning."

"Stop worrying. I promise you're going to enjoy yourself."

She narrowed her gaze but I could tell she wanted to smile. "I'll hold you to that."

* * *

Half an hour later, I was showered, dressed, and standing by my car, waiting for Eilish. She emerged from the building in boots, a jacket, and leggings that molded to every inch of her long, sexy legs. I could barely keep the grin off my face as she walked toward me, a rush of adrenaline followed, knowing I had her all to myself for the rest of the day.

Not touching her is going to be torture.

"You look gorgeous. Hop in," I said and opened the door for her. She flushed a little at the compliment, and I went around to get in the driver's side.

"Did you talk to Patrick?" I asked as we buckled our seatbelts.

Eilish nodded. "Yeah. He's fine. Watching an episode of *Bob the Builder*."

"I need to get to know what he likes. Buy him some stuff."

"Believe me, Sean spoils him enough. He has so many toys I'm running out of places to store them."

"Huh. How about I get some new storage then? Building furniture has actually become a bit of a hobby of mine. I made this giant set of shelves for my living room last week."

Eilish shot me a funny look but didn't say anything.

I glanced between her and the road. "What? What's that look for?"

She shrugged. "It's just, something weird about me. I love assembling furniture, organizing spaces. It's like meditating. I love it."

"Yeah? We should build something together sometime," I said in a low voice.

She looked embarrassed, like I'd just suggested mutual masturbation. Although that *was* something I wouldn't mind trying sometime, too.

"You honestly don't have to buy us anything. Just being there for Patrick, spending time with him, is enough. He really likes you."

"I really like him. Actually, I love him."

"I know you do," Eilish replied quietly. The statement surprised me.

"You do?"

She glanced at me for a second and then back out the window. "When you first saw him, I could just tell. It was like witnessing love at first sight."

I reached out and squeezed her knee. "It was. I never thought to describe it like that, but that's exactly what it felt like."

We shared a weighted look, then I focused on driving. I didn't move my hand, and instead brushed my thumb back and forth over her knee. Out of the corner of my eye, I thought I saw her shiver.

"Bryan?"

"Yeah?"

"What made you decide to quit drinking?" Her curious eyes rested on my profile. My hand reflexively tightened on the steering wheel, and I blew out a breath.

"Kind of a heavy question for our first date," I said.

"I'm sorry. If you don't want to talk about it we can—"

"No, it's fine. You just took me by surprise, that's all."

She chewed on her lip. "It's just, you seem so different now than before. I can't imagine what might've spurred you to make such a massive change."

I turned my head to glance at her, then back to the road. "They were going to fire me."

Her mouth fell open. "From the team?"

"Yep. I showed up on the day of a Six Nations match drunk off my arse and unfit to play. Coach told me if I didn't get on a program and get sober, I could kiss my place on the squad goodbye. Don't get me wrong, I'd been pushing my luck for a while, and Coach was tired of giving me more and more chances that I just ended up throwing back in his face. It was rock bottom for me, especially since a few days previously I'd discovered my girlfriend stole my credit card and ran up almost 50k in spending."

"Oh my goodness, did you call the police?"

I nodded. "Yeah, but she'd left the country by then. Probably purchased herself a one-way ticket to Ibiza."

"That's so awful," she exclaimed, looking truly horrified.

"Those are the kinds of people you attract when you're an addict. Other scumbags."

She frowned. "You weren't a scumbag."

"I appreciate you defending me and all, but I was. Just look at what I did to you."

I expected her to agree with me, but all I saw in her eyes was empathy. Christ, this woman. She really was too good for me.

"Anyway, I'm not gonna lie. It was hard. The hardest thing I've ever done in my life. I fell off the wagon a few times before I eventually found a balance."

She stared me, genuinely interested. "Yeah?"

"It's all in the routine for me. I need predictability. The same thing every day. That's why you saw me get so pissed when my neighbors were throwing that party. They were interrupting my routine."

I thought she might chuckle at the memory. Hell, even I could admit it was funny. I was a thirty-year-old guy acting like a curmudgeonly old codger. But she didn't laugh. Instead, she frowned deeply.

"Surely that's not sustainable though. You need to be able to allow for some spontaneity. You can't predict what each day is going to bring."

"Of course not. I know that. I just need my routine and my comforts, that's all."

Eilish considered me for a long moment. "You should do something spontaneous today. Something out of character."

I shot her a perplexed look. "Why?"

"Because, like I said, it's not healthy to be completely set in your ways. It's too rigid, and life is way too flexible. You could end up losing your rag and breaking your sobriety."

I stared at her, deadly serious. "I'll never drink again, Eilish. I promise you that."

"And I believe you, but I still think you should try it. Besides, doing new things can be fun." She paused and reached over to pinch my cheek. "If you act like a serious, cranky old grandad all the time you might just turn into one. Or worse, develop a penchant for hemorrhoid cream," she teased with a pretty smile.

I couldn't help it. That smile of hers was way too persuasive. My mouth curved as I replied, "Fine, but you have to do it, too. We can embrace a new experience together."

She held out her hand. "It's a deal."

When we arrived at the marina in Howth, we parked and I led her toward the private docks. She walked ahead of me, and I absolutely checked out the round, heart-shaped curve of her arse. My thoughts were running away from me, picturing her bent forward, legs spread, as I—

"Are we going for seafood?" she asked curiously.

I shook my head, my voice tight as I responded. "Nope. We're going out on the water." *Jesus, get a hold of yourself and show some respect. Stop fantasizing about her for two fucking seconds.*

"Oh. Are there some kind of tourist boats that leave from here?"

I shook my head again and didn't speak until we stood in front of the Carver C37 Coupe I'd borrowed from a friend. He only used it a few times a year and mostly it stayed at the marina, going to no good use.

"We're taking this baby out," I told her and hopped on before reaching for her hand. She took a step back.

"That's a yacht." She appeared a little dumbstruck.

"Are you afraid of the water?"

"No. It's just . . . is this yours?"

"No. Belongs to a friend."

"Oh." She sighed, sounding strangely relieved, but then asked, "Do you know how to drive it?"

"Of course. I'm great with boats. I even rowed when I was at school."

She laughed. "A yacht and a row boat are not the same thing, and you know it."

Struck by a sudden impulse to touch her, I stepped one foot off the boat, grabbed her by the waist, lifted her, and deposited her on the vessel. She yelped and gripped me tightly. I didn't let go of her, liking the feel of her in my arms too much.

"Bryan . . ." She exhaled, our mouths inches apart, her wide eyes moving between mine.

THE CAD AND THE CO-ED

I leaned forward and whispered, "Just tell me you can swim."

"Bryan!" She grinned, smacking my arm.

I chuckled. "Relax, I'm joking. You're safe with me. I'll always take good care of you."

Eilish flinched, something flickering behind her eyes at my words, and I released her. I frowned at her expression but before I could question her, she tossed her thumb over her shoulder. "I—uh—need to use the bathroom. I'll be right back."

"Sure, sure. It's downstairs. I'll be up top."

She nodded tightly and left me on the deck. I stared at the spot she'd vacated for a minute, replaying our conversation, trying to figure out where I'd gone wrong. When a couple minutes passed and she still hadn't returned, I went down to make sure she was all right.

She'd just emerged from the bathroom when I reached the bottom of the stairs.

"Is everything okay?" I asked, studying her features. Fuck, she was gorgeous.

"I was just splashing some water over my face," she explained.

"Yeah?" I was hardly listening to a word she said, too engrossed in how she'd taken off her coat to reveal a baggy jumper that hung off one shoulder, exposing smooth, glowing skin.

"Bryan?" She said my name like a question, but there was a slight hitch in her voice.

I reached out and caressed her shoulder. "You've got the most beautiful skin, do you know that?"

She didn't answer, only lowered her eyes to the floor.

"Eilish, look at me."

"I can't."

"Why not?"

She bit her lip. "This is really difficult."

"What is?" My heart beat like a maniac, fear seizing my chest.

Don't. Don't say it. Don't push me away.

"Being alone with you." She closed her eyes, shaking her head. "I—I keep thinking about what happened last week, with us."

"Do you regret it?" The question was out before I could stop myself. I moved an inch closer, needing to be near her.

"No." Her answer sounded desperate and confused. Lifting her eyes to mine, I saw her expression mirrored her voice. "And yes. I . . . ." her stare dropped to my lips, "I can't stop thinking about you."

Yes.

I had a hand in her hair and another on her ass—*how did that get there?*—growling as I pulled her to me, then backed her up against the wall. It was so small in here my head was literally an inch away from the ceiling. Eilish gasped in surprise right before I dropped my mouth to hers.

If she wanted spontaneity, I'd give her spontaneity.

These weeks had been a lesson in endurance and my reserves had finally run dry. By the way her body moved against me when I sank my tongue into her mouth, it had clearly been just as much of a struggle for her.

I liked that, liked the idea of her wanting me this way.

Within seconds, my hand was under her jumper, skimming across the tops of her breasts. They were so *soft*, but the barriers between us frustrated me. I didn't think. Just felt. I tugged her top up over her head. *Oh, fuck me.* She was braless. I groaned, taking just a second to admire her naked breasts before I bent to suck her nipple into my mouth. She made a loud noise of pleasure that reverberated through me, her hands gripping my shoulders.

Mark me, my mind screamed. *Claim me.*

But she didn't. Her hands were hesitant, and her hesitation frustrated me.

My mouth parted from her breast long enough to lift her by the hips and carry her across to the bed. Being alone with Eilish like this, being intimate, made my entire body soar. It coiled tight and relaxed simultaneously. She soothed something inside me and at the same time made me savage.

I drowned in the scent of that seductive fucking perfume. For the rest of my life, the smell of watermelons was going to be an unlikely aphrodisiac.

"Something new, right?" I breathed.

Her eyes were foggy with arousal when she gazed at me, nodding as her moans urged me on.

I kissed my way down her body, tracing the goose pimples that danced along her flesh with my lips. She shuddered. When I reached her belly button, I kissed her stomach as my hands hooked into the band of her leggings. Breath whooshed out of her when I tugged them down over her hips to reveal black lace underwear. I ran my finger under the elastic and shot her a devilish grin.

"I like these. I'm going to keep them."

She flushed and made a low keening sound when I pressed my mouth to the lacy fabric. I dragged her knickers down her thighs until she was bare, tucking them into my pocket, then lifted both her legs and settled them over my shoulders. Damn, she looked amazing. Her sex glistened in the low light as I spread her long legs.

"Eilish," I whispered, dragging my lips over her tender flesh lightly, hardly touching her but still making her shake with pleasure.

"Y-yes?" she whispered back, her voice full of longing and anticipation. Her touch might have been light and hesitant, but she wanted me. That much was clear.

"Feel this."

Her lips parted on an exhale right before I sank my mouth onto her flesh.

She was so soft and wet. I licked and sucked her skin, my cock a steel rod. My jeans weren't tight, but my erection made them stiff to the point of pain. Her moans filled the small cabin but they were muffled. She was holding back and I needed her to scream my name.

I pressed my hand against her inner thigh and used the other to rub circles over her clit. She closed her eyes and arched her hips off the mattress. I growled and ate at her deeper. Her thighs clenched around me and I knew she was nearly there. I lapped at her sensitive nerve endings as my fingers brought her to orgasm. The moment she shattered I felt it rumble through me. The sounds she made, the way she shook, how she cried out my name, it all drove me over the edge.

After that, I was more instinct than man. I lifted my shirt over my head and made quick work of taking off my jeans and boxers. Eilish lay sated on the bed, the movement of the waves causing the boat to rock gently back and forth.

I hooked my fingers behind her knees and moved between her legs, ready to plunge inside when I remembered. I wasn't wearing a condom. *Shit*. Her eyes asked a question. Mine stared right back in agony.

"My bag," she breathed, her words a life raft in a bottomless ocean.

I didn't even hesitate to grab her bag from the floor a few feet from the bed. I handed it to her and a moment later she produced a small foil packet. My lips cracked into a grin as I took it and climbed back between her legs.

"Came prepared, did we?"

She blushed a deep, delectable shade of red. "It's been there a while, if you must know."

I grinned even wider, my eyes catching on her hair, a fiery halo around her shoulders. "You are so beautiful."

"Bryan."

"What is it, gorgeous?" I murmured, palming one breast and then the other, admiring the light sheen of perspiration on her skin.

"Can you please just stop talking," she replied, and I let out a low, throaty chuckle.

"Bossy. I like it."

She started to scowl, but it transformed into a look of pleasure when I grabbed the base of my dick and brushed the head over her sex. I had the condom on now, and though I wished to be with her skin to skin, I knew it was necessary to build trust. One night long ago, I'd had her trust, and from the way she'd steered clear of me when we met again a few weeks ago, I'd clearly crushed it under my boot. I wanted to cherish what she offered me now. I wanted her to know me, trust me. Forgive me. And I'd start with giving her the best boat sex of her life.

Fuck it, I'd give her the best sex of her life. Period.

I rose, bracing my hands on either side of her and pushed forward with my hips. My cock nudged inside her at the same time my head knocked the roof of the boat.

Stupid slanted ceilings, ruining my efforts at expert sexing.

Eilish let out a quiet giggle, and I grinned down at her. We shared a moment of just smiling at one another, finding humor in the moment. Then I slowly pushed into her again, this time filling her inch by inch, and the smile fled her features, desire taking its place.

I'd never forget that look.

I'd never forget seeing her like this.

I'd never forget another moment with her for the rest of my life.

I held myself above her, savoring how hot and perfect and amazing she felt. I trembled, overcome with sensation. My eyes closed. My jaw clenched tight. This was my first time inside a woman in two years and it felt incredible, better than I could've ever imagined.

Because it's her.

Emotion overtook me, my heart drumming away inside my chest. She had no idea how much I felt for her, how deeply I was falling in love with her.

Soft, searching hands found my face, her words gentle and concerned. "Bryan, what's wrong?"

I tried shaking it off. "Nothing. It's just . . . been a while."

She swallowed and nodded. "For me, too."

"I might not last very long," I warned self-deprecatingly.

A husky laugh escaped her. "That's okay."

"No, it's not. I want to make this good for you." I stole a kiss, needing her lips.

She blew out a breath. "Believe me, it is good. More than good."

"I want to last longer than two minutes," I went on.

"Bryan," she said, her voice firmer now.

I stared down at her. She looked so effortlessly sexy. So natural. So made for me. "What?"

"Just shut up and fuck me."

Her order obliterated my fears and with tender affection I lowered my lips to hers. The kiss started out light and playful, but as I started to move, slowly sinking in and out of her, it deepened. Our tongues waged a war as my movements sped up. Her thighs tightened around my hips, her beaded nipples brushing against my bare chest and driving me crazy.

I broke the kiss to suck in a harsh breath, thrusting. She clenched around my dick and I groaned loudly. Jesus. Fuck.

My hand found her neck, so delicate, so breakable. I loved how vulnerable she looked beneath me, how trusting and conquered. Her cheeks flushed, lips red and bruised from my kiss. I gripped her neck gently and the noise she made ricocheted around the cabin. She wasn't quiet; she wasn't hesitating. It was that noise and the sight of her spread wide for me, our bodies joined in the most intimate of ways, that sent me over the edge.

I came with ungraceful thrusts, a rough grunt, capturing her lips again as I spilled inside her. Her arms encircled my shoulders, and she held me until I was empty and sated. I crashed to the bed, disposed of the condom, and pulled her half on top of me, holding her close and burying my nose in the crook of her neck.

Holy shit.

"How was that for spontaneous?" I whispered huskily as my hand wandered down her naked body, finding her clit and rubbing.

"You p-pass with flying colors," she answered on a moan, shifting against me.

I smiled, satisfied, and used my other hand to palm her pert little backside and squeeze. I slid a finger inside her and groaned at the feel of her.

When she came for the second time, it was harder, more intense. The way she breathed, how she shook when she orgasmed was branded into my memory. We lay in peaceful quiet for a little while, just holding each other. I absentmindedly stroked her breasts, her stomach, her collarbone. *Mine now.*

"Are we going to be late?" she asked, breaking the silence.

"For what?"

"For wherever you're taking me."

"Oh." I'd forgotten about our date. Well, the details of it, anyway.

"No. We're not. Not at all."

She bent her neck to smile up at me. "Good."

I waggled my brows at her. "So, are you having a good time on our first proper date?"

This made her laugh. "I think we might be incapable of doing things the normal way around."

"That's only because we're both outstandingly magnificent." I grinned.

"Well, I can't disagree with you there."

I stroked her hair and gazed at her lovingly. It was official. I was in love with this woman.

* * *

Eventually, we did put our clothes back on. It was both a sad and happy moment. Sad because she was covering all that perfect skin; happy because I still held her knickers hostage, so when she bent over to put on her leggings I got a glorious eyeful of her arse.

We climbed the stairs and she went outside to the back lounging area while I claimed the captain's chair. I brought the engine to life and set the course. The day was cold and crisp, but sunny, and there was a light wind. I glanced behind me at Eilish, who was looking around the marina, taking it all in.

Walking back to her, I asked, "Have you something to tie your hair up with? It'll be windy where we're going."

She reached in her pocket and found something. I took it from her and snapped it over my wrist. "Turn around."

Hesitantly, she turned, and I gathered her long tresses in my hands. Then I pushed all her hair over one shoulder and dug my fingertips gently into her neck, massaging.

"You spend your whole day easing other people's aches and pains, but nobody ever eases yours," I whispered and continued working my hands into her tight muscles. She stayed quiet, then after a minute, she relaxed and sank back into me. My heart beat wildly. I ran my thumbs down her neck, back up again, down, up. I did my best to forget the fact that she wasn't wearing a bra or underwear beneath her clothes. And failed.

She trembled, and I wanted to drag her below deck again so badly I practically burned with need.

But I didn't.

I wouldn't.

She deserved a proper date, not more shagging on my friend's boat. If we were going to shag all day, it needed to be on *our* boat. It would have taller ceilings and we'd buy it together once we were married.

Whoa, slow down there.

Eilish let out a tiny sound of pleasure. Unable to help myself, I bent and pressed a light kiss to the base of her skull. Breath whooshed out of her.

I gathered her hair up again, this time pulling the band off my wrist and using it to make a ponytail.

"There," I whispered, not wanting to let her go.

"Thanks," she whispered back.

"Stay here, enjoy the view. I'll start taking us out."

She only nodded, and I made my way to the front again. We were cruising for a good ten minutes when I felt Eilish come up behind me and wrap her arms around my middle. I stood frozen, the affection from her totally unexpected.

"It's so peaceful out here. I rarely get to see Dublin from this angle."

"Yeah, it's pretty," I managed, my voice husky.

We were both quiet then, plowing through the sea. I loved the salty air, the freshness of it. I loved how there was nothing all around but us. Perhaps that had been my motive all along, to get her alone, have her all to myself.

Her hand moved inside my jacket, stroking along my stomach for a second, then dipping under my shirt. Her fingers brushed my skin and I had a hard time holding it together. For a split second I wondered what it'd be like if she just went all out and grabbed my crotch. I knew it wasn't something she'd ever do, but a bloke could dream.

Speaking of dreams.

"Eilish."

"Yeah?"

"Tell me about the night we met."

Her hand paused mid-stroke.

"Why?"

"Because I honestly hate myself for not being able to remember. Sometimes I have these flashes of memory, but I can't tell if they're real. Maybe if you tell me how it all went down it'll come back to me."

"Is it that important?" she whispered.

"So fucking important. Please."

She sucked in a breath, her hand sliding from my body. "Okay then."

"Oh, and Eilish?"

"What?"

"Keep touching me."

There was a moment of silence. Her hand didn't move, but then it did, and I sighed quietly in relief.

"So, it was at Annie and Ronan's wedding," she started.

"Yeah, that much I recall."

"You do?" She sounded surprised, and pleased.

"Yes. You said something about it at dinner when you told me about Patrick, and I've been wracking my brain. I remember asking you to dance."

"Oh," she exclaimed, her voice breathy. A moment of quiet passed before she started speaking again. "I was so excited to be there because I was really into rugby at the time. Like, superfan territory."

That was unexpected. "You were?"

"Yep. I knew every player's name, their stats, basically every single detail about the league. I was such a nerd."

"Did you know about me?" I asked, interested despite the small voice in the back of my head warning me to stop asking questions.

"Of course I did. Like I said, I knew about everyone."

I shouldn't have asked the next question, but I couldn't seem to hold it back. "Did you have a crush on any of the players?"

She went quiet, then answered. "Maybe."

"Who?"

"Never mind."

"Oh, come on. You're a grown-up now. A silly teenage crush is nothing to be embarrassed about," I cajoled, but for some reason I had difficulty swallowing.

She went quiet again and I grew frustrated, turning and pulling her forward so she was in front of me. I slid my arms around her waist and bent to whisper in her ear. "You can tell me."

She let out a little huff and shook her head. "Fine. It was you, if you must know. I had a crush on *you*, Bryan. It's why I was so dumbstruck when you asked me to dance."

I let that sink in for a moment. Eilish had had a crush on me when she was a teenager. *Shit.* And like the opportunistic twenty-five-year-old swine I was, I probably ate it up. I certainly took full advantage of it.

"I should've left you alone."

She tilted her head a little to look up at me. "Why? I was over the moon that you were even acknowledging my existence. It felt like the best night of my life."

My eyes widened in surprise, and the unease that had felt so small a moment ago flared like a fire in my chest. "It did?"

She glanced down. "You were actually really sweet and patient." A pause as she blew out a breath. "God, I was such a love-struck little virgin."

Wait, what?

Holy shit.

Holy fucking shit.

Her cheeks heated as soon as the words were out and I knew she hadn't meant to say them.

Meanwhile, I hadn't recovered from her confession.

Jesus Christ. She'd been a virgin?

I couldn't fucking believe this. I couldn't believe myself. I'd taken something so special without a single care. But that's who I was when I drank, a careless, greedy arsehole.

She twisted in my arms so her back was to me. I pulled her around again and met her gaze, my eyes flickering back and forth between hers, oddly out of breath. "I was your first?"

She swallowed, then nodded.

"Oh, Eilish, I'm so fucking sorry," I said, my tone full of remorse. She must've been so scared when she found out she was pregnant. Pregnant from the one and only time she'd had sex. With me. The biggest bloody arsehole in the whole entire world.

"It's okay," she assured me. "Honestly. Like I said, you were really sweet. You kept telling me how much you loved my hair and how gorgeous I was." Some things didn't change. I still loved her hair. And yeah, I had to admit that there was some tiny part of me that loved the idea of being her first, even if I made an absolute hames of it in the end.

I was quiet for a long moment, my brain working.

An image of her flashed into my mind's eye, the night I saw her at William's birthday party, how she'd acted like she didn't know who I was when the truth was she'd followed my career for years. She'd had a crush on me. And then the first time she met me, we slept together.

Another image, of her friend this time, the way Josey had looked at me last week, how she'd acted. I didn't like the thought of Eilish ever looking at me that way.

"I thought I was in falling in love," she added distractedly, pulling me from my thoughts, her eyes losing focus. "The next morning I woke up, stars in my eyes and everything, and you barely even knew who I was or what we'd done."

I winced. A silence passed between us and I tried putting all the pieces together. As I did, something hit me, a weird memory, and I couldn't tell if it was real.

"I told you to close the curtains," I blurted, and her eyes flared.

"What?"

"That morning, I told you to close the curtains, didn't I? That was you."

She gasped, her hand going to her mouth. "But how . . .?"

My brow creased. "I don't know. I think you recounting the night helped. I wish I could remember more."

Eilish swallowed and turned to stare out at the water for a second, her profile to me, her expression thoughtful. When she finally spoke it was barely a whisper, "Yes, that was me."

I swore under my breath and grabbed her upper arms, my thumbs brushing tenderly back and forth. My face was earnest when I said, "I know I keep repeating myself, but I really am sorry, Eilish. You deserved so much better than that. I was a total prick to you."

"You were an addict, Bryan. And it wasn't like I discouraged your attention. When you flirted with me I flirted right back, and I was stone-cold sober. You were the one under the influence."

I contradicted her automatically. "I was the villain of the piece, and we both know it."

She shook her head and met my gaze pointedly. "There were no villains. Just two misguided people colliding and making something beautiful. I might've been scared at the time, but I wouldn't trade Patrick for the world. He's my everything."

My heart warmed and then burned, the odd nagging of unease and doubt dissipating at her mention of our son.

I loved how much she loved him, and in that moment I realized how much I wanted that love. Her love. I wanted the three of us to be a family so badly my bones ached. Unfortunately, I suspected that if I breathed a word of this to Eilish she'd run a mile. I was some crazy bunny boiler, infatuated with her.

She'd had nearly five years with Patrick, and I thought about my own mother. She'd had twenty-nine with me, but I never saw that type of love and adoration from her eyes. She *needed* me, loved me, but adored me as someone incredibly special she'd made? *That* I wasn't so sure of. Eilish. She was the one who was teaching me about love, and I knew I wanted that in my life. Despite how we began, I wanted her and Patrick as mine.

She turned in my arms to stare at the water again. We'd been heading out to sea but I steered the boat back around in an arc and headed toward Ireland's Eye. Eilish noticed the direction and cocked her head to me with an excited smile.

"We're going to the island?"

I smiled right back. "Yes, love, we're going to the island."

TWENTY
BRYAN

@THEBryanLeech: When you're having the most perfect day because @ECassChoosesPikachu is the most perfect woman <3
@ECassChoosesPikachu to @THEBryanLeech: Sweet talker… go on. ;-)
@SeanCassinova to @THEBryanLeech: I've created a monster. Don't tell me you've abandoned your housecoat and prune addiction?

Once I secured the boat, I grabbed my backpack and helped Eilish off. Her earlier wariness about going out on the water was gone, and she seemed relaxed.

"I thought we could walk up to the Martello Tower and have a picnic," I said as I took her arm and led her away from the shore.

She eyed my backpack. "You brought food?"

"What kind of date would I be if I let you starve?"

"I just never pictured you as the domestic type," she replied, eyes on the ground as we navigated the rocky terrain.

"Well, get picturing it because I cook all the time. Will has put on half a stone in muscle from all the gourmet protein I've been feeding him."

She giggled. "He is very big."

"Not sure I like you commenting on my flatmate's size," I teased.

Eilish rolled her eyes. "You know perfectly well we're just friends."

I shot her a grin, because I did know that. Don't get me wrong, I'd been ready to string Will up by the balls after I heard he was taking her out on a date. I knew he liked Eilish, so I decided to be upfront and tell him I was Patrick's dad. After that he set aside his romantic notions and decided to help me instead. He was a real class act, a true friend.

I was certain Eilish's change of mind about me was half Will's doing. I hadn't been surprised by the news when Eilish informed me in her kitchen last week that she and Will weren't dating, but I had been surprised she'd told me. I'd expected her to hide behind the ruse for a little longer.

"I haven't been out here since I was Patrick's age," she said after we walked a few minutes in quiet. She sounded wistful.

I glanced down at her. "No?"

"My mother was never one for the outdoors. She put an end to activities like this pretty early on. Cocktail parties and soirees were more her thing."

"Yeah, mine too. Though she preferred house parties and night clubs to soirees." I let out a breath. "Speaking of mothers, did Cara give you any grief about us ditching her hoity-toity brunch?"

Eilish adopted an exasperated look. "Yes. But I've been sending her calls to voicemail. I don't have the energy to deal with her." Her expression turned thoughtful. "Are you close with your mother?"

"I am. Dad left when I was three . . ." I thought about that for a moment, remembering my mother's version of the events. Taking a deep breath, I continued, "It's been just the two of us as far back as I can remember. Kind of hard not to be close in a situation like that."

She almost stumbled over a rock but I caught her by the elbow just in time. "I'm the opposite," she said once she found her footing again. "If I'm the Sahara Desert, my mam's the Arctic. We never really saw eye to eye. Still don't."

"I'm not saying we agree on everything," I said. "In fact, I disagree with Mam on a lot of things. She drinks too much for one, and obviously you know how that can be a problem for me. I've been trying to help her get sober, but it's been a losing battle up until recently."

"Oh? What changed?" she asked, curious.

"I told her about Patrick."

Her brows shot up. "You did?"

I nodded. "I didn't expect it to have such an effect on her, but hearing she has a grandchild really put a bit of life back into her eyes. I hadn't seen her look so hopeful in a long time."

"That's great," said Eilish somewhat warily.

"Don't worry. I already told her it'd be a while before she can meet him. I'll make sure she's cleaned up her act before that ever happens."

Eilish bobbed her head, her expression relaxing as a thought passed behind her eyes.

I tucked some hair behind her ear and asked, "Hey, what are you thinking about?"

She bit her lip. "Is that how you developed your addiction? Because of your mother?"

I exhaled a deep breath, going quiet for a moment before I answered. "It certainly had a hand in it, and I'm sure I got my addictive traits from her, but it's not like she forced alcohol down my throat. I did that of my own free will. She probably could've set a better example though."

"Hmm."

"What does 'hmm' mean?"

"You don't blame her. Most people blame their parents for everything, even when they've had it fairly easy growing up. It's unusual."

"Yeah well, I'm not in the business of laying blame. I know what it's like to make mistakes, and I wouldn't be where I am now if the people in my life hadn't forgiven me. She might not have been the best parent, but she was always there for me. And she always came to my games. It was only as I got older that we drifted apart. We were still close, just not as close as we used to be."

Eilish frowned. "I'm not looking forward to Patrick becoming a teenager and drifting away from me. I wish he could just stay little forever."

I gave her a warm look and slid my arm around her waist as we walked. "You're the light of that kid's life. Even when he does grow up I know he'll never stop loving you. No one could ever stop loving someone like you, Eilish."

She sucked in a breath and then went quiet. I saw a hint of a blush color her cheeks. She always went quiet when I spoke the truth about her.

We reached the Martello Tower and took a few moments to look at the view. All I could hear was the wind and the waves knocking against the shore. When I looked at Eilish, she was so bloody beautiful she took my breath away. Bright, vibrant strands of hair blew across her face. Her luscious pink lips parted a little, her tongue dipping out to wet them. It was her eyes that were most beautiful though. The light caught them in such a way that made them seem like glass, the blue of the sea reflecting through and giving them color.

I wanted to kiss her.

Instead, I threw my arm around her shoulders and pulled her close. "We should take a picture," I whispered, reaching down into my pocket for my phone. Our chests brushed and I felt her shudder. I clicked on the camera and held it up in front of us. Eilish wore a vaguely uncomfortable expression so I nudged her a little.

"Hey, are you okay?"

She nodded and her lips started to curve.

I snapped a few shots before sliding the phone back in my jeans pocket.

"What are you going to do with those?" she asked curiously.

"I won't be plastering them all over Facebook if that's what you're worried about," I assured her. "I'm just capturing memories for us."

"Oh," she breathed and then bit her lip.

"I can send them to you if you'd like, that way we'll both have copies."

Her eyes lit up. "Yes, please do."

"Done. Are you hungry?"

"Starving."

"Good. Let's go find a less windy spot where we can eat."

We found some respite from the wind behind a small outcrop, and I pulled the rolled-up blanket from my bag and laid it on the ground. Eilish sat down, but it was too cold for either one of us to even think about removing our coats. I hadn't exactly thought this whole picnic idea through.

When Eilish visibly shivered, I offered her my coat but she declined. "You'll catch your death."

"Then at least come over here so I can warm you up," I said, my gaze darkening.

Her eyes twinkled at the suggestion, and she crawled over to sit next to me. Memories from back in the boat flooded my head at her nearness, and I had a hard time keeping my hands to myself. I kept them occupied by handing her the wrapped sandwiches and the flask. Then, unable to help myself, I threw my arm around her shoulders, rubbing up and down to create some heat. Her scent hit my nose. Watermelon. Maybe having a cold Irish picnic wasn't such a bad idea after all. At least it meant I had an excuse to hold her close like this. She handed me a sandwich and then unwrapped her own.

"Not exactly haute cuisine," I said. "I promise I'll take you out somewhere fancy next time."

She took a bite of the pastrami on rye and closed her eyes to savor it. "No way. This sandwich is amazing. I'll take this over a Michelin-star restaurant any day of the week."

"It only tastes good because you're starving." I chuckled tenderly.

"Nu-uh. I don't lie about food. This sandwich is the best thing I've tasted in forever. Is that American mustard?"

"Yep."

She groaned. "It's *soooo* good. In my past life, growing up, I went to enough fancy restaurants to last ten lifetimes. Nowadays I prefer good old-fashioned home cooking. You don't get many opportunities to eat out when there's a four-year-old living under your roof."

"Eilish, I'm going to take you to dinner. That's happening," I stood firm. "Get Sean to play babysitter."

She laughed. "He doesn't like the term 'babysitter.' He prefers 'child haute couture consultant.'"

I sighed and smiled. "Of course he does."

Eilish swallowed another bite of her sandwich. "Sean's always been eccentric. By the way, maybe you can talk to him for me? Every time he comes to visit he brings presents for Patrick. It's lovely and all, but I don't want my son thinking gifts every week are the norm. I tried to explain this to my cousin, but he won't listen," she said, exasperated.

I was touched she was asking me for help. "Sure. I'll just keep kicking him in the shins during training until he agrees to stop."

She laughed. "Maybe something less extreme?"

"Spoilsport, but okay, leave it to me."

She looked at me then, our lips so close they almost touched. "Thanks."

We continued eating in silence, our eyes finding each other from time to time. When we were finished, I wrapped my other arm around her and pulled her to sit between my thighs. There were a few tourists ambling about, but the outcrop provided us with enough privacy. Eilish exhaled softly and rested her head against my sternum.

"This is nice," she said, her voice relaxed.

I squeezed her a little and pressed my mouth to the top of her head. "Mm-hmm."

Time passed. In spite of the cold I could've fallen asleep. Being with her made everything peaceful.

"Bryan?" she whispered.

"What is it, love?"

"I'm glad I told you about Patrick."

I smiled even though her back was to me and she couldn't see it. "Me, too." Lowering my mouth to the side of her neck, I brought my lips to her skin. She let out a tiny moan and shifted in place.

"I think you're going to make a fantastic dad," she continued, and I kissed her again, feather light.

"I hope so."

"You will. You're s-so good with him."

God, my heart was gonna burst if she kept talking like this. It felt like a dream. Too good to be real. Even when she admitted to me that Patrick was mine, I never imagined we'd end up here.

"Eilish."

"Hmm?"

"Just shut up and kiss me."

She barked a laugh at my use of her earlier words and I flipped her on her back, climbing over her. I took her mouth in a hot, searing kiss. I'd been dying to do this since leaving the boat. How could I miss the taste of her so much? It had only been an hour since we'd arrived.

She melted beneath me, her mouth opening, our tongues dancing. She arched off the ground, her thighs parting and wrapping around my waist. I groaned loudly when our bodies met intimately. Too loudly.

Footsteps started coming our way.

We snapped apart in a flash and I gathered up the blanket, shoving it in my bag. My breathing was still fast and I willed my erection to go down. The footsteps transformed into a small group of German-speaking tourists, and I prayed they didn't glance in the direction of my crotch. When I caught Eilish's gaze I could see she was trying her hardest not to laugh. She was well aware of my predicament.

I cleared my throat. "We should start heading back."

She glanced at her watch, her lips twitching. "Yeah, I told the babysitter I'd be home by eight."

I arched a brow. "Something funny?"

Her mouth formed a tight line. "Nope."

I approached her. "You sure?"

Her gaze flicked to mine, then away. "Uh-huh."

"Okay, then." I turned and headed over to grab the last of our things.

"It's just . . ." Eilish began and then trailed off.

"Yes?"

She shook her head and finally let her giggles flow free. I couldn't help smiling, too, even though I wasn't entirely sure an inconvenient hard-on warranted so much laughter. It was infectious all the same.

She gestured to the retreating group of tourists. "I studied German at school, so I can pick out certain words. One of the women commented about you to her friend."

I smirked. "Oh yeah? What did she say?"

She dabbed the wetness from the corners of her eyes. "Something along the lines of *a bratwurst big enough to feed an army*."

My smirk died. "I wish I hadn't asked."

"Really? I thought men enjoyed compliments about that . . . particular area."

"They do. But armies are generally made up of a bunch of blokes." I arched a brow meaningfully. A loud burst of laughter escaped her, and she clamped her hand over mouth. God, she was too fucking adorable.

She sucked in a breath, finally calming down from her fit of giggles. "You're too much, Bryan Leech."

"That's what the German ladies think anyway," I deadpanned, my smirk returning.

Eilish burst into laughter all over again.

TWENTY-ONE
EILISH

@JoseyInHeels to @ECassChoosesPikachu: Pick up pick up pick up!! I'M LITERALLY DYEING!!
@ECassChoosesPikachu to @JoseyInHeels: What are you dyeing? Your hair? What color?
@JoseyInHeels to @ECassChoosesPikachu: ... really? That's what I get? I'm desperate for info and you joke about my grahmer.
@ECassChoosesPikachu to @JoseyInHeels: Grammar is no joke, but "grahmer" is. ;-)

I didn't exactly regret what we'd done on the boat. Regret wasn't the right word.

I . . . worried about it.

As Bryan drove me home and the streets leading to my apartment loomed before me, reality settled heavy on my shoulders.

We'd had sex. On the boat. *Before* the date. We still hadn't talked about what it meant. We hadn't even made additional plans after tonight.

Unable to draw a complete breath, I clenched my hands together on my lap, my thighs flexing with the memory of what we'd done. Though I didn't have regret, I was disappointed in myself.

The fact of the matter was, I didn't recognize myself with him. His body made me reckless, thoughtless, irresponsible.

That's not true. It's him. It's all of him. I'd happily have sex with him again. Right now. On a boat. Or on a train. Or in the rain.

Man, I really need to read something other than Dr. Seuss.

Trivializing my desire for this man by relegating it to *just his body* was an oversimplification. His voice, a soft compliment, a look, the movement of his hands, a twinkle in his eye, anything he gave me made my nipples hard, my breath short.

That couldn't be normal.

Worst of all, he wasn't some bloke I could test the waters with and move on from should things not work out. This was Patrick's father. For better or for worse, we were stuck with each other for the next thirteen years at least. And if things didn't work out between us, then things might get ugly.

"What's wrong?" Bryan covered my hand with his. I'd been twisting my fingers.

I looked at him and then away, giving him a tight smile. "Nothing is wrong."

I wasn't ready to talk about it, not yet. I needed to think, decide if it was something to worry about at all. Maybe this was great. Maybe I was being silly.

Or maybe this is the big mistake. Because this time, when Bryan leaves, it really will wreck me.

I tried to swallow but couldn't, so I forced to clear my throat against the sudden tightness. His eyes were on me, I felt them on my profile so I tried to relax, deciding I could dwell on this later. No reason to ruin the evening by over-thinking it.

Bryan parked and came around to offer his hand. I took it and we walked to the gate together, our fingers linked.

He was still stealing glances at me, so I decided to redirect our conversation by asking, "Did you send me the picture? Of us on the beach?"

"No, not yet. I want to add one of those Snapchat filters to it first, with the crown of flowers."

I laughed. I loved how easily he could make me laugh. "Fancy a crown, do you?"

He nodded, grinning and standing straighter as we reached my front door. "I think I deserve one, to be honest."

"Do you? What are you the king of then?"

He pulled me to a stop just to the side of the door and guided my back against the wall. Dipping his head to my neck he whispered, "Your body."

I widened my eyes at his arrogance, but then shivered as he tongued my ear. Instinctively, my head fell back as I offered him my neck.

"Send the sitter home, love." He placed a biting kiss just under my jaw, a calloused hand slipping into my leggings and grabbing my backside. He groaned, squeezing me. "You're not wearing any underwear."

"I know. You took them."

Pressing his hard body more insistently to mine, I felt the length of his erection press against my belly. My breathing quickened.

"I'll stay the night," he said, his hand in my leggings sliding around to the front. "I'll make you come."

The sound of my neighbor's door opening hit me like a bucket of ice water. I yanked his hand from my pants and pushed him away. He gazed down at me, rocking back on his heels, his eyes equal parts hot and amused.

I turned, frantically searching for my keys, and lifted my head to make eye contact with Mrs. Francis, the very nice elderly woman from next door. Whenever she saw me she told me she would pray that I found a husband like her Timothy. I'd tried telling her I didn't need a husband and she'd patted my hand, smiling at me like I was a simpleton.

"Hi, Mrs. Francis," I called, my hands shaking and my voice unsteady as I tried to unlock my door.

"Oh. Hullo there, Eilish. And who are you?"

"Bryan Leech, ma'am." Bryan gave her a friendly wave.

"My goodness, you're very tall, aren't you?"

"Everyone says so," Bryan replied evenly, reminding me of Josey's bout of verbal nonsense. I grimaced just as I fit the key into the lock.

"Are you to be Eilish's husband?"

I glanced at my neighbor and shook my head. "No, Mrs. Francis. Like I told you, I don't need a husband."

"Oh. I must be muddled, because I'm sure your son told me you were getting married."

Frowning, I slid my eyes to Bryan. I'm sure my look of confusion mirrored his.

"Well, good night, Mrs. Francis." I opened my door, giving her a tight smile and stepping into the apartment, Bryan trailing after me.

He closed the door and we traded bemused stares.

"What was that about?" Searching my eyes, he smiled. But there was something off about it.

"I have no idea." I dropped my keys in my bag. "She's always going on about me needing a husband. Maybe the talk confused Patrick."

"We should ask him." There was an odd edge to his voice that had me standing a little straighter.

"Sure." I shrugged. "He's not in bed yet, should be having a bath. Let me go relieve Becky."

Bryan swallowed, not quite frowning. "I'll go check in on him."

"Sounds good." I pulled out the cash I'd withdrawn to pay the sitter and counted it to make sure it was all there.

Bryan put his hand over mine. "Let me pay her."

"What? No." I shook off his hand, giving him a sidelong look. "I took this cash out specifically to pay her, and I hate carrying it around."

Bryan's not quite frown became a true frown, yet he nodded, stepping away. "I'll go check on Patrick."

"Okay." I tried to look unconcerned, normal, but didn't quite succeed. The way he was acting, the whole evening, how he'd responded to Mrs. Francis's bizarre pronouncement had me in a tangle of knots.

His gaze moved over my face once more, as though he were searching for something specific, and then he turned for the bathroom. As soon as he was out of sight, I released a quiet breath and leaned against the table, my eyes staring unseeingly at the carpet as I recounted the evening's events.

He'd been acting oddly on the deck, too, after I confessed my crush to him. Or maybe it was after we'd had sex. Maybe *he* was regretting what had happened.

But I didn't think so. No.

If he regretted our time on the boat, then he wouldn't have been grabbing my arse outside and asking to spend the night.

My phone rang, so I pulled it out of my bag and glanced at the screen. It was Josey, so I sent it to voicemail, making a mental note to call her in the morning. Bryan was absolutely *not* spending the night. I needed some time to think, and time with Bryan was not time spent thinking.

At least it wasn't time spent thinking with my brain.

I checked in with Becky and paid her, ignoring the ringing of my phone as I walked her to the door. She was a nice girl of sixteen who lived in our building. I liked her because she was even-tempered and responsible. Patrick liked her because she was pretty and let him have ice cream.

Boys.

After she left, I checked my phone, saw it was Josey again, and crossed to the kitchen, still pushing my worry about the evening's happenings to the back of my mind. Ensuring that Becky had done all the dishes and put the food away, I turned off the light and walked toward the bathroom, again ignoring my phone.

Forks and crackers, Josey. Keep your knickers on!

I shouldn't have told her about the date with Bryan. She wasn't going to stop calling until I checked in and told her about the evening. I had no plans to tell her any of the details; I'd sort through my feelings in my own time.

Bryan was just helping Patrick out of the bath and wrapping him in a towel as I arrived. "Can Bryan spend the night?" was the first thing Patrick said upon seeing me.

My mouth dropped open and my eyes darted to Bryan. He looked just as shocked as me.

"I-I . . ." Bryan stuttered, eventually recovering, looking wide-eyed and innocent. "I don't know where he got the idea."

"Don't you?" I narrowed my gaze on him, not liking that he might use Patrick this way.

But then Bryan huffed an uncomfortable sounding laugh and shook his head firmly. "No. I don't. I swear."

Seeing he was telling the truth, I moved my attention back to Patrick and his hopeful face.

"He can sleep in my bed, and I can sleep in my dinosaur." His dinosaur being his sleeping bag shaped like a T-Rex.

"I'm sorry, honey. But Bryan can't spend the night. He has chores to do in the morning, just like us. But he'll see you in the afternoon." Bryan's eyes bore into me as I said this. I felt the intensity of them even though I wasn't looking at him.

"I understand." Patrick nodded, looking glum but resigned, then to Bryan he said, "Promise you'll come over as soon as you're done with your chores?"

"Absolutely." Bryan ruffled his damp hair.

"And we'll play football?"

"Sure."

"And build a blanket fort?"

"Hey!" I cut in, laughing despite my swirling uncertainty of emotions.

"And have ice cream?" Patrick pushed, ignoring me, speaking solely to Bryan.

Bryan glanced at me and then back to Patrick, choosing his words very carefully, "It depends on what your mam says about the ice cream."

Patrick slumped a little and nodded.

But then Bryan loud whispered, "But definitely yes to the blanket fort."

I shook my head. "Go get your pajamas on, I'll be right in," Patrick's smile was huge as he quickly walked out of the bathroom, past me as though he wanted to leave before I could contradict the older man's promise.

Turning my gaze to Bryan, I crossed my arms over my chest as we swapped stares. A smile lingered behind his eyes but I knew Patrick's antics were the reason. Beyond that, I couldn't tell what he was thinking.

"I'll see you tomorrow?" he asked, again his gaze moving over me searchingly, like he was also having trouble reading me.

I was about to suggest that he stay for a short while after Patrick went to sleep so we could talk about it, but then my phone rang again. I huffed, lifting my eyes to the ceiling.

"Who is that?" Bryan asked, a note of irritation in his tone. "Your mobile's been ringing constantly since we got home."

"I know." I turned for the living room and the offensive phone, planning to place it on silent. "Sorry. It's Josey."

"Josey?"

"That's right. She's driving me nuts." Reaching the phone, I switched it to vibrate and shoved it in my purse.

"Why is she calling?"

I turned back to Bryan, not quite able to meet his eyes as I explained, "I made the mistake of telling her we—you and I—were going on a date."

Bryan was quiet for a moment and I felt a blush rise to my cheeks, embarrassed for reasons I didn't understand.

When I finally found the courage to look at him, he was glaring at the wall behind me, and I didn't like the set of his jaw.

"Bryan?"

"I should go." He nodded at his own assertion, his eyes flickering over me, his smile not reaching them as he strolled toward me and placed a light kiss on my cheek. "Tell Patrick I'll see him tomorrow, yeah?"

"Yeah. Sure," I said, a sinking sensation in my stomach had me wrapping my arms around my torso.

Bryan paused, looking down at me distractedly. But then after a moment, his gaze warmed and his smile became true.

"I had a great time tonight," he whispered, pulling my hand from my body and tangling our fingers together. He bent forward to brush a sensual kiss over my mouth, hot and soft.

I felt myself sway toward him, melt under his touch.

"Me, too," I whispered when he drew away.

"I know," he said, wagging his eyebrows.

And, despite everything—my uncertainties, my worries, my fears—that made me laugh.

"You're wicked."

"The wickedest," he agreed, pulling the neck of my top to one side and peeking down my shirt.

I smacked his hand away, still laughing. "Go. Get out of here, pervert."

"Fine. I'll leave." He held his hands up as though surrendering. But then he pointed at me as he backed away toward the door. "But you should know, I'm only pervy for you."

* * *

Bryan did come over on Saturday and we did build a blanket fort. And then the three of us ate ice cream inside it.

But I caught him giving me strange looks. He'd stare at me, frowning, as though concentrating or working through a problem.

He left after dinner, making an excuse about having work to do around his apartment despite my invitation for him to stay and watch a movie with us. And when he left, he gave me a light peck on the cheek.

A peck. On the cheek. Nearly twenty-four hours ago, he'd had his hand in my pants, begging to stay the night.

His behavior since had continued to be unsettling.

At work he was very polite, but distant. And then he was all friendly flirtation when we were at my apartment. He hadn't asked me on another date, but he came over almost every night to see Patrick.

I wondered if it was the upcoming match that had him acting so strangely. It was the first of the season and everyone seemed to be a little more on edge, talking a little louder, pushing themselves harder.

With these thoughts plaguing and distracting me, I wasn't paying attention to my surroundings. So when I was walking out of the locker room after an urgent session with Daly two hours before the big match, a hand reached out and grabbed me by the wrist, catching me completely off guard. The mysterious hand tugged me firmly behind the wall leading to the showers.

I stumbled, colliding ungracefully into a familiar chest. Bryan's rumbly chuckle met my ears. "Hello, love. Fancy meeting you here."

I glanced up at him, becoming aware of several things all at the same time.

One: he hadn't shaved this morning and it made him devilishly handsome.

Two: his hand had released mine and he was palming and grabbing my arse.

Three: he was wearing just a towel.

"Bryan!"

"Were you expecting someone else? Maybe Alice from the front office?" He grinned wolfishly, then lowered his lips to my neck and squeezed my backside.

"What are you doing?" I whispered harshly. "Daly and Moore are in the locker room. They'll hear us."

"Not if we're really quiet." He grabbed my hand and moved it to the front of his towel. "Can you be quiet?"

Instinctively, I gripped his cock through the fabric, my breathing coming ragged. He felt so good.

And he would feel even better if I just gave in.

Give in!

"Wait," I breathed, shaking my head for some sobriety from my lust. "We shouldn't do this here."

Bryan's reputation would survive a tryst in the locker room, but mine would not. I already had Connors making comments about me *spreading my legs* for players.

"Fine." He rocked his hips forward, pressing himself into my hand. "Where should we go? The showers?"

"I don't know," I said weakly, biting my lip as an image of us taking this to the showers floated through my mind.

God, yes!

Damn.

Damn damn damn.

"Bryan, please," I whimpered, because he'd bent lower, nuzzling my breasts and biting my nipple through the fabric of my long sleeved polo.

"Anything you want." His voice was a rumble, thick with promise. "I need you, I need the feel of you. I miss your taste." His hands delved into my pants, his fingers finding my clit. I was already aching and wet.

FORKS!

"Please," I mewled, tilting my hips mindlessly, the back of my head falling to the wall. This was so wrong. We were at work. He had a match in less than two hours. Why did he always make me so mindless? So thoughtless?

"I love the sounds you make when I touch you." He kissed my eyelids, separating my folds, rubbing my slick center. "I love how you feel."

My breath hitched, and I rubbed him through the towel. He bucked against my hand.

"I love how you touch me," he growled, then softer added, "I love how you look at me. I love how brilliant, strong, and brave you are." His movements slowed and he shifted his hand, caressing my hip as he nipped my jaw.

And then he held very still.

I blinked open my eyes, staring at him in question. It took a moment for the haze of desire to recede, but when it did his stare was intent. Had I done something wrong? How I wish I understood all his looks. His look confused me. He confused me. One minute he was insatiable, and the next a dividing wall.

"I love you."

I could only blink at him, at his fierce gaze and words, dumbfounded.

"You . . . ?"

His eyes dropped to my lips. "I'm in love with you."

TWENTY-TWO
EILISH

@ECassChoosesPikachu: Mirror, mirror on the wall . . .
@THEBryanLeech to @ECassChoosesPikachu: You are. Always.

"Wait. Wait a minute. Just. Wait." I was out of breath.
I couldn't think.
My eyes lost focus.
It's too soon.
"It's too soon," he said, bringing my attention back to him, reading my thoughts. "But it's true. You're perfection."
"No. I'm not."
"You are." He grinned, charming me. "You are noble and genuine and—I feel like I need to be honest here—so goddamn sexy I can't think straight."
I shook my head. "Bryan—"
"Eilish, listen to me." He gripped my face, holding it between his palms. "I'm in love with you. And it's a relief to say it. I've been trying to keep my distance, not scare you, not push you. But I have to tell you. I love you. I've never said it to another person before, and I can't imagine saying it to anyone else."
All the breath left my lungs and I leaned heavily against the wall behind me. My eyes and nose stung, but I was in no danger of crying.
I just felt . . . blindsided.
And scared.

We stared at each other, but his stare was expectant. I knew what he wanted me to say, but I couldn't.

I can't. Not yet. Not yet.

Silence pressed around us as I struggled. He watched me, the expectation in his eyes cooling, growing remote, until finally he released me and stepped back.

My heart twisted, my lungs ached.

I had to say something. So I did.

"I used to stutter."

Bryan's eyebrows rose slowly. "What?"

"I used to have a stutter." His gaze flickered over me and I shrugged, a small, helpless smile on my lips as I explained, "It used to drive my mother crazy. She told me not to speak—at all—because it irritated her so much."

"I'm sorry." His features softened a little, and I straightened my back. I didn't want him to feel sorry for me. That wasn't the point of the story.

"I'm not."

He blinked once and frowned, obviously confused.

"Don't get me wrong. I know my mother is despicable, and I don't condone her behavior. I would never treat Patrick like that. I felt sad about it, but mostly I felt frustrated. And then determined."

"Determined to speak without a stutter." He was openly studying me now, like he was trying to understand this odd alteration in conversation and how it related to his confession.

"Kind of. Yes. I wanted to speak without a stutter." I glanced over my shoulder at the sound of voices behind me, beyond the curtain in the locker room. Lowering my voice, I returned my attention to him and rushed to explain, "But having the speech impediment and overcoming it is something I wouldn't trade for anything in the world. It taught me how to work hard for what I want, to stay the course, to define goals and stick to them."

Bryan's brow cleared as I spoke and his mouth hitched to the side. "So I have your stutter to thank for your extreme stubbornness?"

I laughed lightly, liking this, talking to him this way, hoping he would understand. "I suppose you do. But that's not all."

"There's more?"

"Yes. There's more." I hesitated, studying him.

His eyes were jade green today, and he was looking at me like I'd invented rugby and cake.

He loves you.

I braced myself, because what I needed to tell him next might diminish his opinion or change his mind. We had limited time to talk and the clock was running out.

"Don't keep me in suspense," he prompted, clearly interested in where I was leading this conversation.

"I wasn't a nice person," I blurted.

His eyebrows jumped. "Excuse me?"

I swallowed an unexpected dryness in my throat. "I found it was easier to speak without a stutter when I was being sardonic and insincere. Being genuine, being . . . vulnerable, made it worse. So I grew up making jokes and being snarky."

Bryan's gaze searched mine. "That doesn't make you a bad person."

"You don't know what I was like as a teenager. I wasn't nice. And when other kids made fun of me for the way I spoke, I never forgave them."

"You were also a kid." Bryan gave me a funny look, like I was crazy.

"I was, but I never forgave them. Even when the teasing stopped and we weren't kids anymore, I held a grudge."

"What are you saying? That your grudge extended to revenge?"

I shook my head. "No. Nothing like that, not really. I just—" I tilted my head back and forth, trying to find the right words, keenly aware that he was still in a towel and needed to get ready for the match. "I was derisive, sarcastic, mean. Bitchy. But it wasn't because I wanted revenge, I couldn't bring myself to be sincere with people who'd hurt me."

He blinked at that, his expression softening further. His affection hadn't waned. If anything, his gaze warmed.

"You don't trust easily." His voice was low, not quite a whisper, and he said the words as though they'd just occurred to him.

"No. I don't." I tried to smile, but I couldn't. I needed him to understand why I couldn't return his love. Not yet. I wasn't there yet. I needed time, free from the murkiness of my desire for him. Because I desired him so completely I was suffocating with it.

As we continued to stare at each other, I thought I saw something like comprehension pass over his features. I hoped he understood that my inability to say the words wasn't him; *he* wasn't the problem.

I'm the problem.

And we're out of time.

"Listen," I reached out, squeezing his arm, needing to touch him. "You need to get ready. Can we talk about this after the match?"

"Of course," he nodded thoughtfully, adding, "It's too bad you didn't make an exception for your mother."

"What?" I frowned at him. "You think I should trust her?"

"No. Not at all. I was talking about revenge. You should make an exception and use your sarcasm superpowers to take revenge on your mother."

I chuckled lightly. "I guess I did take small revenges on my mother."

"What? Don't hold out on me. What did you do?"

Pleased he was joking, I admitted, "When she praised me for *finally* speaking so well, I made a point to discuss topics she found distasteful with my perfect diction."

He grinned, this news apparently tremendously agreeable. "Like what?"

"Everything, from describing the worst-case scenario for wound sepsis in great detail—"

"That's disgusting."

"—to using the word 'salivate' during Sunday brunch. She hates that word or anything having to do with bodily fluids, so I try to speak about them in front of her as much as possible. As soon as my mother remarked on how nice a voice I had when I wasn't butchering words, I made it a point to be as politely offensive as possible."

"Good for you." He smiled, looking proud. But then something dark flashed behind his eyes, a secret knowledge of some sort. "She certainly deserves it, and much worse."

* * *

This would be the first time I'd seen Bryan play in over five years.

Actually, that's not true. I'd seen him scrimmage over the last few months, in practice and drills, but this was the first match I would watch. Avoiding rugby in the States wasn't difficult, most of the country doesn't know much about it, can't tell the difference between league and union rules.

"Oh, Christ." Connors winced from his spot on the bench next to me. We were on call and on the sidelines, ready to jump into action should we be needed. "That looked painful."

Ronan Fitzpatrick had just gotten trampled in a ruck, and I tensed in readiness. But the play moved on and he stood, running back into the fray once the giant huddle dispersed. I noted he was sporting blood over one eye, and he was opening and closing his right hand. Someone must've stepped on it.

"Say what you will," Connors said as he gnawed on his thumbnail, his eyes wide as he followed the action of the game, "but these blokes are tough bastards."

I didn't respond.

Since calling my coworker out on his behavior last Friday, we'd reached an uneasy truce. I was using the therapy room for sessions, pushing his mess over to his side, and wiping down the tables with disinfectant every morning, afternoon, and evening. As well, I ensured the floors and standing mats were cleaned daily, the supplies restocked, and the trash removed every night.

But I still charted in the office on the admin floor.

As the match progressed, I became aware of twisting knots in my stomach and had to stand and pace, finding it difficult to keep my eyes on the match. Bryan was playing brilliantly, but witnessing the brutality up close, hearing the grunts, the crunch of bone against bone, made me cringe. Each time he took a tackle, each time he shouldered a ruck, I worried my lip. Eventually, I drew blood.

At the end of the first forty-minute half, I was relieved when Coach Brian had me stay back in the locker room to attend to Daly. Poor bloke would be out for the remainder of the match with an ACL injury.

"Is it bad?" he asked, bracing for bad news.

I shook my head. "I don't think so. You have full range of motion without pain. It's a strain. We'll do a full set of X-rays, and you'll need extra therapy this week."

"Oh, that doesn't sound so bad." Daly winked at me, his eyebrows bouncing once.

But then all cheerfulness leached out of his expression as he caught sight of something over my shoulder. I turned, spotting Bryan with an ear turned toward the offensive coordinator, giving Daly a look meant to incinerate.

He moved his eyes to me meaningfully and then back to his teammate, his jaw working.

Meanwhile, I slid my teeth to the side and tried not to roll my eyes.

Too much testosterone. I'd seen the fellas hyped on its effect before—after they'd had a particularly rough practice—but never like this. The locker room reeked of it—of the violence of sport, of winning and losing and testing limits. Of giving and taking punches.

Boys.

I spent the second half with Daly, taking him through gentle exercises, icing, and rubbing down his legs. We watched the remainder of the match on a TV mounted to the wall. Ireland won. It wasn't even close. But still, when the last minute drew to a close, I could see Daly's features relax.

Soon the room was full of players and reporters, coaches and support staff. I was tasked with administering massages, applying stitch strips to cuts, and disinfecting wounds. Everyone was high on victory, the room vibrated with celebratory male energy. Their eyes were a little wild, looking at me like untamed marauders instead of professional athletes. No one seemed to mind their abrasions or bruises. Quite the opposite.

As an example, Ronan had a black eye, but he seemed pleased as punch about it.

"Isn't it painful?" I asked, handing over an icepack.

"It's not bad." He shrugged, then winced as the pack made contact with his swollen brow. "I'm getting too old for this shite, but it'll all be worth it when my Annie gets hold of me."

I grinned at this. "She'll take good care of you?"

"The best." His grin turned playful, happy, and I laughed at him.

The crowd thinned. Reporters, happy with their stories, departed. Some players hit the showers, others left without cleaning up. Eventually, near midnight, it was Bryan's turn. He sat on the physio table in the locker room, a hungry, unsmiling glare trained on me. My skin buzzed at his nearness, at the raw intensity of his gaze. I felt a little intoxicated by both.

"Hey," I said quietly, my own gaze moving over him. His knuckles were split on one hand and a nasty bruise was forming on the right side of his jaw. Other than that, and being covered in dirt and sweat, he was perfect.

I cleared my throat, my senses coming alive under his perusal. His silence, paired with the concentration of his stare, agitated me, made my hands shake.

"What's wrong?" I whispered, using a cool disinfecting compress to remove the grime from the back of his fingers.

"Meet me in the therapy room."

I lifted my eyes from his hand, frowning at him. "Are you hurt?"

He shook his head. "Meet me when you're finished."

Bryan gripped my wrist, turned it toward him, and placed an open-mouthed kiss on the skin. His tongue traced a light circle over my veins, and then he stood, forcing me to back up. His height dwarfed me, his powerful body and rugged features would have been intimidating if I didn't know better.

Actually, no.

Tonight, he was intimidating.

"Ten minutes," he whispered darkly, stepping forward, crowding me, and brushing his chest against mine as he turned and left.

I leaned heavily against the counter at my back, chasing my breath.

"I think we're done." Coach Brian's voice met my ears, pulling my attention back to the room and reminding me that Bryan and I were not the only two people in the world. "Why don't you go home and get some sleep? Great job tonight."

I nodded dumbly, giving my boss a small smile. "I'll just—I'll just grab my things."

Leaving the locker room, I glanced behind me, ensuring the hall was clear of spectators, then hurried to the physio room. Once there, I knocked gently, again looking over my shoulder. Before I could speak or try the knob, the door opened and a hand reached out, pulling me inside.

And then my back was against the closed door, his hands were everywhere, and his mouth was moving over mine. His kiss was hungry, punishing, demanding, and my head swam with the feel of him. He smelled of clean earth and sweat, his skin still slick with it.

Needing to breathe, I turned my head to the side, gasping, "Bryan . . ."

Saying nothing, he picked me up, his hands on my arse, encouraging my legs to wrap around his torso, and his mouth bit and sucked my neck. I was so turned on, ready for him. *How does he do this?*

He carried me to the physio table and dropped me in an inelegant, hurried movement. His fingers were in my pants, pulling them down my legs without my assistance, my knickers and tennis shoes, too. Then he bent, his mouth hungry, biting my breast.

A sharp cry of pleasure and pain slipped past my lips and I arched, offering myself more fully.

Before I could comprehend his intent, Bryan was kneeling on the mat between my legs, widening my thighs, tonguing my slit. I gasped, leaning back and catching myself on the edge of the table, movement behind him snagging my attention.

The mirror.

I saw the reflection, our reflection. Bryan kneeling before me, his head bent between my legs, his arms wrapped around me. He was still fully dressed in his uniform, the only items he'd removed were his shoes and socks. And I saw myself, naked, spread open, my mouth parted in surprise, a flush high on my cheeks.

He lifted his hand, palming and squeezing my breast, pinching and twisting my nipple between his thumb and finger, forcing my attention to his eyes. He was studying me, my face, and I watched as he tongued my clit. He wanted my eyes on him, on what he was doing. I moaned. Trembled.

Heat spread up my neck to the base of my skull, but I couldn't help it. My attention was drawn back to our reflection. I witnessed him lift his head, turning over his shoulder, asking, "What are you looking . . . ?"

Our eyes met in the mirror. Understanding dawned. He smirked.

"Right," he said, standing, taking my mouth with a searing kiss before separating long enough to whip off his shirt and shorts.

Again, my betraying eyes flickered to the mirror where his stunning backside was on full display. His back was muscled, his shoulders wide, his waist tapered to his hips ending at two perfectly formed orbs of grade-A man-arse.

A shallow breath escaped me as I consumed him with my eyes. I wanted to touch him, but he had different plans.

Kissing me, he wrapped his arms around my waist and lifted me off the table, carrying me toward the mirror. Gently—but firmly—he lowered me to my knees, facing my reflection.

"Bend over," he demand-whispered in my ear from behind and pressed me forward until I was on all fours. The friction of his chest hair against my back, his hot breath falling on my neck, and the growly quality in his voice sent shivers racing over my skin. He spread my knees apart with one of his.

"What are you doing?" I asked breathlessly, moving as instructed and watching him in the mirror with wide eyes.

"Let's give ourselves a show." I stared at his reflection as he rose behind me, his dark hand on my waist, his eyes on my arse, dirt under his fingernails, blood on his knuckles.

I was so clean and smooth. He was not. He was bloodied and bruised, sweaty and stained. He hadn't shaved.

Leaning forward over my back, he bit my neck where it met my spine then worked his way down, biting and kissing until he reached my arse. Then he took a bite of that, too. Sending spikes of sensation along my nerve endings, his eyes on my skin, his fingers digging into my hips as he nudged my entrance with the head of his dick. I gasped, watching him, watching us.

With one swift movement he filled me, and I instinctively pressed back, wanting more. He groaned, his eyes finding mine in the mirror.

"Fuck," he gasped, his gaze blazing, lowering to my lips then breasts, greedily devouring the sight of me on all fours. His stare was hazy, dark and determined, wild and raw.

I tilted my hips, rolling them as he entered me, his thighs slap, slap, slapping against my arse. He held my hips firmly in place, even so, my body jolted with his movements, which were just shy of painful. Sighs of pleasure escaped my lips. I moaned, I begged, my breath hitching. God, it was too much seeing us together, watching him watch me.

Abruptly, he wrapped his arm around my waist and straightened me, sitting on his heels as I sat back, straddled his lap, closing my eyes as my head fell to his shoulder.

"Open your eyes," he commanded.

Doing as instructed, I forced my head up and our gazes tangled in the mirror. His was fierce, dark, and insatiably wild.

"Do you like watching?" the question asked through gritted teeth. "Do you like watching me fuck you?"

I could only nod, my throat dry, too overwhelmed by the sights, sensations, and sounds of our mating.

My gaze drifted lower, his dirty hands possessively kneading my breasts and leaving smudges, the scuff of his beard sandpaper against my shoulder. I rolled my pelvis, entranced by the sight of his cock sliding in and out of my pussy.

"Touch yourself," he growled, biting my ear, holding me upright. "And bounce for me."

So I did. I spread my folds and rubbed my middle finger around my clit, finding myself wet and swollen, and so incredibly sensitive to my touch. I bounced on his lap, increasing our tempo as a shudder wracked his perfect, strong body. I moaned, my other hand covering his where he rolled my nipple between his fingers.

"You're a goddess," he exhaled, his legs flexing beneath my thighs as he thrust upward to meet me.

"Bryan, I can't—I'm so close."

"Pinch your clit." His voice was a dominating growl, as though he were barely controlling some base instinct. "Hard."

I did and I threw my head back, seeing stars as my climax overtook me, paralyzed me, wound its threads of ecstasy through my veins and nerves and bones. His hands slid to my hips, lifting me up and down over his cock, using my body, and I let him, too lost to my pleasure to help. As he surged upward a low, guttural groan erupted from him as he came.

"Fuck, fuck, fuck," he chanted, breathed. His jaw was clenched, his fingers dug into my flesh.

I couldn't catch my breath, my lungs strained, my body limp, useless. His chest rose and fell against my back as he held me, his rough exhales hot along my skin.

"God, Eilish. That was incredible. You're incredible." He gripped my chin, turning my head over my shoulder to capture my mouth with a deep, savoring kiss. He sipped me, sucked on my lips, caught my tongue with his teeth. "I love you."

I stared at him, slowly sobering, feeling him everywhere: his arms around me, his body behind and beneath me, and he was still inside me.

It wasn't enough. I wanted—

I want . . .

I didn't even know. We'd just had crazy, dirty, voyeuristic sex, and I loved it. My body felt used and sore and spent in the best way.

But still, it wasn't enough.

Bryan's brow furrowed as he stared at me. His eyes grew searching. Turning me in his arms so he could hold me against him, he tugged on my hair to keep me from hiding my face.

"Hey. Are you okay? Did I cross a line?"

"No, God no. That was wonderful. You're wonderful. I'm just—"

I didn't know how to finish, how to answer. I wanted him forever. I never wanted to let him go. But I doubted myself, my feelings, the desperation of my want.

Was this love? *Or was this lust?*

"What's wrong? And don't say nothing."

I shook my head, thoughts and words spilling from my lips. "It's too soon, Bryan. This is too soon. I feel like we're m-m-moving too f-f-fast and I d-d-don't—I want us t-t-to—"

"Shh." He pressed me to his chest, squeezing me tighter. "I'm sorry. I didn't mean to rush you into something you're not ready for."

"You didn't." I shook my head vehemently, my nails digging into his back. "Not at all. I wanted it. I want you. But I feel like I don't recognize myself. For Christ's sake, Bryan, we're at work. This is where we work. It's completely irresponsible."

"And hot?"

I exhaled a short laugh, squeezing my eyes shut. "Yes. And hot."

He petted my hair, his other hand rubbing my lower back in a soothing motion. We sat like that, him on the floor, me on his lap, and he cradled me, giving me soft kisses and tender touches.

I felt cherished, sated. I felt amazing.

But how long will it last?

He's only known you for a few months. How can he possibly love you?

He didn't know what I was passionate about. He didn't know the true extent of my family's abhorrence toward my choice to keep Patrick, and how that had burnt layers off my thick skin of self-preservation. He didn't know of my need to sit quietly at the end of each day to regroup, my love for both art and open-source coding projects. He didn't know that I was a data nerd, that I spent my free time reading peer-reviewed medical journals for best practices and new techniques.

He doesn't know me.

Whereas I'd known of him for years. I knew all about the carelessness in which he threw people away—when he wasn't sober. I knew of his darkness, his playboy ways.

He's not that person anymore. Trust him!

At length, I felt his chest rise and fall, and then he said, "You want to take things slow."

It wasn't a question.

I nodded. "Yes."

He swallowed, and I heard an edge of anxiety in his voice as he asked, "What does that mean, exactly?"

TWENTY-THREE
BRYAN

@THEBryanLeech: Just spent five hours organizing my non-perishables in alphabetical order by country of origin #killinit
@ECassChoosesPikachu to @THEBryanLeech: Oooh! Tell me more.
@WillthebrickhouseMoore to @THEBryanLeech @ECassChoosesPikachu: When you guys want some alone time with the kitchen cabinets give me a heads up and I'll make myself scarce...

No sex.
    No oral play.
No fingering.
No making out.
Fuck my life, but don't fuck my gorgeous girlfriend.
It was worth it.
She was worth it.

One, two, three weeks passed, and Eilish and I stuck to our agreement to take things slow. Over the course of those weeks I had unfettered access to my boy.

My boy.

With each passing day, Patrick felt more and more like mine, claimed more and more of my heart. Not only that, but Eilish felt more like mine, too. I had to hold myself back, the need to touch or claim her in some way was overwhelming. But I was determined to go at her pace.

Even if her pace felt like cruel and unusual punishment. I couldn't stop thinking about all the orgasms I wasn't giving her. But more than that, I couldn't stop missing the moments of intensity when I could look into her eyes while I held her.

When she'd stood by the sink doing dishes, I'd wanted to grab her from behind, lift her skirt, kiss her neck, touch her, and feel her sex pulse around my fingers. Or when she'd bend over to get something from the bottom of the fridge, I couldn't take my eyes off her backside, dirty thoughts invading my mind and pumping through my veins.

And don't even get me started on the times she treated me at the sports complex. Eilish touching any part of my body was a lesson in patience and endurance. My attraction to her was becoming a problem. A distracting problem.

I had two crystal-clear, very recent memories of being with her, worshipping her body, and I almost wished I couldn't remember. Now I knew what we were missing.

So, you could see my predicament.

Though saying that, having a kid around was a good method of prevention. Even if I'd wanted to come up behind Eilish, bend her over the kitchen table and have my wicked way with her, I couldn't when there was a four-year-old hanging about. A four-year-old who was far smarter than he had any right being.

"What were you two doing in there?" Patrick asked one evening after dinner when I was over for a visit. I'd taken advantage of a moment of opportunity and pulled Eilish behind the kitchen door for a quick kiss. About three seconds later, Patrick had peeked his curious little head into the room.

"Nothing," said Eilish as she reached down to ruffle his hair. "Come on. You can play Pokémon on my phone for a while."

"Fine," said Patrick. "But I know you two were kissing."

See? Clever little bugger. Half of me grumbled irritably, the other half was proud as punch.

Fast forward a couple weeks, and I arrived outside Eilish's for another of my scheduled visits. I was parking the car when my phone rang. Sarah's name flashed on the screen. This woman. It was like she had a sixth sense or something.

I knew she was only calling to check up on me, but a feeling of guilt hit me all the same. After all this time, I hadn't made a single move toward getting a paternity test, and she was going to give me hell for it. I sighed and hit "accept." Might as well face the music.

"Hey, Sar-bear, how's it going?" I answered, hoping my playful tone might distract her from tearing me a new one.

"Hi Bryan, I'm good. Been busy with work. Don't call me that again."

I chuckled. "Fine. I'll just call you Sarah the Magnificent then, how does that sound? Though technically, the point of a nickname is to abbreviate rather than to lengthen."

I heard her exhale on a sigh. "Quit trying to butter me up. It won't work."

I mustered my most innocent tone. "What won't work?"

"Lavishing me with charm. I still want to know how things have been with you. Have you made any progress with that thing we discussed before?"

"Some," I hedged.

"None, then."

"No, not none. If thinking about it constitutes progress, then I've made lots."

"Oh Christ, you're fucking her, aren't you?"

How the hell did she—?

"I know you, Bryan," Sarah went on before I could even ask the question. "And I've never quite heard that happy-go-lucky tone you're currently sporting. You're getting some. It's obvious."

"Well, if you must know, I'm not getting any, actually. We decided to slow things down. We're not having sex. Not anymore."

"But you were?" Sarah sounded appalled. "Bloody hell, Bryan. Please tell me you at least took her out on a date first."

Well . . . technically . . .

"Of course I did. What do you take me for?"

"I take you for a rugby-playing horndog; that's what I take you for."

"Hey! That's not fair. I was celibate for two whole years. Cut a fella some slack."

"Yes, and there was a reason for that. The majority of women you used to sleep with were users. They encouraged your addiction because keeping you shitfaced meant they could run around spending your money. Remember Jennifer? Remember Kylie?"

I grit my teeth. "Yes, I remember them, and you seem to love reminding me, but Eilish is nothing like those two. She's a good person, Sarah. She . . ."

I was about to say *she loves me*.

But I didn't.

Because she hadn't said the words.

I'd been battling doubt for weeks, ever since I'd admitted the truth and she'd stared at me blankly in return.

My poor decision-making in the past was something that always haunted me. I could distinctly remember thinking the sun shone out of Jennifer's backside. Kylie's, too. I could remember thinking they'd never set a foot wrong, similar to how I thought of Eilish.

But, no.

Things were different. *She* was different. She was honorable. And I was sober now. I was levelheaded enough to know a genuine person when I saw one and Eilish was as authentic as they came.

"So, you said you two have decided to take things slow," said Sarah. "Was that her decision or yours?"

I thought on that a second, and then answered, "Hers. But mine, too. Well, I agreed with her logic, that is."

"Of course it was hers," Sarah mumbled under her breath like I was thick or something.

I grit my teeth but said nothing, not liking her tone. But she was my sponsor. She'd been there for me through dark times. I owed her a listen.

She blew out a breath. "Look, I'm only trying to play devil's advocate here, but have you ever considered that withholding sex could be her way of stringing you along?"

"Sarah," I growled, warning in my tone.

"Just hear me out. This is all purely hypothetical. So, she lets you have her, gives you a taste of what you've been missing all these years, then pulls the brakes. She knows you've had problems with addiction and she's using it against you, only this time through sex. If she keeps dangling that cherry over your head, she knows you'll do whatever she wants, including accepting Patrick as yours without a paternity test. Next thing you know, you're married with a kid that's not even yours."

That was a laugh. There was no doubt Patrick was mine. "You're letting your imagination run away with you. He's the spitting image of me," I said, at the same time remembering the incident after our first date, when Eilish's neighbor had mentioned Patrick telling her his mummy was going to get married. I hadn't had the chance to question him about it, had tried to brush it off as childish folly.

Now I began to doubt myself, just like I always did.

No.

No, no, no.

Sarah didn't know Eilish like I did. She was seeing all this through a tiny lens. She'd never seen how it was when we were together. She didn't know how *right* it felt.

"You're wrong, Sarah," I told her flatly. "Eilish would never come up with something so convoluted, something so manipulative. If you ever met her in person, you'd know it's true."

There was a long moment of silence on her end of the line, and I thought she was going to argue with me until I was blue in the face. But then all she said was, "Okay."

Okay? That was it?

"If you trust her then I'll trust her," she went on. "You're a grown-up and I guess there comes a point when every sponsor has to let their sponsee make their own choices. Maybe I'm just being overprotective. Maybe you know better than I do."

I felt strange. I'd been trying to get her to accept Eilish all this time, and now that she was relenting it felt like she was giving up on me. I didn't like it, and my confidence wavered.

"Come on, don't be like that."

"I'm not being like anything. Just know that I care about what happens to you. Think about it, Bryan."

With that she hung up and I sat staring at my phone for a long while, a feeling of unease building within me. Finally, I managed to shake it off and emerged from the car.

I knocked on Eilish's door and heard little feet running down the hallway. Bigger feet followed and then she opened the door to greet me, Patrick in front of her.

"Bryan!" he roared and ran forward to throw his arms around my legs. His excitement took me by surprise, and instantly the lingering bad vibes from Sarah's phone call melted away. *He was mine.* In my heart of hearts, I knew it was true. I met Eilish's gaze, and she was shaking her head at our son's antics.

"I made the mistake of letting him have ice cream after lunch about an hour ago. He's been running about like a crazed monkey ever since."

I took his hand and stepped inside. He was practically hopping with energy.

"How about I take him across to the park, and we can throw a ball around for a bit? That'll burn off some of the hyper."

"Yes! Let's go now," Patrick yelled enthusiastically.

Eilish blew out a breath, looking relieved at the suggestion. "That'd be great, actually. It'll give me a chance to put dinner together."

"Take your time," I told her and bent to press a kiss on her cheek. As I pulled away, I caught her eye and found her looking at me strangely, like she was disappointed or frustrated.

But then Patrick exclaimed, "You're kissing again!" breaking the moment, and both Eilish and I started laughing.

"Yep, we are, and now you're getting one, too," I said, lifting him and laying a big smacker on his cheek. He giggled loudly, and I set him back down. Eilish wore a warm expression as she took in the two of us. I felt that same warmth suffuse my chest. It was such a normal, everyday moment, and I couldn't remember the last time I felt so light, like life was full of good things, endless possibilities. Sarah was wrong about Eilish, so fucking wrong.

"We'll be back in half an hour," I said as I took Patrick's hand and led him over the road to the park. I made a quick stop at my car to grab a rugby ball from the trunk.

"I'm cold," said Patrick, and I realized in his excitement he'd forgotten to put on a coat. I didn't want to bother Eilish so I grabbed a clean rugby shirt I had stashed in the car.

"You want to wear this?" I said, holding it up to him.

"Okay," he nodded, completely unaware of the significance. I bent down on one knee and pulled the shirt over his head. The thing was huge on him so I tied it at the end to make it fit better and rolled up the sleeves. It still swam on him but it was the best I could do. Patrick stared up at me with his big, trusting green eyes and emotion smacked me right in the chest. There was something about seeing him in my colors, my number on his back, that had me choking up. Yes, that's right, I was a grown man, and I was welling up at the sight of a little kid wearing my shirt.

"You warmer now?" I asked gruffly, too much love for this boy.

Patrick wriggled around in the shirt for a second, getting comfortable, then said, "Yep."

I smiled so hard my jaw hurt. "Okay, let's go play some rugby."

By the time the half hour was up, both of us were covered in mud and grass stains. I couldn't remember the last time I'd had so much fun. The kid's hyperactivity was infectious. Eilish gaped at us when she opened the door, and held up a hand. "Wait. You both need to take your shoes off. I don't want grass trampled all over the house."

I quickly helped Patrick off with his shoes and then removed my own. Whatever Eilish had made for dinner smelled delicious.

"Is that your shirt he's wearing?" she asked in surprise.

"I wanna play rugby like Bryan and Monkey Sean when I get older," Patrick said.

"He forgot his coat," I answered softly. "I hope it's okay I let him wear it."

"Of course. It's way too big for him, but he looks adorable," Eilish said, reaching down to rub some mud off his face. "He also needs to wash all this mud off. I'll take him into my en-suite and you can use the main bathroom," she went on, plucking a tuft of grass from my hair and winking. I liked her like this, easy-going, flirtatious. She was different when she was at home, definitely a lot more relaxed than at work.

About twenty minutes later, we sat down to eat. Eilish made Spanish omelets, and I devoured everything on my plate. The three of us talked and laughed. It was an unexpected moment of blissful domesticity. I was surprised how much I enjoyed it. Just this.

I looked across the table at Eilish, and she gave me a small smile. Maybe she liked it, too. Me being here with them. I caught her feet between mine under the table, my gaze darkening. She pulled at the collar of her top, like she was too hot all of a sudden. I grinned and continued cradling her legs between mine. She shot me a look that said *quit it*.

I didn't.

By the time we'd all finished eating, I had her truly flustered and was enjoying myself immensely. I loved winding her up. But more than that, our lack of physical interaction was really starting to weigh on me. I didn't *need* sex, not if she wasn't ready, but I felt like I needed to touch her more than I needed to breathe.

She went to settle Patrick in the living room and I made a start on the dishes. I was almost done when she came back in.

"Were you sent from heaven?" she asked, flopping onto a chair as I wiped down the counter.

I shot her a devilish look. "Household chores and orgasms are the way to a woman's heart, right?"

She flushed and I grinned in triumph. I dried my hands with a dish cloth and strode across the room to kneel before her. "Speaking of the latter," I whispered and leaned forward to kiss her neck.

She let out a quiet moan and wriggled in place. "We can't."

"Let me touch you," I pleaded. "Just for a little while."

My hands roamed her thighs, her hips. She trembled. I licked a line from her neck to her earlobe, sucking it into my mouth and loving how she gripped my shoulders in response.

"Bryan," she gasped when I kissed my way to her chin and gave her a little nip with my teeth.

"If you let me, I'd make you come for the entire night. I don't know if you're aware of this, but I have incredible stamina." I spoke low and husky, trying to keep the mood light, and her skin flushed red with desire.

In that moment I thought she might give in, but then her grip on my shoulders tightened, and she pushed me away. She was shaking her head, and I frowned. It had been *weeks* since we'd kissed, really kissed.

"Patrick's in the next room. We really can't do this. I'm sorry," she said, worrying her lip like she was afraid I'd be angry, but I wasn't.

Not really. Just tremendously frustrated and crazy in love with a woman who didn't love me back.

No big deal.

I stood, gritting my teeth, and glanced at the clock, catching sight of the time. I had an evening training session I needed to get to and, honestly, I was relieved for the excuse to leave.

"Don't apologize. You're right, and I need to get going anyway."

"Will we see you this week?" she asked, and seeing the knit of her brow, the plain frustration on her features, my uneasiness actually eased.

I lifted Eilish's hand and pressed a kiss to the inside of her wrist. "Yes. Absolutely. Does tomorrow work?"

Eilish rubbed at her brow. "I'm working all day tomorrow, and Patrick will be at school, but you're welcome to stop by the day after. We could watch a movie and order pizza?"

"Sure, sounds great," I told her and dipped down to give her a quick peck on the lips. "I'll see you then."

I left, already anticipating the next time we'd all be together, but I couldn't seem to master the pressing doubt in the back of my mind.

I loved her. I was in love with her. It had happened so organically, so naturally as I got to know her, but I couldn't help notice that she was constantly pushing me away. We hadn't gone on any more dates since our first and I wondered if, maybe if I took her out and we had a proper chance to talk, *maybe* . .

On the drive my phone rang, pulling me from my frustrated thoughts. I thought it might be Mam calling to catch up. She'd started making an attempt to lower her alcohol intake, but she wasn't sober yet, not by a long shot. Still, she was down from three bottles of wine a night to one, and that was a huge improvement.

I frowned when I saw the number wasn't my mother's, but Eilish's. *Again.* What the hell was she calling for? I hoped like hell I wasn't being summoned to another family brunch. Hitting "accept," I put the phone on speaker.

"Cara, good to hear from you," I lied. "How have you been?"

"Hello, Bryan. I'm quite well. And you?"

"Just dandy."

She cleared her throat. "I thought I'd call since I hear you and Eilish have been spending a lot of time together."

My mouth formed a thin line. Just who, exactly had she been hearing this from? "We've been seeing each other, yes."

"*Dating* is the term I believe they use nowadays."

I frowned at the phone, then at the road, then back at the phone again. Where was she going with this? "That's right. I like your daughter a lot, Mrs. Cassidy."

"And the child? Am I to assume you've accepted him as your own?"

The child? What the fuck was this woman on?

"Cara, not to sound blunt, but what's this phone call about? You can be upfront with me. I don't need empty pleasantries."

There was a long moment of silence and I wondered if I'd offended her. I just didn't see the point of beating around the bush. I might have a decent name thanks to my father, who was rich enough to be considered respectable in Cara Cassidy's eyes, but I was under no illusions that she liked me. I already knew she was aware of my past and found it all distasteful.

"As you wish," she said, recovering. "Now that you are aware you have a son, I was simply wondering what you plan to do about it?"

"*Do* about it?"

My vaguely hostile tone didn't faze her as she continued. "The respectable thing would be to marry my daughter and solidify her position in society. She's gone long enough as a black mark on our name, and even though we can't restore her image completely we can at least salvage some of—"

"Okay, I'm going to stop you right there, Cara. This isn't the nineteenth century, and I'm not going to be manipulated, guilt-tripped, or bullied into marrying your daughter just because you think it will somehow restore her virtue. There's no restoration needed. Eilish is a wonderful person, and she's done an amazing job bringing up our son. You're the only one who can't see it."

Now she laughed. It was a cold, cruel sort of laughter. "I see she has you wrapped around her little finger."

"Excuse me?"

"She had your posters plastered all over her bedroom wall as a teenager, you know. Completely infatuated. I suppose it's no surprise what happened. If I didn't know any better, I'd say she planned all this from the very beginning."

A weird feeling crept over me and I hesitated, unsure what to say next.

She was lying. She had to be. Eilish would never plan something so calculated. She wouldn't. Christ, it was like the phone call with Sarah all over again, only without the person on the other end actually giving a damn about me.

"You've got a sick mind, do you know that?"

"What on earth are you talking about?" asked Cara, like butter wouldn't melt. "I'm only trying to let you know how much Eilish adores you and how she's wanted to marry you since she was a young girl. Now all you have to do is man up and propose. It's really quite simple, Bryan."

"I'm hanging up now," I told her.

"Don't you dare—"

I pressed the "end" button before she could finish her sentence, my gut all twisted up in knots. I wished I'd never answered the call. Doubts crawled all over me, like spiders spinning a web.

Yeah, I'd found the idea of Eilish having a teenage crush on me a little unsettling, but mostly cute. What I didn't find cute was the notion of her planning to bed me, to get pregnant.

This is madness. You love her.

But then, my insecurities took hold, my past mistakes. I'd been wrong about people before and it had cost me not just money, but entire chunks of my life, too. Sarah's warnings rushed back as well, her words a foreboding echo in my mind.

The majority of women you used to sleep with were users. They encouraged your addiction because keeping you shitfaced meant they could run around spending your money. Remember Jennifer? Remember Kylie?

I pulled at my hair, unable to make sense of my thoughts. Did I believe Cara and Sarah, or did I trust the Eilish I knew now, the grown woman as opposed to the teenage girl?

This was nuts. Of course I trusted Eilish.

Then again . . .

I may have trusted her, but could I trust my own judgment? By her own admission, she hadn't been a good person when she was younger. Was that her way of telling me she'd done this on purpose?

How could one phone call send a perfect day spiraling so far down the toilet?

Fucking hell.

Again, I wished I'd never answered that bloody phone call. But I knew what I had to do. Even if I did trust the Eilish I'd come to know, I needed to put this doubt to rest. Set straight everyone who thought they had a say in our relationship so that we could finally be happy together. In the grand scale of things, that's all I really wanted. To be with Eilish, the reserved girl who always surprised me with her humor and sass, the one who snuck a peek at medical journals between washing the dishes and taking care of our son, the one who understood my love of home comforts, who looked into my eyes and seemed to see right into me like no one else ever had.

And in order for us to be together we needed to talk about what really happened five years ago, what she hasn't told me about her life since then, and *maybe* I needed to get the goddamn paternity test, if only to shut up Cara Cassidy and Sarah and anyone else who thought they had a say in our business.

TWENTY-FOUR
EILISH

@ECassChoosesPikachu: What does not kill us merely lowers our defenses for the next shit storm to finish us off.
@SeanCassinova to @ECassChoosesPikachu: I still have my "Free Hugs" sign.

"I don't understand." I moved the cell from my left hand to my right, cradling the phone against my ear. "Sorry, could you repeat that?"

It happened on Tuesday.

Monday came and went without seeing or speaking to Bryan, but that wasn't unusual. Mondays were busy, catching up with the team after the weekend, setting the priorities and schedule for the week leading up to the game.

I'd texted him on Monday evening, just a quick note letting him know I was thinking about him.

EILISH
Missing you today.

BRYAN
Are you free for lunch tomorrow? We should talk.

EILISH
Not tomorrow, we have the roundup. Wednesday?

BRYAN
Wednesday works.

EILISH

> Good. I'll miss you until then.

He hadn't texted back.

I missed him every second of every day we weren't together. I missed how grumpy he became around teenagers at the park and how particular he was about his tea. I missed how books about birds got him excited and how proud he'd looked giving Patrick a kid-sized housecoat and fur lined slippers.

It disconcerted me. We hadn't been physically intimate, yet I still felt out of control, but in a different way. Instead of sex, seeing him was my new drug. Seeing him, talking to him, learning about him, laughing with him, and taking care of him eased the ache, but his light kisses and thoughtless touches had been torture.

Things weren't getting better, they were worse. Much worse.

Maybe you do love him, you loon. Maybe this is love. Maybe you should trust him and yourself.

And then this.

"Certainly," the woman said. "I'm Bryan Leech's solicitor, Ms. Cassidy. I'll be representing his interests in the custody case between you and Mr. Leech."

"The . . . custody case?" My ears were ringing and something had invaded my chest, making it impossible for me to breathe. I rejected these sensations, convinced I was overreacting.

There's a perfectly good explanation for this. She's confused.

"That's right. Do you have representation, Ms. Cassidy? Someone I should be calling about this matter?"

"I still don't understand." I rubbed my forehead because my brain hurt. I couldn't wrap it around this woman's words. "There is no custody case."

"Yes, technically you are correct. Not until you've submitted the child to the court-ordered DNA testing, which is why I'm calling you now. You see . . ." she continued, but I didn't hear her, not really. I caught snippets here and there, something about taking Patrick to a clinic so he could have his cheek swabbed.

"Stop." I straightened in my seat, holding my free hand out in front of me. "No. That's not right. Bryan has Patrick's hair. I gave it to him weeks ago for the test."

"Correct. But, with all due respect, Ms. Cassidy, we have no way to confirm the hair came from the child in question. In order for the child's parentage to be independently established, a new sample must be collected in front of a witness of Mr. Leech's choosing."

"Did he—?" I blurted, then stopped myself, needing a minute to gather my thoughts.

Did he request this? I wanted to ask. And if so, when? Weeks ago?

It must've been weeks ago. Over a month ago, most likely.

"How long ago did Bryan make this request?" I asked evenly, ready to explain to his solicitor that her information was old.

"Monday," she said.

I blinked.

"Monday," I repeated. The ringing in my ears returned as I choked out, "He requested this, this new test, on Monday? As in yesterday?"

"Yes."

"But how did he get a court order so fast?" I asked and thought at the same time. Surely there was some error here. Surely I should be doubting the legitimacy of this woman's claim.

She's a reporter . . . I stiffened at the new theory, a different kind of worry flooding my veins. It was only a matter of time before reporters started sniffing around. I knew this. Once word got out that Bryan had a son, there would be interest from the fans.

"I can share with you that Mr. Leech's father had a hand in aiding the order through the system, but no additional details will be forthcoming." The woman sighed, as though she were losing patience. "May I suggest you find a solicitor, Ms. Cassidy? This process will be greatly expedited if you secure representation."

This last part gave me pause. Why would a reporter push for me to hire a solicitor? *That makes no sense. Shouldn't she be trying to pump me for information?*

She was still talking. "In my experience, it's in the interest of both parties to communicate exclusively through their representative. It greatly increases the likelihood of an amicable agreement."

Amicable agreement?

AMICABLE AGREEMENT?

WHAT THE FUCK?

Staring at my desk, the truth tsunami crashed over me.

Bryan wanted a paternity test. He'd asked his father to rush it through the courts. He wanted a witness present to ensure I didn't try to tamper with the results.

And then, once the results came back . . . *custody case.*

"Oh my God." I covered my mouth with my hand as a sob escaped my lips before I could catch it, tears of panic stinging my eyes.

Bryan *was* going to try to take Patrick from me. This was my every nightmare come true, just like I'd feared, just like I'd told Sean.

Why is he doing this?

What happened to Bryan's profession of love? Had that just been an act?

If so, that meant I was still the same gullible fool I'd been five years ago.

The woman was speaking again but I didn't hear her. I couldn't see. I couldn't think. I felt too much—anger, resolve, anger again, fear, anger a third time—and the feeling of too many emotions at once muted my other senses.

I let the phone drop from my ear, leaving it on my desk as I fumbled to stand. Numbly, I left the physio room, stumbling into the hall and robotically walking to the locker room. He would be there. It was after drills, and he would be with his teammates.

Or he might be with the offensive coordinator, going over notes. Or he might be at home. Or he might be off somewhere with another woman. Who knows?

Clearly I didn't. Clearly I didn't know him.

Propelled by irrational fear, I crossed the threshold, glancing at his locker. It was open. He was there, or at least close by.

"Who you looking for?" Ronan called to me. I glanced at him. He was huddled close to Daly and Malloy, watching something on an iPad, likely game footage.

I moved my mouth but no sound came out. Ronan frowned, his eyes flickering over me with concern.

"Oi, are you okay?" He broke from the huddle, crossing to me and placing a brotherly hand on my shoulder. "Do you need Sean?"

I nodded wordlessly, because I did need Sean. I needed him. I could trust Sean, but no one else.

No one else.

"Daly, page Cassidy. Tell him to hurry." Ronan led me over to a bench and guided me to sit, squatting in front of me and asking gently, "Hey now, do you want to tell me what happened?"

I didn't know how to respond and, as it turns out, I didn't get a chance. Bryan entered the room at just that moment, dressed casually in jeans and a long-sleeved T-shirt, toweling his hair dry.

My eyes snagged on him immediately and my heart leapt.

I love him. The thought burst through my mind, grabbed and seized my heart. For a fraction of a second I rejected my earlier conclusion. I rejected it completely, to the marrow of my bones.

Trust him! He loves you. He would never do that. He would never take Patrick from me. He would never—

But then our gazes locked and he stiffened. The lines around his mouth and between his eyebrows creased with unhappiness and resolve.

And I knew.

Of course you love him. You only love people who hurt you.

Unbidden tears filled my eyes, tears I couldn't manage or control though I made no sound. They ran down my face, rolling—fat and sloppy—to my neck. Through the blur I witnessed Bryan's gaze shutter. His chin came up.

Ronan glanced between us, his forehead wrinkling with confusion. "Would someone tell me what the feck is going on?"

"Why? Why are you doing this?" The question was a ragged croak, my throat was dry, my tongue felt useless.

Bryan swallowed, his eyes moving to the other people in the room as though to remind me we weren't alone, but he said nothing.

A burst of hysterical laughter slipped past my lips and I shook my head, wiping my nose with the back of my hand as I stood and squared my shoulders. Maybe if I didn't love him I would've been able to calm down, think clearly. But the word *betrayal* echoed between my ears with every beat of my heart, driving me mad.

Focusing on my rage as a mother, the insanity that is borne from the desperation for my child, finally gave me back my voice.

"You're not taking him away from me."

"I don't want to take him from you," Bryan countered immediately. His eyes again moved meaningfully to the crowd surrounding us, his tone and expression losing some of its aloofness.

"Then what do you want?" I asked desperately, wanting to trust his frigid assurance, but knowing I couldn't. My madness told me I could never trust another word out of his mouth ever again.

"Just the test."

"Fine," I readily agreed, even though wretched pain sliced straight through my heart.

He didn't trust me. Why else would he want the test? He thought I was lying, that I'd lied to him, that Patrick wasn't his. *He doesn't love me.*

I swallowed with difficulty and forced myself to ask, "And when the results come back, what then?"

"We'll cross that bridge when we come to it," he answered evenly, his eyes never wavering from my face.

I stared at him, my mind racing and panic re-emerging. "You're not taking him," I blurted, repeating the words before I could stop myself. "You will *never* take him from me. He is my son, do you hear me?"

Maybe it was my imagination, or maybe it was really there, but I thought I saw a flicker of emotion pass behind his eyes. Something resembling regret. Or guilt. Or desire. Or respect.

I didn't know. I couldn't read him. I could barely see.

"Let's . . . let's talk about this somewhere else." Bryan took a step toward me, reaching out.

I twisted away, moving quickly out of his reach. "Don't touch me. Don't you dare touch me."

He stopped, his hand dropping to his side as a frown claimed his handsome features. "Eilish . . ."

Tangentially, I heard the door to the locker room open and close. I listened to the quick fall of footsteps, and I sensed someone stand next to me. And I knew that someone was Sean. He didn't touch me, just stood there, at my left and close by, backing me up, showing his support.

I felt stronger just having him there. Knowing I wouldn't have to do this alone made me stronger. I would accept Sean's help. Damn my pride, I would accept his money if it meant keeping my son. I would do anything.

Clearing my throat and hastily wiping the tracks left by my tears, I straightened my spine and shot daggers at Bryan Leech, the man I loved, the man who had betrayed me.

But I wouldn't think about that now.

"If you want to talk to me," I said slowly, quietly, carefully, because I could barely control the fury singing through my veins, "you can talk to my solicitor."

* * *

BRYAN

Talk to me.

BRYAN

Pick up your phone.

BRYAN

You are jumping to the worst possible conclusions and you need to give me a chance to explain what this is all about.

BRYAN

Stop being so goddamn stubborn.

I blocked his number after the fourth text and left work early, then packed some of Patrick's and my things so we could stay with Sean for the week.

Patrick took the DNA test on Wednesday, and I took the entire day off. The witness Bryan had selected was a woman named Sarah. I wondered who she was to Bryan, but I didn't ask. I couldn't look at her without wanting to scream, so I imagined speaking to her might endanger her life.

Afterward, I took Patrick for ice cream and tried to pretend everything was normal. He let me pretend, though I could tell he knew something was up when he offered me the last few bites of his ice cream. And then Patrick had asked about Bryan, breaking my heart into smaller pieces.

God, I'd been so stupid.

Word spread quickly around the office and the team. By the time I returned on Thursday, everyone knew. I couldn't muster enough energy to care. Their stares and whispers didn't bother me. Gossip is trivial compared to a broken heart.

I didn't cry again.

Not when I lay in the dark Tuesday night, staring at the ceiling in the hotel Sean had let for us temporarily, wondering where I went wrong.

Not when I walked into work on Thursday and was informed by Coach Brian that they'd decided to move me to a research position for the time being. I would provide literature support to Connors for the next month, take over all charting, and the older physiotherapist would handle all therapy sessions.

Not when I received the phone call from my newly acquired solicitor—courtesy of Sean—Thursday afternoon informing me that the DNA results had come back as expected. Which meant we would be moving forward with mediation. Bryan, apparently, wanted things settled so a meeting was planned for Friday.

Not when I spotted Bryan walking off the lift on the admin floor. As soon as I saw him, I turned on my heel and walked into the women's locker room, texting Alice and asking her to let me know when he left.

I couldn't talk to anyone about it. I ignored Josey's calls. Sean and I sat up together Tuesday, Wednesday, and Thursday night in the hotel suite, but we didn't discuss it. Instead, we chatted about insignificant things, or watched a movie. He seemed to intuitively know that I couldn't—I physically *could not*—talk about what had happened.

But then Friday morning brought a reprieve.

My solicitor emailed me a copy of Bryan's suggested custody agreement, and I almost fell off my chair with relief.

Fridays and weekends during the off season, Tuesday through Thursdays during the season.

Every other Christmas and major holiday.

Medical decisions would require his approval, which was normal.

And we would discuss schooling and other matters on an as-needed basis, but all day-to-day decisions would continue to be mine.

That was it.

I read it ten times to be sure, then let my face fall to my hands, needing the darkness to process my deliverance from despair.

"Thank you," I said to no one, to God, to the empty room, to my absent cousin, to the solicitor who had sent me the email. "Thank you so much."

I dwelled with my thanks and gratitude, immersing myself in it for a long time, before lifting my head and reading the rest of the message.

And that's when I saw the suggested child support payment. I gaped at my screen, feeling intense irritation.

The number was too big.

It was so big, it felt like . . .

Like . . .

Like a payoff.

Like an assuaging of guilt.

Like something his father had done to his mother, or something my father would do to my mother.

And I didn't want it.

Riding high on the wings of righteous indignation, I typed a quick reply to my solicitor, giving him my edits to the agreement:

Mr. Temple,
Please pass along the following:

1. *Terms of custody are acceptable. Mr. Leech should pick up Patrick from school Friday nights and take him to school Monday mornings so as to limit unnecessary interactions between parents.*
2. *Disciplinary procedures must be agreed upon in writing prior to the first weekend visitation.*
3. *Patrick should have his own bedroom and space at Mr. Leech's home.*
4. *Non-emergent decisions requiring discussion are to be handled through solicitors.*
5. *Mr. Leech can take his money and shove it up his arse.*

Sincerely, Eilish Cassidy

TWENTY-FIVE
BRYAN

@THEBryanLeech: Life is shit and a bird just crapped on me and we're all screwed and everything is pointless.
@WillthebrickhouseMoore to @THEBryanLeech: So…is this the title of your new self-help book?

R unning drills was a *fantastic* way to burn off anger.
More specifically, it was a great way to kick the living shit out of Sean Cassidy without getting arrested.

I'd been gunning for him ever since he'd pulled Eilish out of the locker rooms. Afterward, he told me in no unspoken terms I was to leave her alone unless she came to me. No calls, no home visits, not until she decided she wanted to see me. The fucker.

He'd told me to pursue her. He'd told me she needed to be cared for, so why the sudden one-eighty?

Of course, I hadn't listened. I stopped by her place, but she never answered the door.

"Leech, take it easy. We don't want you ruining Cassidy's pretty face. He needs it for all those magazine spreads he likes to pose for," Coach Brian called from the side of the pitch. A couple lads chuckled.

"Yeah, take it easy on me," Sean agreed, out of breath. "I don't want to get cut from shooting the cover of *Men's Health* next month."

"Don't worry," I said, eyes flashing at him viciously. "A month's more than enough time to heal." And then I tackled him to the ground. We scuffled, and I heard Coach Brian yelling again for me to ease up. Fuck that. Sean was the wall between Eilish and me, why I hadn't been able to explain myself. He was lucky I hadn't slashed his tires and replaced all his favorite lotions with foot cream. Or God forbid, generic-brand equivalents.

"I'm not your enemy," he grunted when my elbow made contact with his trapezius.

"Oh yeah? Then—" I sucked in a breath when the big bastard dug his heel into my shin. "Five bloody minutes to explain myself."

"It's not up to me," he grunted. "It's up to Eilish."

"You can convince her. You've just decided not to."

"Maybe I'm not sure you deserve a second chance," he bit out. "You went behind her back and started working on a custody case—"

"I didn't! This is why she needs to hear me out. I called my dad to ask if he could recommend a decent family law firm, and he decided to fast-track the process without consulting me first. I had no idea my solicitor had called Eilish until right before she came barreling into the locker rooms, all guns blazing."

Even in his struggle, Sean managed to arch a quizzical eyebrow. "That was your father's doing?"

"Yes!" I bit out.

"Well, that changes everything."

"Oh, it does, does it? It's not like I've been trying to explain this to Eilish since Tuesday. She won't answer any of my calls, and she's never home."

"I put her up in a hotel for the week, you pig-headed arse, and she blocked your number."

I blinked at him, at this information, thinking and saying in unison, "She's fucking crazy."

"No. She's heartbroken."

"She's being irrational, stubborn."

"Maybe." Sean laughed, shaking his head. "She loves you."

My heart stopped, and I asked before I could catch myself, "She said that?"

Sean smirked. "She's not talking at all. I caught her staring at a picture of you two on her phone."

"So?"

"For a half hour. Just . . . staring."

Staring.

Fuck. Just thinking of that made my heart burn like crazy. I needed to see her.

"Parents can be meddlesome creatures," Sean went on thoughtfully. "Especially when it comes to relationships."

He didn't have to tell me twice. Mine had unintentionally poured gasoline all over my life and set it alight.

I loosened my hold on Sean, and we finally broke apart.

"It's about time," Ronan called out. "I thought we were gonna have to book you two a room."

"Shut your trap, Fitzpatrick," Sean called back as we both endeavored to catch our breaths.

"So, will you explain what happened to Eilish?" I asked, eyeing him hopefully.

He ran a hand through his short-cropped hair. "Little problem with that. She's officially banned all talk of you. If I bring up your name, I get the icy stare of death."

"She's about half your size, Cassidy. I'm sure you can handle a few mean looks."

At this he chuckled. "You obviously haven't experienced the ire of the Cassidy women. Actually, strike that, you are experiencing it, you just haven't had the pleasure of going through it up close."

"And I never will if you don't help me."

He gave me a sidelong look, wiping his brow.

"Come on, Sean, you know I deserve a chance to explain myself."

He glanced over my shoulder. "It *would* be a travesty if you lived the rest of your life without a good tongue lashing from a Cassidy woman," he said with a glint in his eye before he realized the innuendo.

I shot him a look. "Wrong choice of words, my friend. But since I need your help, I'll let that one slide."

He studied me a moment. "Fine, I'll help you."

I came forward and gripped him by the shoulders. "Thank you. Seriously, you're my last hope."

"Yeah, yeah, just remember you owe me a new pair of cufflinks for my birthday. Take Eilish with you, she has impeccable taste."

"Noted."

He started to walk away and was halfway across the pitch when I cupped my hands around my mouth and shouted, "And don't you worry. If all goes to plan there'll be plenty of tongue lashings from a Cassidy woman in my future."

He didn't turn around. However, his hand did shoot up into the air as he flipped me off.

I smiled, feeling hopeful for the first time in days.

***

"What? How . . . how can she do that?"

My solicitor cleared her throat and glanced at her notes again. "I can try and push for it, but it seems she's quite set in her decision."

"No. No way." I shook my head vehemently. "She can't do that. It's my right as Patrick's father to provide for him."

"Ms. Cassidy is under no legal obligation to accept your financial support." Mrs. Feelan's words and expression were apologetic but also matter-of-fact.

I huffed out an irritable breath and clasped my hands together, glancing briefly at the clock on the wall. Eilish and her solicitor were due any minute. We were waiting for them to arrive so that we could discuss the custody agreement and put an end to this absolute clusterfuck of a situation.

I was just about ready to pull my hair out with the ridiculousness of it all.

One conversation and I could fix everything. But she wouldn't talk to me.

She is so fucking stubborn.

The door opened and I sat up straight. Three people walked into the room. Eilish, Sean, and her solicitor, but I only had eyes for Eilish. She wore a navy pencil skirt, a cream blouse, and a long gray coat. Her hair fell over her shoulders in long waves. She looked beautiful. So beautiful I had to take a moment to catch my breath.

I stood before I knew what I was doing. "Eilish," I breathed. Those crystal blue eyes came to me, and I hated the neutrality in them, the careful mask she'd put in place. It reminded me of William's party all those weeks ago, before she'd come to know the man I am now. Before I'd come to know her. Before I fell in love with the kind, generous, and warm woman I knew she was.

"Mr. Leech, please sit down," Mrs. Feelan urged, a note of caution in her voice, like I might cause a scene or something.

I grimaced and sat while the three newcomers took their seats on the opposite side of the table. Eilish's solicitor started to speak, but I barely heard a word he said. My focus was too fixed on the stunning redhead sitting across from me. I stared at her until she sensed my attention, and her gaze flicked momentarily to mine. A touch of crimson colored her cheeks, and she glanced away again.

Look at me. Please.

I was also irritated that she felt the need to bring Sean along, like she needed protection from me. I'd never hurt her, not in a million years. A flash of memory hit me, of how she'd looked when she confronted me in the lockers, the hurt so palpable I could almost touch it. She thought I'd committed the ultimate betrayal, so maybe in a small way I could understand why she brought him.

Still, I eyed my teammate in annoyance. Judging from Eilish's refusal to look at me, it didn't appear he'd made any headway in explaining things to her, even though he said he'd try. Though funnily enough, when I looked at him he smirked.

Huh.

"Sign here, please, Mr. Leech," Mrs. Feelan instructed after a few minutes of back and forth. The custody agreement was in front of me. I picked up the pen, then hesitated. I put the pen down and looked across the table at Eilish again. Not at Sean. Not at the solicitor. Just at her.

"I want you to reconsider the support payments. If you won't accept all of it, then at least think about taking half."

Eilish didn't breathe a word, only shifted uncomfortably in her seat.

"Ms. Cassidy does not wish to receive any child support payments, Mr. Leech," her solicitor cut in. "We already informed Mrs. Feelan of this before the final agreement was drawn up."

"Well, nobody informed me." I crossed my arms over my chest, her stubbornness rubbing off on me.

"I informed you earlier, Mr. Leech. Remember? I would've done so sooner but it was all very last minute," said Mrs. Feelan. "We did what we could in the time provided."

"But why?" I asked, still only addressing Eilish. "You can talk to me, you know. I'm sitting right here."

"Mr. Leech—" Mrs. Feelan cut in, but then Eilish spoke, her voice calm and measured. It was only the slight catch when she said my name that alerted me to her nervousness.

"It's too much, B-Bryan."

"It's not too much, nothing is ever too much when it comes to Patrick, or you for that matter," I said with passion as my eyes bore into hers. "You can't give this to me? You keep him from me for years and you won't let me support him now?"

I hit a nerve. I could see it in how she glanced at the table and worried her lip, her eyes stormy and uncertain.

"Mrs. Feelan, can you please control your client," Eilish's solicitor requested.

Mrs. Feelan placed a hand at my elbow. "Mr. Leech, please."

"I'll agree to support payments," Eilish blurted, surprising everyone in the room. "But they need to be a smaller sum. *Much* smaller."

I exhaled and shot her a grateful look. "I can work with that." If I had my way, the amount wouldn't matter in any case.

"Given this information," Mrs. Feelan stacked her papers, "we'll need to draw up a new agreement and schedule a further meeting."

"Very well," said Eilish's solicitor. "I'll talk through the options with my client and get back to you in due course."

Everybody started getting up to leave. Both solicitors hung back to discuss something while Eilish and Sean approached the door. They were already gone before I realized this might be my only chance to talk to Eilish in person. Jumping into action, I chased after them to the bank of lifts. Sean pressed the button to go down as I caught up to them.

"Talk to me. Give me ten minutes."

She turned to look at me, a galaxy of emotion in her eyes. "There's nothing—"

"*Please,*" I urged, almost begging.

The lift doors slid open and she stepped inside. I followed suit, while Sean hung back. "Actually, I need to use the bathroom. I'll meet you in the lobby, Eilish," he said just as the doors closed.

"Sean!" she yelled, but he was already gone.

If looks could kill, Cassidy would be six feet under. Eilish glared at the smooth, polished metal with absolute murder in her eyes.

I, on the other hand, could've fucking kissed her cousin. With tongue.

The lift started to descend, and Eilish blew out a heavy breath. Her arms were folded over her chest, and she stared dead ahead, totally on the defensive.

"Eilish, will you please just look at me? This is all so messed up, and you're not even giving me the chance to explain."

"What on earth is there to explain? You don't trust me. There's nothing to talk about."

I stared at her profile, so entirely closed off, and an unexpected surge of anger flared in my chest.

"I don't trust you? Really? That's how you're justifying all this?"

"All what?" she bit out, still not looking at me.

Before I could respond the lift shuddered to a halt.

"Oh my God, are we stuck?" Eilish exclaimed in horror.

Usually, such an incident would bother me, but not today. Today the gods seemed to be smiling upon me, because getting stuck with Eilish was exactly what I needed, what *we* needed. I remembered the knowing look Sean gave me right before we got on and suspected this was his doing. I definitely wouldn't put it past him. After all, he had said he'd try to help me.

I blew out a breath. "Looks like it."

She tugged nervously at her collar. "Wonderful."

I turned to stare her down. "Yeah, wonderful. Because now you might have to admit you're just as much to blame for this clusterfuck as I am."

She spun, disbelief and rage twisting her features.

Both intensified as I added, "Maybe even more so."

"How am I to carry the blame for any of this?" She gestured around us widely. "I gave you his hair for the test weeks ago. I encouraged you to get a lawyer from the very beginning. And you said no. No, we could work it out between us. I trusted you."

Ignoring the hurt and betrayal saturating her words and piercing me from her eyes, I pressed forward. "That's a lie. You never trusted me. Never. You were determined to think the worst of me. I told you I love you—and I do, God help me, I'm so fucking in love with you—and you pushed me away. We make love in the physio room—"

She scoffed, laughing derisively. "Oh? Was that what we were doing?"

"Yes," I answered immediately, desperately. "At least, that's what I was doing for the last few weeks. I can't keep my hands to myself, and every time I steal a kiss, it's because I'm so bloody in love with you I can't think straight."

"That's not love, Bryan. That's infatuation. That's lust."

"No. It's a symptom of being over the moon gone for another person and wanting them to be happy, wanting to be the one to make them happy."

She stared at me, her face no longer a mask of dispassion. Her features were a mess of conflicting emotions—raw pain warred with hope and despair. She inhaled an unsteady breath, her eyes shining with unshed tears.

"I love you," she said on a tortured exhale. "I love you."

She loves me?

"Eilish . . ." I wanted to touch her, but she had her arms wrapped around her torso as though holding herself together.

"And you're right, I pushed you away. I closed myself off. I thought, if we removed physical intimacy from the equation, I would be able to see clearly. I would be able to trust that what we had between us was real."

I stepped forward, intent on reaching for her, but she flinched. "No. Don't . . ." She shook her head, her words trailed off, and her lip quivered. Jesus. I hated seeing her upset like this, but at same time I just wanted to shake some sense into her.

She took another visible breath, her gaze lowering to the floor. "I'm sorry for pushing you away. I was wrong, but, Bryan," she shook her head, "what you did was wrong, too. You could have come to me if you wanted the test, the formal agreement. Going behind my back—"

"I called my father on Monday. I had no idea he'd fast-tracked the process. He arranged everything without consulting me. I planned to take you out to lunch Wednesday so we could talk about it. That's not an excuse, but it is the truth."

"Why?" Her voice cracked on the word, and she still wouldn't give me her eyes. "Why did you want the test? Did you think I lied to you?"

"No. God, no." I balled my hands into fists, frustration eating me from the inside. "This whole situation is a fuck-up," I breathed.

She lifted her gaze to mine, her blue eyes wide, sad. She didn't disagree.

I sighed heavily and continued speaking. "Last week, after I left your house, I got a call from your mother."

Her eyebrows jumped, her eyes flashed with anger. "My mother?"

I nodded. "She wanted to know what I was going to do about Patrick. Basically, she was pushing me to propose to you."

"Bryan, oh my God," she exclaimed, her hand going to her mouth in shock. "You have to believe I would never—"

"Yes. I know that now, but my head was all over the place at the time. I had your mother calling me, and my sponsor was breathing down my neck. You remember the woman you met at the hospital?" She bobbed her head. "That's

Sarah. She's been so great in helping me stay sober, but when she found out about you and Patrick, she was adamant I get a paternity test. I've had a lot of bad luck with girlfriends in the past, you see, women—addicts—who encouraged my addiction to feed their own. She was worried about me, that you were after money."

She let out a joyless laugh. "I don't and never have wanted your money."

"I know. But you're the first person I've been with since I've been sober and I couldn't help doubting myself, wondering if I could trust my own judgment. That's on me. I'm still learning how to live life sober. But when you pushed me away . . ."

Eilish studied me, her face understanding but wary.

Both of us went quiet then, silence filling the confines of the lift. I tried to think of the best way to proceed. In the end I decided a truce was needed. Casting her a tender glance, I said, "Thank you for changing your mind about the child support. I know it might not seem like such a big thing, but it's important to me to be able to contribute."

Some of the anguish left her face as she dropped her arms to her sides. "I wouldn't have declined if you'd been more reasonable. Thirty thousand a month is ridiculous."

I ran a hand over my face. "I don't agree. I've contributed nothing for five years. And you live in a very upscale neighborhood, Eilish. It can't be cheap, especially not in today's market."

"It isn't," she allowed, her mouth tugging to the side ruefully. "And, honestly, I do need the money. Sean made me promise to accept his help financially for twelve months, and that was eight months ago. He's been paying the rent."

"Then why couldn't you—?"

"Because, don't you see? *I* feel guilty about what happened between us. *I* was sober, *you* were drunk. Patrick is my responsibility. I hate taking money from Sean, but I can't ask you—"

"No." I shook my head. "No, no, no. You're not asking me, I'm insisting. He's ours. He's my responsibility and yours. You have to start thinking of him in this way."

She nodded again, and it was clear she was fighting back tears. "I'm so sorry."

Seeing my window of opportunity, I closed the rest of the distance between us. When my chest met hers, a tension I hadn't even realized released from deep in my bones. It had only been a few days, but I'd missed her so bloody much. Being close to her now was an odd but welcome relief.

"So, can we start over?" I asked, my voice a gentle caress.

"Yes, of course, but—"

Before she could finish the sentence, I kissed her, my relief propelling me forward. She gasped into my mouth. I lost myself a little in how soft her lips were. I pressed my entire body to hers, like I couldn't get enough. I pressed so close I could feel her heartbeat pounding against my chest.

I teased her mouth into opening for me, and after only a second's hesitation she let me in. I slid my tongue along hers, tasted her with every fiber of my being. She arched her back, and I felt her breasts push into me. My cock stirred instantly. I lifted my hand and took hold of her neck, brushing my thumb back and forth over the hollow of her throat. A strangled moan escaped her. I groaned and kissed her deeper, wishing I could be inside her.

Her hands came to my shoulders, and even though I was so lost in kissing her, I still felt them shake. She pulled away, her eyes pleading. I knew she'd let me take her here, I knew she wanted me as fiercely as I wanted her. But this wasn't the place.

Still, I couldn't help teasing her, lowering my voice to a rough whisper, "Eilish, we might be stuck on this lift for hours. We can do what we like."

She whimpered. I grinned.

Whispering in her ear, I said, "And I would. I would take you here, against this wall, make love to you with your skirt around your waist, your knickers torn off, but . . ."

Her breathing was shallow, frantic, and her hands tugged at my shirt. I caught them before she could undress me, sucking and biting her lip into my mouth.

"I'm sure the security guards wouldn't be amused. But turned on? Maybe," I teased with a tender smile.

Her eyes widened in realization as she stared at me, lucidity warring with mortification. "Oh my goodness. They've probably been watching this whole time."

"Probably," I agreed, loving how embarrassed she got over a few kisses.

"And we never even pressed the emergency button," she went on, rushing by me to slam her hand down on the red button.

I approached her from behind, brushed her hair over one shoulder, and kissed her neck. "God, I love you," I whispered fervently. It wasn't even a slip of the tongue. I'd meant to say it. I wanted her to know. I didn't want any more misunderstandings between us ever again.

Her back arched instinctively against my body as she said, "I love you, too, Bryan."

And that was the moment the lift decided to jolt back to life.

TWENTY-SIX
EILISH

@SeanCassinova to @ECassChoosesPikachu and @THEBryanLeech: YOU'RE WELCOME.

"I wouldn't have trapped you in the lift if you hadn't insisted on being so stubborn." Sean twisted his cufflinks and cocked an eyebrow at me. "I accept your apology."

"I didn't apologize."

"Yes, I know, darling. But I can tell you want to."

I grinned, very reluctantly. "You overstepped."

"Someone needed to do it." He shrugged.

My cousin and I were in the extra office on the top floor of the sports complex. Bryan had driven me back, and I needed the lift since Sean had *abandoned me* at the solicitor's.

Of course, I didn't at all mind spending the extra time with Bryan, and we'd made plans to meet up after work. But that didn't change the fact that Sean had locked us in a lift and then proceeded to spy on us via the security camera.

The last thing I wanted to do was finish my day at work, preferring instead to spend the rest of the afternoon snogging with my boyfriend.

That's right. *Snogging.* With my *boyfriend.* You might have heard of him? Bryan Leech? He loves me. Just FYI.

My desires were completely unprofessional and maybe not very adult, but I didn't care. I embraced these whimsical wishes as a reawakened facet of my personality.

"Someone needed to put you two in a room together and lock the door, throw away the key, etcetera, etcetera."

God, I loved my cousin. There was no one else in the world like him, I was sure of it.

"Thank you," I said softly, leaning forward and on my tiptoes to give him a peck on the cheek.

"You're very welcome," he responded warmly, catching my shoulders before I could step away. "You know I love you, don't you? I only want what's best for you and Patrick. You're my family."

He sounded so earnest, maybe a little vulnerable, I felt a lump rise in my throat. "I know, Sean. And we love you, too."

He nodded, his eyes moving over my face as he hesitated a moment before saying, "Don't let Bryan get rid of those suits."

"What?"

"Patrick's suits. I had them tailored so that we can let them out as he grows."

"Why would Bryan get rid of Patrick's suits?" I shook my head at my cousin, giving him a bewildered look, the inner workings of his head worried and astonished me.

"Because he's going to be a proper father now, to Patrick." Again, Sean hesitated, clearing his throat before adding, "You mustn't forget, he's a Cassidy, too."

My heart constricted, and I also had to clear my throat before speaking. "Patrick will never forget you, you know. Bryan is his father, but you'll always be his Monkey Sean."

He nodded tightly, releasing my shoulders, not looking convinced. "Yes. I know."

I sighed, and I'm afraid to admit the sigh was a touch unsteady and watery, but before I could give the big doofus additional assurances, my phone rang.

"You better get that." Sean shuffled away. "I have to check in with the defensive team about tomorrow's match."

"Fine, but I'll see you tomorrow?"

"Of course." He grinned, looking more himself. "And hopefully, now that this silly business is behind us, you'll be back to your post where you belong."

I didn't get a chance to respond as he hurried out the door, so I glanced at my phone screen, spotting Josey's avatar and number.

"Hello?"

"Eilish! Tell me what happened. Are you okay? Did he get custody? Or what's happening?"

"Calm down," I walked to the office door and closed it, frowning because I hadn't told Josey about the DNA test or the custody case. The last time I'd spoken to her was Sunday, eons ago.

"Firstly, who told you about the custody case?"

Her side went quiet for a protracted moment, and then she said, "Don't be mad."

That gave me pause.

"Why would I be mad?"

"Because your mother told me about the custody case."

I felt my frown morph into a confused scowl. "My mother? Since when are you speaking to my mother?"

"Since she called me after you moved back to Ireland."

What?

"What?"

"I can explain. She was worried about you, I was worried about you. So I may have let it slip that Bryan is Patrick's father—"

I gasped, my hand flying to my mouth. I couldn't believe my ears.

"—but, I swear, it was only because I thought, maybe if she knew she could help. You know, help Bryan do the right thing and step up. I had no idea he would file for custody instead. I thought things were going well when I saw you at the café, I am so sorry."

"Stop. Just, stop talking." I shook my head, willing these facts to be untrue.

How could she?

"Eilish?"

"Give me a minute here, Josey. I mean, how . . . why . . . what could possibly possess you to tell her? You know what she's like."

"She seemed genuinely happy when she found out Bryan was the father," Josey rushed to defend herself, "and, I'm sorry, but he did need to step up."

"But that's between Bryan and me, not you, and definitely not my mother."

"I thought she could help," came her small voice from the other end, making me sigh again.

"Cara Cassidy only helps herself," I responded harshly. "You know that. I can't believe you would do this."

"Well, what else was I supposed to do, Eilish? I never see you. I just thought, you know, if Bryan was in the picture. I mean, you've liked him for so long, you deserve happiness, and if your mother could help him see reason—"

"But she didn't, Josey. She didn't. She just spewed her poison all over the situation and made everything worse."

She was quiet for a beat, then asked, "Did he get custody?"

"No."

"He didn't?"

"No, I'm not discussing this with you." I hated how cold I sounded, but how could I trust her now?

"What?"

"I can't talk to you about this. Not if you're informing my mother."

"You make it sound like I'm a snitch; I'm not. I just want you to have some free time to have fun, like before you got pregnant and everything went to shit." Now she was yelling at me.

I yelled right back, "Everything did not go to shit, Josey. My life is not shit, it never has been. Patrick is the best thing—"

"See, you say that, but you can't possibly mean it. Not unless it gets you Bryan, otherwise what's the point?"

"Oh my God." I sat down at the desk, my anger mounting to near uncontrollable levels. "That's it. We cannot talk anymore."

"Why? Because you don't like hearing the truth?" she spat.

"No. Because you don't listen. Patrick is precious to me. He is the most precious, the most wonderful, the most important person in my life. I love him soul deep and oceans wide. And you've never been happy for me."

"How can I be happy for you? You gave everything up, *everything*."

"You're wrong. I am so lucky, so blessed."

"You wouldn't be saying that if Sean hadn't come to your rescue, would you? Then where would your love for your precious Patrick be?"

"I'm hanging up now. I love you Josey, I do, but I can't keep doing this with you."

"Wait, I—"

I didn't wait. I hung up, tossing my phone to the desk, wanting it out of my hand, which was shaking with anger.

"Eilish?"

I turned at the sound of my name, relieved to find Bryan hovering just inside the door.

"I knocked," he tossed his thumb over his shoulder, "but you didn't hear me. Are you okay?"

I nodded. But then, realizing I didn't want or need to pretend with Bryan, I shook my head. "No. No, I'm not."

"Then why are you over there?" He opened his arms and admonished me softly, "Come here."

I huffed a laugh, I couldn't help it. He sounded so serious. I stood and walked into his embrace, melting against him as he gathered me to him.

"Are you going to tell me who that was on the phone?"

I snuggled closer. "It was my friend Josey."

"She upset you?"

"She just admitted to being the one who told my mother about you being Patrick's father."

I felt Bryan stiffen and then gather a deep inhale. "Wow."

"Yes. Wow. I had no idea until just now. She heard about the custody case somehow and called to ask what happened." I filled Bryan in on the rest of the conversation.

When I was finished, and I was marinating in my anger and exhaustion and

THE CAD AND THE CO-ED

hurt, Bryan leaned away and slipped his fingers under my chin, tilting my head back. Then he placed a sweetly seductive kiss on my lips, sweeping his tongue out and catching my bottom lip with a soft bite.

When he moved slightly back so he could see me, I gazed up at him and smiled. "What was that for?"

"You've been through a lot today."

"So have you."

"Yes. We've been through a lot together. So we should kiss each other until it's all better."

Despite everything, that made me laugh.

"You think so?" I gave him a quizzical smile. I especially appreciated that he didn't jump in and try to tell me what to do. He just offered his support.

"What's that look for?"

"It's just, I'm impressed with you. Instead of giving me unsolicited advice or trying to fix things for me, you listened. And then you gave me a kiss. That's impressive."

Bryan stood a little straighter, looking pleased with himself. "One thing we learn in recovery is that no one can fight our battles for us, and we can't fight other people's battles either. I'm—or I haven't been—so great at keeping my nose out of your battles. But what happened this last week, with everyone thinking our business was their business . . ." he paused, his expression growing contemplative, "I'm going to trust you. You let me know if you need my help and I'll be there."

A sense of rightness and wonder fell over me, like a gossamer blanket. I couldn't help my smile, which had grown so large it made my cheeks ache.

"Bryan—"

"Oh!" He released me, stepping away and taking a folded up piece of paper from his back pocket. "I have some good news."

I accepted the paper, casting him an amused and suspicious glare. "What is it?"

"Take a look." He dipped his chin toward the sheet in my hands.

Carefully unfolding it, I skimmed its contents. It was a memo from Coach Brian to the entire team announcing that Connors had resigned effective immediately.

My eyes darted to Bryan's. "What is this?"

"You know how Connors kept stealing people's lunches?"

"Yes, but I didn't think it was widely known."

"It is . . . and it isn't. Anyway, Alice didn't know it was him who'd been stealing lunches, so she put dye on her bento box and caught him—literally—red-handed."

I sputtered a laugh at Alice's detective work, then said, "But I thought he was related to the general manager? I can't imagine it'd be easy to have him let go."

"He is. Connors is his cousin, but Alice is our GM's niece."

I shook my head at the absurdity of it all. "So he was fired for taking Alice's lunch?"

"No. He was fired for threatening Alice because she had the audacity to put dye on her lunch container, waving around red hands like a madman. Coach Brian witnessed the whole thing and gave him two choices: either he'd be fired or he could resign."

"Wow."

"Yeah. Wow. And thank fuck. Not sure I could handle another season with his grubby paws on me," he said with a shudder and then winked at me. "I'd much rather yours."

I swiped him on the shoulder, though I had to admit his flirting gave me a little thrill in my belly. "And this all happened while we were gone this afternoon?" I went on, still curious.

"No. This happened on Wednesday, while you had the day off. The resignation just came through today." His hand traveled from my neck, wandering down my spine to rest on my lower back. I shivered.

"Oh! So, what does that mean—"

"I ran into Coach downstairs," Bryan gave me a wry smile, "he told me to put my *goddamn personal drama on the shelf for the sake of the team.*"

I winced. "Sorry about that."

"No, no. It's fine. I told him I never wanted you benched in the first place—which is the truth—and now he thinks I'm Mother Teresa. I come out of this smelling like a rose."

Chuckling at his good humor, I slid my arms around his neck and nuzzled his jaw with my nose, then whispered in his ear, "You do smell like roses. Actually no, you smell woodsy, like a forest, so much better than roses."

He groaned, his hands coming to my waist and squeezing. The action had me clenching my thighs together with need. It felt like a lifetime since we'd been together, and I desperately needed to reconnect. It wasn't just physical either. No, sex with Bryan Leech was so much more than that. It was emotional, passionate, a balm for my soul.

"Can we leave now?" he asked huskily. "Or do you need to stay?"

I shook my head. "We can go."

"Good." Bryan cupped my face between his palms and gave me a quick kiss. "We need to go. Now. So grab your stuff. We'll pick up Patrick, then I'm driving us home."

* * *

After the emotional rollercoaster of the last week, pizza for dinner with my two guys was exactly what I needed. Unfortunately, Bryan couldn't eat the pizza, not with a match the following day. He flexed his self-control muscle and ate a clean meal of veggies, fish, and quinoa salad.

Bryan offered to do the dishes, but I waved him off, insisting that he help Patrick through the bedtime routine. Truth be told, I enjoyed my quiet moments at the end of the day while doing the dishes. The sound of the water was soothing, and I liked heating my hands under the warm tap.

Once I was finished, I checked on Patrick and Bryan, and found that Bryan had fallen asleep in our son's bed. Patrick, however, was sitting on the floor playing with his train set.

As soon as he spotted me, he held a finger to his lips. "Be quiet, Mummy. Bryan needs his beautiful sleep, even though my bed is too small."

I smiled at my son. "You mean beauty sleep?"

He nodded.

"Where did you hear that?"

"Monkey Sean said sleep is why he's so stunningly handsome."

I covered my mouth to smother my laugh. When I recovered, I threaded my fingers through Patrick's hair and placed a kiss on his forehead. "You need to go to sleep."

"But where will Bryan sleep?" He frowned.

I hesitated a moment, then said, "With me. I have a big bed. There's enough room for both of us."

Patrick nodded, like this made a lot of sense, then his eyes lit up. "Does this mean Bryan will be here in the morning? Can he watch cartoons with me? Or maybe we can build another fort."

"I hope he's here in the morning, but no fort. Unfortunately, we won't have time for that since we have the match in the afternoon." I hugged my son to me and placed another kiss on his head. "Come on. Help me move Bryan to my room. I can't carry him by myself."

Patrick gave me a funny look and gestured to his dad. *His dad.* A rush of emotion ran through me at the thought and my heart pounded.

"You can't carry him. He's too heavy."

I chuckled at that, then moved to wake the big man up. Bending over him, I whispered in his ear. "Time to go to bed, sleepyhead."

"What?" Bryan's eyes fluttered open, and he seemed surprised by his surroundings.

"I said, time to go to bed," I repeated softly.

"Oh. Is it?" He glanced around the room. "I guess I should be going."

"No. You're staying." Patrick tugged on Bryan's hand, clearly trying to get him to stand up. "You're sleeping in Mummy's big bed."

Bryan turned a confused, questioning, and still hazy gaze to me. "I am?"

"You are." I nodded, grinning at his expression. "So come on, time for bed."

In a daze, Bryan let us pull him to his feet and steer him towards my room. Once there, Patrick very solemnly pulled back the blankets, motioned for Bryan to climb in, then covered him back up.

"Good night, Bryan," Patrick said, kissing him on the forehead. "Sweet dreams."

A dreamy smile arrested Bryan's features as he gazed at our son, but his tone was a little rough as he responded, "You, too."

Patrick then tugged me out of my bedroom and back to his. I cast a longing glance at Bryan, who was watching us go with equal parts amusement and mischief as he lay lazily on my bed. The sleepy tired look on his face was incredibly sexy.

Once I had Patrick all tucked in, lights off, bedtime hugs and kisses at an end, I mussed Patrick's hair and asked, "What do you think if Bryan spends the night more often?"

"How often?" Patrick asked between a yawn.

"A few times a week, maybe."

"Why doesn't he just move in? We could get bunk beds, and he can share my room."

Laughing at his adorable antics, I gave him one last kiss and shut off the light. "Sweet dreams, my love."

"Sweet dreams, Mummy."

Leaving his door cracked, I tip-toed down the hall back to my room, not wanting to wake Bryan if he was already asleep.

But when I entered the room, I found he wasn't asleep. In fact, he was up, sitting on the edge of the bed, waiting for me.

"Hey," I whispered as I closed the door, a surge of excitement and happiness —and also horny expectation—rushing through my veins.

"Hey," he said, standing. "I didn't know what to do."

"About what?" I asked, pulling off my shirt, my eyes moving over his as I wondered why he would still be wearing clothes.

Bryan hesitated, his eyes dropping to my chest and then back to my eyes. "Am I . . . ?"

"Are you . . . ?" I tugged off my pants, removing my earrings and placing them in a dish on top of my jewelry box.

"Am I spending the night?" he asked, still looking confused.

"Of course," I grinned, but then paused, "Unless you don't want to sp—"

I didn't get to finish, because Bryan was up and on, his mouth crashing onto mine, his hands roaming over my body. I trembled at the feel of his rough palms against my bare skin. How I'd yearned for these hands. Thinking I might never feel his touch ever again had been agony.

"Christ, I've missed you." He pulled away just long enough to say, "I've missed you so fucking much."

I tilted my head to the side, offering him more of my neck as he trailed biting, hungry kisses from my jaw to my shoulder. The sensation of his stubbly jaw and hot, wet mouth moving over my skin sent pinpricks of awareness racing in every direction.

But mostly south.

"Forking," I mumbled.

"What?"

"You'll get used to saying forking instead of fucking."

"I don't care what you call it—forking, sporking, ducking, fucking—as long as we're doing it."

A laugh bubbled up from my chest, which he cut off with another searing kiss, his fingers sliding down my ribcage and into my panties.

I gasped.

"I need you, Eilish." His voice was rough, his strokes were skilled. Perfect. "Let me make love to you."

"Yes," I answered on a sigh, my nails digging into his shoulders.

He bent as though he were going to pick me up, and I stilled his movements, holding him in place. "No, not on the bed."

His eyebrows jumped. "Not the bed?"

I shook my head, grinning, then turned, facing the dresser and bracing my hands on it. I found his eyes in the reflection of my mirror and grinned.

"Well then," he also grinned, removing his belt, his gaze blazing a trail over my body, "let's give ourselves a show."

* * *

Later, much later, after we'd spent some measure of our exuberance at being reunited, Bryan and I lay in bed wrapped around each other. He was trailing his fingertips along my arm, up to my shoulder, then down my back, raising goose pimples wherever he touched.

"You know," he said, his voice roughened and sleepy, "this is the first time we've been able to lay together, afterward."

I snuggled against his chest, enjoying the feel of his legs—his luscious legs—tangled with mine.

"We've cuddled before," I said absentmindedly, too relaxed to think better of my words.

"We have?"

"Yes. The first time."

His movements stilled and he stiffened. And that's when I realized what I'd said.

I lifted my head and gave him a bracing look. "I'm sorry. I shouldn't have—"

"No. No more apologies." He rolled me to my back and hovered over me, stealing a kiss, then running his nose along mine. "You should be able to speak about it without feeling guilty, and I should be able to hear about it without feeling guilty. I want to know, and I want you to tell me."

I smiled at that, warmth suffusing my chest paired with a sense of weightlessness, like a burden had been taken from me, one I didn't know I'd been carrying. I lifted my hand and tousled his dark hair.

"Thank you."

"For what?"

"For being wonderful."

A grin bloomed on his face and he wagged his eyebrows. "Wonderful? Or impressive?"

"Both," I laughed lightly, tilting my head to the side. "I want to talk about it, I want to tell you. Because—for me—it was an amazing night. You were wonderful, and impressive," I quickly added, causing his smile to widen further, "and I've always treasured the memory of it, even though I had a hard time separating the guilt. But I've always felt . . ."

"Go on," he encouraged, rapt with interest.

"Like my treasuring it, my wanting to remember and think fondly of that night, made me a weak person. Or a daft person. One or the other."

He was shaking his head before I'd finished. "No. Absolutely not. I am so jealous of your memory." His eyes drifted over my lips, nose, and forehead. "I wish I could remember. But I guess I'll have to settle for listening to you tell me instead."

"Are you sure you want to hear about it? I was pretty naïve."

"Yes," he replied firmly, shifting to his side and propping his elbow against the mattress, his head in his hand. "Start at the beginning and leave nothing out."

Seeing he was serious, I tried to recall the evening, the night I'd thought about so many times and, just as many times, tried to bury. Tried to hide from myself.

"We danced."

"I remember a bit of that. What happened after?"

"You took me to the garden and kissed me."

"That sounds good."

"It was." I grinned at the memory.

"What happened next?" Bryan palmed my breast, rubbing a light circle around the peak with his thumb.

"You said I was beautiful, and then . . ."

"And then?"

I looked at Bryan, studied the image of him next to me, right then, as we were in that moment, and I realized the story I was about to tell him was more fantasy than reality.

Though I would always think back on that night with a twinge of some unknown emotion, what we had now was real.

And the reality of us, of our son, of our life together, the unknowns, the ups and downs of our past, and the ups and downs yet to come, were far superior to any fantasy.

EPILOGUE
BRYAN

@THEBryanLeech to @ECassChoosesPikachu: I love you.
@ECassChoosesPikachu to @THEBryanLeech: We're in the same room you nutter. And I love you, too <3

~Several weeks later~

"It's going to be fine," Eilish reassured me, taking my hand and giving it a squeeze.

I glanced down at her, so much love for this amazing woman, and gave her a tender smile. I wasn't usually lacking in confidence, but today was different. Today we were going to tell Patrick I was his dad. So many nightmare outcomes ran through my head.

Patrick bursting into tears at the news.
Patrick shouting, "You're not my daddy!" at top volume.
Patrick shutting himself in his room and refusing to see me ever again.

I knew it was all in my head, but I couldn't seem to stop thinking the worst would happen.

"What if he gets upset?" I asked, fretting.

"Are you serious? He loves you, Bryan. At this point I'm fairly sure he wouldn't even notice if I was gone for days so long as he could spend time with you." She chuckled affectionately.

I shot her a soft look, running a finger down her cheek. "That's not true, and we both know it."

"He adores you."

"He adores his buddy Bryan who comes to play rugby with him and lets him find Pokémon on his phone. I'm not so sure about Daddy Bryan who tells him he has to go to bed early and that he can't have a second serving of ice cream after his dinner."

"My God, you're adorable."

"I am not adorable. I'm brooding and sexy and masculine," I said, effecting a manly expression. It was all in the brow.

"Oh, yes you are. I never expected you to be so nervous to tell a little boy you're his dad. A little boy who's already head over heels in love with you. You, Bryan Leech, fullback, reformed party boy, who shows no mercy on the rugby field, are nervous, and it's the most adorable thing I've ever witnessed."

I scowled at her. "You're enjoying this way too much."

She went up on her tiptoes to press a kiss to the underside of my jaw, smiling widely. "Yes, I am."

I exhaled and ran my hand seductively down her back, pressing firmly into the base of her spine. "I fucking love you."

She shivered a little but quickly shook it off, those bright blue eyes of her sparkling. So much for delaying the inevitable with sex.

"I love you, too. Now let's get this over with. Pull off the Band-Aid."

I met her gaze and steeled myself. "Pull off the Band-Aid. Okay."

We went inside the living room where Patrick was sitting on the floor playing with his Legos. I'd gotten him a kid-sized version of my jersey and he was wearing it. I knew that was Eilish's doing. She was trying to bolster my confidence, and seeing Patrick in my shirt definitely helped. This kid was mine. *Mine.* I might have missed out on his early years, but I was determined to be there for him every single day from here on out. I was determined to be there for both of them. And Mam, too. I'd finally managed to get her into a rehabilitation clinic. As soon as she was better, I planned on introducing her to Patrick. I knew how much it meant to her. I knew his existence was half the reason she was so determined to get sober.

"Bryan!" he exclaimed when he saw me, jumping up and running at me full force. I plucked him up before he could crash into my legs and swung him around in my arms.

"Hey buddy," I rasped. My chest felt heavy with the words I was about to speak. He was always so happy to see me. I hoped that didn't change once he learned the truth.

"Bryan and I have something we'd like to tell you, baby," said Eilish, her calm, sweet voice soothing my nerves.

"Are we going to Disneyland?" he asked, and I chuckled. This kid. Such a chancer.

"No, we aren't going to Disneyland," Eilish replied with an indulgent smile.

"But if you behave for the rest of the year we might think about going for your birthday."

"Deal! I'm going to Disney for my birthday," Patrick yelled with glee, and I chuckled. I was well aware of his Disneyland fixation by now. He'd been asking to go for weeks, ever since he saw an ad for it on TV.

"I said *might*," Eilish warned. "Only if you're good."

"I'll be good," he promised, but the shine of mischief in his green eyes said otherwise. *My* green eyes. It was still hard to get used to how much he looked like me.

I carried him over to the couch and sat, placing him on my lap. He started fiddling with the collar of my shirt, and his comfort with me, his familiarity, warmed my heart. From the very first day we met there had always been this comfort, this sense of destiny, like we were meant to be in each other's lives. Eilish came and sat down next to us, and for a moment I relished the three of us being so close. A family. *My* family.

Eilish reached out and affectionately stroked Patrick's hair back from his face. He needed to get it cut. I made a note to ask if I could start taking him with me to my barber each month.

I was constantly making note of the things we could do together—father and son things.

"Bryan has something he'd like to tell you," she said in a gentle voice.

Patrick's big, expectant eyes met mine and my throat ran dry. Of course I'd choose this exact moment to forget how to speak. I'd never felt so jittery. Not even when I was coming off alcohol. Cold turkey had nothing on this.

"You . . ." I paused, and cleared my throat. "You know how your mates Jack and Harry sometimes get picked up from school by their dad?"

Patrick nodded. "His name's Carl. He drives a tractor."

"Yes, that's because he owns a farm."

"I'd like to drive a tractor someday. Do you think Carl would let us borrow his?"

I chuckled, unable to keep up with how his mind jumped from one subject to the next. "We'll see. But first, how would you like me to pick you up from school some days?"

"Like Jack and Harry's dad?"

"Yes, just like Jack and Harry's dad."

I glanced at Eilish. She made a "keep going" gesture, and I knew I was beating around the bush. It was hard to pick the right words.

Patrick fiddled with my collar some more. "Okay. Could we go for ice cream afterward?"

"Maybe."

Patrick's expression turned stern, disappointed. I relented. "Okay, but only on Fridays."

I heard Eilish exhale a long, exasperated breath. At this rate it'd be Easter before I actually got around to telling him. She shifted closer and lifted Patrick so he was sitting half on her lap and half on mine. I brought my arm to rest around her shoulders and squeezed while she gave Patrick a kind, motherly expression.

"How would you like it if Bryan was your daddy, just like Carl is Jack and Harry's daddy?" she asked softly, and Patrick's eyes went huge.

"But . . . how can he just become my daddy?"

"Well," Eilish started, then hesitated.

"I can because I am your dad," I said, my voice uncharacteristically croaky. "I've always been your dad."

He furrowed his small brows, confused. "You have?"

I swallowed and took his hand in mine. I couldn't get over how tiny he was. If he took after Eilish and me, he was going to be as tall as a house when he got older. I mustered a smile. "Yeah. It just took me a while to find my way back to you."

He went quiet while Eilish emitted an odd watery sound. I knew she had to be feeling just as emotional as I was. Patrick stayed quiet for a long few moments, his brain working overtime to make sense of what he was being told.

At last he said, "Is that why we have the same hair?"

And just like that my nerves evaporated. I let out a scratchy laugh and answered, "Yeah, buddy, that's why we have the same hair."

"Not to mention the same eyes," Eilish put in.

Patrick went back to mulling things over. I rubbed my thumb over the inside of his soft palm and asked, "What do you think, buddy?"

I was surprised and disappointed when his mouth dipped down in a frown.

"B-b-but you're my best friend," he exclaimed. "You can't be my daddy *and* my best friend, can you?"

What was that sound, I hear you ask? Just my heart cracking in two. No big deal. His earnestness really did a number on me.

"Yes, I can definitely be your dad *and* your best friend," I answered, choking up a little. Okay, choking up *a lot*.

Patrick started bopping up and down in our laps excitedly as his smile returned. "Then yes! I want you to be my daddy. This is awesome!"

Eilish chuckled, at the same time moisture filled her eyes. "Hey! I thought I was your best friend."

Patrick made a face like the idea was preposterous, and I couldn't help chuckling. This kid really was too much sometimes.

"Does this mean you'll come to Disneyland with us?" he asked, looking back at me now.

"I only said maybe," Eilish reminded him.

"And I said I'd be good. That means we're going."

Eilish sniffled and laughed, shooting me a dry look to cover her emotion. "He gets that from you."

I plastered on an innocent expression. "What?"

"The brazenness. I can't imagine what he'll be like in a few years' time."

I tightened my arm around her shoulders and pulled her closer. "Oh, whatever. You love it."

"See?" said Eilish. "Brazen."

I flashed her a confident smile, not arguing. We stared at each other over Patrick's head, and I didn't think I'd ever loved anyone as much as I loved the two people sitting in my arms. They were my whole world. I knew they always would be.

"Can I go play with my Legos again?" Patrick asked, looking up at me with wide, guileless eyes.

"Yeah, go play. But I'm here if you need to talk or have any more questions."

He started sliding off our laps and when he casually replied, "Thanks, Daddy," I welled up all over again. This day was determined to see me bawling like a baby. It just felt bizarre to have imagined so many nightmare scenarios and then have him take it all in his stride. But he was young. I guess the world was much simpler when all you had to worry about were your friends at school and catching Pokémon.

I glanced back at Eilish, who was staring at Patrick now, her eyes just as watery as mine.

I wrapped both my arms around her, pulled her to my chest, and gave her another squeeze. "We're such a pair of wusses," I said with a gruff breath.

Her lips curved in a smile as she pulled her gaze away from Patrick to look up at me with the most open, affectionate expression. "Yeah," she whispered, "but I wouldn't have us any other way."

"Me neither," I whispered back.

"I told you it would be fine."

"I know."

"See how happy he looks?"

"Yeah."

"That's because he loves you."

"Eilish."

She bit her lip as she bent her neck to stare long and deep into my eyes. She didn't speak, but I wondered if she could read my mind by the intense expression she wore.

"Marry me," I blurted.

A gasp escaped her. Patrick was still playing over by the window, completely oblivious.

I lowered my mouth to kiss her softly. "Marry me," I said again, a whisper this time.

"Bryan, I—"

I kissed her deeper. "Don't make me say it again."

"But—"

"*Eilish*."

She let out a small, whimpering sound, a steeliness in her eyes when she finally responded, "With all my heart, yes."

THE END

ABOUT THE AUTHORS

L.H. Cosway has a BA in English Literature and Greek and Roman Civilisation, and an MA in Postcolonial Literature. She lives in Dublin city. Her inspiration to write comes from music. Her favourite things in life include writing stories, vintage clothing, dark cabaret music, food, musical comedy, and of course, books. She thinks that imperfect people are the most interesting kind. They tell the best stories.

Come find L.H. Cosway-
Facebook: https://www.facebook.com/LHCosway
Twitter: https://twitter.com/LHCosway
Mailing List: http://www.lhcoswayauthor.com/p/mailing-list.html
Pinterest: http://www.pinterest.com/lhcosway13/
Website: www.lhcoswayauthor.com

Penny Reid is the *New York Times*, *Wall Street Journal*, and *USA Today* bestselling author of the Winston Brothers and Knitting in the City series. She used to spend her days writing federal grant proposals as a biomedical researcher, but now she writes kissing books. Penny is an obsessive knitter and manages the #OwnVoices-focused mentorship incubator / publishing imprint, Smartypants Romance. She lives in Seattle Washington with her husband, three kids, and dog named Hazel.

Come find Penny -
Mailing List: http://pennyreid.ninja/newsletter/
Goodreads: http://www.goodreads.com/ReidRomance
Facebook: www.facebook.com/pennyreidwriter
Instagram: www.instagram.com/reidromance
Twitter: www.twitter.com/reidromance
TikTok: https://www.tiktok.com/@authorpennyreid
Patreon: https://www.patreon.com/smartypantsromance
Email: pennreid@gmail.com …hey, you! Email me ;-)

OTHER BOOKS BY L.H. COSWAY

Contemporary Romance

Painted Faces

Killer Queen

The Nature of Cruelty

Still Life with Strings

Showmance

Fauxmance

Happy-Go-Lucky

Beyond the Sea

Sidequest for Love

The Cracks Duet

A Crack in Everything (#1)

How the Light Gets In (#2)

The Hearts Series

Six of Hearts (#1)

Hearts of Fire (#2)

King of Hearts (#3)

Hearts of Blue (#4)

Thief of Hearts (#5)

Cross My Heart (5.75)

Hearts on Air (#6)

The Running on Air Series

Air Kiss (#0.5)

Off the Air (#1)

Something in the Air (#2)

The Rugby Series with Penny Reid

The Hooker & the Hermit (#1)

The Player & the Pixie (#2)
The Cad & the Co-ed (#3)
The Varlet & the Voyeur (#4)

The Blood Magic Series
Nightfall (#1)
Moonglow (#2)
Witching Hour (#3)
Sunlight (#4)

St. Bastian Institute Series
Foretold

OTHER BOOKS BY PENNY REID

Knitting in the City Series
(Interconnected Standalones, Adult Contemporary Romantic Comedy)

Neanderthal Seeks Human: A Smart Romance (#1)

Neanderthal Marries Human: A Smarter Romance (#1.5)

Friends without Benefits: An Unrequited Romance (#2)

Love Hacked: A Reluctant Romance (#3)

Beauty and the Mustache: A Philosophical Romance (#4)

Ninja at First Sight (#4.75)

Happily Ever Ninja: A Married Romance (#5)

Dating-ish: A Humanoid Romance (#6)

Marriage of Inconvenience: (#7)

Neanderthal Seeks Extra Yarns (#8)

Knitting in the City Coloring Book (#9)

Winston Brothers Series
(Interconnected Standalones, Adult Contemporary Romantic Comedy, spinoff of Beauty and the Mustache)

Beauty and the Mustache (#0.5)

Truth or Beard (#1)

Grin and Beard It (#2)

Beard Science (#3)

Beard in Mind (#4)

Beard In Hiding (#4.5)

Dr. Strange Beard (#5)

Beard with Me (#6)

Beard Necessities (#7)

Winston Brothers Paper Doll Book (#8)

Hypothesis Series
(New Adult Romantic Comedy Trilogies)

Elements of Chemistry (#1)

Laws of Physics (#2)

Irish Players (Rugby) Series – by L.H. Cosway and Penny Reid

(Interconnected Standalones, Adult Contemporary Sports Romance)

The Hooker and the Hermit (#1)

The Pixie and the Player (#2)

The Cad and the Co-ed (#3)

The Varlet and the Voyeur (#4)

Dear Professor Series

(New Adult Romantic Comedy)

Kissing Tolstoy (#1)

Kissing Galileo (#2)

Ideal Man Series

(Interconnected Standalones, Adult Contemporary Romance Series of Jane Austen Reimaginings)

Pride and Dad Jokes (#1, TBD)

Man Buns and Sensibility (#2, TBD)

Sense and Manscaping (#3, TBD)

Persuasion and Man Hands (#4, TBD)

Mantuary Abbey (#5, TBD)

Mancave Park (#6, TBD)

Emmanuel (#7, TBD)

Handcrafted Mysteries Series

(A Romantic Cozy Mystery Series, spinoff of *The Winston Brothers Series*)

Engagement and Espionage (#1)

Marriage and Murder (#2)

Home and Heist (TBD)

Baby and Ballistics (TBD)

Pie Crimes and Misdemeanors (TBD)

Good Folks Series

(Interconnected Standalones, Adult Contemporary Romantic Comedy, spinoff of *The Winston Brothers Series*)

Totally Folked (#1)

Folk Around and Find Out (#2)

Three Kings Series

(Interconnected Standalones, Holiday-themed Adult Contemporary Romantic Comedies)

Homecoming King (#1)

Drama King (#2)

Prom King (#3, coming Christmas 2023)

Standalones

Ten Trends to Seduce Your Best Friend

Made in United States
North Haven, CT
23 February 2025